Berkley Sensation Titles by Cheryl Ann Smith

THE SCHOOL FOR BRIDES
THE ACCIDENTAL COURTESAN
THE SCARLET BRIDE

The Scarlet Bride

CHERYL ANN SMITH

BERKLEY SENSATION, NEW YORK

THE BERKLEY PUBLISHING GROUP
Published by the Penguin Group
Penguin Group (USA) Inc.
375 Hudson Street, New York, New York 10014, USA
Penguin Group (Canada), 90 Eglinton Avenue East, Suite 700, Toronto, Ontario M4P 2Y3, Canada
(a division of Pearson Penguin Canada Inc.) • Penguin Books Ltd., 80 Strand, London WC2R 0RL,
England • Penguin Group Ireland, 25 St. Stephen's Green, Dublin 2, Ireland (a division of Penguin
Books Ltd.) • Penguin Group (Australia), 250 Camberwell Road, Camberwell, Victoria 3124, Australia
(a division of Pearson Australia Group Pty. Ltd.) • Penguin Books India Pvt. Ltd., 11 Community
Centre, Panchsheel Park, New Delhi—110 017, India • Penguin Group (NZ), 67 Apollo Drive,
Rosedale, Auckland 0632, New Zealand (a division of Pearson New Zealand Ltd.) • Penguin Books
(South Africa) (Pty.) Ltd., 24 Sturdee Avenue, Rosebank, Johannesburg 2196, South Africa

Penguin Books Ltd., Registered Offices: 80 Strand, London WC2R 0RL, England

This is a work of fiction. Names, characters, places, and incidents either are the product of the author's
imagination or are used fictitiously, and any resemblance to actual persons, living or dead, business
establishments, events, or locales is entirely coincidental. The publisher does not have any control over
and does not assume any responsibility for author or third-party websites or their content.

THE SCARLET BRIDE

A Berkley Sensation Book / published by arrangement with the author.

PUBLISHING HISTORY
Berkley Sensation mass-market edition / June 2012

Copyright © 2012 by Cheryl Ann Smith.
Excerpt from *A Convenient Bride* by Cheryl Ann Smith copyright © 2012 by Cheryl Ann Smith.
Cover art by Judy York.
Hand lettering by Ron Zinn.
Cover design by George Long.
Interior text design by Laura K. Corless.

ISBN: 978-0-425-25081-5

BERKLEY SENSATION®
Berkley Sensation Books are published by The Berkley Publishing Group,
a division of Penguin Group (USA) Inc.,
375 Hudson Street, New York, New York 10014.
BERKLEY SENSATION® is a registered trademark of Penguin Group (USA) Inc.
The "B" design is a trademark of Penguin Group (USA) Inc.

PRINTED IN THE UNITED STATES OF AMERICA

10 9 8 7 6 5 4 3 2 1

ALWAYS LEARNING   **PEARSON**

For Duane, Regan, Paige, and Ethan.
All my love.

Chapter One

Simon Harrington, an ill-tempered brute if Lady Jeanette Abbot was to be believed, rode down the deserted streets of London with no particular destination in mind. Lamplight flickered in fresh puddles gathered from the same light rain that splattered his coat, dripped off the brim of his hat, and trickled in cold rivulets down the back of his neck. The discomfort fit his mood, as his sober expression was on the edge of turning grim.

The blasted wench had refused his suit again, calling him untamed and beneath her consideration as a husband, in spite of his family's wealth. She'd flashed an abundance of tiny albeit slightly crooked teeth, stepped away from his bent knee as if he had some horrid disease, and politely asked him to leave lest she have him tossed out into the street by her footmen.

Now as the horse beneath him ambled freely down the street, he considered letting the beast carry him all the way to Scotland, where no one knew his history, and the women had much less starch in their drawers. His father had married Irish, so taking a Scotswoman as his wife wouldn't shock the Ton. The path to scandal had already been paved with the bodies of all the disreputable Harringtons before him.

Unfortunately, as the elder son of his branch of the family oak tree, he had to make a wise marriage. If his uncle and father decided to drop over dead, he'd be the earl and head of the notorious clan of bounders and rakes. Without Lady Jeanette, his chances of dragging the family firmly into societal favor were slim. Tonight's rejection was certainly a blow to his carefully laid plans. Though a few Harringtons had risen to prominence in society, Simon's Irish blood and lack of a title made the path nearly impossible for him. He'd not care what anyone thought of his family if not for his sister, Brenna.

"Onward to Scotland then, er, Horse," Simon commanded, his voice a touch slurred from several pints downed at a bawdy pub somewhere near Whitechapel.

He really should name the beast, he decided, as he peered down at the pair of furry ears that had turned backward to listen for his commands. After all, he'd owned the large gray for over a week now. The finely bred animal needed something majestic to make him stand out among less well-bred and costly beasts.

But the search for a name was to be delayed, as a piteous sound, carried on the wind, immediately brought him upright, sober, and nearly off his horse. Horse himself nearly leapt out of his hide and braced to bolt. Only sawing at the reins kept the gelding in check.

It was the cry of a child in distress. Wait, no. Not of an infant but of a woman in trouble. Serious trouble, if the second louder cry was to be believed.

Simon jerked up the reins, startled the horse a second time, and kneed the beast in the direction of the sound. As soon as he rounded a corner, he spotted two large men in footmen's livery, struggling with a woman in rumpled clothing. She appeared to be fighting for her life, or perhaps only her virtue. Truthfully, it didn't matter which. Trouble was trouble, and she was outnumbered.

At least that was how Simon saw it. He wasted no time

on further speculation. The damsel was in danger, and by the looks of the empty street, he would be pressed into service as her knight in damp armor.

She struggled mightily against two brawny pairs of hands as the men did their best to unwrap her arms from a streetlamp. She wasn't weeping and her cries were more of the desperate sort. Simon was impressed by her determination to succeed against greater forces than she.

"No! You will not take me back!" she cried as one arm was finally dislodged. It would be but a matter of seconds before she was carried away in the waiting coach.

Simon wasted no time. He kicked Horse to a run and barreled down on the trio in a clatter of racing hooves. The two men had just a moment to register their surprise when one of them took Simon's knee to the chest. The man flew up with a pained grunt, landing awkwardly backward on cobblestones. The other jumped back to avoid the horse. Simon shot out a foot and kicked him in the face. His nose shattered.

The woman swayed but reclaimed the pole. Simon spun Horse around as the first man shook his head and began to rise. The other cupped his broken nose and groaned.

There was no time to spare. He edged the horse close to the woman and reached out a gloved hand.

"If you don't intend to embrace the pole all evening, then perhaps you should allow me to rescue you."

Wide eyes peered from beneath tangled and soaked sable hair. Her confusion over the sudden turn of events showed in her face. She hesitated for a heartbeat, and then shoved her slender hand into his. She lifted her foot and placed it on his in the stirrup. He pulled her up behind him.

"Hold tight," he commanded, and she grabbed for his coat. Then, with a sharp tap of his heels, they were off.

A bellow of outrage followed, with a trail of curses to show deep displeasure from the two ruffians. Simon grinned. After the evening he'd had, it was pure enjoyment knowing there were two men in London who were unhappier and more put out than he.

Two hands clung to him as the horse sped through the streets, the cool breeze forcing out the lingering effects of imbibing too much cheap ale. The excitement of the rescue sent his blood racing and cleared the fog of whiskey from his brain. It wasn't until he was certain they weren't followed that he stopped the horse.

The gelding bobbed his head and snorted.

Simon glanced over his shoulder to see the woman twisted around to peer behind them. She'd clearly lost some of her starch. Her body trembled as she clung to his sodden coat. He thought of offering her the item; however, she wasn't nearly as wet as he. Better just to leave her as she was for the moment.

"We must go," she urged and turned back to dig her fingers tighter into his coat. "They will come."

There was such terror in her voice that Simon was taken aback. No simple runaway was she.

"You must tell me your story," he said, resisting the urge to kick the horse back into motion. He needed to know if she was not a victim but a criminal before he became further mired in the situation.

"There is no time," she pleaded and clawed at his arm. "If his lordship finds me, it will mean my death."

His lordship? Death? The words ripped through his brain. "Who are you? Who is this man who would kill you?"

"He was my patron; I was his courtesan." She shook uncontrollably until her teeth chattered. "I ran away."

Simon reconsidered offering his coat but had no time to shrug out of the wet wool. Her eyes pleaded with him. "Please, you m-must t-take me to safety. I have money to pay y-you for y-your help."

Simon swept his gaze down her face. There was nothing untoward in her pale features to give him pause. No deception, no untruths. She was truly in fear for her life.

"I know a place where you'll be protected." He nudged his horse into motion. The animal easily complied. Horse was probably eager to get out of the misty cold.

Simon quickly navigated the rain-slick streets. Though

the brim of his hat kept the rain from his eyes, the grim weather made keeping on course difficult.

Thankfully the destination wasn't far. He knew Eva and Noelle would be displeased with this unexpected arrival. However, his mysterious passenger would be safe there. There was no other option. Bringing her to his family home was out of the question. To show up with a courtesan in tow would certainly press the boundaries of what his mother would consider proper.

It took several wrong turns to finally find the correct street, as the increasing rain made navigation challenging. Thankfully, within minutes, he came upon the address he sought.

The town house was as he remembered—dull, nondescript, and dark. The household was asleep. By now the woman was dazed and half-frozen. He dislodged her fingers from his coat and swung down from the horse. She was thistledown light as Simon removed her from behind the saddle and she slid limply down his body. Her toes had barely brushed solid earth when her knees buckled.

Alarmed, Simon caught her about the waist and noticed her unfocused eyes. He scooped her up into his arms and carried her toward the darkened town house.

The door was locked. He kicked the panel several times with his boot, rattling the door on its hinges. After a brief delay, candlelight flickered through a narrow window.

A man of middle years cautiously opened the door and peered through the crack, a nightcap covering his hair. He stared first at Simon and then at the woman, clearly confused by their appearance at the late hour.

"I need to see Miss Eva," Simon demanded.

The man shook his head, his face stern and his eyes puffy from sleep. "Miss Eva is not here and Miss Sophie is sleeping. Go away."

Simon didn't have the patience for further conversation. He tucked his damsel higher on his chest and forcefully brushed past the servant.

The man sputtered. "Sir, you cannot come inside." He

slammed the door closed and scurried after them. His bare feet slapped on the parquet floor. "This is unseemly."

Unfamiliar with the floor plan of the house, Simon strode down the hallway with only the muted candlelight to keep him from stumbling about. He quickly found a dark room with a settee near a cold fireplace.

"Get Sophie," Simon ground out.

"What is happening here?"

Simon spun to see a shadowed blond woman hurrying down the stairs, clutching a robe protectively around her body. A trio of women gathered at the upper landing behind her.

"How dare you force your way into this house." She shot the servant a glance and demanded, "Primm, get Thomas."

The man took a step. Simon's voice brought him upright. "Miss Noelle is my cousin. I need your help."

Sophie started, then paused, uncertain. Finally she turned to the women on the landing above and snapped, "Return to bed. I will take care of this."

Simon wasted no more time. He entered the room and eased the courtesan down on the settee. Sophie took the candle and lit a pair of wall sconces. She spoke to Primm in low tones and the servant left the room.

When they were alone, Sophie scowled at him and walked over to check on the woman. She took a blanket from a nearby chair and tucked the edges around his charge. The courtesan's eyes fluttered when Sophie's warm hand pressed against her cheek.

"You are safe now," Sophie said softly and brushed damp hair from the courtesan's pale face. "Rest."

The woman settled back as Sophie stepped away. She indicated for Simon to join her, and they moved to a corner of the small room. She crossed her arms.

"Tell me who you are and what happened to her." Her whispered tone was sharp and her glare sharper.

"I am Simon Harrington." He looked toward the settee and lowered his voice. "I apologize for the intrusion but I had nowhere else to go."

"Who is she?" Sophie asked.

"I don't know." He shrugged. "She was in danger and I rescued her. She claims to be a courtesan who fears for her life. Otherwise, I have no more information."

Sophie scanned his face. After a long moment, she sighed. "You've done the right thing by bringing her here. You can explain yourself to Miss Eva later."

Simon grimaced as she returned to the courtesan and sat beside her on the settee. Forgiveness was the least of his concerns. Eva owned the school and fiercely protected her privacy. She would be livid to find out he'd been spying on her. Worse, he hated to think how his cousin Noelle would take the news. She volunteered at the school and was just as protective of the young women. Coming here had breached their sanctuary and both women would have his hide.

Laura peered into the stranger's face and saw compassion in the woman's wary eyes. She hadn't any idea where she was, but suspected her rescuer had delivered her to a safe place.

"Where am I?" she asked weakly. Her body shivered beneath her wet clothes and she struggled to keep her teeth from clacking together. She was so cold that she couldn't move, and her limbs felt frozen in place.

The woman smiled and her face softened slightly beneath a fringe of blond hair. "My name is Sophie. We run a school that rescues courtesans."

Laura glanced around the small and tidy blue parlor. She wanted to laugh at the irony of the information but didn't have the strength. She shifted her attention to the tall man near the fireplace. His face was shadowed by his hat, but she knew by his sodden appearance that he was the man who had swooped in and rescued her.

"Thank you," she said and managed a weak but very grateful smile. If not for him, she'd be dead. He could have ridden off, minding his business. Instead he'd provided her assistance, protection, and a haven from her demons. "You truly did save my life."

He tipped his black hat and bowed slightly. "I shall leave you now in capable hands." Without another word, he crossed the room and vanished out the door.

Laura felt slightly bereft with the absence of her savior. Still, she couldn't ask for more than he'd already given.

"I'm sorry to cause such trouble," she said softly.

Sophie patted her hand and stood. "Not to worry. We are used to dealing with the misfortunes of women here." She tightened the tie at her waist and darted a quick glance over Laura. "When is the last time you've eaten?"

Laura scrunched up her face. The veil of exhaustion kept her from an immediate answer. "Two days. I think."

It was clear that Sophie wanted to ask questions about her history, but wisely held her tongue. Laura was relieved. She was too tired to think, much less speak, of her horrible ordeal. She needed rest, food, and dry clothes. Tomorrow she would explain everything with a clear and rested mind.

Now that she was free, she would die before she'd ever return to the clutches of the Earl of Westwick again, the vile bastard. She'd kill him first.

"Let me help you up." Sophie assisted her to sit, then stand. Sophie wasn't large but she was surprisingly strong. She bore much of Laura's weight as the two women gingerly crossed into the hallway and up the stairs, to a room halfway down the narrow corridor. Sophie had no difficulty managing the distance without a candle or while supporting the wobbly Laura.

Sophie walked her inside a tiny room, lit with a single candle. The man at the front door had clearly prepared the space for her. There was a nightdress on the bed and a tray of hot, fragrant broth and biscuits on a bedside table. A shudder racked Laura's body, her wet gown clinging to her every curve.

"Let me help you undress." Sophie quickly stripped her to the skin with quiet efficiency. Once her chemise and drawers were removed, Laura heard Sophie's breath catch.

She knew exactly when the woman saw them—black and purple bruises, some old, some still fresh upon her skin. She'd felt every blow.

"Whoever did this to you needs to be horsewhipped."

Laura smiled wryly. "Or worse."

Their eyes connected and held. Sophie pulled the nightdress down over Laura's head and helped her into the bed. Laura felt understanding and sympathy in this stranger. She wondered if their stories were not so different.

"I do not know your name." Sophie collected the tray and settled it over Laura's lap. The aroma of the broth caused her stomach to grumble with anticipation of the simple meal. At this moment, even biscuits would be a delicious feast.

There were many things his lordship had taken from her—her innocence, her dignity, and nearly her life. But he could not take the one thing from her she'd held on to during all these months of torment and torture at his hands. Her name.

"I was called Sabine," Laura said softly and felt a thin thread of hope and strength rise beneath her battered ribs. She smiled into Sophie's eyes. "But you may call me Laura."

Chapter Two

"S imon. What have you done?"

His cousin Noelle's sharp voice caused Simon to stiffen. He turned away from the window to see her angry amber eyes pin him against the windowpane with a hard stare.

Expecting the wrath of Eva when he arrived the next morning, he wasn't sure if Noelle's surprising presence at the courtesan school was better or worse than facing Eva.

When they were children, Noelle used to take a nip of flesh out of his hide if he crossed her or teased her too much. He had several scars to prove it. Hopefully, she'd outgrown biting.

"I didn't expect to see you today," he said, sighing. "I thought you were in Kent."

"My husband is in Kent on business. I stayed home," she said through gritted teeth. "Do not change the subject. Answer the question."

What could he say? When he'd heard family gossip about a new cousin that Noelle had uncovered, he had to find out more. Unfortunately, all leads led nowhere. Cousin Eva was a mystery. Adding this information to the fact that

Noelle was keeping Eva largely a secret further notched up his curiosity. The only way to gain information was to spy on Noelle and discover what she was hiding.

Through his investigation, he'd discovered that not only was Eva a duchess but she disguised herself as a spinster and ran a courtesan rescue school. The bigger surprise was finding out that Noelle was secretly helping Eva with the courtesans.

"I suppose you deserve an explanation—" he began, but she cut him off midsentence.

"How could you? Eva trusted me to keep her secret." Noelle stalked across the room and looked up. She had one hand on her hip and the other uplifted to his chest, one finger pointing in the direction of his heart. "How did you find out about this place? I've told no one about its existence, save Gavin, and I trust my husband completely."

Of all his cousins, Noelle was more like a sister to him than a cousin. Though she was several years his junior, he'd always felt a special bond with her, as they were both the mischief makers in the family. And as she'd grown, she'd flaunted convention where she could, and accepted people not because of their monetary worth but by their character. And gads, she'd actually married a man in trade.

Simon admired her for her independence, and he and her husband, Gavin Blackwell, were quickly becoming fast friends.

"I didn't follow you exactly." He rubbed the side of his neck. "I followed your mysterious cousin Eva one afternoon after I saw her leaving your town house. I'd heard of her through family gossip and had to know if she truly was kin or some sort of charlatan intent on causing trouble." A smile crept across his face. "I must say, I was shocked to learn that my newly discovered cousin ran a school for wayward courtesans."

Noelle's lids lowered to narrow slits. "What else do you know about Eva?" she demanded, her voice brittle. "How long have you been spying into our affairs?"

"Not long, I assure you." The little spitfire had certainly

grown into a formidable adversary. Simon wanted to discuss his courtesan but knew Noelle would not be put off until all her questions were answered. "I know she is a duchess."

Her small hands closed into tight fists. "What else?"

He braced himself. Noelle was teetering on irate. "And she might be your long-lost bastard sister."

"Do not call her that," Noelle snapped, and one surprisingly hard fist made contact with his breastbone. "Don't you ever call her a bastard." Fury welled heavily in her eyes, and she pulled back for another whack. "I do not care if she is the natural daughter of my father and his mistress. She is my sister and I'll not have you disparage her."

Simon caught her hand. Regardless of Eva's questionable parentage, he felt like a cad for his unfortunate choice of words. Clearly, Noelle loved Eva.

"I apologize, Noelle. I shouldn't have pried into your business." He placed her hand over his heart and tapped a finger under her chin. "I do find having the duchess-matchmaker as kin amusing, no matter her unusual connection to our family."

With his apology, Noelle settled from enraged to merely bristling as she dislodged her hand from his grip. The matter of Eva had been settled somewhat amicably with his apology.

"But will she accept *you* as her family?" she said, frowning. "I have shared with her how difficult you can be. Your latest adventure will not put you on firm ground with my sister."

He settled back on his heels and crossed his arms. "So you heard about the courtesan rescue? I should have known Sophie would not keep quiet about my part in the adventure."

"Eva sent me a note this morning after Sophie sent her a note. I rushed over ahead of Eva, expecting your chivalrous nature to override your good sense. I knew you'd return here to check on your distressed damsel."

Noelle turned and walked over to a chair. She slumped

into it and pressed her fingertips to her scrunched brow. "Eva is livid. The school and her connection to it are supposed to be her secret."

"But she *will* protect the courtesan?" Simon asked. After her ordeal, he'd been unable to shake his concern over her continued safety.

Noelle's eyes snapped up. "Of course she's being protected. I assured her myself this morning. Eva would never leave a courtesan in danger."

He sighed, relieved. Despite her vigorous fight to save herself from the footmen, the woman had been terrified. Whatever she'd been through had been more than just a squabble with a lover. He believed her when she said the man would kill her.

"I must thank Eva for her assistance." He met Noelle's eyes and his mouth twitched. "Besides, I think it is high time I meet this mysterious duchess-cousin of mine."

"Do so at your own peril, Simon. My sister is with child and ornerier than an injured wolf. You breached her sanctuary without invitation, even if your motive was pure. She will not allow you to get away without a much-deserved dressing-down."

Simon grinned. Why couldn't the Harrington family have one single simpering miss among them? Did they all have to possess fire in their britches?

"I shall take my chances." He winked and Noelle pressed her mouth into a disapproving line. "I shall enjoy sparring with the ornery duchess."

Simon wanted to take back those words when faced with the outraged courtesan-rescuing duchess. Her amber eyes, so like Noelle's, pierced him with an icy stare. He suspected any attempts to charm her would fail miserably.

"So you are Simon?" Eva walked into the parlor, her face tight. She pushed her spectacles up on the bridge of her nose and stared. "The same man who terrified Sophie and my courtesans with your midnight visit?"

He enjoyed a good verbal sparring as much as anyone, but his new cousin was with child and needed to be treated with care. The sober disguise only added to her grim demeanor.

Simon knew she disguised herself at the school and passed herself off as a spinster to keep her two lives separate. However, he also knew she was a beauty beneath the dull costume.

Gossip about the duke's beautiful new bride had covered all of England, although the pregnancy was still a secret. For now. It would only be a matter of time before her full skirts could no longer hide evidence of her condition.

It would also be a difficult matter for a spinster to explain to her courtesans.

"I did not mean to frighten them," he said, contrite. "I was in fear for the life of the courtesan. I had to find her a safe haven."

"And you discovered this school how?"

"Through curiosity and a desire to protect my family," he admitted. "I had to learn about you for myself."

"You thought I was trouble?"

He nodded slowly. "Yes."

She crossed her arms. "Noelle found me. I did not seek her out. She insisted we know each other."

"I'm not surprised. Noelle is not one to let a small thing like the wishes of others deter her from her wants."

For a long moment, he watched her watch him. She wasn't nearly as put out as he'd expected. Yes, she was annoyed. And yes, she wasn't happy he'd taken it upon himself to put his aristocratic nose into her privacy. But as she laid her hand over her belly, he saw in her a level of contentment and calm.

"And did you discover I am all you expected—the grasping bastard daughter of one of your long-dead uncles, come to cause havoc on the Harrington good name?"

A second hand followed the first until she was protectively guarding the life growing in her womb. Simon knew then that this thorny duchess would be a fierce and devoted mother.

"Truthfully, you aren't at all what I imagined," he admitted. "I'd expected to find a crass and lowborn wench without scruples who'd taken advantage of Noelle and somehow hooked herself a duke. What I discovered was a woman who truly cares for her courtesans and wants a better life for them."

"And my marriage?" she asked tightly.

"A love match by all accounts," he said. He leaned back on his heels and squarely met her gaze. "I see the joy you've brought to Noelle and her sister, Margaret. How can I fault their happiness?"

He watched her eyes well with tears before she turned away. Though he had very little experience with expectant mothers, he knew their emotions ran pell-mell from one day to the next.

"It is my sisters who have brought *me* great joy." She swiped her hand over her face, sniffed, and turned, composed again. She looked him over and grimaced. "I am not entirely certain what I feel about you, however."

Simon frowned back. "I can be difficult."

"So I understand."

He grinned. "Welcome to the family."

The grimace dissolved into a look of exasperation. "I'm not so certain counting me as kin is a worthy idea. My history is quite scandalous. If not for my sister and husband, I would have lived my life quite contently with just my mother for company."

"Then we shall let this play out naturally, one relative at a time," Simon conceded. He brushed a piece of lint off his black coat. He suspected his family would welcome the duchess. With a long history of Harrington rakes and bounders to choose from, the bastard daughter of his uncle and a former courtesan wouldn't be highly scandalous.

Perhaps a connection to the Duchess Evangeline could also lift his sister, Brenna, in the eyes of society. But until Eva decided to publicly claim her twig on the family tree, he was left to continue his hunt for a suitable wife.

Eva's posture loosened. "We'll see." She uncrossed her

arms. "I'm certain you didn't invade my school, again, to discuss your family. I assume you have come to see Laura?"

Laura? Pretty name. "I'd like to assure myself that she has suffered no ill-effects from last evening's unsettling adventure. She was quite weak when I left her."

There was a slight hesitation in her face. Eva was clearly worried about the courtesan. "You must not upset her. She has already suffered enough unhappiness."

He shook his head. "Upsetting Laura isn't my intention. I promise my visit will not cause her any distress."

It took her a moment before she agreed. "She is in the upstairs parlor, the last door on the left." She scanned her eyes over him. "And if you pass a courtesan along the way, I ask that you refrain from flirting. They should not be distracted from their studies."

Simon bowed. "I will be a pillar of propriety."

A slight smile tugged Eva's mouth as her hand returned to her belly. With a nod, he left his new cousin to ponder his foibles privately. He'd gotten through the meeting without injury. Noelle would be sorely disappointed.

Per Eva's instructions, he found the parlor with no difficulty. As with the rest of the house, it was bland and functional. The walls were papered a muted green, with paintings of birds hung to add interest. A narrow desk sat against one wall, a faded rug lay near a small fireplace, and two narrow settees faced each other and took up much of what was left of the space. But it wasn't the lack of finery in the room that caught and held his interest.

It was the woman who stood at the parlor's one window. The side of her head rested against the glass in a relaxed stance. She was framed by the late morning sun and the green backdrop of a large tree just beyond the windowpane.

He was taken aback by the change in her. She was no longer the bedraggled waif of last evening who smelled of inexpensive perfume, damp clothing, and fear.

Her thick sable hair was pulled back into a loose braid that fell to mid back. Her dress was a pale gray and a size or two too large, yet it didn't distract from her graceful curves.

Simon didn't need to see her full face to realize she was lovely—a fact he'd missed previously. And she didn't appear to possess the hardness one usually found in women of her profession. Truthfully, she seemed almost . . . innocent.

But it was the deep sadness in her eyes and wistful expression that held him silent and still in the open doorway as a stunning desire to protect her welled inside him.

He knew he should make his presence known, but he couldn't speak, for this lovely courtesan caused his breath to catch deep in his lungs.

Laura watched the courtesans from the window above them as they laughed and chatted while enjoying tea in the garden. They seemed so carefree, as if they hadn't a single concern to worry them. Soon they'd be matched with husbands and on to new lives. They'd have children, or travel perhaps, and their futures would be full and happy.

How she envied them.

A small sigh escaped her. Not one of them would suffer the nightmare of misuse and abuse. Miss Eva would see them well cared for.

From what she'd learned from Sophie, Miss Eva chose their future husbands with great care. If she even suspected a man had darkness in him or possessed a less than sterling character, he was forever banned from her Husbands Book.

If only Miss Eva had been at their ramshackle cottage when her father eagerly matched her with the earl, thinking he was doing right by her. Miss Eva would have quickly seen into the earl's black heart and done her formidable best to dissuade Father from his course.

Bleak images flashed unbidden into her mind of the long months that followed the marriage agreement. She closed her eyes and bit her lip to fight a whimper. A prickle of revulsion raised gooseflesh on her skin, and she rubbed the chill from her flesh with her hands.

She would not think of *him*! She could not think of *him*!

When the earl slipped unwelcome into her thoughts, it was as if he still controlled her mind. She wouldn't allow it. Fourteen months of suffering were now behind her.

She was free, never again to be controlled by the vile whims of a man.

Then why couldn't she keep the nightmares away?

A small sound jerked her head upright, and she spun around to see a large body framed in the doorway. All she saw was the cut of an expensive coat and a crown of dark hair before the room spun and terror clouded her vision.

The earl! He'd found her!

She let out a small distressed cry and felt the floor drop out from beneath her feet.

Chapter Three

A pair of hands caught Laura's arms before she crumpled. Fury instantly replaced terror.

"No!" She struggled violently against the hard chest, only to be quickly subdued by a familiar voice forcing its way into her consciousness.

"Easy, Laura," he urged. "I'll not hurt you."

She stilled, tipped up her chin, and stared at the face above her. It wasn't the earl! He'd not found her whereabouts after all! The man was her rescuer from last evening.

She slumped with relief.

Blurry memories of him flashed in disjointed pieces—starting from the moment he appeared out of the dark atop a large gray horse, to when his gloved hand had reached down to her as the footmen roused from somewhere behind her. And she'd taken his hand, putting her faith in a stranger.

She remembered his kindness as he carried her into the town house, her body limp, her strength drained from her desperate flight from the earl. What she didn't remember was that his eyes were a striking icy blue.

She trembled. His hands tightened on her arms as he eased her toward a settee. "Let me help you," he said softly.

Laura curled up on the padded surface, tucking her slippered feet under her. She refused to meet his eyes. The shame of weakness filtered through her. She'd always been so strong, so unafraid. Not anymore. She didn't have any strength left in her achy and abused body.

"My name is Simon. Simon Harrington." His voice was deep and soothing. "Do you remember me?"

She nodded, her eyes downcast. "I remember."

He took a seat across from her on the empty settee and leaned forward with his elbows on his thighs. "I didn't mean to cause you any alarm," he said gently. "I just wanted to see you settled."

Laura lifted her gaze. Suspicion welled. There was no hint of salacious intentions in his face, so why then did he come back? His moment as her rescuer was over.

Did he expect something in return for his help? She'd told him that she was a courtesan. Might he ask for services as payment for his efforts?

She blanched at the thought and hiked up her chin. Never again would a man use her in such a way. Never. He needed to know that her gratitude was the only payment he'd receive. "Miss Eva has provided me clothes, food, and shelter. I need nothing else."

The abrupt and dismissive comment didn't change his expression. He continued to look at her as though she were a curiosity. His size didn't help her unease. Still, he remained unthreatening. Were his motives truly pure?

"What about your family?" He locked and unlocked his fingers and continued, "Can I send for someone for you?"

"I have no one." The last word lodged bitterly in her throat. She should be married and planning for children. Her dying father had been pleased to find her a suitable match, a husband of wealth and position who could provide her with everything she desired. How could he have known how his best-laid plans would end so horribly for his only child?

"Isn't there anyone who can take you in?" he pressed, frowning. Clearly he wouldn't be satisfied until he explored all avenues for her.

"Anywhere I go would jeopardize the safety of those who give me shelter." She expelled a deep breath. "I cannot ask anyone to take that risk."

His face tightened. Perhaps he was feeling some regret for involving himself in her troubles. It was no longer a matter of dropping her off on a relative's stoop and riding away.

Laura had to relieve this stranger of his misguided desire to protect her. She would dig free of the darkness on her own.

With the security of the school to shelter her while she healed both her mind and her body, she knew that one day soon she would no longer flinch at every noise, no longer need to accept the kindness of strangers, and no longer fear the twisted desire of the Earl of Westwick.

Her eyes burned, and she looked away. With Miss Eva's, Miss Noelle's, and Sophie's assistance, she'd learn to walk again on sturdy feet.

Quickly composing herself, she faced him. "I will always be grateful for your assistance. You saved my life. But you may go now. There is no need to worry yourself any further on my behalf."

Mister Harrington sat silently for a moment, several emotions warring on his face. Finally he nodded and stood. "If you ever need anything, Miss Eva knows where to reach me." With a brief nod, he left the room.

Laura listened to his footfalls all the way down the stairs before succumbing to the grief she'd held back for such a long time. Curling into a ball on the settee, she cried for her father and her mother. She cried for the innocent squire's daughter who'd been sold into a false marriage that left her ruined and abused.

But mostly she cried for the girl who'd become an unrecognizable hollow shell, without light and life, and wondered if she could ever truly free herself of Sabine.

* * *

Simon was certain he heard muted sobs when he reached the landing but knew his interference in her grief wouldn't be welcome. He was a stranger. He had no right to comfort her or to inject himself into her life. Whatever ills she'd suffered were not his to correct. She was safe. He'd offered help and been rebuffed. He could do nothing more for her.

Eva and Noelle were absent when he passed the parlor and decided not to seek them out. His meeting with the courtesan hadn't gone at all how he'd expected. His visceral reaction to her beauty had taken him aback.

She was a seductive package as a whole, though not intentionally so. There was simplicity to her loveliness, as it came without artifice. She was in possession of a raw sensuality that defied explanation.

Perhaps it was the curve of her blush pink lips, or the smoky gray of her eyes—eyes a color the like of which he'd never seen before. Perhaps it was her vulnerability mixed with the hint of strength he'd seen as she fought off the footmen. Whatever it was, he knew he should keep his distance. She could easily become an unwelcome distraction.

Simon took his hat and coat from the peg by the door and left the town house.

The ride back to his family's Berkeley Square address wasn't long. His family and the social whirl of London should push Laura from his mind. The brief spate of chivalry was now over. He needed to find a wife.

As a boy he'd wanted to be an adventurer. Unfortunately fate had intervened and left him closely aligned to inherit a title. So instead, his younger brother Gabriel had taken up the reins of family adventurer and left home some time ago to see the world.

Uncle Arthur was the earl of record, though he'd fled his responsibilities when Simon was still a child. The man had been so long buried in the wilds of India, studying plants and insects, that Simon's memories of him were faded.

Approaching sixty, Arthur had no intention of ever returning to England and begetting an heir. He was quite content to leave his holdings in the care of family and a vast selection of employees.

Simon's father, Walter, was in robust health and had no desire to leave Simon's beautiful mother, Kathleen, widowed. The idea that several men of the Ton would gladly take his place at Kathleen's side, and in her bed, was enough motivation for Father to keep hale and hearty.

Thankfully, this left Simon time to woo and win Lady Jeanette, if he could get past her ridiculous concerns. He'd not be inheriting the title for, hopefully, many more years.

However, it wasn't his future title or Lady Jeanette on his mind as he left Horse with a stable boy and walked into the house. It was a certain courtesan with wounded eyes and incredible sensuality that left him entirely too engaged in woolgathering.

It took several sharp headshakes to clear her from his mind and firmly return his thoughts to the lovely, if slightly dull, Lady Jeanette. It took a brandy and conversation with his father some minutes later to regain his focus.

"I understand Lady Jeanette refused you again?" His father lifted a brow and looked at him askance. Just north of fifty, Walter Harrington was what one would call distinguished, with a bit of gray at his temples and a face that women still found handsome.

Simon grumbled under his breath, then, "The chit thinks I intend to take her to the wilds of Ireland and have her bearing my children in some dirt hovel. No amount of explanation will convince her I am not some wild animal whelped in a field of rye grass."

Walter cocked a half smile and shrugged. "How could the chit possibly know you were conceived in a meadow?" he teased, and Simon scowled in response. "I thought that was a carefully guarded secret."

"Father, please," Simon begged. It was difficult enough to live under the same roof as his openly affectionate parents without having his father talk frankly of his supposed conception. "There are some things a son does not need to know about his parents. What debauchery you practice with Mother is one of them."

He was rewarded with a bark of laughter from the other side of the room. He glared.

There was a time when Simon longed for a love match like his parents shared. Unfortunately, his current situation left that fanciful notion dying on the vine. His sister, Brenna, was growing long of tooth while waiting for true love to find her. If he didn't intervene, she'd grow old and stooped while waiting for a prince to wed her.

Simon had vowed to himself, and promised his father, he'd be the one to make his own acceptable match and lead the Harrington family back into the good graces of society. And he had the perfect husband picked out for Brenna, too.

This was a vow easier to undertake in his head than to apply it to his pursuit of the proper Lady Jeanette.

"Her interest appears to lie with men who spout poetry and follow her about like lapdogs." He peered at his father's amused expression. "I tried to woo her with a sonnet, but the words clogged bitterly in my throat."

Father chuckled. "The inability of Harrington men to spout poetry is long-standing," he jested. "We would much rather hunt for game or rob a coach. And there is not one Harrington who ever played the lute for a woman."

Simon nodded. "If not for her family's close connection to the king and Lord Chester, who is a rattling cough away from inheriting a dukedom from his sick father, I'd leave the Lady Jeanette alone and spend several more years enjoying my bachelorhood."

"Perhaps you should give up Lady Jeanette and move on to another lovely," Father suggested. "Or will you continue to chase her all around London until she is eventually too exhausted to flee your pursuit?" Walter rose from his place behind the desk and joined Simon in an open chair by the fireplace.

Simon locked his jaw in a stubborn set and ground his teeth. He knew it was only a matter of time before his apparently fruitless endeavor to win the hand of the chit left him the laughingstock of all London. But he had to press on. It was high time he became a dutiful son.

"If I wed Lady Jeanette, Lord Chester will be family and Brenna will be a step closer to becoming his wife. Then we shall gain the favor of the king and all that entails." He paused and scratched his jaw. "I'm weary of listening to unflattering whispers about my scandalous family."

Father leaned his elbow on the arm of the chair and seemed to escape in thought. Simon sipped his brandy and waited for his father to impart some parental wisdom. It took several sips before Walter spoke.

"You can have tea with the king once a week for the rest of your life and it won't stop the whispers. We Harringtons have been the source of gossip for generations. I've not let it undermine me and neither should you. Enjoy your life and find your happiness. And be damned what anyone else thinks."

"It's not so easy to do when I have a sister who is tumbling pell-mell toward spinsterhood," Simon remarked.

Father frowned. "Your sister is my responsibility."

Simon countered, "And someday she will be mine. I will not have her unhappily dried up and hidden away in Kent when I can help her by making this match."

"And you think porridge-faced Chester Abbot is the man for her?" Father tapped a fingertip on his chin. "You know your sister. Do you truly think she would be happy with the marquess?"

The marquess *was* sadly lacking in bold masculinity. Hell, he was one step away from wearing corsets. "Spending his days breeding roses isn't doing anything to ruddy out his extremely pale skin or to build up his muscles. However, he is male, and that is enough to get Brenna with child and secure her future."

"Dear lord." A sharp feminine voice interrupted from the doorway. Simon looked around the chair back to see Brenna standing just inside the library, her face aghast. "You plan to wed me off to that toad, Chester Abbot?" She walked, or rather stalked, into the room in a flurry of russet skirts. She stared down at him in the chair. "Could you find anyone less fitting to be my husband than Chester Abbot?" She darted a glance at their father, her green eyes accusing. "How long did you plan to wait before you dropped this anvil upon my head?"

Father shrugged and looked back at Simon. "It is your brother's idea." He leveled a mischievous smile at the elder of his two sons. "Keep me out of this argument."

Simon rewarded him with a scathing glare. He'd get no help from that quarter. "Chester may not be a man who will hunt a stag for your dinner table, but he is pleasant enough and you will never need to worry that he'll gamble away your future."

"Hunt a stag? Pleasant? What about love?" Brenna grimaced. "I'd rather marry a pirate or highwayman. At least then I'll not fall into a bored stupor every time I'm in my husband's presence."

Irked over her flat refusal to consider the idea, Simon pushed to his feet. "And where is this interesting husband-to-be of yours? You certainly have not brought him around for tea. He hasn't begged Father for your hand. You'd refuse a future duke in order to seek a love that may never happen?"

Brenna looked as if she'd been slapped. She crossed her arms over her chest and glared at him from beneath a fringe of black hair. "When did you become so cruel? If Gabriel were home, he'd put a stop to this travesty."

Simon winced. He'd adored his little sister from the moment he first saw her tiny red face and bald head. He'd always had her interests at heart. She might not realize it now, but he knew that once she was wed, she'd settle in to her new life and be happy. It was what he sincerely wanted for her.

His defenses rose. "That is not my intention. And fortunately, our brother is not here for you to twist around your finger. If I have my way, you will be wed before he returns from wherever his most recent adventure has gotten him off to."

The comment did nothing to settle her anger. Instead, she pressed her open palms briefly to her forehead. "You say cruelty isn't your intention, yet you'd wed me to Lord Abbot?" She turned her back on her father. "I see the only way to remove myself from this travesty is to find a highwayman or pirate and get myself caught with his child." She shot Simon one last scowl. "Then the marquess will refuse to wed me."

With a huff, she stalked to the door. Then with a voice high enough for the entire household to hear, she said, "Mary, collect my most expensive jewels and call for a coach. We have some dangerous roads to travel!"

Both father and son looked at each other with alarm as Brenna's stomping footsteps faded into the bowels of the house. "You don't think she would actually seek out a highwayman, do you?" Simon asked, uncertain. With his sister, it was impossible to know how far she'd go to get her way. He hoped the threat was anger based and wouldn't lead her into a situation she'd regret.

"No telling with your sister. Thankfully, we will be away in the country for a few days. That should be enough time to calm her." Father stood. He adjusted his coat and glanced at the open door. There was worry in his eyes. Brenna seldom made threats, but when she did, they usually turned out badly for them all. "However, I shall make sure the coachmen know their heads are on the block if they dare think of taking her anywhere outside the city boundaries."

Chapter Four

❦

W hat do you think of this one?" Bess asked. The former courtesan shook out the deep green gown and held it up to herself for inspection. The cloth shimmered in the daylight and glowed against her flawless skin.

Laura politely examined the gown and nodded. "It's lovely. The color suits you." With Bess's raven hair and the deep emerald of the gown, the effect was stunning.

"You should wear that to the party. The men will not be able to take their eyes from you," Jane said, and then frowned and shook her blond head. "No. It's much too formal for the garden party. You must save it for a grander occasion. Your wedding perhaps?"

Bess smiled knowingly. "Perhaps. Though, I'd much rather wear the cream for that. It portrays a touch of innocence."

The courtesans had returned from shopping a half hour earlier and were twittering about their purchases. While they were away, Laura had enjoyed the quiet few hours alone. She'd read two chapters of a novel she found shelved in the sitting room and taken a walk in the garden. She hadn't realized how used to the other women she'd become until they were absent.

The silence had been deafening. But the last year of guards and locked doors made the quiet all the more precious. She'd truly enjoyed having a few hours to herself.

Sitting alone in the small garden had been heavenly.

She'd never had sisters. After her mother died when she was thirteen, her father was her main source of companionship. Though she did have a few friends in the village, her father's long illness had kept her from enjoying too many social gatherings. And without a dowry, she'd never had a serious beau come courting.

Her meeting with the earl had been accidental. Had she returned home a few minutes earlier, or later, they wouldn't have met on the trail and her life wouldn't have taken such an awful downward turn.

Now she was overwhelmed with women. They were arriving daily. Every time she spun about, she tripped over a new one.

Truthfully, their kindness and endless chatter kept her mind occupied and off darker thoughts. This in itself was a blessing.

"We shall let Laura choose."

The sound of her name brought her attention back around. She looked up to find Mariette and Bess holding up two gowns, one rose with cream lace trim, and the other pale blue with white ribbon woven through the bodice.

At her questioning glance, Bess smiled. "Which dress do you think Mariette should wear to the party?" She pointed to the blue in front of Mariette while she held the rose up. "She wants to make a positive impression on her future husband."

Mariette flushed. Two years working as a courtesan and she was still painfully shy. Impoverished, her mother had taken advantage of her daughter's dark beauty and had arranged for Mariette to take a lover—a married man with a dozen children and still enough energy to enjoy a mistress.

Looking at her now, it was impossible to imagine the young woman as a seductress.

"Hmm." Laura lifted her clasped hands to her chin and frowned. Both gowns suited Mariette nicely, but one more so than the other. "I think the rose. It goes well with your coloring and brings out the delightful pink in your cheeks."

Bess, Jane, and Mariette agreed and began the process of picking out fripperies and slippers to match their gowns. Soon every surface of the parlor was covered with discarded frilly items.

Miss Eva made a brief appearance in the open doorway, smiled sympathetically at Laura, who was nearly buried behind the open boxes, and escaped to another part of the house.

When the conversation turned to wedding nights and lacy nightwear, Laura excused herself. She felt the overwhelming need to remove herself from that conversation.

Walking aimlessly through the house, Laura tried to find something to occupy herself. The bread was baked, the washing was finished, and the mending was completed yesterday. She ran a fingertip across a gleaming picture frame. The house was well kept by a small staff, so her skills with a dust cloth were not needed.

Sitting down on the stairs, she sighed. It had been two weeks since her escape and the town house had begun to feel cloying. Miss Eva was wonderful, but the lack of purpose lost its charm as the days passed slowly by.

Desperate to venture out, well covered, of course, Laura felt the tug of freedom beyond the town house and its tiny garden. But where could she go?

She dared not wander about London for fear of the earl and his henchmen. It was too soon. Truthfully, there might never be the right time to do so. Perhaps an outing outside of London would be acceptable?

Eventually, she would settle deep in the country to begin her new life. Until then, it was imperative she remain hidden. It was impossible to gauge what the earl would do if he discovered her whereabouts, and London was right under his patrician nose. It was a peril she couldn't risk. She'd have to leave the city to find her adventure.

She wandered into the kitchen, explained to Sophie her intention to take the gig out, and assured her new friend she'd be careful.

"I promise I will not speak to anyone and will remain covered until I am well away from London." Laura picked up a fig and popped it into her mouth.

"You should take Thomas," Sophie urged. "You will not be safe on the roads alone."

Laura claimed a second fig. "It is daylight and the roads are well traveled." She sent Sophie a pleading glance. "I have been cloistered for months behind locked doors, my every movement watched dare I try to escape. I need to see a field, a hill, a hawk, something other than plastered walls and fenced gardens."

Sophie twisted her mouth disapprovingly. "You would take a risk just for a few hours outside?"

"I promise to be careful," Laura said and ate the fig. "If it eases your fears, you can ask Thomas to escort me out of town. Once we are free of the city, I shall be safe as a babe."

Clearly Sophie wasn't convinced. Still, Laura was twenty-three and capable of making decisions for herself.

She walked over, pressed a kiss on Sophie's cheek, and squeezed her hand. Cook watched the exchange, a large wooden spoon gripped in her fist. Cook's eyes showed that she, too, wasn't confident with Laura's plan.

"Truly, you two needn't worry," Laura said. "I shall return to you the same as when I left."

With the countryside calling, Laura changed into a borrowed white day dress that hid her shape beneath heavy adornments of lace and bows. Then she collected her shawl, her bonnet, a borrowed cloak, and a picnic basket Cook pressed into her hands. She found her way to the stable, met up with the stern-faced Thomas, and soon left the bustle and noise of London behind.

The two-wheeled gig squeaked and rattled as the fat pony, Muffin, ambled slowly down the road, as if piqued that she'd been pressed into service. Still, Laura had been informed that the pony was a dependable sort and perfect for a daylong adventure.

Sometime later, she'd waved off Thomas with the promise to return to the school well before dark. A useless vow, certainly, as she suspected he'd be following behind her, at a discreet distance, to make certain she came to no harm.

That suited her just fine. If he wanted to waste an entire day dawdling, it was up to him. She planned to think of nothing but sunshine and green meadows.

Since the day was warm, she shucked off the hot hooded cloak, her disguise, and tossed it over the seat beside her. The sun prickled delightfully on her bare forearms as the oversized bonnet kept her nose from freckling—and prying eyes from a close examination of her face.

There was no one to hover or tend to her needs. Nothing would keep her from running pell-mell across meadows like a wild thing if she wished. She had no destination in mind or a set time frame for which she had to be back. She had a few coins in her pocket, stolen during her planned escape from the earl. She'd brought them with her in case she stumbled across a village and wanted to make some purchase.

For the first time in what seemed like forever, a genuine smile graced her mouth and she tipped back her head. The sun spilled over her cheeks and she sighed happily.

"Onward, dearest Muffin," Laura said and clicked her tongue. The pony shook her head to dislodge a fly and snorted, her tiny hooves thumping on hard-packed earth. Laura grinned and eased her around a rut. "I promise to have you back in the stable by evening for oats, if that suits your mood."

With persistence, Laura managed to get Muffin into a trot. She kept her head down when passing other conveyances and spent an hour or so enjoying the sweet fresh air of the countryside without incident. It had been too long since she'd breathed anything but London soot. The scent of wildflowers and mown fields was a rare treat.

Eventually, the grumbling in her belly won out over

exploration and she began a search for a place out of the sun to eat. She glanced longingly at the picnic basket.

A young girl leading a brown cow on a rope came into view. Laura eased Muffin past them and then quickly edged back to the side of the road to allow an oncoming horse and rider to pass.

In an instant, she realized there was something familiar about the dappled-gray horse as it trotted by. It took another second or two to realize the rider had turned the beast around and was pulling up beside her. She lifted startled eyes to his face and jerked the reins at the same time. The gig stopped abruptly and she was nearly pitched from the seat!

Thus began an awkward scramble to recover her balance. A burning flush stained her cheeks as she righted herself. Gads.

There was no point pretending not to notice him, or that she did not recognize his face. She had a feeling Mister Harrington was not the sort of man who would be ignored. And he certainly wasn't the kind of man whom women easily forgot.

"Imagine my surprise, Miss Laura, to discover you out here, alone, and quite some distance from London." He peered at her from beneath the brim of his hat and leaned down to brace an elbow on his thigh for a better view of her. "Are you lost?"

She felt a tingle of annoyance. Her day had been perfect and all her own. Until now. "No, Mister Harrington, I am not lost." Then a worrisome thought rushed into her head. "How did you recognize me? I thought I was well disguised." She put her hand to her mouth and scanned the road behind her. The girl and cow had vanished.

"You needn't worry." He followed her gaze before turning back to point to Muffin. "It was the pony. She belongs to Eva. I matched her with the way you carry yourself and came to a correct conclusion; the woman buried under the large bonnet was indeed Miss Laura."

Laura narrowed her eyes skeptically. If she didn't know better, she'd suspect he'd followed her. However, he had come upon her from the other direction. She concluded that their meeting had to be by chance. She settled back and stared.

"I thought it would be safe to venture out for a few hours." She looked at his face, really noticing his striking features for the first time. He cut a fine figure on his grand horse. "I promised to be back before dark."

Continuing her perusal, she noted that his hair was lighter in the sunshine, not quite black now, and was a bit long where it brushed the collar of his charcoal gray coat. His white breeches skimmed his thighs casually and left little to the imagination. His blue eyes were amused, and she knew it had to be her graceless near fall from the gig that brought his humor.

"Excellent plan, this adventure," he said, tightening his grip on the reins. "I think I shall join you."

He started to urge the horse forward, but drew up when she held Muffin back. "I don't mean to be rude, sir, but this journey involves one woman and one pony. Now if you will excuse us."

Laura flicked the reins and clicked her tongue. The gig jolted into motion. The pony managed a full dozen steps before the gray moved up alongside them with a dancing gait. Laura stopped again, planting her feet so not to commit a second almost-tumble.

The man lacked the good sense not to grin at her vexed glare. "I think it best you have an escort. These are dangerous roads for a woman alone."

Her gloved hands tightened on the reins. "In spite of recent events, I am not entirely helpless and am very handy with a whip. I can assure you I am quite safe."

The saddle creaked as he adjusted his seat and held her stare. "Still, you cannot begrudge me an afternoon spent in the delightful company of a lovely woman?"

This argument was getting her nowhere. He had made up his mind to accompany her and wasn't about to be put off. Hopefully, he'd quickly become bored with her aimless wanderings and leave her alone.

"As you wish," she said with a sigh and urged Muffin onward. "But let me assure you, if you expect an exciting frolic around the countryside, you'll be disappointed. Muffin, and I, do not frolic."

She could feel the weight of his gaze on her. Oddly, though, she wasn't uneasy with him, in spite of the way he'd quickly subdued her attackers. With evil footmen, he was a clear threat. The two men were likely still licking their wounds. With her, he was well contained and non-threatening.

If he planned to drag her off into the bushes and violate her, there was no hint of that darkness on his face.

"The excitement will come from spending time in your charming company," Mister Harrington said. "I believe we two will not suffer a single dull moment."

Laura tried to look at him askance, but the brim of the bonnet proved an effective barrier. She impatiently pushed it back, then squinted under the attack of sunlight in her eyes.

"You, sir, do not know a thing about me." She lifted one hand to shade her eyes. "I could be very, very dull."

His smile was wide and disarming, the sort that made women swoon.

Thankfully, she was immune. There wouldn't be any swooning today, or any other day.

"Are you *really* dull, Miss Laura?" He asked the question with mock sincerity. "Please tell me that you are not dreadfully dull."

She shrugged. "If I say yes, then you will think I am dull and my womanly pride will not allow it. And if I say no, then I am filled with conceit for thinking myself a fascinating creature. I cannot win either way."

He fell silent for a moment, and then smoothed down his artfully knotted white cravat before cocking up one brow. "Can I offer my opinion on the matter?"

"Would it gain me anything to say no?"

"I fear not."

"Then proceed."

Truthfully, she wanted to know his opinion. At the same time, he was much like the fly currently buzzing around Muffin's pointed ears. If she waved him away, he'd keep coming back with equal determination to pester her until a swat ended the matter.

They came upon a split in the road and he headed left. Laura reluctantly followed. Once they were again side by side, he picked up the conversation.

"When one thinks of a person as dull, there are usually several reasons on which to base such an opinion, don't you think?" He waited for her nod. "A person's lack of conversational skills or endless pontificating on one especially dull topic can breed a dullard. Perhaps even a crushing shyness that makes lively conversation impossible. All of these do a person discredit when socializing. One, or even the whole, can lead one to become reputed to be dull and therefore avoided in social situations."

"I suppose that is correct." Laura couldn't fault his reasoning thus far. But what did this have to do with her?

To Laura, this conversation itself was growing tiresome. "Sir, you really must get to the point. Am I dull or am I not?"

There wasn't a need to look up to know he was smiling. Her impatience would only add to his wry humor.

"I have seen you face down footmen with fierce courage, half-frozen with fear and cold. You forge ahead with your life, in spite of having no family support or a clear path to follow. And today you have given me glimpses into your sharp and fascinating mind." He shook his head. "My Lady Laura, you are most certainly not dull."

Laura sat in the bobbing seat and thought about his observation. She once considered herself witty and carefree. There had been friendships and young men to flirt with and a father who taught her to enjoy books and lively conversation. She'd laughed and danced and was hopeful of her future. Unfortunately, her father's illness had worsened. Everything had changed once he realized he was dying.

The frivolity of her life had vanished.

Her chest tightened as the bright sky seemed to darken around her. "Sometimes it is safer to cling to dullness. It allows one to go through life without notice."

Simon heard an underlying current of something in her voice—a deep sadness. It notched up his curiosity about her.

"Perhaps." He let his eyes drift over her hair and noticed there was a hint of red in the sable. Her lashes were long and dark and effectively shaded her eyes. From his position above, he could see the graceful curve of her neck and the straight line of her pert nose. But it was the upward press of her full white bosom against her modest neckline that caused the most interest. She possessed delightful curves.

Beneath his breeches, he felt a stir, and silently cursed his reaction. If he wanted her to trust him, openly lusting after her was not the way to go about earning favor.

"I see you have a basket," he asked, changing the conversation. He needed to lighten her mood. "Dare I hope you are in possession of food?"

She looked at the basket and frowned. She was clearly nearing the end of her patience. He should ride away, but found he couldn't. He was curious to know her better.

"I suppose I *could* share with you. . . ." She let her voice trail off, leaving him the perfect opening to excuse himself.

Instead, he nodded toward a nearby copse of trees. "Then I think that field yonder is a perfect spot for a picnic."

Simon ignored her exasperated sigh and nudged Horse off the road. He dismounted and tied both Horse and the pony to a crooked fence post.

The two animals regarded each other warily before the weeds waving near their muzzles proved more interesting than each other. They both settled down to eat.

Holding out his arm, Simon led Laura across the meadow to a pair of oak trees. The light scent of flowers drifted up from her and he grinned. If he could soothe her annoyance, then perhaps the picnic would be a success.

He shucked off his coat and smoothed his gray-striped waistcoat into place. They didn't have a blanket, and her white dress wasn't practical for sitting on bare earth.

"Allow me." He spread the coat out for her. She murmured her thanks and settled down on the makeshift seat. Simon sat on a patch of prickly grass and lifted the lid of the basket.

"Are those tarts I smell?" If the delightful scent was any indication, the cook at the courtesan school possessed excellent culinary skills. But it wasn't food he found first. Brows aloft, he closed his hand over polished steel and lifted a pistol to the light. "Someone is expecting trouble."

Laura gasped, screwed up her face, and shook her head. "Sophie is very protective. Clearly she expected me to be overrun by highwaymen and thieves."

Simon turned it in the light. It was loaded. "These are only useful when one knows how to use them."

Laura smirked. She reached for the pistol and he reluctantly put the weapon in her outstretched hand. It took him a few seconds to realize she knew exactly how to handle a pistol as she skillfully examined the piece.

At his surprised look, she shrugged. "My father always hoped for a son. Sadly, my parents had no other children. So he taught me everything a son should know."

Simon grinned and reclaimed the pistol. "I am impressed." And he was. She was quite an interesting puzzle. "Now we eat."

As he pulled out each food item, he eagerly anticipated the next. Slices of fresh bread filled with ham and slices of cheese, the strawberry tarts, and some sort of crusty meat pie that he suspected by the aroma was pigeon, rounded out the fare. "Your cook expected you to feed an army. There is enough food here for a half dozen hearty appetites."

A smile tugged one corner of her mouth. "Miss Eva makes sure her courtesans eat well. She is very considerate of her young ladies." She reached out for the cheese and popped a wedge into her mouth. Simon watched, fascinated, as she delicately chewed before reaching for a sandwich.

Watching her eat was a dangerous thing to do. She had a mouth meant for kisses. It took a huge measure of discipline to turn his eyes from her full lips to the treats spread out near his knees. The food was certainly less fascinating than his lovely companion.

Simon took a fork to the meat pie and put a large bite into his mouth. The taste was delicious. After he swallowed it down, he grinned. "Do you think Eva would be piqued if I stole away her cook?"

Laura looked at him sidelong. "I think you have pushed her patience too far already. If you abscond with Cook, I think she will set the hounds on you."

"She has hounds?" Simon asked, frowning.

"If she doesn't, I'm sure she can find some."

Simon realized Laura was teasing him, and he chuckled. It showed him, in spite of her sober demeanor, that she didn't despise him. Not completely anyway. If she could banter with him, surely smiles and laughter would follow. Someday.

"Then I shall leave the cook to the school." He made a face. "I do not relish the thought of being torn to bits."

The corners of her mouth twitched. He froze, watching and waiting for the smile. It didn't come.

They ate in companionable silence until a good half of the food had disappeared. Once satisfied, Laura leaned back on her hands and lifted her eyes to the blue sky, mottled through the expanse of leaves overhead. For an unguarded moment, she seemed relaxed and carefree.

The wary strain around her eyes and mouth vanished, and Simon wondered what it would be like to hear her laugh—a full, open, belly laugh. He considered recent events and suspected she hadn't had much cause for laughter.

He'd treaded into a perilous tide and knew spending the day with her was a terrible idea. He had Brenna's future to consider. He should be in London courting Lady Jeanette. But for a few hours he wanted to forget the weight of his responsibilities and simply enjoy Laura's company.

They sat quietly for several minutes. She watched the

birds and he watched her. Her every innocent movement drew his attention, from the way she tipped her head, to the motion of her hand as she twirled a length of grass between her fingers.

Eventually he forgot himself when her seductive draw proved too much for his male urges to resist. Her perfect mouth was a beacon for his attention. He leaned forward and stepped over an invisible boundary.

"Now that our appetites have been sated, what shall we do next?" Without thinking, he reached out and drew a pair of fluttering hairs away from her lips. His fingertips brushed her silky skin and his mouth parted. The overwhelming ache to kiss her overcame his good sense.

He lifted his eyes to her face for some sign that she wanted to kiss him, too. What he saw was not sensual hunger. She was stock-still, her eyes wide.

Panic flashed across her features. She blinked, scrambled backward off his coat, stood, and jumped away from him like a startled deer. "Don't touch me," she cried and lifted her hands to hold him off.

Simon was stunned by her reaction to a simple touch. Did she think his plan was to violate her here in the grassy meadow? Did he look to her like the sort of man who'd force himself on a woman?

He felt a rush of annoyance and stood.

"Keep back," she ordered. Her eyes darted to the horses as she appeared to assess her chances of escape.

"Laura." He lifted his hands, too. The encounter was teetering on odd and he was darn certain he had no idea why she'd reacted to him so vehemently.

Laura shook as though she'd fallen into an icy pond. "Don't you come near me or I'll scream."

"Laura." He turned his hands palms up and open in a gesture he hoped would appease her. "I didn't mean anything untoward by touching your face."

Whether it was because of his tone or the words or his calm voice, something changed in her. She blinked and her shoulders drooped as she openly struggled to regain her composure. Her nose notched up. "Just keep your hands to yourself."

Simon nodded. "I shall try and remember." He shoved his hands into his pockets. She seemed satisfied with his compliance.

As he looked into her eyes, he suspected that his lusty thoughts and his clear desire to kiss her had panicked her. But why? Maybe she *had* thought he planned to make use of the privacy to press her down in the grass.

Slowly, she crossed her arms protectively over her bosom. The movement shifted the neckline of the day dress and it gaped slightly away from her body.

There, on the lovely pale skin of her collarbone, skimmed by sunlight, was a puckered scar. The shock of the dreadful mark took him aback. He suspected that if he pulled back her gown, he'd find further injuries.

It explained clearer than words her panicked reaction to his touch.

And the urge to murder welled hot in his chest.

Chapter Five

Laura saw his face tighten with rage. She followed his gaze to the exposed scar. No longer red, it was letter-opener shaped—the kind of burn one gets when that metal object is held over a candle and pressed against the skin.

The kind of punishment that came with disobedience.

She quickly jerked the gown over the place and lifted her nose. "This is none of your concern." She turned away and took a few deep breaths.

Her mind whirled. It wasn't his reaction to the scar that occupied her rioting emotions but her visceral reaction to his touch. Her body had shockingly responded to the simple brush of his fingertips on her face in a way that had both enticed and terrified her.

The shiver that he'd sent across her skin had been followed quickly by alarm. Until that moment, she'd been indifferent to his attention. Clearly her body had other ideas. And finding herself drawn to his touch was worrisome. Very, very worrisome.

A stick crunched and she felt him move up behind her. Her wary body tightened. Of course she'd known he was attractive. She wasn't blind to it. And he'd touched her before.

Somehow the intimacy of his fingertips on her face had snapped her out of the cold reserve she'd developed with Westwick, as if Mister Harrington had reached through the outer shell of Sabine and touched a small piece of Laura.

She pinched her arm to collect herself and forced herself not to flinch at his nearness.

"I cannot forget what I saw," he responded softly. He stepped around her and bent to look into her eyes. "Tell me who did this to you."

"And you will do what? Call him out with pistols? Beat him senseless?" She placed her hand over where the dress covered the mark. "There has already been enough violence. Leave it be, Mister Harrington."

With that, she turned and stalked off toward the gig. Behind her she heard him quickly collect the remains of their picnic and hurry after her. By the time he got back to the road, she was perched on her seat with the reins in her hands and her bonnet firmly in place. He had just enough time to drop the basket onto the cart when Muffin lurched into motion, turned around in the road, and headed back toward London.

He'd been soundly dismissed. Laura could only hope it would keep him from pursuing further contact.

Thankfully, she didn't hear the horse following. Perhaps he was a gentleman after all. Yet somehow, she knew she hadn't seen the last of him.

She touched the scar.

Why couldn't the past stay buried? It was as if everything that was her life was reduced to her time in captivity, those months of hell at the hands of a devil.

Laura glanced at the basket and the pistol within. And for a moment, and only for a moment, she considered turning the gig toward the earl's town house and exacting her own revenge.

The idea vanished as quickly as it had come. Killing him would not erase what he'd done or satisfy her desire to see him punished. With luck, he'd get his comeuppance someday. However, it wouldn't be at her hand.

She forced herself not to look back to see if Mister Harrington was following. She suspected he was. The man had a strong, if misguided, sense of chivalry.

Simon untied Horse and swung up into the saddle. Anger festered in his blood, and all he saw on the return to London was the shadowy face of a man he wanted to hang from a high branch by his feet and take a whip to. Had Laura shared the name, he'd have the deed done by nightfall.

He kept close enough distance behind the gig to keep Laura in sight but far enough not to invade her privacy. There had been plenty of that today.

Their meeting had been entirely accidental. He was considering purchasing a ramshackle property that had been repossessed for unpaid taxes. The owner had died without heirs. The stable and grounds were in need of attention, but the house was solid and the land was excellent for planting. And the tenants were desperate for a new master. It was an ideal country home. He planned to make an offer on the place when he returned to town.

Spotting Laura on the road had been a pleasing bonus to his productive day. And now he'd ruined hers.

He followed until a servant joined her just outside the city, then Simon pointed Horse toward White's. If ever he needed a brandy, it was now.

The club was quiet when he arrived, and soon he was slumped in a chair before a fire, a glass of fine port in his hand. Within a quarter of an hour, the spirit softened the edges of his frustration.

He felt pulled in two directions—not only toward Lady Jeanette, his intended bride, but also toward Laura, the damaged courtesan.

There was no easy remedy to the situation.

"There is Harrington." A slurred voice snapped him from his musing and he looked around to see the Goodrich twins, Sherman and Shaw, weaving their way across the room. "And he looks like he requires company."

Clearly the Goodrich duo were fully into their cups as they wobbled over in a drunken dance to claim a pair of open overstuffed leather chairs nearby. His scowl didn't deter them from joining him.

He squelched a groan as the affable pair settled, stretched out their skinny legs, and released a pair of silly grins. Orange freckles dotted their matching faces beneath thick mops of matching hair on each head.

Only casually acquainted, Simon didn't know who'd spoken. The Goodrich brothers were the sons of a viscount, known for heavy drinking and heavier losses at cards. In social settings, they were a generally amusing pair. Well, to all except their exasperated father.

"We haven't seen you around in days, old boy," one brother said jovially. "You missed the Hurst musicale."

The second brother nodded. "It was quite a row. Lady Tew caught Lord Tew nuzzling the neck of Miss Lacey out on the veranda. The harridan dragged her wayward husband out of the house by his thinning hair."

Simon snorted. Both Lord and Lady Tew were as round as they were tall, and Lady Tew was known for her temper. "It is nigh on impossible to understand why the lovely Miss Lacey would nuzzle in the dark with Tew. More than likely he'd snuck up behind her and taken advantage of the absence of her chaperone."

The lecher.

"Too true," said one twin. "No one believes the lady asked for his attention. She is highly marriageable and has offers. Still, you missed the fun."

"I've been busy with business matters," Simon replied, his mood lightening considerably. "But I will be at the Stanwood rout this evening. I certainly hope Lord Tew will behave. He has little hair left for Lady Tew to pull."

The two brothers laughed wholeheartedly, much more so than his small jest required. It attested to the depth of their drunken state. Well, that and the heavy scent of brandy and wine clinging to them.

"The party should be entertaining." The first brother

leaned forward in his chair. "It is rumored Lady Stanwood has hired the services of a woman who can tell fortunes."

Simon wanted to openly scoff, but the pair seemed genuinely excited at the prospect. "The woman is likely a charlatan who will spend the evening separating the nobility from their money."

"She is rumored to be Romany," twin two protested. "They are known for having the sight."

"Save your coin, lads. I can tell you your future." He lifted his glass and gulped down the last swallow. "I see wine, debutantes, and dancing, followed by drunken snores. Then tomorrow morning will follow with cold compresses for your heads and your mother lecturing you on imbibing too much."

The two men looked at each other, nodded, and laughed again. "Bravo," they said in unison. Then the first brother added, "That is exactly the evening we have planned."

The second brother begged, "Tell us more!"

Simon smiled indulgently. "Alas, I must beg off. If I don't leave now, I will not get to the bank before it closes."

He settled his glass on the table and moved to push up from the chair. However, the pair wasn't finished with him.

"I understand Lady Jeanette Abbot will be there," one brother said. The Goodrich pair shared an exaggerated wink. "We understand the delightful miss has led you on quite a chase, Harrington. You must run faster if you plan to catch the chit."

Annoyance replaced amusement and tightened Simon's chest. He hated to be the brunt of gossip.

The second brother piped in, "It is said that she is encouraging Lord Vincent, though he has neither your fortune nor handsome visage to recommend him."

"You might want to nudge her along if you plan to wed and bed the girl," the first brother added with flourish. "There are several scoundrels sniffing after her."

The pair sniggered. Simon wanted to clack their orange heads together. If the Goodrich brothers were privy to his pursuit of the girl, then his interest in Lady Jeanette was causing a stir. A humiliating fact, surely.

A Harrington who couldn't land the bride of his choice? The entire family tree would shake and shudder. Not even the blackest blackguard in Harrington history ever failed to snag a wife once he set his cap for her. In fact, most Harrington males had their pick from many beauties.

That was the problem. The questionable reputations of an entire clan of Harrington men had tarnished him in the eyes of suspicious mothers.

"I wouldn't bet against me yet, gentlemen." Simon gave them a slight bow. "Until the lady has said vows before a parson, she is still open for the taking."

The two brothers chuckled and called out encouragement as he left them to finish their journey to complete intoxication. While he gathered up his coat, hat, and cane, a low-voiced conversation filtered over to him. He froze.

"His lordship is quite upset over losing his courtesan," a tall man in a blue coat said, his face grim. "In fact, he is livid. His footmen are searching all of London for her."

"She has disappeared?" the shorter, stouter man asked, his florid face awash with curiosity.

The taller man leaned to take his companion into his confidence. Thankfully, Simon was close enough to hear. His stomach rolled and his fist balled. Were they discussing Laura? If he could get the name of her abuser, then he could hunt him down and change the position of his nose.

"She up and vanished, ran off, same as Lord Marsden's mistress did last year." The tall man scowled. "I never thought the day would come when a man couldn't control his courtesan."

The shorter man matched his scowl. "Clayworth is obscenely wealthy. He can clap his hands and the courtesans will line up to bed him. What has piqued his ire about losing this one?"

Simon's shoulders slumped. He left the club.

Lord Clayworth was seventy if he was a day. The man couldn't be Laura's patron. He could hardly stand, much less beat a woman, even with his cane. Simon speculated that the loss of Clayworth's courtesan had less to do with losing her than with his pride. He wouldn't want his companions to think him too old to keep a young lovely satisfied.

It was possible Eva was sheltering the young woman the two men spoke of. Either that or the missing courtesan had simply tired of icy hands and had gone off to seek a younger buck for her bed.

Laura's abuser would keep his face for another day.

He said a muffled curse as he collected Horse and left White's behind.

A s Simon expected, the Stanwood rout was a lively party. Lady Stanwood liked to invite too many guests, and the house was packed with bodies and too little air. Still, there were very few invitees who ever declined her invitations. The festivities always brewed up some sort of scandal, and no one wanted to miss a moment of fun.

"There you are, Harrington." Jace Jones slapped him on the shoulder. "I've been searching all over for you."

Simon smiled at his friend. Jace was an American and wealthy. They'd met two years previously in a scuffle over the same pretty tavern wench and often found trouble when they came together. However, tonight Simon was focused on courtship.

"I see your future fiancée has arrived." Jace pointed across the room. "And she isn't alone."

Simon spotted Lady Jeanette almost immediately, surrounded by a clutch of admirers. She looked lovely in pink, with her pale hair swept up and her eyes dancing with good humor.

"Since the day she rolled out of the schoolroom to start her season, she's been the center of attention," Simon remarked as he watched Lord David take her hand. "As the belle of society this year, the chit certainly doesn't lack for confidence."

"Then you should dash over and claim her before some other buck takes your place in her affections," Jace said, smirking. "She is ripe to be plucked."

Simon frowned. Jace wasn't fond of the young lady and

thought Simon a fool for pursuing her. "You are treading on treacherous ground, friend," Simon warned. "You know my reasons for the courtship."

Jace sighed. "I do. Though I do not think Brenna is headed for spinsterhood. She is still young."

"That is my concern, not yours."

"Then I shall put aside my misgivings and help you, old man," Jace said. "I am well known for my success with women."

Simon shook his head as Jace focused on Jeanette. Perhaps it would take his friend to see what mistakes he was making. He couldn't. The courtship was failing.

A minute or two passed before Jace spoke. "Do you see how the eager bucks are ignored and the more aloof fellows earn the most interest? Lady Jeanette sees a challenge in drawing out attention from the less engaged among her admirers."

Why hadn't Simon noticed that before? Perhaps it was his own confidence that his charm would bring her to heel that kept him from seeing the sly way Jeanette manipulated the men around her.

"Of course." He *had* played the game from a wrong angle. She was used to men chasing after her. He'd show disinterest and see what happened.

"A woman like Jeanette would despise being ignored," Simon said, more to himself than to Jace, and then grinned at his friend. "Well done. I bow to your superior knowledge of the fairer sex."

With this new idea in place, he spent the next two hours searching out other women who fit his requirements for a bride. He wholly ignored Jeanette and, upon doing so, added two names to his list of potential wives. Though neither was as well placed or as wealthy as Jeanette, they were both acceptable.

Simon collected a glass of wine from a passing servant when a clatter behind him brought him around. Jeanette stood one pace behind him, her body turned just enough to allow her to pretend she didn't see him.

He followed the path of her eyes and spotted her fan just off the tip of her right slipper.

"Oh, dear," she said prettily and bent to retrieve the item. Simon was quicker. He scooped up the fan and handed it to her with a flourish.

"Your fan, Milady." With that, he turned and took a step away from her. An exasperated breath sounded. Simon smirked.

"Mister Harrington."

Simon sobered before turning about for a second time. He cocked a brow. "Milady?"

Her pouty lips showed her displeasure and he knew his plan had worked brilliantly. She was displeased with him, even after refusing his suit only days before.

For the third time.

A dawning came then. Jace was correct. She *had* refused him in order to pique his interest. She'd wanted him begging for her hand like a queen on a throne. She wanted a pet who would come when she whistled and who'd totter along on her heels like a well-trained mutt.

Anger welled.

"You have not yet asked me to dance, Mister Harrington." The lip pulled in and her pout melted into a smile. "You must correct the matter soon before my dance card is filled."

Simon reined in his temper. "You made your position clear the last time we spoke. As I recall, you called me untamed and lacking charm. Then you called for a footman to put me out." He watched her flinch and took satisfaction from her reaction. "I thought it best if we had no further contact."

Chapter Six

Simon knew his abrupt dismissal forever harmed his cause. However, all he could think about was the scar on Laura's collarbone. Dancing in attendance to the spoiled child was a grim prospect when his mind was engaged elsewhere.

"I was correct about you, sir," said the pouting pink confection. "You are boorish and rude."

He shrugged. "I'm a Harrington."

The chit left him in a huff. As he headed home, he knew he'd suffer for his callous behavior.

There was little chance of ever repairing things with the girl.

Worse, he realized that until he recovered from his fascination with Laura, there would be no other woman in his life. This did not bode well for his sister.

Brenna might never get a chance to marry Chester Abbot. That was his biggest regret as he wandered to his room and readied himself for bed. The match would have been perfect for his sister.

After a night spent staring at the ceiling and counting the minutes until dawn, Simon finally eked out two hours of rest before dragging himself from the bed.

Dunston, his valet, helped him dress and poured some coffee into him. The dark brew did nothing to ease the threads of red in the whites of his eyes. He looked like he'd spent the evening drinking and wenching, without the rollicking good memories of doing either.

"Is there anything else you require, sir?" Dunston asked when Simon was properly tucked into his coat and the item smoothed out over his shoulders. That man was nothing if not efficient. After eight years of loyal service, the valet was worth his extensive experience in gold pieces.

"You have done all you can, my good man, unless you have a tonic for red eyes?" Simon looked into the mirror. The haggard face peering back at him would probably terrify dogs and small children. "Have I ever told you how much I value your service?"

"Sadly, I've no tonic, and once or twice." Dunston answered both questions with a patient grin. "Usually you speak of your appreciation when well into your cups."

Simon chuckled. "Ah, yes. My misspent youth." He had more than earned his Wild Harrington title. But those days were behind him. At twenty-nine, it was time to grow up.

Sleeplessness had given him clarity. He had to untangle his life, and quickly. Brenna was withering.

"Do you have sisters, Dunston?" Simon asked.

"No, sir." The valet smiled. "Though my pa was a faithless scoundrel, he produced no other issue. Thus far no one has come forward to claim him as kin."

Simon clapped him on the back. "You are a lucky man. Sisters have a way of aging a fellow. I will be lucky to get Brenna wed before I am stooped and gray."

Chester Abbot's father, the duke, was said to be near death from consumption. Chester would soon be required to find a wife and produce heirs, a feat that Simon wasn't entirely certain the man could accomplish. Still, if Simon couldn't find Brenna another acceptable mate before the old duke died, he planned to throw his sister at Chester's oversized feet.

* * *

Simon dismissed Dunston and called for his horse. It was a fine morning for visiting his new estate in Surrey. Though he'd been pleased to find a home far enough from London to be considered a country estate, it was close enough to visit and return in a day's ride.

With his day planned, he urged Horse onward for several minutes until he realized he was traveling in the wrong direction. He pulled Horse to a stop, taking a second to orient himself. Somehow, he'd sent his horse toward the courtesan school, as if somewhere in the back of his mind he knew he couldn't let another day pass without apologizing to Laura.

He smiled and nudged the beast forward. "Off we go."

The town house was as he remembered as he approached the door, again without an invitation. He'd made certain he hadn't been followed, nor did he intend for these visits to continue.

He just had to assure himself Laura hadn't suffered any ill effects of their prior conversation.

It was a thin excuse to see her again, but he hadn't the time to come up with something more substantial.

What he hadn't counted on was Noelle's face at the door.

"Simon." Her voice was heavy with censure, and his name was spoken through gritted teeth.

"Cousin. Again I find you here," he said, biting back a smirk. "Your husband must miss having you at home."

She expelled a breath. "Not that it is any of your business, but Eva had a household emergency so I offered to come this morning in her stead. And though I appreciate your concern for the state of my home situation," she said tartly, "Gavin is quite content with our marriage."

Grimly, he nodded. "The man clearly has low expectations."

He knew by the look on her face she was teetering on the brink of killing him. He fought a grin. He shouldn't tease her, but found a lifetime of doing so hard to change.

"What do you want, Simon?" she asked impatiently, though they both knew the answer.

"I have come to see Laura," he answered in a matching tone.

She scowled. "I know who you've come to see. The question is, why can't you leave the poor woman alone?"

"If you let me in, I'll explain." He waited for her to let him pass. However, that was not her intention. She blocked the narrow opening. Only her face and a thin bit of her gray-clad body showed.

"You'll explain from there."

For the second time in recent weeks, he wished for a more biddable female relation. "I bumped into her on the road the other morning and I fear that our conversation, though unintentional I assure you, upset her. I have come to apologize."

"And that is all?" Suspicion edged the scowl. "Her loveliness has nothing to do with your continued interest?"

This time the door opened and Noelle stepped outside, closing the door behind her. She crossed her arms and looked up at him. "Laura is not the sort of woman you can play games with, Simon. Her life has been difficult. If you intend to do her any sort of disservice by taking advantage of her situation, I assure you Eva and I will not be pleased."

Her words took him aback. "You think I want to make her my mistress?" She said nothing. "You do." He scrubbed his hand down his face. "That is not my intention."

Noelle stared for a long moment. Finally, she spoke. "In spite of her circumstances, Laura was not a courtesan by choice." She paused and her eyes clouded. "I'll not break her confidence when I say that she was meant for a better life."

Not once had Simon considered the reason why Laura became a courtesan. He assumed she sold herself for the same reasons most women did: money, sex, or desperation. Obviously, he'd been wrong. There was much more to his courtesan than he'd seen thus far.

His curiosity rose. "I fear I have mistaken her situation.

Still, my intentions are not dishonorable." What were his intentions? That was a question he couldn't answer. "In some cultures, when you save a life, you are responsible for that person forever." He smiled. "I suppose you can consider me her champion."

"Hmm." Her scowl faded but her suspicion stayed put. "Laura grows stronger every day. She needs no one to fight her battles, Simon. But you may see her, if only to ease your mind. Then perhaps you'll never again darken this stoop."

Laura should have been surprised when Miss Noelle announced that she had a visitor, and who it was, but she wasn't. For some unfathomable reason, Mister Harrington had decided his presence was needed in her life. And unfortunately, her frequent dismissals were not enough to dissuade him from that notion.

The courtesans whispered among themselves, a flock of hens anticipating the arrival of a fox. They'd been curious about her rescuer since the night she'd arrived, and his visits did nothing to quell their interest.

Laura ignored their whispers, brushed bits of flour off her dress, and walked to the parlor. She was hot from the kitchen and did not want to make frivolous conversation with an unwelcome guest. He had to be sent away.

Forever.

He was examining a painting over the fireplace, his back to the door. She noticed immediately how much he imposed on the feminine space. "Mister Harrington."

He turned. "Miss Laura." His smile warmed the room.

She ignored his charm. "I believe I have made myself very clear, Mister Harrington," she said sharply. "I no longer need your assistance or companionship. And yet here you are again. Were my wishes unclear?"

"Indeed they were not." He shrugged. "My family calls me stubborn. Sadly, it's an incurable trait."

A lock of damp hair fell over her right eye. The strands were too short to stay tied in the ribbon at her nape. She tried to brush it back, but the hair was persistent. Frustrated, she dropped her hand.

"Stubbornness is no excuse for ignoring my wants," she countered. "You must stay away."

Mister Harrington took a few steps forward. She forced herself to remain still under his regard.

"I felt compelled to come," he said. "I can't explain it, but I had to make certain you suffered no ill-effects of our argument."

Fatigue from the morning's work took some of the starch out of Laura. It was baking day and the smell of fresh bread filled the town house. She found the coolness of the parlor refreshing after hours in the kitchen. It was Mister Harrington who kept her from completely enjoying this brief respite.

She scanned his handsome face, and her heart beat a little faster. It was impossible not to notice how well he fit the cut of his clothing. This observation added to her aggravation. Next to his polished perfection, she was a wet cat.

Sticky dough clung to her fingernails. She frowned and hid her hands behind her. "As you can see, I am quite well. Truly, there is no more need for you to concern yourself about my welfare."

Light twinkled in his eyes. "I can see you are a step up from the bedraggled young woman who clung so valiantly to the back of my horse."

Reluctantly, she followed the downward path of his eyes. There was a damp patch in the center of her dress, marred by flour and a trio of red strawberry-filling finger marks.

Though she'd assured him she was well, she looked a fright. No wonder the man had his concerns. It appeared as though she'd been under attack by a tray of strawberry tarts.

Somewhere deep within her, laughter began to well. Before she could catch herself, giggles broke free as she reached up to rub at the stains. She heard his chuckle and lifted her eyes to his face, their laughter mingling in the small room.

"When you arrive unexpected, you must accept whatever condition I am in."

His chuckle faded to a smile. "I am not disappointed."

Beneath her corset, her stomach flipped. His warm eyes reconfirmed his words. He wasn't the least bit horrified by her condition. It was the intensity of his stare that rattled her emotions. She didn't need him to gather her into his arms and kiss her to feel a surprising and most unwelcome attraction to this appealing stranger.

She sobered and cleared her throat. "Don't come again."

"I can't make that promise."

Impatience flared. She glanced over her shoulder. There was no sound of chatter coming from the kitchen. The women likely had their ears pressed to the door. "Men are welcome only at the party. You are breaking Miss Eva's strict rules."

Beneath unruly dark hair, his face sobered. "Then I should leave at once. Miss Eva can be positively frightening."

Laura's lips twitched. The man was a rake. An utterly charming rake. Why couldn't she hold on to her anger? "Only because she cares."

"Yes, she does."

Silence fell between them. Then, "Mister Harrington—"

He interrupted, "The real reason for my visit was to ask you a favor." He crossed the room and stopped a respectable distance from her. "I have purchased a property in Surrey and it requires renovations and a woman's eye for decoration." He leaned back on his heels. "Would you ride out with me and give your opinion on what needs to be done to make it inhabitable?"

Laura stared. She couldn't get rid of the man no matter what she tried. "Don't you have a female relative you can press into service?"

"I'd ask my sister but she is put out with me at the moment." He grinned. "Right now she is out searching for highwaymen and pirates."

Pirates? Laura let the odd comment pass. "I don't think

that wandering about Surrey with you is a good idea. We would be alone and Miss Eva has her rules—"

"I promise not to take advantage," he interjected and rushed to assuage her fears. "I will be a proper gentleman."

"I suspect you have never been proper, sir." She wanted to refuse. Knew she should refuse. However, something inside her felt an obligation to him. If not for his timely arrival that night, she'd have been returned to her nightmare. What he asked of her was small in comparison. She nodded and sighed. "I will help. But you must have me back by nightfall."

"It is a promise."

Another promise? Why then did she have the feeling she was about to crawl into a bucket of snakes?

Chapter Seven

※❦❧

Simon was surprised by Laura's agreement to accompany him. He expected her resistance and lined up several arguments in hope of changing her mind. Thankfully, he didn't have to use them. Though she wasn't pleased, she'd agreed, and he was relieved.

"I can retrieve a carriage if you have an aversion to horses or would like to bring a chaperone." He hadn't considered that she might be unable to ride. Clinging to Horse out of fright did not make her a skilled rider. "For the sake of propriety, of course."

A cheerless smile tugged her lips. "The maid has gone off to purchase eggs and the courtesans are better off kept away from you. Besides, I am well beyond the age and circumstance where I need to concern myself with propriety. Being a courtesan allows me the freedom to wander about as I wish."

Simon grimaced. There was no bitterness in her words, just cold acceptance. How had she come to this? He found that he wanted to know her story—every last detail.

"You are no longer a courtesan," he said tightly. It

annoyed him to think of her that way. As if "courtesan" was all she could claim. She was so much more.

She settled her beautiful eyes on him, and an undercurrent of desire shifted through his body. He tamped it down.

"Current or former, it really matters not, does it?"

He wanted to say it did matter, but she was correct. It didn't matter if her father was a king or her mother a duchess. Once she was labeled a courtesan, she'd always be considered tarnished in the eyes of society.

It was a shame. With her beauty, she could have been much sought after by men of the Ton. Add a huge dowry and she'd have her pick of husbands. They'd line up to charm her and beg to wed her. She'd choose her favorite and that one man would be lucky to spend the rest of his life in her bed.

There was no chance of that now.

Simon shook his head and silently scoffed at the thought. When had he become a romantic, and where had he put his lute?

Instead of answering her, he looked over her serviceable dress. "Can you ride?" He wanted the day to be light and enjoyable. No dismal topics, no arguments.

"Passibly." She looked down and grimaced. "I shall tell Miss Noelle of our plans, and change."

With that, she left the room. Simon listened to her footsteps fade away. He walked to the window. Laura might not welcome his visits, but she wasn't entirely cold to him either. He'd seen a slight spark of appreciation when she'd flicked her gaze over him.

Damn. He knew he was floundering through dangerous seas with Laura. Still, he couldn't seem to keep away from this damaged former courtesan.

Laura took only twenty minutes to ready herself for the ride. She came down the stairs in an unadorned brown gown and gloves. Her hair was swept back into a tight chignon and topped with a serviceable black bonnet that framed her lovely face.

Despite the severity of her appearance, his breath caught.

Yes, he was in deep danger.

He'd never felt such an intense attraction to a woman, and he'd spent time with plenty of beauties. Her subtle seductive pull drew him in and refused to release him.

There were bedrooms aplenty upstairs and Simon ached to make use of one. Instead, he silently cursed his thoughts, walked over to her, and held out his arm. "Shall we?"

Laura hesitated, then took his arm. He felt her hand tremble slightly as she touched him. Clearly, she was remembering the afternoon in the meadow.

"I do not bite," he teased, hoping to set her at ease.

She met his eyes and wrinkled her nose. "Of that, I am not convinced."

Chuckling, Simon escorted her from the room and spotted Noelle at the end of the hallway. She leveled a pointed frown at him, a silent warning to return Laura in the condition in which she left. He frowned back at her. Then he smiled and led Laura out the door.

I am impressed by how quickly you were able to secure a second horse, Mister Harrington. I thought your hunt for a mount would prove futile."

He'd led her through the tiny garden and disappeared into the mews behind the row of town houses. She renewed her acquaintance with Horse with several minutes of neck and ear scratching, before spotting Mister Harrington walking toward her, leading a saddled and pretty little gray mare.

"You must call me Simon. I think we are well past the need for formality." He dismissed Miss Eva's groom and adjusted the stirrup himself, shortening the length.

Laura wasn't comfortable with using his given name, though she often thought of him that way. However, she'd not argue. The weather was divine and she hadn't been riding in such a long time.

"Where did you find her?" Laura asked and brushed her cheek against the mare's soft nuzzle.

"The right number of coins can rent almost anything," Simon remarked as he walked over and gave her a hand up.

She settled in the sidesaddle and accepted the reins. "She was residing in a stable three houses down. According to the stable boy, the owner is elderly and bedridden. She keeps the mare in hopes of one day riding again. The lad assures me his mistress will not notice her missing."

Smiling, Laura leaned down to rub the mare's neck and murmured soft words. The mare and Horse were a matched set of grays and a lively pair. She smiled at her companion, pleased that she'd not have to ride Muffin.

"What is her name?" she asked softly. Her world brightened with the feel of the fine animal beneath her.

Simon paused. "I'm afraid I didn't ask."

Laura looked from the unnamed mare to Horse and back. She grinned slyly. "For today, I'll call her Mare." She ran her gloved hand down Mare's mane. "I do apologize for this slight, lovely girl. I am certain your real name is far more beautiful."

She tapped the mare with her heels. "Lead on, Mister Harrington." She ignored his disapproving grunt. "You promised to have me back before nightfall."

"Indeed I did." He darted a glance at the courtesan school and set Horse into motion. "Eva and Noelle will have me drawn and quartered if I break my promise."

His affection for the women was clear. The orphaned Laura envied his kinship with Noelle. She remembered that on the night of her escape, he'd mentioned they were cousins. And she'd begun to believe Miss Noelle and Miss Eva were more than just two women working toward saving courtesans. No, there were too many subtle exchanges between them not to suspect they were at least very dear friends.

"They have Thomas to do the torturing." Laura looked at him askance and teased, "I believe he is capable of tearing off limbs and heads."

He returned her glance and she shivered. The unwelcome reaction of her body to Mister Harrington unnerved her a bit, so she ignored the feeling. If she was to get through the afternoon without incident, she had to keep control of her traitorous body.

"Don't worry about my limbs," he said confidently. "I am a fast runner."

Laura snorted and a giggle escaped. "I suspect you aren't the kind of man to run from danger. I have seen no sign of cowardice during our short acquaintance."

In the cloud-filtered sunlight, she noticed a small scar through his left brow and another just beneath his chin. Either he'd been a very clumsy child, or he'd been in scrapes that involved fists or weapons. She believed it was the latter.

He hadn't hesitated in securing her from the footmen. He'd barreled over the two men with Horse and honed skill. He was no weak-kneed ninny.

"How little you know of my nature, dear lady, to be able to make such an observation." He sighed deeply. "I am afraid of mice and the dark and I shriek like a banshee when lightning cracks overhead. It is most shameful to admit."

She smiled and shook her head. "None of that is true."

He flashed a grin. "Alas, you have indeed caught me in a lie." He pressed Horse into a trot. Mare followed suit. "Though if I see an animal frothing at the mouth, I flee like the wind in the opposite direction."

Giggles followed as she imagined a foaming fox chasing him across hill and dale, his coattails flapping as he fled. Oddly, the image didn't fit at all. He was entirely too manly for such matters. However, the silly chatter had put her at ease. Soon London was behind them.

"So what is it you do, Mister Harrington?" Laura asked after a quiet stretch passed between them. His clothes did not come from a peddler's cart. They were fitted and costly. "Let me guess. Barrister? Ship captain?"

He shook his head. "Until recently, I did as little as possible beyond seeking my pleasures. Now that I am in the shadow of thirty, and my uncle seems unwilling to beget an heir, my father has begun grooming me for the eventuality that I will inherit a title."

"Title?" Laura's chest tightened. It was easy to be comfortable in the presence of a barrister or captain. Courtesans did not befriend noblemen.

"Should I outlive my uncle and father, I will be Lord Seymour someday." He shifted in the saddle. "I find it difficult to imagine myself as an earl. I was not born to expect it. There were two uncles born before my father, and we expected their sons to inherit. The oldest died without male issue and the second has no children."

The shine left the day. Her few contacts with the noble classes had left her with an unfavorable impression. They were spoiled, indulged, and took what they wanted without consequence.

Westwick had promised her a life free of worries and instead nearly destroyed her. His friends were no better. They knew his character and mirrored it without hesitation. The whole were a despicable lot.

"Pity," she remarked before realizing she'd spoken aloud. Her eyes opened wide and she slapped a gloved hand over her mouth. She'd just insulted a future earl.

She waited for him to take her to task.

"It *is* a pity," he said soberly. "It is the curse of the eldest son to carry the weight of the family." He looked up to the growing clouds. "If only Uncle Arthur had chased skirts rather than exotic plants, I'd be free."

Puzzlement brought her eyes to his. This was an odd turn.

"One would think most men pray for the day when they become titled," she said suspiciously. "I am surprised by your lack of enthusiasm."

Simon shrugged. "Some men are born with estate books in one hand and a sense of entitlement in the other. I wasn't. Uncle Arthur almost married once, but the woman died of a fever before the wedding. After her death, he lost his appetite for the institution."

Laura likened the doomed romance to a Shakespearian tragedy. "Your poor uncle. He must have loved her."

"Since childhood."

Having never been in love herself, she could only see the matter in an abstract way. "I understand that some people love only once in their lifetime. To lose that love is terrible. How different his life might have been had she lived."

Simon shrugged again. "Now he is content to spend his life as an adventurer, ever seeking new plant species and avoiding romantic entanglements."

That Laura could understand. She planned to spend the rest of her life content to be alone. "Even though you were not born buried in estate books, you do have the sense of entitlement. I have sent you away several times, and yet you return again. I'm not certain what you want from me. However, if you have salacious intentions, you may think again."

He chuckled. "I am a man. We always think salacious thoughts about women. But no, I am not taking you to Surrey to seduce you in my drafty old house. I thought you might like another outing, and I knew that I would enjoy your company. I see I was right. You are charming."

"Charming? I've never been called charming. And I have been nothing but contrary to you since your first visit," she said, her mouth twitching. "I'm quite out of practice when speaking to men I don't despise. Perhaps you should reserve your opinion until after you've returned me to the school."

Horse snorted and shook his head.

"I live with contrary women," Simon countered grimly. "My mother has a temper and my sister lives to make me miserable. You, my dear Laura, could learn much from them."

Laura smiled behind her hand. "I think they sound wonderful. Any woman who can ruffle you is someone to admire."

With a pained expression, he scowled. "Now I think I *shall* reserve my opinion until I return you to Eva."

Feeling his consternation, and knowing she'd caused it, she laughed brightly. "That is an excellent idea."

They passed the time on lighter topics. She learned that he hated figs, rats, and wasps. She told him about her aversions to pickled eel, crows, and tea without sugar.

His stories about his childhood were delightfully entertaining. Despite his comment about his mother and sister, she saw in his eyes his love for his family and envied the affectionate-squabbling relationship he shared with his younger sister and brother.

"Did your sister really tell Miss Sally Pemberton that you caught some contagious disease from eating worms?" Laura gasp-giggled as she pictured the incident he described.

Simon winced. "She did. That was the last time Sally ever spoke to me. Twelve-year-old girls already know that twelve-year-old boys are covered with icky stuff. Add an unnamed worm disease to the mix and she ran home so fast, she kicked up dust in her wake."

She shook her head. The young Miss Harrington had certainly given her older brother quite a time of it growing up. "I think your sister sounds delightful."

He glared. "That isn't the word I would choose."

"And yet you love her."

"That I do."

Laura pondered all she'd heard. "I wonder what stories your sister would tell." Laura said. "Did you dip her braid in an inkwell? Toss her in a puddle? Put a toad down the back of her gown?"

"I was always a perfect gentleman," he said.

"I find that very difficult to believe."

She pondered the man as he pulled Horse to a stop. Mister Harrington was certainly full of contradictions: charming yet dangerous; amusing yet sober, too. The more she knew of him, the less she understood him.

Something she did understand was the way she felt out of sorts when he looked at her with his intense blue eyes. Though he promised this trip was not about seduction, she wasn't certain that he wouldn't take advantage if pressed.

Her body wasn't repulsed as she'd been with Westwick. In fact, it was constantly aware of him beside her, as if on alert and eager for his touch.

This would not do. She'd fight the attraction with everything within her.

"It looks like rain," he said, pulling her from her musing. "The good news is that we have arrived."

Laura startled and looked around. All she saw was a long, overgrown driveway curving through a patch of trees. There was something oddly familiar about the area but the trees kept her from making a connection to the house beyond. He urged Horse onward and Mare plodded in line. As the lane opened up to the first glimpse of stone and roof, Laura felt a swell of familiarity she couldn't quite grasp. Did she know this estate?

They finally broke from the tree line into a clearing and Laura saw the stone monolith that stood looming from atop a low hill.

She gasped.

Chapter Eight

◈

"Laura, what is it?" She said nothing but sat frozen in the saddle with an odd look on her face. He pulled Horse to a stop, dismounted, and secured the horse to a tree.

Walking over to help her down, he noticed she was staring off toward the back of the house. Her eyes had a far-off cast. It was as if she were lost in a private world where he was not invited.

Worried, he touched her knee. "Laura, are you ill?"

She blinked, and then without a word, she kicked the mare into motion. Simon stumbled backward to avoid the moving horse. The pair launched across the weeded yard, around the manor, and disappeared with a thud of receding hooves.

Stunned, it took Simon a moment to recover from his surprise. What in the hell was happening?

Fearful for her safety, he grabbed his reins, swung up on the gelding, and took off after them.

As he circled the house, he noticed a narrow trail behind the manor. There was no sign of her, so he headed for the trail. Thankfully her direction was clear as he neared the opening. Broken twigs marked her passage into the forest.

Horse plunged forward, narrowly dodging tree branches and ruts and overgrown weeds.

"Damn woman," he cursed as a leaf hit him in the eye. Had she lost her senses? What was her destination, or had she decided to steal the mare and escape to a new life somewhere?

He barely had time to brace himself for flight when Horse bunched up beneath him and sailed over a log lying across the trail. Horse landed with an awkward thud, nearly unseating him. Skill kept Simon upright. At that speed, they should be narrowing the distance between them and the fleeing Laura, even with her head start. Horse was the superior animal. If she was running off, he should catch her soon enough.

"A passable rider?" Simon snorted, and ducked. A passable rider would have killed herself racing at such a breakneck speed. Laura was likely born atop a saddle. The mare had wings.

Up ahead, he saw enough light to expose a clearing before the gelding burst out of the trees and into an overgrown area where a building loomed before them. Simon sawed on the reins and Horse came to a hopping stop.

Standing beside the mare, reins dragging loosely on the ground, stood Laura, her attention transfixed on the small ramshackle cottage at the edge of a glen.

"Thank God you're safe," he growled. "You could have killed yourself running off like that."

She said nothing under his scold. It was as if he hadn't spoken at all.

"Laura?" he queried and slid to the ground. Then louder, "Laura!"

He hurried toward her, worried she'd suffered some sort of ailment of the mind. She didn't turn to him but acknowledged his presence with a simple, "I grew up here."

"What?"

"I grew up here," she repeated.

This time his brain processed her words. This was her
home? The day was full of surprises. "When?"

"Until just over a year ago."

Her voice was emotionless. "A year ago?" Confusion
welled as he stared at the abandoned building. Was this
really her home or had she hit her head on a tree branch in
the trail and addled her mind? He needed to shake her from
the trance in order to get answers.

He reached to place a hand on her shoulder. She moved
away before he made contact. She was stiff as she walked
toward the narrow door that was hanging slightly askew on
crumbling hinges.

Curiosity overcame concern and Simon followed, weeds
tugging at his breeches and scraping his boots as he walked
briskly after her.

He caught up at the door and placed a hand on her arm
to stop her advance. She didn't flinch. He moved around her
and pushed open the damaged panel. Instinctively, he knew
that whatever was troubling her, she'd tell him eventually.

"Let me go first." He looked in, finding no visible signs
of wild beasts, before stepping over the threshold.

The general smell of dust and decay filled his senses. It
had been some time since anyone had cared for the modest
structure. Light filtered in through the few windows,
exposing the stark emptiness of the house.

Laura followed him in, then passed by, her boots scattering dust as she walked into a room just off the entryway.
Wary, he kept a close watch for unwelcome surprises.

The room Laura entered was a parlor and likely the
largest room in the cottage. A sizable stone fireplace stood
at one end. Coal and burnt peat from a last fire was scattered over the hearth, likely caused by animals foraging for
food.

The few remaining pieces of furniture were shabby,
ruined by rodents and rain from the damaged ceiling.

Simon watched as Laura walked to the fireplace, her
boots crunching across bits of damaged roof. She didn't

look down. Her attention was on a dusty painting above the mantle of a child and a dog. In the girl's features, he could see Laura.

"She is you?" His question was more a statement. She'd told him that this was her home. There were likely more paintings, more trinkets, and more memories of Laura within these walls.

She pushed her bonnet back on her shoulders, nodded, and spoke. "Yes."

From her position, Simon couldn't see her face but felt her sadness, saw it in the droop of her carriage. There was no stiffness in her body as she crossed and rubbed her arms.

"The last day I spent here was the day before my father died." She turned to scan the room. Grief lined her features. "I was married that afternoon in this very parlor."

Married? "You are married?"

For days he'd spent all his time lustily thinking of her eyes, her face, the curves of her body, and she was a married woman? The idea of her legally belonging to another man was inconceivable. How had she gone from wife to courtesan?

She lifted her eyes to his. "The marriage was a sham to appease my dying father. The parson was a drunkard and not truly a parson at all. I did not know the truth until days later, after—" She cast her eyes downward. "My husband took great joy in informing me that I was, in fact, not his wife but his courtesan. He gleefully assured me that he'd never marry a lowly squire's daughter."

Simon gnashed his teeth. "And your father?"

Laura clasped her palms together and lifted them to her mouth. "By the time the truth came out, my 'husband' had already dragged me to London after a brief farewell. My father never knew of the betrayal. I received word some two days later that Father had died." She swallowed deeply. "I wasn't allowed to attend the funeral. My 'husband' thought I would solicit help and flee."

A grave impish light slowly filled her eyes. "But I did

flee. I suffered his punishments and bided my time. And when the moment came, I didn't hesitate."

The story certainly explained why she was clad in only a gown and slippers when he'd found her. Simon imagined her sneaking down some dark servants' staircase and into the night, a pair of footmen on her trail. Her false husband may have thought he owned her body, but her spirit had remained intact.

And knowing that she'd only been with one man filled him with a strange sense of relief.

"Had you been armed, the footmen wouldn't have had a chance of reclaiming you," he said, his admiration growing.

A shy smile tugged at her mouth. "I think you have mistaken me for a woman with more courage. I did what I needed to survive, nothing more."

Simon walked to her and took her hands. "You underestimate yourself, Laura." He rubbed his thumbs over her gloved knuckles. "You have more strength than you realize."

She briefly allowed his touch before pulling her hands free. Her chin went up. "I cannot allow *him* to take any more from my life. Otherwise he will continue to own me."

There was steel in her; he'd seen only brief glimpses of it until now. Her false husband had bent her and tried to break her will. When she'd fled, she proved herself stronger than he. The man was probably still raging about how he'd lost the game to his missing courtesan.

"You have the spirit of ten men." Simon smiled. He wanted to pull her into his arms and inhale her sweet floral scent. He wanted to show her what it was to be held with tenderness and affection. He longed to teach her that pleasure was to be found in bed, not force.

However, she was gently born, raised to be a wife, not a mistress. She needed friendship from him, not seduction. So no matter how much he ached for her, he would not seduce her to his will. If she wanted him, it would be Laura who made the decision.

"You see me as more than I see myself," she said, looking into his eyes. "Though I thank you for the compliment."

Simon tipped his hat. "Now you promised to assist me with my new home. I intend to hold you at your word."

Laura matched his smile, chasing the shadows from her mind. She could either spend the rest of her days with a cloud of gloom over her head, or turn her life into one of purpose.

Although being in this cottage brought her sadness and renewed her grief over losing Father, from this moment forward she planned to tuck away their sad last days together and remember happier times instead.

"I will fulfill my promise, but first . . ." She walked past him and out the door. "I am growing weary of wearing the same three borrowed gowns. The one I wore the night of the escape has been given away and the others came from Sophie. While I'm here, I shall collect some of my things. I long to wear my own clothes."

"It *will* be nice to see you in something that fits."

"It *will* be nice to wear something I chose for myself," she said and looked down. "Sadly, I have lost some weight. Alterations may be required."

Mister Harrington followed her through the cottage and up the stairs as she went to her room. Dust covered everything and gave the cottage an eerie feel. But she focused on her mission. Without asking for help, she dropped to her knees and dragged a valise out from under the bed. She heard Mister Harrington lean against the doorframe.

"I do not need help," she said firmly.

A soft chuckle followed her order. "As I am beginning to learn."

For the next several minutes, Laura dug through her belongings, taking a few favorite gowns, stockings, slippers, and other important items. Though her gowns were simple and unadorned, they were hers.

She couldn't pack much into the valise. Still, she was satisfied with her choices. The last items she chose were a pair of tiny paintings of her parents. She stared down at them, tears welling, before gently placing them atop the tidy pile and snapping the valise closed.

She spun to face Simon. "Now you may assist."

He bowed and collected her valise. He made a mock pained expression when he lifted the item and she shook her head with a smirk.

"It isn't that heavy."

"I think I've strained my back," he teased as she walked past him, leveling a glare on him as she went.

The next stop was her father's room. Laura averted her eyes from his crumpled bed. Their staff had been minimal in the end, as his modest pension dwindled with his care. After the funeral, the servants would have left to seek other employment. There would be no reason to tidy up behind them.

Laura went to his wardrobe and opened the doors. Most of his clothing was gone, taken by servants or thieves, but for a few musty old pieces. Odd that there was anything left at all.

The earl must have decided the contents of the cottage not worth his consideration. He'd left it all to rot rather than auction the lot. And as the cottage belonged to the estate, it wasn't his to sell.

She slumped with relief and picked through the few remaining coats until she found the one with the missing button. A quick check of the pockets revealed what she was looking for: a purse filled with coins.

Glancing back, she smiled. "Buried treasure."

She pulled out the purse and shook it. Coins clanked. "Father did not fully trust banks." She pulled it open and looked inside. "Of course, there wasn't a need to use one. There was never much."

Simon took the item from her and poured the coins in his hand. "Still, it is something."

"Miss Eva will allow me to stay until I find employment," Laura said. "However, I cannot accept her hospitality indefinitely. Space is limited at the school. One less room means one less courtesan helped."

"Eva would never turn you out," Simon replied.

Laura nodded. "I know she wouldn't. However, the school is for courtesans seeking husbands. I am not seeking a husband. And there are no other positions open. I must find a way to support myself."

He clanked the coins. "You have some funds."

"It's only enough to live on for a few weeks." Laura reclaimed the coins and put them back in the purse. "I find it unlikely that Father had secret investments somewhere."

Mister Harrington nodded. "There might be a way to claim part of his pension, or maybe a long-lost relative left him a forgotten account. If you'd like, I can check into it for you."

She met his eyes. "Thank you."

His kindness had no end. Laura had worried about visiting the banks for fear of discovery. She didn't know how far the earl's spies reached. Right at this moment, eyes could be peering out of the forest surrounding this cottage, ready to report her arrival.

Her stomach soured. "We should leave now."

Laura tucked the purse into her pocket and hurried through the cottage. She barely noticed the darkening sky as her eyes darted into the shadows of the trees. There was no sign of watchers, yet she couldn't be certain. The earl would not accept her defection with grace.

Mister Harrington helped her into the saddle. She darted another glance around her. Though there was no sign anyone had been there, Laura suspected that the earl had sent someone to check the cottage.

"It has been weeks since your escape," Mister Harrington said as if reading her mind. "If someone was sent after you, he has long given up looking here."

A cold chill dusted over her. Whether it was from fear or from the wind in a threatening sky, gooseflesh dotted her skin.

"The danger he poses is real, no matter how many weeks have passed. I cannot fall into his clutches again."

Simon reached up to touch her hand. "You have friends to help watch over you: Eva, Noelle, Sophie, and me. We will fight to keep you safe. You are no longer alone, Laura."

The words went right to her heart. Tears welled and she blinked to keep them at bay. Unable to trust her voice, she instead turned her wrist and clasped his hand in hers.

Their eyes locked. They stayed that way for a moment until Laura flushed and looked away.

Mister Harrington released her hand and handed her the reins. "Let's see to the house, shall we?"

He mounted Horse and turned back toward the manor. Laura nudged the mare into a trot and followed at a reasonable pace, back up the trail.

"You must be familiar with this house," Simon asked after they'd arrived and she'd slid down unaided from the mare. "The cottage is part of the property."

Untying the bonnet and removing it, Laura looked up at the four-story structure. "The owner was distantly related to my father. Some sort of cousin by marriage." She brushed loose hair from her eyes. "He had little use for his poor relations, though he did send over food when it amused him, and allowed us to live in the cottage. I visited only a half dozen times to return picnic baskets and never ventured beyond the kitchen."

The manor was lovely. She remembered occasionally dawdling in the kitchen as a child, wondering what it was like to live there. "The grounds were never cared for properly, as my cousin was unable to hire a decent groundskeeper. Edgar was reputed to expect much from his servants and paid them very little. No one stayed long."

She paused and scanned the weed-choked lawn. "It was one of those times that I drew the attention of my husband." She grimaced. "He was a visiting friend from Eton. They'd gone to school together. My cousin and he were quite alike, both the worst sort of bounders. Edgar died without heirs several months after my father died, from a fall off his horse." She paused. "Or so I've been told."

"You think it wasn't an accident?"

Laura scrunched up her face. "He was the sort of man who had enemies. One of them could have easily broken his neck."

Chapter Nine

From all he'd learned about Laura today, Simon was surprised she'd not been broken. The life of poverty, a sham marriage, abuse, all cobbled together to kill a spirit. And yet here she was, continuing onward in spite of the burdens she carried on her trim shoulders.

"Was there an investigation into his death?" Simon asked.

Laura shrugged. "I do not know. I was told of his accident and nothing more." The wind ruffled her hair. "He callously seduced young women all over Surrey and beyond, leaving outraged fathers in his wake. If there was an investigation, I suspected it warranted only a cursory glance."

It was difficult to prove murder under the best circumstances. In this case, the clues would be minimal.

"Then we shall accept it was an accident and move forward with our exploration." Simon led Laura to the front door. A thought crossed his mind. He stopped. "I've not asked if this manor holds painful memories for you."

Laura looked up at the stone façade. "Not painful. I do have some misgivings, though not enough to overcome my curiosity. I have always wondered about the rooms beyond the kitchen."

Simon smiled. "Then we shall continue." He paused and looked up. "The door is the tallest I've ever seen, as if the entry was meant to rival a castle of old. It was part of what drew my interest when I first saw the manor." The door was actually not one but two panels, which protested loudly on their neglected hinges when he pushed them open. Laura preceded him inside.

"It is as I remembered." She smiled wickedly. "I did manage a quick peek of the hall once when my cousin was away." She ran a gloved finger across a table by the door. "Though the dust is new. My cousin was a tyrant when it came to both his clothes and his home. The kitchen was immaculate and the staff harried. He ran the household with a heavy hand."

"The servants were fond of him then?" Simon jested. Her smile lit up the dim entry. He longed to touch the corner of her delightful mouth with a fingertip right before he kissed her soundly. He silently cursed the noble intentions that kept him from acting on his impulse. The last time he'd almost kissed her had ended badly. He'd not frighten her again.

"Oh, yes," Laura said. "Immensely. If it wasn't for the lack of employment opportunities in the area, he'd have had to remove his own spiderwebs from his ceilings." She looked up to where several spiders had taken up residence in the high crevasses of the two-story space.

"You said he had no other relatives?" Simon asked.

"None that I know of," Laura said. "His mother died when he was young and his father a few years ago. He had no siblings."

"Why then did his estate not go to your father? Or you?"

Laura shrugged and walked farther into the foyer. "Rumor swirled that he'd made some questionable financial transactions and owed money to some powerful men. Whether that is true, I don't know for certain, but I assumed his estate went to pay his debts."

"I did purchase this property from the bank," Simon said. "It went for far less than it's worth."

She ran her fingertips over a narrow rosewood table and looked at him over her shoulder. "I am pleased the property went to someone who will care for it."

Simon moved away from the door and walked over to examine the pair of staircases that led to the second floor. "I made a cursory examination of the manor when I bought the place, but have not looked at the draperies or peered into every nook. I want to see my new home through your eyes."

The dread that Laura had expected when she followed Simon around the manor did not come, in spite of the fact that she'd met the earl on these grounds. No, the fluttering in her stomach came from being alone in this huge manor with Mister Harrington. Simon. The idea of spending the hours ahead with the unsettling man left her uneasy.

It was becoming difficult to keep her thoughts of this near stranger in check. He occupied her mind more than he should. He was charming and amusing and a bit dangerous. Though he was a gentleman, she knew if he ever crossed paths with the earl, he'd inflict damage on the bastard.

"Shall we continue?" His voice brought her attention back. She'd been woolgathering quite frequently today.

"The house is as beautiful as I suspected," Laura remarked.

Whether by accident or design, the tour did not include the bedrooms. She wondered if his thoughts had been as inappropriate as hers and he didn't want to add the temptation of beds to their time together.

She followed as he led her from room to room, pointing out this rug or that gilt-and-glass candlestick, while her mind was fully elsewhere. Once, she noticed, to her chagrin, that she was staring at his bum when he bent to right a tipped-over vase. She jerked her eyes away, only to dart them back for another quick glance.

For the first time since their meeting, she freely saw him not as just her rescuer but as a man—a very desirable man.

Though there couldn't be anything more than friend-ship between them, she enjoyed his company. And he was pleasing to the eyes with his wind-ruffled hair, squared jaw, and excellent form.

It took her a moment to realize he'd stopped talking and was looking at her with amusement.

"What is it?" she asked, puzzled.

"I'm boring you," he said and lowered a vase back onto the cherry fireplace mantle.

"No. No, it isn't that." She flushed, caught admiring his manly perfection. "I was, I, drat." The warmth in her cheeks deepened. "I wasn't paying attention. I do apologize."

He rubbed his chin. "We do not have to continue the tour."

Laura sighed. "I do want to see the manor. I suppose being so close to home has tangled up my thoughts." She squared her shoulders. "Please let us go on. I promise to admire each and every room with great enthusiasm."

It took focus to keep her mind on his words as they con-tinued up from floor to floor. By the time they got to the attic, the wind was howling outside, setting the shutters on the attic windows to rattling.

Laura was certain by the conclusion of the tour that she could name all the finer points of his male form, and noth-ing about the house.

"The attic at last," Mister Harrington said, then teased, "I'm sure, if pressed, you wouldn't know Hepplewhite from Sheraton, as you have spent the last two hours nod-ding politely and staring off, at what I can't imagine."

Cheeks warming, she wondered if he suspected where her thoughts had really been. "I—I have been thinking of my poor departed cousin. He would hate the dust."

He crossed his arms and narrowed his lids. "Truly? Two

hours of thinking about that. Then my tour was duller than I imagined."

"It wasn't dull at all," she hurried to assure him. Goodness, how to get out of this without revealing her true distraction! "I was merely admiring the fine craftsmanship of the pieces. My cousin had a grand collection."

"Then it wasn't the dust?" His mouth twitched.

Flustered, she glared. "Why must you be privy to my thoughts? I am allowed to think whatever I wish without sharing them with you."

His grin was wicked. "You seem a bit flustered."

In an instant, she knew that he knew she'd been admiring him. How, she couldn't know. Perhaps he'd seen her reflection studying him in a mirror? Gads, had he seen her admiring his bum?

"It's shameful to not cling to your host's every word. But to have it rudely pointed out is worse."

Simon chuckled. He leaned to peer into her eyes. He was close enough for her to feel his breath . . . to touch her.

"I shouldn't tease," he said, his eyes dropping to her mouth. "Unfortunately, I find intense enjoyment watching your eyes flash when I do."

Laura opened, closed, and opened her mouth again. She couldn't speak with him so close.

What was wrong with her? Her breath quivered in her chest and she felt shivery from toe to head. He'd done nothing to warrant such a reaction, and yet, she was so intensely aware of him that she could do nothing but stare into his eyes.

The roof creaked, and with it, her voice returned.

"Ha, I long suspected that you liked to see me flustered and annoyed," she said breathlessly. "Now you have confirmed it."

His eyes stayed on her mouth. "You are not easily flustered."

Would he kiss her? He shouldn't!

To put distance between them, Laura walked to the end of the immense room and looked out. The sky was bleak and she could see rain moving across the landscape. She rubbed her arms. "A storm is coming."

Simon joined her. She could feel his heat, and her body responded with a ripple of something primal. A half step back and she'd be against the warmth of his chest, in his arms, feeling comforted and secure.

It had been a long time since she'd been held, touched in a way that wasn't forced and unpleasant. It took all her will not to take that step backward.

Why had she become so attuned to him today? Perhaps it was the bleak fog she'd lived in this past year that had kept her from seeing much beyond her fear and pain. These last few weeks at the courtesan school had lifted some of those shadows. Time spent with Simon today had opened her eyes to the color and light around her. It was a wonderful place to be.

She turned to him. "It's so dark out."

His face was grim. "It might not blow over quickly. We may have to spend the night."

Spend the night together?

"It has to blow over," she said, staring at the trees, which were fighting against the wind and rain that lashed through their branches. "I told Sophie and Miss Noelle I'd return before nightfall."

She pulled her bottom lip between her teeth. Though the two women knew she was safe, Laura wasn't quite as sure of her safety herself. Even now, she could smell his subtle scent.

"We can't ride back in this," he replied.

A distant rumble confirmed his words. "If I didn't know better, I'd suspect that you brought the rain to keep us trapped here." She narrowed her eyes. "This has all the makings of a romantic novel. A lowly governess or maid is trapped alone with the brooding master of a huge manor house while a storm brews outside. She tries to resist his charms but cannot, as he is already too powerfully hand-some to resist."

Humor filled his eyes. "I am pleased to know that you

liken me to the powerfully handsome hero of a romantic novel."

Her mouth quirked as she casually examined his face and said dryly, "I shall try to keep my wits about me lest I become taken in by your manly charms."

Mister Harrington chuckled. "And I shall do my best not to tempt you to misbehave."

Smiling, Laura shook her head. "You are a rogue, Mister Harrington. Thankfully, there are no governesses in residence."

Lud, he *was* handsome. Perhaps the empty house and the encroaching storm *were* setting her mind abuzz with less than innocent thoughts.

Of course, rain was as common as breathing in England, so this wasn't part of some sinister and seductive plan he'd hatched. Still, the weather was working against her.

He leaned forward to examine the sky, and the movement brought the side of his face near to hers. With a slight head turn, she could press her cheek to his.

It took concentration to keep her attention on the sky.

"I should tend the horses." He pulled back. "We can decide our next course in an hour or two. Perhaps by then, the rain will have moved off."

Laura nodded. "I shall pray for sunshine."

"Then I shall leave you to your prayers."

Without his presence, the room felt empty. She rubbed her cool hands together, the air having taken on a chill without the sun. If they were to be imprisoned until the weather cleared, she should aid in their comfort. But where to start?

A few droplets of rain clicked against the glass and brought her upright. The storm had kicked up. Though Simon was wearing a coat and hat, he would be drenched by the time he finished his chore. She could certainly help with that.

With one last glance outside, she started to turn when an odd shadow beneath a tree stopped her. It looked like the dim silhouette of man. She squinted and leaned toward the glass, but the shadow had vanished.

Her heart raced. She quelled images of Westwick hiding in the shadow of the trees, plotting his revenge.

"It must have been Mister Harrington," she murmured, not entirely convinced. He was with the horses. "My eyes are tricking me."

Shaking off her overworked imagination, she put her focus into making him comfortable when he returned.

In spite of concerns that she'd get lost in this enormous house, she managed to find her way down to the second floor with only one wrong turn. It took less time to find the library.

The makings of a fire were still laid out beside the huge fireplace. Edgar's servants had been efficient.

"Excellent." Growing up, Laura had learned to do much for herself. Her family didn't have a full household staff to tend to their needs. They were lucky to keep a housekeeper and maid. Fire starting was a skill she'd learned as a child. Soon the blaze lit the room and chased away the cold.

"Where are you?" Simon's voice and footsteps carried up from the vicinity of the staircase.

Laura crossed to the doorway and called out, "I'm in the library."

She walked back inside. It took him less than a minute to find her. As expected, he was quite wet and bedraggled.

The top of his head was dry when he pulled off his hat. The rest of him hadn't fared so well.

Laura hid a smile. "You should have taken an overcoat and umbrella when you went out. I'm sure my cousin left one somewhere."

"There was no time to look for one. The horses were suffering the elements. The tree offered very little protection from the pelting rain." He pulled off his hat and gloves and tossed them onto the desk. Then he turned to the fire and back to her. One dark brow cocked up.

"You did this?" he asked, amused.

"I am known throughout the land for my fire-making skills." Laura watched his grin and the body-racking shiver that followed. Worry changed her teasing tone to one of seriousness. "If you don't get warm, you'll catch a chill."

"Yes, ma'am."

Adding a few more sticks and some peat, Laura stoked the flame high. Still, despite the heat, his lips had a slightly blue hue. "You need to get out of that coat." Without waiting for his agreement, or a gentlemanly refusal, she came around him and dragged the sodden coat off his shoulders. A damp trail of rainwater stained his waistcoat from neck to waist.

He grunted when she freed his arms.

"Oh, dear. Has something happened?" She took the coat to the nearest chair and hung it over the back to dry. She returned to him, concerned by his pained expression.

"I led Horse into a stall, when scurrying critters in the loft overhead startled the beast." He flexed his shoulder and winced. "The nag jumped sideways and knocked me into the wall. My shoulder bore the brunt of his actions."

Laura gently touched his arm. She felt no obvious damage. "Are you seriously injured?"

He shook his head. "It is nothing a day or two of rest will not cure." He looked down at her hand on him and followed the path of her arm back to her. Their eyes met and his eyes danced. "If there is an attack launched on this castle, I fear it will be up to you to vanquish the invaders."

Her heart softened. His face was damp and boyish beneath his mop of damp-dry hair. "I can use both pistol and sword with some skill. I believe I can fight off a few invaders."

"I have faith," he replied, his eyes on her mouth.

Laura's stomach quivered. Her stomach had been quivering frequently today. He was very, very close. There was power in his torso beneath his shirtsleeves and waistcoat. She could see it when he moved. She suspected the whole of his body was the same hard muscle.

Thinking of him in such a sensual way filled her with a

rush of nerves. Clearing her throat, she pulled her hand
from his arm, her eyes from his sculpted mouth, and took
a half step back.

The area around his perfect mouth was still an odd
shade of blue. "You are freezing." She ran a critical eye
over the rest of his clothing. The entire front of his waistcoat and his cravat were wet, and his shirt clung in wet
patches to his skin. In as much as her sensibilities protested
her next thought, she had to consider his comfort before
herself. "Your shirt and waistcoat will have to come off."
Laura flushed when she realized his breeches were also
sodden. However, she did have her limits. "You may keep
on your breeches."

A low chuckle deepened the heat on her cheeks. One
would think she'd never seen a naked male figure. She
should be well beyond girlish blushes.

Simon tugged at his cravat, his fingers white from the
cold. "The knot is soaked." He pulled at it, shivered again,
and still the item refused to budge.

Laura sighed. "Allow me."

Forcing her attention to the cravat, she tried not to notice
how close their bodies were. For every inhalation she took,
he took one, too. His breath occasionally touched her face,
her forehead, as she dug into the knot.

"You must pay your manservant well," she said through
gritted teeth. "A hurricane could not get this loose."

She didn't need to look up to know he was smiling.

Finally, Laura managed to get a finger into the knot. At
almost the same time she felt cold seeping through her
dress at her waist. She looked down to find his hands there,
just above her hips, splayed open and holding tight.

In fact, they were standing thigh to thigh. The intimacy
of the contact had gone unnoticed as she'd attacked the
cravat.

Slowly, she looked into his eyes and the pure, innocent
stare she found there.

He shrugged. "My hands were cold."

Laura frowned. "You are certainly free with them."

"And you are no longer afraid of my touch."

Not even her glare loosened his hold or wiped the satisfaction from his face. She wasn't about to show her discomfort. He'd admitted enjoyment in seeing her flustered. So she turned back to the knot and pretended to ignore his touch.

A notion better put to thought than to actual application. The cold from his hands tingled across her skin and caused her legs to wobble, just a bit. Fortunately, his hold kept her from stumbling when her fingers slipped from the knot. She frowned and attacked the cravat, her elbows braced against his body, her annoyance rising from both the knot and his touch.

Soon, the wet cloth was loose. She unwound the cravat from around his neck and tossed it toward the coat. It dropped to the floor a full step short.

"You are free," she said. "You can release me now."

He did so without argument and removed his waistcoat. She took it from him and hung it next to the coat.

She watched, fascinated, as he reached for the bottom of his shirt. Several quick tugs managed to do little more than crinkle the material.

"I seem to have difficulty working both my shoulder and fingers." He closed and opened his hands several times to ease the stiffness. "Gloves do little to keep hands warm when they're rain soaked." He wriggled his fingers, then blew into his cupped palms. "They are chilled to the bone."

Laura's eyes narrowed suspiciously. He was either excessively susceptible to cold, or he was playing with her. The latter seemed likely. But his shoulder had been injured and he could have an underlying sensitivity to cold of which she was unaware. To mock him could be hurtful.

With a sigh, she moved back to tend to the shirt. The linen offered resistance in the wet waistband of his breeches. With determination, she loosened it at his hips. She slid her fingertips under the hem and froze. The texture of his supple skin and the warmth of his body against her knuckles sent a shock through her. Clearly not all parts of him were suffering from the cold.

She couldn't breathe beyond shallow, uneven pulls. She didn't look up out of fear of falling into his eyes. She knew the intimacy of the moment wasn't lost on him either. He was tense beneath her hands.

Laura wasn't about to satisfy her unwelcome desire to caress his skin. She forced herself to finish the task with a forceful jerk. "You should be capable of removing your shirt now, sore shoulder notwithstanding."

He didn't move. "I prefer you undress me." His voice was a soft caress over her skin.

Oddly, she wanted to refuse, knew she should refuse. Yet she stayed planted in place, unable to step away from him or remove her eyes from where the open shirt teased her to look at the hint of bare chest. His was a sensuous draw she couldn't resist. Curiosity drove her onward and her hands upward of their own volition.

"I should leave you now," she whispered.

"You should," he said softly. "It will save us both."

"And yet . . ." Her voice trailed off. She was lost in something more powerful than she. Simon would have to end the madness.

With her lips parted slightly, she flattened her palms on his waist and began a slow breathless progression up along his rib cage, the shirt sliding effortlessly as she went. His rippled stomach came into view, and below the shirttail, a thin trickle of fine hair traveled from his navel downward to vanish into his breeches.

"I cannot continue," she protested. Her words were without bite.

"You can."

The spot at the juncture of her legs pulsed as she imagined him without a stitch of clothing on, his eyes heavy with desire as he kissed and caressed her eager body.

Losing all sense of sanity, she lifted the shirt, and her gaze went to his firm chest and the sprinkle of fine hair she discovered there. Slowly, deliberately, she splayed her hands open, unable to help herself. His muscles flexed and his breath caught.

Once the shirt was at his neck and his torso fully exposed to her hands and eyes, her body swayed forward and her boldness faltered.

Mister Simon Harrington was completely and truly magnificent.

Chapter Ten

It took several rapid heartbeats for Laura to realize she was a moment away from pressing forward against him. Her body ached to feel his arms around her, his thigh tucked between her legs, her breasts flattened against the broad expanse. He was so sinfully warm, so shockingly male.

Her mouth went dry.

Yet even as she struggled to steel herself from wicked thoughts, it proved impossible not to give his body, in the flickering firelight, a more thorough perusal. Her hands remained where they were, infused by his heat.

"Are you having some difficulty getting my shirt off?" Simon asked, his voice low and gruff.

"If your shoulders were not so broad," she snapped weakly, and removed her hands, "I might have an easier time of it." She flushed, realizing she had just offered up an offhanded compliment. Now he knew she'd been admiring his body. "Surely you can help?"

Angry over her lack of control, she cursed herself under her breath and helped him free one arm. He wobbled slightly and stabilized himself by returning the freed hand to her waist.

"A success, My Lady. Well done."

An exasperated sound escaped her clenched teeth. "I am pleased you are enjoying yourself."

The hand flexed. "Yes, indeed, I am."

This time she finally looked up, to meet his heated expression. How she ever found him charming was a mystery. "I cannot believe I thought you a gentleman. I have recalled that notion."

Simon chuckled. "Certainly you cannot blame me for this. I did not cause the storm, nor did I frighten Horse into knocking me into the stall wall. If you were a kind soul, you would pity me. I am in terrible pain."

Suspecting he was exaggerating his injury in order to touch her, or for her to touch him, she released a small harrumph.

"Lift your arm," she commanded. He did so. She placed her hands on his bicep and slowly slid them along his arm from shoulder to elbow, while he pulled the arm downward. Once the entire arm was removed, Laura slid the shirt off his head.

Her mind turned to mush and she might have even moaned just a little bit. The deepest, most female part of her was aflame.

He stood over her, flesh golden in the firelight, his breeches low on his hips, and Laura was helpless to do anything but stare like a besotted maiden.

Embarrassment flared hotly to sour her stomach as she clutched the shirt to her bosom. Oddly, or perhaps not so, Simon appeared completely comfortable with her attentions.

Truthfully, the warmth in his eyes told her he was quite content to have her admiration.

"You would make an excellent valet," he said softly and reached toward the shirt. Before he could take it from her, he stopped and looked into her eyes. Her heart fluttered.

She handed him the item, purposely brushing her fingertips against his. In the span of less than an hour, she'd not only touched him but accepted his touch without flinching.

"I certainly have become comfortable with you. There will be no repeat of that moment in the meadow."

"You do not need to explain. I understand—"

"No," she said. The bond of seduction was broken. "You don't understand. You can't understand."

Laura looked away and walked over to the fireplace. Wind whistled down the chimney and the flames danced. She crossed her arms around her waist and closed her eyes. For the first time since her freedom, she allowed herself to fully remember her months in captivity.

She swallowed, then began her tale. "The abuse started soon after he brought me to London. He quickly tired of my strong will and made it his mission to break me."

"Laura." Simon moved up behind her.

"No. Please let me speak." No one knew the full story of her life. Not even Miss Eva. She was deeply ashamed of her past but felt an overwhelming desire to tell someone, to share her burden. "He took great pleasure in using his fists and insults to keep me cowed. He was a powerful monster. I was unable to flee. I was kept locked in my room. During the few times I was allowed out for meals or walks about the grounds, footmen guarded me. The staff was well paid to ignore my pleas for help. I was a prisoner."

"And yet he failed to tame you." Simon's voice was filled with admiration. "You fled."

A smile flickered across her lips. "Owning my body is not the same as owning my mind. I knew one day I'd be free."

Curiosity led him to ask, "Tell me what happened. How did you escape?"

Laura hesitated. It was easy to talk to Misses Eva or Noelle or Sophie. They knew the difficulties courtesans faced. Sharing her worst moments with Simon was much harder. And yet she felt, somehow, he wouldn't judge her negatively.

"I discovered where he kept the funds for his household accounts. I took small amounts from that cabinet and from his pockets. I believed that he owed far more for what he'd done to me. I hid it away and waited."

She closed her eyes and memories flooded her mind. "Two weeks before you found me, I overheard him speaking to his horrible friends about an auction. They were too happy, too pleased with themselves, too secretive. This aroused my suspicion. So I spied for several days until I managed to put their veiled comments and whispers together. I then realized the plan was to sell me to the highest bidder—noblemen, slavers, anyone who had the money to bid."

"Oh, Laura." He slid an arm around her shoulders.

She leaned back against him and realized tears were trailing down her face. "Men came from all over. They filled the house. He paraded me about as if I were an expensive, ignorant toy, yet always keeping me in shadow. He wanted their curiosity to entice them to loosen their purses."

"They would fight to have you," he said.

Laura brushed her cheek against his arm. "The bastard thought he was so clever. His simpleminded country mouse would never figure out his brilliant plan. He became confident. How could I escape with so many men under his roof watching me? So I waited until a moment in the kitchen when the cook's back was turned and I ran out the door."

The terror of that year with the earl spilled through her and she cried, her heart breaking. Simon turned her and pulled her into his arms. She buried her face against his chest.

He made soothing sounds and ran his hand over her hair, allowing her to cry away all the abuse, her lost innocence, the fears for her life. He gave her himself, something solid to hold on to, and she clung to his strength.

Eventually her sobs subsided. He held her tightly as she listened to his heartbeat. After a moment, she sniffed and lifted her head. What she saw were the crisp hairs on his chest, which were now very damp. Again. She snort-laughed and lifted her hand to rub the wetness off.

"You just cannot seem to get dry," she quipped.

Simon looked down and frowned. "I think most of our

encounters involve rain, or tears." He watched her use her sleeve on the wet patch. When she was satisfied with her efforts, she flattened out her palm and looked up into his eyes.

Touched by his kindness, Laura wanted to tell him how much she valued him as a friend, for friends they had become. But she couldn't speak, lost as she was in his gaze. The humor on their faces faded and changed into something far more intimate. They were locked together, hip to hip.

"Laura," he whispered and moved to release her.

She shook her head. "Please hold on to me, Simon."

So he held her, pressing his mouth against her hair, running his hands across her back, while she sighed and splayed her open palms on his hard-muscled back.

Desperately, she wanted to feel something other than cold misery and pain. So when he pulled back and lowered his blue eyes to first capture her gaze and then drift down to stare at her lips, she rose onto her tiptoes and met his kiss halfway.

The feel of his mouth shattered her body and sent a wave of heat through her bones. He slanted his mouth over hers for a brief teasing moment before pulling back.

"We must not do this," he said regretfully.

"No regrets," she whispered and slid her hand around his neck to keep him close. The tiny hairs she discovered at the base of his neck felt soft beneath her hands. "I want you to kiss me, Simon," she pleaded. "I need you to kiss me."

He hesitated for no more than a blink before reclaiming her lips in a passionate and searing kiss. Laura's knees shook as she pressed more fully against him. She opened her mouth to deepen the kiss and he plunged his tongue within. Hunger exploded inside her.

Laura moaned deep in her throat as their tongues mated and shivery warmth flooded low between her legs. She arched her body against him, knowing she was likely making a grave mistake, but also realizing that she wanted to feel again. She wanted to know what it was like to be desired, not for brutal possession but for affection and true desire.

She wanted to feel him against her, loving her, if only for this one stormy afternoon.

Laura broke the kiss and reached to ruffle her hands through his hair before moving to cup the sides of his face. She wanted him to see how much she desired him. "Simon, make love to me." Her boldness shocked even her.

He released his hold and brought his hands up to circle her wrists. He bent his head and looked deeply into her eyes. "Are you certain?"

She nodded. "More certain than I have ever been."

For a moment, she thought he'd refuse her. He expelled a very long, deep breath. Then he bent at the waist, lifted her in his arms, and carried her, laughing, from the room.

Laura was certain. Simon wasn't as much so. He desired her, yes, from her soft mouth, to her silky skin, to her toes. But she had been damaged. How much of this seduction was to erase the other man from her body, and what measure of her eagerness was truly for him?

"Do not put too much thought into this moment," Laura said softly as he carried her down the hallway toward a row of bedrooms and kicked open the last door on the right. She pressed her mouth against his neck and trailed kisses up along his jaw to the corner of his mouth. "There will be no one but us two in that bed."

Swinging her about, he paused, and she followed his gaze. The bed was massive, with a deep blue and white coverlet and four posts carved by a master craftsman. They stared, incredulous. "An entire family could sleep comfortably there," he said with a snort.

Laura screwed up her face. "And the staff and a few of the neighbors, too," she added. "This kingly bed must have been a strong consideration when you decided to purchase the manor."

"Truthfully, I didn't give it much notice." His eyes were warm on her. "Until now."

"Then we shall explore it together."

The lightness in her tone uplifted his spirits. In the days since they'd met, this beautiful woman had flourished under the care of the women at the courtesan school. She was healing well and was not the same terrified woman fleeing for her life.

Her scent claimed his attention away from the bed and he leaned to press a kiss at the base of her throat. "Thankfully, there is only you and I. I'd hate to love you with an audience in attendance."

Laura giggled, both from his comment and from the light brush of stubble against her skin. "I, too, am thankful."

If Eva or Noelle found out about this seduction, they'd rip him apart. However, now was not the time to think of his two cousins, the school, or Laura's past. He had a seduction to deliver and he wanted it to be all she'd hoped.

Simon lowered her feet to the floor and turned her in his arms. He captured her soft mouth in another hungry kiss.

Once before, he'd suspected that her mouth was made for kissing. He was right. The softness of her lips, her sweet taste, and the touch of innocence in her kisses were burning fire through his senses. It was impossible to believe she'd held on to any measure of purity through her trials, yet she had. The seductive Laura was only in her exotic eyes and lush body.

"You are very beautiful," he said as he drew his mouth away from her lips and down to nuzzle the spot below her ear. She tipped her head back and sighed.

"I have been told I resemble my mother," she replied and slowly ran her hands from his waist to his hips. "Your shoulder seems to have recovered."

"I can ignore the pain with you in my arms."

Simon relished the feel of her hands on his body. Her scent, light and floral, drifted from her and made him think of making love to her in a meadow of wildflowers. Perhaps on some future sunny day, he could make that happen.

He lightly nibbled the spot where her dress ended on her shoulder and pushed the material away from where he'd seen the scar. The spot was healed and fading. Still, it would always be a reminder of her past.

Kissing it gently, he felt her tense.

"I intend to kiss every one, love." Simon lifted his head to see concern on her face. He locked on to her eyes. "Trust me."

Very slowly, her body relaxed. She reached up to gently touch his face. "Simon, I do."

They stood for a moment before Simon reached for the ties at the neckline of her dress. He pulled the ribbon loose and the bodice sagged slightly, exposing her chemise and the swell of velvety flesh.

He put his hands on her shoulders and slid the gown down her arms to her waist. Once freed of her trim hips, it dropped to the floor in a whisper of fabric.

Simon awaited her cues. There was no fear in her eyes, only an open curiosity. Simon was taken aback. Had she never been gently undressed by her abuser?

Likely he'd taken her without preliminaries.

It made Simon angry to think of anyone not treasuring Laura as she deserved. She was a rarity among women, and he vowed to always treat her like a gift.

"You are thinking again," Laura said softly, bringing his thoughts back to her. She frowned and crossed her arms. "I am beginning to feel neglected."

Her teasing tone belied the set-down and he grinned. "I apologize, darling Laura. Your loveliness has muddled my brain."

She shook her head. "You possess a silver tongue, rogue, but I am feeling chilled. Perhaps you should continue with my unwrapping before my teeth start to chatter."

Simon shot her a heated stare. "Yes, Milady."

With measured steps, he placed a hand on her hip and drew it over her as he walked around behind her. He encompassed her in his embrace, nibbling her neck and splaying his hands over her stomach. At her moan, he slid them upward to cup her delightful and perfect breasts.

Her breath caught. "Warmer now, love?" he asked.

"Much," she breathed.

The husky sound ravaged through his senses, making him steely hard. It took extreme control not to carry her to the bed and bury himself between her legs. He'd vowed to make this afternoon memorable, and impatience would ruin the moment.

He eased her chemise down and kissed her silky white shoulder. Her sweet scent drew him to the curve on her neck. He pressed his mouth there, earning a sigh. He grinned against her skin and tangled his hand in the knot at her nape. With a deftness he didn't realize he possessed, he freed the silky strands with one hand.

It tumbled down her back in a riot of sable and light.

His breath caught. In that moment, she possessed him completely.

Moving onward, Simon discovered a small scar between her shoulder blades and struggled to keep from cursing. He'd made a promise to himself to keep his attention on her and not tangle this moment up with dark thoughts. There would be time to exact revenge for her mistreatment later.

"You have on too many clothes still." Simon had to get her naked to distract him from the urge to kill. He continued around her until they were facing each other again and began the work of divesting her of her undergarments.

The chemise and corset proved to be no obstacle and soon she was bared to his view.

In the cool air of the room, her rosy nipples pebbled to tight peaks and her pale skin glowed in the dim room. Mottled along her skin were imperfections, each building a map of the suffering she'd experienced. There was a peculiar long and oddly shaped scuff-scar on her upper thigh, as if she'd been pressed down with the heel of a boot.

Rage ripped through Simon.

Chapter Eleven

Fighting the desire to flinch under the fierce anger on Simon's face, Laura knew his reaction had nothing to do with her. Nor did she have to look down to see what had caused the change in him. Her body was marred, damaged by evil.

"Please. Do not allow him to ruin this moment." Laura moved against Simon and took his face in her hands. She stared hard into his eyes. "He has taken enough from me. I cannot bear it if he takes you, too."

Her plea had the desired effect. His lids closed briefly as he drew a deep breath. When his eyes opened again, they were clear blue and the anger was gone. He reached out to span her waist with his hands and passion flared again.

"Nothing will change my desire for you. Not scars, not anger, not my need to kill for you." He ran a fingertip across her lower lip. "You are lovely in my eyes."

She'd felt, seen, his protective nature before. If she named her abuser, he'd be off, storm be damned, exacting revenge on her behalf.

At this moment, she didn't need a chest-thumping,

woman-in-distress-saving knight. She needed him. She needed to be desired, marks and all. She wanted to see the intensity in his eyes as he looked at her, kissed her, a look that was not tinged by the desire to punish with a fist if she didn't comply with any demand.

Her confidence wavered. Simon was telling her that she was lovely. Was it because he knew compliments were required when a naked woman was standing in front of you? Could he really look past the scars?

Suddenly shy, she bent and pulled her chemise back up. She kept her eyes averted, knowing if she were to see distaste on his face, she couldn't bear it.

She had the straps of the chemise halfway up her arms when his hands stopped her progress. Finally she lifted her gaze.

"Do not cover yourself, love." He brushed aside her hands to allow the chemise to return to the floor. He lifted her hand to press a kiss on her palm. "Your beauty steals my breath."

Laura trembled at the tenderness she saw when he looked at her. In spite of her flaws, her lingering imperfections, he desired her. And she sensed that it had nothing to do with her lack of clothing or a simple eagerness to bed her.

Simon smiled and bent to lift her into his arms. He carried her to the bed in a few long strides and gently placed her on the downy mattress with its endless blue and white coverlet.

The musty scent of the unused room did not distract Laura from her focus. As Simon straightened and began the process of removing his boots and breeches, she stared at him hungrily, eager to see the last bits of his magnificent body.

Not even when he freed his erection and tossed his breeches aside did she falter. Her nipples tingled in anticipation of his touch. Her core pulsed with need. When he climbed onto the bed and covered her with his hard body, she reached up and pulled him down for a kiss.

She was no longer a virgin, nor could she save herself for a husband. No amount of wishing could make her that innocent girl she once was.

This time was for her. Her choice. Her desire.

Later, she'd return to the school and make plans for her future. Today, she wanted passion.

He slid up and over her, reclaiming her mouth. Laura caressed her hands over him, from hip to waist, to his muscled rib cage, letting her fingers explore the dips and planes of his body.

The spicy scent of his skin teased her senses, and his hungry kiss added to the delightful mix of sensations that left her breathless.

When he broke the tender kiss, his warm eyes focused on hers. "From now until dawn, I intend to kiss away every mark, every dark memory for you. By morning, you will know what it feels like to be treasured, adored."

Laura felt the prickle of tears behind her lids. "I ask for nothing more than to feel desire. Real desire." She lifted her hand to cup the space below his ear and brushed her thumb across his strong jaw. Moving farther forward, she touched his bottom lip as she held on to his gaze. She arched slightly against him. "I want you desperately," she breathed.

Amusement tugged one side of his mouth into a crooked grin. He looked down between their bodies and reached to brush a fingertip over one erect nipple. She twitched. "Your desire is only half as great as mine, my seductive Laura." He shifted slightly and she felt the full press of his thick erection on her stomach. "I think we should start here." He pressed a kiss on her neck. "And continue here." He kissed the other side. "Before moving down here." He kissed the hollow of her throat.

"Excellent choices," she said with a sigh. His mouth tickled on her skin. "Where do you go from there?"

He lifted his head to once more capture her eyes and grinned. "I was thinking here." He didn't look away as he lowered his head to capture her nipple, suckling it between his lips and teasing the peak with his tongue.

Laura gasped and arched back on the bed. Still, she could not break contact with his eyes as he released the nipple and moved across to the other. He drew his tongue around the firm peak, then nipped gently on the tip.

A small moan escaped her parted lips. Simon cupped the other breast, playing with the damp nipple between his fingers until her breathing turned ragged.

"I assume you like this?" Simon said, lifting his head.

"Very much." Laura grinned at his teasing tone. "However, there are other areas sadly in need of attention."

"Is that so?" He cocked a brow.

She nodded. "Several areas."

Sobering, he frowned. "Then I will be remiss if I do not explore every inch of you."

Laura watched with soft eyes as he moved down her body, kissing his way to her toes. When he finished the front, he rolled her over and kissed her back, caressing and kneading her flesh until she was groaning with the sheer pleasure of his ministrations.

Her body tingled with each kiss and caress. He rolled her back over and kneeled between her legs.

"Did I miss anything?" he said, sliding his gaze up and down her body. "I wouldn't want to be taken to task for any errors."

There was only one place he'd clearly avoided. She looked down at the thatch of sable hair. Heat crept into her cheeks. The juncture between her legs pulsed, but she dared not ask him to kiss and touch her there. He would be scandalized and think her wanton.

"Oh, dear." He looked down to where her gaze rested. "I overlooked one important area."

Before Laura could lift her head to see where his intentions lay, she felt his hand move downward from her stomach to caress over the soft curls between her legs.

From some disembodied place, she thought she heard

someone whisper, "Oh, yes," followed in short order by a deep male chuckle. But she wasn't at all certain it was she who had spoken. All that came from her throat, when he slipped a finger between the folds to caress the throbbing nub, was some sort of mewling noise.

"That's it, love." He caressed her, adjusting his movements and position by the pleasured sounds she made.

Laura writhed and clutched the sheet as he quickly brought her to the pinnacle of her release. She cried out with both surprise and delight before falling back on the bed.

Simon chuckled and bent to kiss her. "Clearly, we need to do that more often."

"Yes, please," she said and smiled a grateful, dreamy smile.

He, however, wasn't finished. She watched through heavy lids as he cupped her hips and positioned her body beneath him. The sight of his erection chased aside the lingering fog of pleasure and she feasted eagerly on the sight.

"Hurry," she said softly, blushing at her boldness.

"As My Lady commands," he said, low and harsh. He slid inside her ready body and buried himself deep.

Laura let out a glad cry as her body closed around his shaft. He groaned and rocked his powerful body against her. As he plunged and withdrew, she wrapped her legs around his waist and clutched his shoulders. Her second release was as welcome as the first. Her body shuddered and she whimpered.

Simon leaned to kiss her, tangling their tongues together as he slowly built to his own release. He finally buried himself inside her with one last deep thrust, before pulling out to spill himself on the sheet. He was only gone for a brief moment before dropping next to her on the bed and pulling her into the cradle of his strong arms.

"Happy?" he asked, his hand moving down her arm.

"Very much so," she answered honestly. She *was* truly happy. Turning her head, she pressed a few firm kisses on his warm skin. When she lifted her face to look into his eyes, her hair fell in casual disarray over her line of vision.

Simon brushed the hair aside and tucked it behind one ear. There was tenderness to his attentions and Laura felt her heart tug again.

Though she couldn't love him, for a time he'd made her feel, and forget. For that he would always hold a special place in her mind and heart.

"The storm seems to be gaining intensity," he said. "It confirms that we will be spending the night after all."

This time, she didn't protest. Not rain or wind or an angry Miss Eva could draw her from this bed. She was exactly where she wanted to be.

"We will starve without food," she said.

He cocked a brow. "There must be something in the pantry. We can search once I've regained my strength. Who knew you'd prove to be such a demanding lover?"

"It was all because of you," she protested lightly. "You have a certain way with your mouth and hands."

"You mean like this?" He caressed her waist, her hip, her thigh, following with his eyes. His movements were not to inflame passion but felt more like he was making his own memories of her.

"Just like that," she replied as he lifted her hand to his mouth and nibbled her wrist. "Though you did miss a few places," she teased.

Simon smiled against her skin. "Fortunately, we have many hours until dawn." He touched his tongue on her palm. "I intend to make love to you until you are unable to stand unaided."

Laura laughed, the sound carrying through the empty room. Then she shot him a sultry stare and reached between them to run her fingernail gently down his growing erection. He twitched.

"Then let us not waste a moment talking."

The storm stopped sometime during the evening, but Laura hardly noticed the change in the weather. Simon had done just as he promised. He loved her all night. When she finally fell asleep near dawn, she didn't have the energy to roll over, much less rise from the bed. So when he left the room, and then returned sometime later, all she could offer was a muffled groan, lying as she was, facedown, her head buried in the pillow.

"As enticing as it is to spend my time staring at your perfect and bare bottom, you have to eat." His pronouncement was immediately followed by a clunk on the bed table. "The pantry hadn't much for food, but I did find some wine and canned meat. Getting the can open proved quite difficult."

At the mention of food, Laura lifted her head to sniff. She screwed up her face. "I've never had canned meat."

Simon looked into the bowl. "I understand it's popular with the army. I had to use a sword to break the blasted thing open."

"Then we should try it." Laura reached for a fork and gingerly stabbed a piece of meat and placed it on her tongue. "Hmm. It isn't horrible."

Simon chuckled. "I think you made that exact sound several times last night." He took a bite. "What is this?"

"I'm not certain," Laura replied. "Lamb, I think."

They ate quietly for several minutes. She thought it doubtful that she'd ever choose to serve this at her table; however, it was food and she was famished.

"The next time I spend the night here, I will have hired a cook," Simon remarked, reaching for the wine bottle. "I'll be pleased to never eat canned meat again."

Once Laura had recovered a reserve of energy, she slowly pushed up on her bum. Her hair tangled over her eyes and she pulled the sheet up to cover her bare breasts.

"It is a shame to hide them," he protested and rubbed a hint of hair on his unshaven face. At her curious look, he pointedly stared at the covered pair.

Her body warmed. "If I don't, we will never rise from this bed." Her narrowed eyes warned him off.

Simon indulged her comment with good humor and cleaned up the meal. "I'll hire a woman in the village to tidy up behind us after we leave." He looked over the mussed sheets and even more mussed Laura with obvious regret. "I wish we could stay the day but I have an appointment I cannot miss."

"And you are already in danger from Miss Eva. If you do not return me to the courtesan school soon, you'll risk your head."

"Sadly, it may already be too late."

Laura nodded under the weighted twinge of disappointment when a ray of sunlight finally broke above the horizon and cast light into the room. "I have decided I truly hate the dawn. It comes at the most regretful moments." She kicked away the sheet and slid from the bed. Simon wrapped his arms around her. "The night has too few hours."

They kissed. It was Simon's turn to groan when he finally pulled back. "I hate to waste such nakedness, but I will be late if we don't leave immediately." He smiled at her frown and moved to collect her clothing. With the efficiency of a well-trained maid, he soon had her dressed.

"You have as much skill dressing as undressing me, even with a sore shoulder," Laura said, returning the favor by straightening his cravat. "You would make an excellent lady's maid."

He bent to brush her lips one last time. "If I had my way, you'd never wear a stitch."

Laura grinned and pulled on the borrowed bonnet. "That would certainly shock anyone who crosses my path."

They shared a smile before Simon escorted her from the room and manor. As they rode off, she looked back one last time at the stone monolith. The house had been both the beginning of her darkest days and now, with Simon, the place of her most precious memories.

"Laura?" He slowed his horse beside her and examined her face. "Is there something the matter?"

She smiled and shook her head. "No, nothing. Truly."

And she meant it. He'd given her a gift she'd always

cherish. She couldn't marry him, have his children, or spend her life with him. But she had the stolen moments in his arms. Nothing could take this newfound happiness away from her.

Chapter Twelve

Thankfully, Miss Eva wasn't standing at the door of the school, wringing her hands with worry, when Simon dropped Laura at the back gate. The courtesans were still abed, and neither Miss Eva nor Miss Noelle had arrived yet. Sophie frowned but kept her tongue, not sure of what role to play as Laura's protector.

"We took shelter from the storm at a manor," Laura said simply. She turned away to claim a freshly baked scone and to hide her blush and smile. "The owner of the house was most accommodating."

"Accommodating" was such a simple word for what Simon had done to her and what she'd done to him, so it wasn't quite a full lie. Simon did not complain over her presence in his house. In fact, he seemed extremely happy to have hosted her.

Sophie didn't need to know they'd spent the night alone in *his* manor. It was best to let her think they'd accepted the kindness of strangers.

Laura was entitled to her privacy.

"You returned safely," Sophie said stiffly. "That is what's important."

"I am sorry if you worried." She offered Sophie a tepid smile. "However, there was no way to send off a note in the storm. The roads were quite treacherous to travel."

Whether Sophie believed her or not, the explanation was reluctantly accepted. The woman nodded and left her to her meal.

Laura wasn't one of Miss Eva's courtesans to be schooled and matched with a husband. She was a temporary guest and therefore not subject to the same rules as the other women. Still, Laura knew that her behavior would be noted by the courtesans if they saw her arrive at this early hour. It was a negative example to set. The school was meant to set rules of propriety, not break them.

With discretion in mind, she snuck up the narrow servants' stairs to her room, with hopefully no one the wiser.

Miss Eva would not allow her to flaunt a love affair under this roof. Laura needed to tread carefully or risk being asked to leave. This was a school to help courtesans escape that life. She'd not look away if Laura openly took a lover.

Thankfully, the courtesans were still sleeping and only Sophie knew she hadn't returned late last evening.

The bed called to her and she took the opportunity for a few hours of sleep. When she joined the courtesans later, she discovered them in the kitchen, hunched over a newspaper, shock and worry on their collective faces.

"Laura, there's been a murder."

The newspapers were often out of date by the time Cook or Thomas brought them in. By then, the news could be weeks old. And murders were not uncommon in certain areas of London. Usually they did not garner such excitement.

Laura leaned over the freshly baked bread and inhaled. Her stomach growled happily. She took a slice and slathered it with butter. Taking a bite, she sat at the long table.

"That is why we must stay in the safe areas of London," she said and took another bite. The bread was delicious.

"No, Miss Laura," Bess said, her pretty face serious. "It was a lord who was murdered."

This finally drew Laura's attention. "A lord?" Noblemen were seldom murdered—a broken neck from a fall from a horse, perhaps, but not murder. "This is big news."

Mariette nodded vigorously and wrung her hands. "Can you believe that Lord Westwick was murdered in the library of his very own town house!"

Laura coughed, the bread forming a dry clog in her throat. Lord Westwick was dead? Murdered? Her stomach soured. She dropped her breakfast and stood. "Let me see that."

She took the paper and scanned the page. Lord Westwick, late of Mayfair, was found murdered by a footman in a town house he owned in Cheapside, a knife plunged into his back.

Quickly, Laura looked at the date and dropped back on the bench. As she had suspected, and feared, the *Times*, in fact, *was* old. Westwick was discovered dead on the morning after her escape. Sometime in the wee hours after she'd fled, someone had killed him.

Stunned, she read ahead with sickening dread as the article went further into detail of his violent death. But it was the final paragraph that burned bile in her throat.

"The Bow Street Runners discovered an ear bob next to the body," Bess said, reading over Laura's shoulder. "They believe that His Lordship's missing courtesan, a mysterious woman known only as Sabine, had killed him in a fit of rage and fled."

"I cannot imagine a woman committing such a terrible crime," Jane added.

The world around Laura spun, and only her hands clutching the edge of the table kept her upright in her seat. She heard distant voices but could no longer make out what was said. She stared blankly at the name, Sabine, those six letters mocking her with their clarity.

Somehow she stumbled to her feet and made her way out of the room. The stairs proved a bigger obstacle as she used the rail to pull herself upward.

How tragic the last few weeks seemed now. She'd thought

she'd escaped from Westwick, only to discover that he'd exacted the ultimate revenge. He managed to get himself murdered, and she was wanted for his death.

Even in death, the bastard wouldn't set her free.

If only she had the strength to run away, she thought, as she stumbled along the hallway to her room. Shutting the door behind her, she lay down on the bed. Rolling into a tight ball, she stared off, her eyes unfocused.

She was no longer a false wife, an abused courtesan, the lover of Simon Harrington. She was again the mysterious Sabine.

Murderess.

Simon whistled a nonsensical tune as he wandered through the house, his mind on Laura. Calling for his valet and water for a bath, he shucked out of his rumpled still-damp coat and poured himself a brandy.

Laura. He would never again sleep in that ridiculously large bed without thinking of her, sleep disheveled and lovely, with the sheet drawn up modestly over her breasts and a half smile showing beneath a tangle of sable hair.

An hour later, fully bathed, polished, and famished, he wandered into the breakfast room, only to find his sullen sister pushing coddled eggs around on her plate.

"Are Mother and Father still abed?" he asked.

A sour grunt was Brenna's response. Simon smirked and began to ladle foodstuffs from the buffet onto his plate. He needed something to banish the taste of canned meat from his tongue.

"Having no luck in your hunt for a pirate?" He purposefully took the seat across from her, if only to raise her ire. He began the vigorous task of eating while she glared at him. "You might want to check at the docks. There might be one or two there. Check for a man with a wooden leg and a patch over his eye."

Brenna was pretty in a pink frock. The color went well with her dark hair. Chester Abbot would be delighted to have her as his wife. Well, as delighted as that milksop could be.

"I am so happy to know that you find pleasure in my misery, Brother. One day soon, I hope you are just as miserable as I." She stabbed a piece of ham and tore off a corner with her teeth. "I hope you are forced to marry a woman you despise and spend your life dancing attendance to her whiny demands."

Brenna *was* in a dark mood this morning.

"Your troubles are your own doing, Brenna." He leaned forward onto his elbows. "Several men have asked to court you and you find fault with all of them. You are pushing spinsterhood and have yet to find your one great love. How much longer do you have before you are no longer considered marriageable?"

"I am barely into my twenties," she protested. "Surely I am not in immediate danger of turning into a stooped old hag?"

"That isn't the point." He sighed. Why did his sister have to be so contrary? "I want to see you settled and happy. There is no reason you shouldn't already be a wife and mother. You've had chances, many chances. Several of those rejected men were both handsome and wealthy, and yet you refused them."

She slapped her hands on the table and rattled her plate. Her green eyes flashed. "Who? Who of my suitors do you think was my match? Albert Finley? He was three times my age. Hamish O'Reily wanted to take me to Ireland to raise his seven children. And Phillip Weaton? I saw him holding hands in his darkened theater box with his sixth cousin, William. You think that he is my perfect match? Certainly even you can see that our marriage would never work."

Phillip Weaton and William Brooks? Simon shook his head to clear that disturbing image. "What about Mister Sylvan? He was an amiable sort and both handsome and wealthy."

"Mister Sylvan cannot decide if he wants cream in his

tea without first consulting his mother." Brenna's voice had
gone up a pitch. "I'll not have a husband so inept he'll need
to invite his mother to sit by our marriage bed and bark out
instructions on the proper way to deflower his wife."

Brenna stood abruptly, nearly upending her chair. "I
will find a way to forever remove Chester Abbot as a potential suitor if I have to travel from here to Northumberland
to find my highwayman!"

Simon waited until she was well away from the room
before succumbing to his mirth. He chuckled and finished
his breakfast.

W ith every knock on the town house door, Laura
would startle and her heart stop, certain arrest was
imminent. Though in her mind she knew that the chances
of the Runners finding her were practically nonexistent,
she still couldn't derive any comfort from the knowledge.

"The Runners are known for their dogged investiga-
tions into crimes. The murder of Westwick would be a top
priority." Laura met Sophie's gaze. "How long will it be
until they discover my identity?"

"I will never reveal your secret," Sophie assured her.
"Not even Miss Eva knows you were once called Sabine."

They were sitting on Laura's bed speaking in whispered
tones. A full day had passed since Laura discovered the news.
She'd hoped to keep Sophie from finding out the truth. Sophie
couldn't read. She'd only come to Laura after she heard the
courtesans discussing the murder and realized that Laura
was the missing courtesan.

"I swear I am innocent," Laura said softly. "I hated him,
but I didn't kill him."

Sophie took her hand. "I know you didn't, though no
one would fault you if you did. Even if you had arrived here
covered with blood, I would not have called for the Runners. Westwick deserved his fate."

On this they could agree. "It sounds cold, but I do not
grieve his loss. He was a horrible man. And yet, he had

moments of kindness, though they were few. During those times, I almost felt as if he truly cared for me. Then when I'd think he might be convinced to free me, the darkness would come again."

"There are men like him all over this city," Sophie said. "I have had the misfortune of encountering one myself. But we are both here and safe." She stood and squeezed Laura's hand. "So you must think of him no more."

After the door closed behind Sophie, Laura tried to take comfort in knowing her friend would keep her confidence.

The earl had kept her real identity secret, not to protect her but because he liked possessing a mysterious lover all his friends coveted. That was why he called her Sabine. Still, she knew that one of his friends, Henry, was well aware of who she was. He'd arranged the false marriage and had spent many evenings staring at her over the table, with an evil smirk on his ugly face.

The only thing saving her from arrest was the fact that he wouldn't know where to find her.

M iss Laura is indisposed." Sophie's voice carried up the stairs to where Laura stood stock-still on the landing. "She is not taking visitors."

Laura pressed back against the wall.

"She has been indisposed since Monday," Simon replied with tightly controlled anger. "If she is so ill, I must insist she see a physician."

"She has a cold," Sophie lied again. "I am sure as soon as she is well, she will send around a note. Until then, we expect you to respect this household and find another form of entertainment."

Simon grumbled something that Laura couldn't make out and then took his leave. Sophie started to walk past the staircase but paused when she saw Laura hiding there.

"He is determined." Sophie frowned. "This has become unacceptable, Laura. Either you find a way to be rid of him or I will have to speak to Miss Eva. The courtesans are only a few days from their matching party. I will not have their day disturbed by Mister Harrington's continued presence."

Laura nodded. "I'll see this matter settled immediately." She wouldn't ruin the happiness of the day when the former courtesans were matched with husbands. Worse yet, if she kept seeing Simon, she might let a word slip here or there, talk in her sleep, or say something that would clue him in to her identity and leave her open for arrest.

It was a chance she couldn't take. Simon cared for her, but could he overlook the murder charges against her?

She went to the library and found a sheet of parchment, an inkwell, and a pen. She took them out to the garden and sat at a table under a tree.

The day was slightly overcast, which fit her mood. She looked at the page, trying to come up with just the right words to tell Simon that their friendship had to end.

The idea of never seeing him again left holes in her heart, further convincing her that what she was doing was right. Not only would her attachment deepen each time they were together, but if she was arrested for murder, their connection might come to light and hurt him and his family. Rejecting him would save them all much grief.

She reached for the pen and began to write.

This is absurd." Simon looked down at the servant, Thomas, who stood stoically on the stoop. "Laura didn't write this."

"I assure you, sir, that she handed me the note herself." With that, the man turned and walked back to the carriage. Simon stood, dumbfounded, as the servant drove away.

He backed up and closed the door. Anger and outrage had replaced the frustration he'd felt all week, while Laura hid away at the courtesan school. He'd tried twice to see her and knew the news of the lingering illness were false. Now she claimed to have fallen in love with a man from Eva's Husbands Book and was running off to marry him.

The notion was laughable. Laura was too practical to fall in love with a drawing in a book. She'd been hurt badly. She'd want to know the man very well before ever considering marriage.

Still, he had seen hints of a romantic heart in her. Could she have actually fallen in love with a face in a book?

He folded the note and tucked it into his coat. If Laura had truly gone against her character and found herself a husband, the truth shouldn't be difficult to confirm.

"Dunston!" he bellowed. "Come. I need you!"

Chapter Thirteen

❧❦❧

Laura stayed hidden in the town house for three days. She avoided windows and spoke to no one outside the school. Every time she saw a man walk past the town house, or loiter against a fence, or rest out of the sun beneath a tree along the street, she was certain she was being watched.

Only the furor of the party had kept her from hiding under her bed, chewing her nails to the quick. She helped the young ladies prepare for their party and would watch the festivities from a window overlooking the garden.

"You all look lovely," she said, blinking back tears. She'd become fond of the women in the weeks she'd known them. Her happiness for them was genuine. "I know the men will be eager to win your hearts."

Jane smiled and smoothed her hand over her pale blue dress. "You should be joining us. There are enough husbands for everyone."

Miss Eva stepped forward. "Laura is not ready for a husband. I shall offer again, in time for the next party."

Miss Eva was now aware that Laura and Simon had spent the night together and wasn't pleased. Sophie had thought it her place to share the news with her employer.

Thankfully, Miss Eva had accepted Laura's assurance that she'd taken care of the problem of his visits.

Simon had stayed away, further attesting to the persuasion of her note, though neither she nor Miss Eva was certain he'd gone for good. And Miss Noelle was convinced he was waiting for a right time to return, thinking kidnapping wasn't beyond him to get what he wanted.

Mariette pulled on her gloves. "If you change your mind, Laura, I have a pretty cream frock that would look perfect on you."

Laura held up her hands, palms open. "I appreciate your concern, everyone, but I think I shall wait a bit longer before considering marriage."

The party was a gay event, with two matches made before the party's close and another two women close to choosing their husbands. The last one, Mariette, wanted to consider her options for a few days before choosing between three suitors.

The young women were the pillars of propriety and Miss Eva beamed with pride over their accomplishments.

Later Laura joined Eva in the parlor after the women had retired to their rooms at the end of the exciting day. The town house was oddly quiet for the first time since sunrise.

"I do not know how you do this over and over," Laura said, flopping down in a chair. She was exhausted, and she had done very little to help. "And end the day still standing."

Eva smiled and sipped her tea. "I know the desperation that forces women to sell their bodies. I believe they should have another choice. To know that I can help is what drives me onward during those times when I'd rather curl up in bed with a book."

Laura nodded. "I do admire you, Miss Noelle, and Sophie. I have seen firsthand how happy you make your former courtesans. I do not think a single one stopped smiling for a minute today."

Eva put the cup down. "I will continue to match them for as long as good health allows." She rose slowly and smoothed out her gown. It was the first sign of fatigue Laura had seen. "I believe my carriage has arrived. It is time for me to return home and soak my tired feet."

Curiosity drove Laura to a window. She knew almost nothing about Miss Eva. She was a mystery to all save Sophie. And Sophie was fiercely protective of the secrets of her employer.

An unadorned coach stood waiting, a tall man in black leaning casually against it. Laura couldn't see him well in the dim light, but did see a flash of a smile when Eva went down the steps. He took her hand and drew it to his mouth before assisting her into the dark interior and following her inside.

Laura smiled. The spinster rescuer had secrets, too. The man with the coach was clearly fond of her. Perhaps Miss Eva was about to lose her spinster title.

Collecting the teacups, Laura returned them to the kitchen and went upstairs. There was nary a whisper from behind closed doors as she walked to her room. The young women were likely sound asleep, or very close to it. There had been several squelched yawns behind gloved hands as they'd said their goodnights.

She quietly opened the door, only to let out a squeak of alarm at the sight greeting her on her bed. Fearful her cry would alert Sophie and lead to a devastating discovery, she glanced quickly down the hallway, then hurried inside and clicked the door closed behind her.

"What are you doing here?" she demanded in a harsh whisper and turned the lock. Simon was sitting on her bed, leaning casually against the wall, one leg bent, supporting his crossed arms. The other leg was stretched out on the coverlet. "Get out."

He frowned. "Imagine my surprise to discover that you had not run off to Gretna Green with your mysterious suitor as you claimed in your letter. But that wasn't the worst of your deception." He pulled a stack of newspapers out from behind him and held up the one on top for her to see. "I have discovered that the courtesan I rescued is a murderess."

Laura's knees buckled and she fell back against the door. Her blood pooled at her feet. "I am no murderess."

"Oh?" He held up the papers one at a time. The lamplight illuminated each horrible headline. "The murder happened the same night that I rescued you. Coincidence? I suspect not."

Bile burned in her throat. He thought her a killer. Why then had he not brought the Bow Street Runners?

Laura stumbled over to the small wooden stool next to the writing table and sat. She drew in deep breaths to keep from being ill and to collect her rioting thoughts.

If she fumbled over her explanation and he took it as confirmation of her guilt, these next few moments could be her last of freedom.

"I know this looks suspicious. But I assure you that I did not kill him." She dropped her hands and clenched them in her lap. "The last time I saw him, he was, unfortunately, very much alive."

His hooded gaze offered no clue as to his thoughts. She grimaced. "After all the time we've spent together, you should know me incapable of this crime."

"They found an ear bob beside the body," he pressed. His voice was cold and flat.

"That is not difficult to explain," she admitted, shuddering beneath his suspicion. She had to make him believe her! "I was in the house for over a year. My things are everywhere. One lost ear bob does not make me guilty."

Simon met her eyes. Mistrust and anger played on his face. "How long have you known about Westwick's death?"

"Since the week I sent you the letter. I knew that until the real killer is caught, I will be in danger of arrest. The Runners have spies all over London. Any time I venture outside, I may be spotted." Her shoulders slumped. "If you are caught with me, you'll be subjected to scrutiny, too. I thought it best if you forgot you ever knew me."

His mouth twisted downward. He flipped through the stack of papers until he found what he was looking for. He sighed and turned it toward her. Sketched on the page was a likeness of . . . her.

Laura whimpered. The temperature in the room dropped. Though the sketch was only vaguely accurate and some-what cartoonish, it was close enough. The earl had insisted she paint her face and add a beauty mark for the men. He thought it made her look more like a courtesan.

The likeness on the sketch had neither. It had to be a servant who had provided information about the unadorned Sabine to the Runners.

"I will be hanged for a crime I had no part of." She closed her eyes tightly and trembled. "I'll never be free of him. I'll go to my death knowing that somewhere in hell he is laughing."

Simon caught her up against him, moving so swiftly that she didn't hear him coming. He helped her to the bed and brought her down with him, snuggling her against his long body.

"I will not allow that to happen," he said softly.

Laura twisted her fingertips into his shirt. It was com-forting to be held in his arms. "A moment ago, you thought I was guilty. Why would you help me now?"

Simon tipped up her chin with a fingertip. "I never thought you were guilty. I was angry that you'd kept this secret from me. I wanted to see you deny this while facing me, to assure myself that I wasn't wrong about you."

She locked on to his gaze. "You were not wrong. Though I wanted to kill him, dreamed every night of killing him, in the end, another person did what I could not do. And I am not sorry he's dead."

Simon snorted. "Then it's just I who's regretful. I wanted to beat him bloody. The bastard went too easily. He should have suffered a long and painful death."

The venom in his voice made her thankful that Simon wouldn't have the chance to confront the earl. "For a gently born man, there is a streak of darkness in you."

He shrugged. "Lady Jeanette once called me an ill-tempered brute."

"She knows you well," Laura said dryly.

"She thinks she does." Simon shifted so that they were lying side by side on the bed, her back to him, his body molded against hers. "How well can anyone know another person?"

He had a point. Everyone had secrets.

Fatigue finally overwhelmed her, and she dozed for a bit. It was nearing midnight when a shout from the street awakened her. She listened for signs of trouble, but there was no repeat of the sound.

She liked the feel of Simon's arm around her waist and his body warm against hers. He hadn't tried to take advantage of the situation or attempt a seduction, and she wasn't sure if she was relieved or disappointed.

Making love to Simon under this roof would betray everything the house stood for. The fact that he'd somehow slipped inside undetected, likely sometime during the party, was enough to get them both banned from the household. To repeat their night in the manor while the courtesans slept nearby was, well, unforgivable.

"I should go," Simon whispered, nuzzling her ear.

Laura shivered and turned her head to look into his eyes. "I thought you were sleeping."

He smiled. "Sleep is difficult with you pressed up against me." He moved slightly, and she felt his erection.

"We cannot do that here," Laura said.

"I know." He kissed her forehead and pushed up on the bed. Laura sat up and took a place beside him. "That is why I should go."

Simon stood and quickly righted his clothing. There was little he could do about the creases in his coat. He finally gave up with a sigh.

"My valet will not be pleased. It is the second coat I've ruined this week." He gave her a sidelong glance as he tugged his cuffs into place. When he'd finished, he crossed his arms and leaned back on his heels. "Meet me in the alley behind this house at two o'clock this afternoon. I need to know more about your Lord Westwick."

"He was not *my* Lord Westwick," she protested, then

frowned. "Why do you want to discuss him? The man is dead."

If she never heard the name Westwick again, she'd be content. When he died, her past died. There wasn't any reason she could think of to revisit those months with him. "I have no intention of speaking his name ever again. He is better left buried."

Simon pulled her off the bed and faced her. "I barely knew the earl, as he kept more salacious company than I." He fingered her stray curl and continued, "You didn't kill him; someone else did. But you are the only suspect in the murder, and the Runners won't rest until you're caught and hanged. Killing a peer is a hanging offense."

"I know." She touched her neck and winced, imagining her last moments on earth as the life was choked out of her. "I should flee to Scotland or America, where they can never find me. It would simplify things for all of us."

He took her hands. "If you run, then you will never be free." He squeezed her fingers. "That is why I need to know every detail about Westwick. The more I know, the better prepared I will be to implement my plan."

"And that is?" Laura didn't like the intense look in his eyes. Her stomach tightened painfully.

"To find and capture Westwick's killer."

Chapter Fourteen

Laura paced at the garden gate, her gray skirt and petticoats swishing around her legs. The hours since midnight had been dreadfully long. All night, she'd had the uneasy sensation of being watched and made several trips to the window to peer out. As expected, there were no eyes staring back from the darkness.

Still, the feeling—and Simon's desire to hunt the killer—melded together to leave her restless. She hadn't slept a wink after he left, and even the delicious food served at breakfast had tasted unappealing on her tongue.

Worried, that's what she was. The killer had had no qualms about murdering a peer. He wouldn't think twice about murdering Simon to keep his secret.

A hackney rolled slowly down the alley. Laura stepped through the gate, and the driver pulled to a stop.

Simon alighted and helped her inside, his expression grim.

"I thought a man of your stature would travel in grander style. I was hoping for gilt trim and velvet squabs," she quipped, trying to overcome the knot lingering in her stomach. The jest fell flat. The second the door to the hackney thudded closed behind her, she rushed ahead: "You cannot risk your life to save mine. I'll not allow it!"

Simon smiled cynically. "You have little faith in my abilities, love. I'm disappointed."

The coach jerked into motion. Laura scowled. "I know you can rescue damsels and fight footmen with great skill. My issue is with a killer who would just as willingly kill you as brush lint off his coat."

His face turned stony. "I've fought men for both sport and entertainment. I can handle a cowardly killer who would stab a man in the back."

Why were men so stubborn? "You mistake my argument. I know you are strong and manly and capable of vast strength," she snapped. "My worry is that you may not see him coming. He managed to enter the earl's town house, kill him, and exit without capture. As you said, he is cowardly, like a tiny dog that nips your heels and darts away before you see his intention."

Simon watched her through narrow slits. "Who said he snuck into the town house? Have you considered that the killer was an invited guest?"

This took her aback. She slumped against the squabs. Had the culprit been staying under the roof with her? Did she know him? Was he one of the many faces that had come to bid for her?

Another notion came to mind. It was hard to fathom that Westwick hadn't been killed over his own evil deeds but for another unrelated reason. It was something she hadn't thought about until now.

Laura pressed a hand to her forehead. "Could this murder be about me?"

"I've considered it. Perhaps the man became obsessed with you and knew he hadn't the means to play Westwick's game. He decided to forgo the auction, kill Westwick, and kidnap you, saving himself from the chance of losing you to a higher bidder."

Bile burned up her throat. "Is that possible?" She closed

her eyes. "I'm a simple country girl, not the sort to inspire men to kill to possess me."

Simon stared. "Men have gone to war over women," he said. "You are beautiful, Laura. To those men, you were a mystery, an unattainable prize. I'm sure Westwick kept you sequestered before the auction to entice them further. There were likely several men frenzied enough to kill to have you."

A headache pulsed in her temples. "Westwick *had* only allowed the men a glimpse or two of me, from a distance and in shadow. At the time, I'd thought he was protecting his prize until the bidding concluded."

"Westwick wasn't a stupid man. He knew the minds of men."

"I was terribly naïve," she said softly. "I should have known."

He leaned forward and placed a hand on her knee. "You were an innocent. He stole you from your sheltered life and forced his will on you. When he tired of your spirit, he decided to sell you. How could you know the depths he would go to break you?"

The earl *had* tried to break her, with fists and words, many times. She was less attractive, less intelligent, and less seductive than any woman he'd ever met. And when she'd remarked that he was welcome to find comfort elsewhere, she'd been backhanded for her impertinence.

"He was evil," Laura said. "The earl's handsome face hid a black soul. His companions hated him as much as they were drawn to him. The staff feared him, scattering like sheep from a wolf whenever he ranted about even the smallest mistake."

"He took advantage of your naïveté," Simon pressed again. "Your father should have sent him away."

"My father was ill," Laura countered protectively. "But it wouldn't have mattered even had his wits been sharp. He wouldn't have seen the darkness in Westwick. He thought the best in all people. He was nearly giddy to have snagged a peer for his daughter."

Simon touched her hand. "I know you met Westwick through your cousin. Tell me how it happened exactly."

She saw where the questioning was going. He wanted to learn all she knew about the man to help with his investigation and wouldn't be dissuaded from his course.

"You will use my memories to hunt the killer."

"I will hunt him with or without your help," Simon assured her. "The more I know, the more I can be prepared for any eventuality."

Laura sighed. "There is nothing I can do to change your mind?"

"Nothing." He grinned wryly. "I have a need to dust off my chain mail and ride my magnificent steed into battle for you. Surely you will not keep me from my knightly course?"

She wanted to argue that she could take care of herself. However, Simon wasn't the sort of man to stand in the background when a woman was in trouble. Their history proved it. So she steeled herself to relive her nightmare and looked down at her cupped hands.

"I was returning a picnic basket to my cousin's cook when he stepped out onto the path in front of me. The look in his eyes made me uneasy. When I tried to pass, he took my arm. I threatened to scream but he only laughed and released me." She sighed. "That evening he came to the cottage, full of charm, and spoke to my father about what a match between us could provide me. Within hours I was betrothed."

"Your father didn't ask your opinion on the matter?"

"He knew he had no more than a few days left to live. He was so weak. After he died, I would have no one."

"Westwick knew how desperate your situation would become," Simon agreed. "The bastard."

Laura sighed. "The next afternoon we were wed at Father's bedside. We spent our wedding night in the woodcutter's cottage to be close to Father. Westwick wanted to stay at an inn. That night was the only time he ever gave in to my wishes." She turned her eyes away. "I was miserable. I begged the earl to let me stay with Father during his last hours. Instead he dragged me off to London with only a brief good-bye."

Her throat tightened and she swallowed. "The first beating was two days later, after I'd heard of Father's death. Westwick despised my tears and punished me for failing to stop weeping when he commanded. That was also the night he told me our wedding was false."

"The bastard," Simon muttered. His jaw clenched.

For the first time, Laura realized that Westwick was lucky to be dead. There was something nefarious happening behind those icy blue eyes. Simon Harrington was clearly contemplating murder.

Simon saw wariness on Laura's face and struggled to settle his temper. It was a difficult task. He couldn't soothe her when he wanted to kill the already dead Westwick.

Beating a woman for grieving? His blood pumped hot through his veins. In spite of this, he managed to unclench his fists and jaw.

He braced himself. "Tell me everything."

As the coach rumbled through the streets of London with no particular destination, Laura emotionlessly told him everything she knew about Westwick. Unveiled was a tragic play: his opium abuse, his gambling, his common street prostitutes, all of which he flaunted under her nose.

"He thought I would be inflamed with jealousy over the women." Her mouth twitched and her eyes took on a wicked gleam. "I pretended hurt and anger, playing his game. Truthfully, they gave me a reprieve from his attentions. So the more he thought he'd hurt me, the more he sought them out. It meant less time I spent in his bed."

Simon smiled. "He never could tame his courtesan."

At the statement, she smiled back. "Had the auction

gone through, he would have broken me. I couldn't allow that to happen. I had to be free."

The coach turned into Hyde Park. Simon had paid the driver well to keep driving until he indicated otherwise.

"I remember a story about a Frenchman who tamed tigers. He put on a show in Paris. One day a tiger, tired of the whip and the cage, turned on the man and killed him." Simon cupped his hand on her face. "You cannot tame a wild thing. It was his fatal mistake."

She looked sidelong at him. In her eyes was an invitation he couldn't misinterpret.

He dipped his head and kissed her, her lips soft and pliant beneath his. She moaned. Simon tangled his hand in her hair, and she opened up to deepen the kiss.

She was so sweet, so strong, and so beautiful.

When he ended the kiss, she smiled softly. "I will never tire of your kisses."

Simon grinned. "I do like to please."

Her smile turned pensive. She glanced out the window as a well-sprung coach and four passed at a fine clip. "What a pair we are. A courtesan"—she turned back to him with an apologetic shrug at his scowl—"and a future earl. Had we met under different circumstances, you might have asked me to dance or to take a turn around a drawing room, under the watchful eye of a chaperone, of course. You may have kissed my hand or asked my father if I could take a drive in your carriage."

"I'm not fond of chaperones," he offered. "You cannot steal kisses while they hover."

Her lovely gray eyes sparkled in the dim coach. "Of course, as a poor squire's daughter, I would have been beneath your notice in a room full of fine noble ladies."

"It is impossible to think you could be in any room, no matter how crowded, and not catch my eye."

"You were born to make a prudent match, Simon, with a woman like Lady Jeanette. Once you tire of this desire to save me from my ills, you will convince her to marry you and forget me. That is how it should be."

Laura was right. This was not his future. Though he knew he couldn't rest until she was saved from a hangman's noose, anything beyond was not possible. She'd never consent to be his mistress indefinitely, and he needed Lady Jeanette to help Brenna make a match with Lord Abbot.

She reached out to touch his hand. "Simon, please forget about catching the killer. Miss Eva will help me flee somewhere far away where I can begin a new life. Eventually, the murder will be forgotten."

"And a killer will go free," Simon countered bitterly. "I cannot allow it. There may be future victims. How can I know if a man who dances with Brenna or takes tea with my parents or sits across from me at White's isn't a killer?"

"Simon, please," she beseeched. "Let the Runners do their job. I cannot bear the thought of you in danger."

He scowled and withdrew his hand. "The Runners are singularly focused on Sabine. They will not look elsewhere when they have their suspect set in their minds."

Laura slumped back, defeated. "You are a stubborn man." She ignored his frown. She fell silent as they passed out of the park. She hated the idea of Simon running around London, digging into dark alleys and under piles of refuse for clues. But it was her next thought that brought her head up. The solution was right at hand.

She crossed her arms. "How will you know where to start your investigation? The men at the party have not come forward as witnesses. They will be one in their silence. To admit their presence could make them suspects."

From his expression, she knew she'd hit her mark.

Satisfied she'd stopped his investigation before it began, Laura smiled slyly. "Only I have seen them. Several anyway, and I will not put you in danger."

Simon met her eyes. "I have ways of getting the information from you." He kissed her again.

She smiled under his lips, then drew back. "You can seduce me senseless, and I will still keep my secrets. You must find a way to both assuage my fears and allow me to play a part in the investigation. It will help if I know you will not do anything foolish."

"I never do anything foolish."

Laura expelled a quick unbelieving laugh. "You attacked a pair of burly footmen to save me. You have risked the wrath of both your cousin and Miss Eva to befriend me, and you seduced me against all your reservations. Now you want to hunt down a murderer? And you tell me that you do not act foolishly?"

He leveled a frown at her and backed out of reach. "I would not consider saving you foolish," he said, his voice tight. "As for the latter, I am disappointed over your certainty that I am to end this caper . . . dead."

Realizing that no man wanted to be seen as less than strong and virile, she shook her head. "I spoke out of turn. I know that you can vanquish dragons and save damsels from locked towers with your manly sword and steed. But you are a man of honor. Murderers work from a different set of rules. This man will not hesitate to plunge a knife into your back. He has done so before."

"Westwick was unaware of the danger."

Laura flinched under his anger. She had certainly botched things up. She might well have called him a milksop or a whey-faced ninny.

Knowing there was only one way to redeem herself, she stood and pulled down first one shade, then the other. With a face full of apology, she climbed into his lap.

"I do want you to save me from the hangman, Milord." She clutched his shoulders and pressed a kiss on his neck. "I need you to use your brute strength and cunning to find him and see him punished." She kissed his chin before moving to the other side of his neck. "I will be very grateful for your assistance in the matter."

His hands slipped up to cup her bottom. "You are mocking me."

"Never." She tugged at the buttons of his coat. "It has been a very long time since a man offered me his protection. I fear I am unused to such chivalry." Once his coat was open, she pressed her breasts against his chest and stared into his eyes. "I will give you the information you seek under this condition." Laura skimmed her lips over his. "I will be involved in the investigation."

Chapter Fifteen

Simon eased her back by the shoulders and frowned. "What exactly do you mean by 'involved'? I thought you were against me endangering myself. Suddenly, you want to put yourself in danger, too?"

Laura pursed her lips. When she'd made the stipulation, she hadn't put any thought into where her involvement would take her. She only knew that she didn't want to hide away and let Simon take care of her. She'd had the strength to survive captivity with Westwick. She'd have the strength to follow the trail of the real killer, wherever it led.

"My life is already in danger. As long as a possible hanging looms over me, I cannot really start a new life." She paused and smoothed his shirt. "I know the faces but not the names of the guests. I need to be where society congregates to put the two together. Once we uncover the identity of some of the auction invitees, you can confront the men to see what they know."

She thought he'd refuse outright but knew that unless they could get the servants to speak to him, she was the only other witness to what happened in that house.

Hopeful, she continued, "Merchants and slavers also

came to bid. Finding those men will be harder and more dangerous. If we keep to men of society, then the danger will be minimal—unless one of them is the killer."

It took a moment for his response. He stared at her mouth. His eyes softened. "Do you promise not to get yourself into mischief?"

"Certainly." She smiled innocently. Simon's left brow went up. He looked down to where her hands rested on his chest. She could feel the strength of his heartbeat.

His mouth twitched. "Why do I feel like I'm being led to the guillotine?" His hands caressed her bottom.

Laura made a face and tried to focus. It was difficult to keep her mind clear when he misbehaved.

A sensual assault rippled through her body. "What a dismal image. We should think of something else less grim."

Simon grinned. "I can imagine a few more pleasant things to concentrate on." He gently squeezed the rounded flesh. Her fingers flexed on his chest. In a moment, he'd have her on her back and panting with need. It was proving difficult to keep to her vow of chastity.

"You could charm a nun out of her habit," she said soberly.

"I only want you." He nuzzled her neck. "I wish I'd never let you seduce me. I cannot think while knowing what delights can be found under your clothing."

At his growl, she giggled. "Would it help you to know how much I appreciate your restraint?"

"Not in the least." He slid his mouth up to her ear. She wriggled as he tickled her skin. How easy it would be to let him love her as she wanted. But she was still an innocent squire's daughter in spite of all that she'd suffered with Westwick. She'd taken her one night with Simon, a gift to herself. The next time she went to a man, it would be in their marital bed.

Years from now, she didn't want to feel a single regret when she thought back on these stolen moments with Simon.

Laura looked forward to getting out of the courtesan

school and clearing her name. Well, Sabine's name. And since they were one and the same, it would be her neck stretched if anything went awry. But she had confidence in Simon, and in herself.

"Well, I do," she said softly. "Sharing your bed, though delightful, muddles the situation. I cannot think clearly when my life is so unsettled." He lifted his head and stared into her eyes. "I look forward to the day when I am truly free to make clear and confident decisions on my own, about my future, and about you. I hope you understand?"

"I know you long for freedom. It will happen." He released her and drew back. The coach paused before making a right turn. "And if it means I must submit to cold baths in order to keep my armor shining bright, then so be it."

She giggled. "You are a very honorable knight."

"It's a curse." He took her hand and turned her arm up. He nibbled from her wrist to the crook of her arm and back. She watched him with a gentle smile as he tickled her skin.

"If you ever find that mixing yourself up in my troubles is too much of a trial and wish to step away, I will understand." Laura eased her arm free. "You have already far exceeded your duties to me."

Simon dipped his head and looked straight into her eyes. "We started this together, love. We will finish it together."

Smiling, Laura leaned in and sealed their pact with a kiss.

Collingwood House?" Laura asked, her eyes wide. The mansion loomed as the coach drew to a halt on the drive. Three days had passed since their outing in the hackney with no word from Simon. She'd grown concerned about his absence.

Where was he? Had he been hurt? Then he'd shown up at the courtesan school and spirited her away without justifying his disappearance. Now they were pulling up to one of the grandest houses in London and she was very confused.

"Why are we at Collingwood House?" she demanded. "I am not leaving this coach without an explanation."

He frowned. "You know this house?"

"I have never been inside, but the earl drove me past it once and noted it with envy." The place was beautiful. Stone and brick, it was the grand home of a duke and duchess. "It is impossible to forget."

The coachman opened the door, but Simon waved him off.

Laura's puzzlement grew. She stubbornly crossed her arms and glared. "If you have some sinister reason for bringing me here, you'll have to drag me out."

Simon shook his head. "It is nothing as dismal as that. You will understand in a few moments." He pinned her with a hard stare. "Before we go inside, I need your word that everything you are about to see and hear must be kept in strictest confidence."

"And if I refuse?"

"You won't," he said. "You are all aquiver with curiosity." It wouldn't change a thing if she tried to deny his comment. He was correct. She'd risk almost anything for a peek inside the fine home.

"You are such an exasperating man." She scowled and nodded reluctantly. "I promise."

Reaching out, he tugged one of her tightly clenched hands free and tucked it in his. "I am not taking you into a lion's den," Simon remarked lightly. "You'll not be locked in a secret dungeon or stretched out on a rack. In fact, I'm certain Collingwood House has no dungeon."

She shot him a scathing glare. "You shroud this all in mystery and expect me not to have misgivings?"

"Have I ever harmed you?"

"You have not."

He tucked her hand under his arm. "You'll learn some things today that must remain secret. Once this visit is concluded, you will be returned to the courtesan school unscathed—unless, of course, I decide to drag you to the nearest inn and ravish you senseless."

Laura flushed. Since the night at his manor, they'd limited their sensual contact to a few stolen kisses and an occasional caress. She was torn over her growing feelings for Simon and the knowledge that the more liberties she allowed, the harder their eventual break would be. And what if there was a child?

The door loomed and a butler swung open the panel. She drew Simon to a halt a few feet away. "You agreed to behave. I am suspected of murder, and you need to focus on finding a bride. There will be no seduction."

She didn't want to tell him the true reason for her desire to keep him at arm's length. Respectability. She'd been an innocent when she'd married. The earl had turned her into a courtesan.

The night with Simon had given her another piece of herself back: the ability to choose for herself. But she wanted all of Laura back—the girl who'd dreamed of love, marriage, and children. Though her innocence was gone, she would take back her respectability with both hands.

Taking a lover was not part of that, even a desperately handsome and skilled lover.

"I wasn't—" He stopped, his gaze turning from seductive to dark. He scanned her face and must have noted the set of her jaw. "I did agree. I'm not Westwick, who would force you into my bed."

Laura winced. She wanted to assure him that she'd never see him that way, to ease the sting of her rejection, but decided to leave the matter alone. "Thank you again for understanding."

A grunt was his reply.

Turning, Simon escorted her up the stairs, and the butler nodded. "Welcome, Mister Harrington. Miss Prescott. His Grace and Her Grace are waiting in the library. This way."

The duke and duchess? He was taking her to meet the duke and duchess? Laura's stomach twisted painfully. What sort of insanity was this? You did not bring a former courtesan to meet a duke and duchess, even if she wasn't a courtesan by choice. "Simon," she hissed under her breath. "You cannot introduce me to the duke and duchess. It is unseemly."

"You were invited," he said sharply and followed the butler. "I wouldn't bring you here otherwise."

Laura hurried to keep up. He'd never spoken to her so harshly. Obviously her comment had stung deeper than she'd expected. He was clearly angry. Still, she couldn't worry about him at present. The butler paused outside a room.

It was too late to flee! All she could do was brace herself as the butler reached for the door handles.

The servant swung open the set of double doors and stood back to let them pass. Laura shifted her gaze briefly over the fine furnishings, the huge fireplace, and the high ceiling, before dropping her attention to the couple sitting comfortably together on a settee.

The duke stood. He was handsome to a fault. Tall and impeccably dressed in black, he cut an imposing figure. The duchess was shorter, petite, and lovely. Her reddish-gold hair was upswept in a fashionable twist, and her gown was green and costly.

Standing there in a simple cream frock, her slippers worn and her gloves threadbare, Laura wanted to hide under their beautiful Oriental rug.

"Harrington." The duke walked over and offered his hand to Simon. "I understand you have fallen into an offal pit. Murder? Surely you could find a better use for your time?"

"Your Grace." Simon frowned and glanced at Her Grace. "I see my cousin has filled you in on our troubles. I assure you that getting involved in a murder was never my intention."

The duchess was Simon's cousin? She almost groaned aloud and stared with longing at the rug, mentally measuring it for size. It was certainly large enough for her to wriggle under.

Simon had other ideas for her. He turned to her and pulled her forward. "Your Grace, this is Miss Laura Prescott."

The duke stared.

Laura dropped to a deep bow. "Your Grace." If the duke and duchess knew about the murder, they must know her story, too.

Her face burned. With her eyes downturned, she desperately wished for an open window, an unlatched terrace door, some avenue of escape. Alas, with Simon at her elbow and the doors closed behind her, she was trapped.

She straightened, her tongue tangled. There was nothing she could say. The situation was shameful.

"Welcome to Collingwood House, Miss Prescott," the duke said graciously. "The duchess has spoken fondly of you."

Fondly? Her puzzlement grew.

His Grace led her to the duchess, who watched the interaction with hooded eyes. When Laura got within reach, she realized there was something familiar about the woman, though she was positive they'd never met.

It was the amber eyes. She knew she'd seen them before, but where? Simon moved up behind her before she could make a connection.

"Your Grace, this is Miss Laura Prescott." There was humor in his voice. The duchess scowled at him.

"Simon, you are a bore," she said. "Noelle said you were troublesome, and you have confirmed her observation time and time again. Now you have brought your difficulties into my home. Wasn't it enough that you invaded my school, as though my rules were meant to be ignored? Now you have tumbled into a murder plot and have decided to include my family in your mess."

Laura felt her blood pool in her feet. Miss Eva. The duchess was Miss Eva. She'd spent weeks with a duchess and hadn't gleaned a single clue as to her real identity.

Light-headed from the shocking discovery, she wobbled slightly. The shame of her past was never as great as now. A duchess knew her most scandalous secrets.

"Laura?" Miss Eva took her hand and quickly led her to the settee. "Simon, get her some tea. No, make it a brandy."

A moment later, a glass was thrust into her hand. "Drink this," Miss Eva commanded.

Laura took a sip, and then tossed back the contents. Unused to spirits, it burned. She coughed and pressed the back of her hand to her lips.

The spirit worked. Her eyes regained focus.

She stared at the duchess and found her voice. "Miss Eva. Then you are cousin to Miss Noelle, too?" She knew from Simon that he was Miss Noelle's cousin. Now there were two. The family was certainly an unusual mix.

Her Grace nodded and took her hand. "Simon didn't tell you about our connection on the ride over?" Laura shook her head. The duchess scowled again. "No wonder you are in shock. I shall have my footmen take him into the garden and beat him."

Laura sighed. "Yes, please."

The duke chuckled. "I'd make a run for the door if I were you, Harrington. The footmen are a sizable lot."

Simon walked to a sideboard and poured himself a drink. Then another. He appeared slightly uneasy and Laura took some satisfaction in that.

"I do apologize for my cousin," Miss Eva said. "Though I haven't known Simon long, he grew up with Noelle. According to her, he was a horrid tease. That has obviously not changed. I have myself discovered that he is both a bother and without manners. I cannot understand why you put up with him."

"He saved my life," Laura said weakly. She was certain that at any moment she'd wake up from this very odd dream and find herself in bed at the school, relieved that this was all only part of her imaginative mind.

The duchess harrumphed. "I suppose we should all be grateful for the intervention that saved your life." She stared at Simon. "Obviously, he does have his uses."

This time Simon grinned.

Laura frowned and ignored him. Curiosity drew her

back to Her Grace. She gave the duchess a quick look-over. Her Miss Eva disguise had worked well. If not for her eyes and voice, Laura would never have put them together as one person.

"You are both Miss Eva and a duchess? How can that be?"

Her Grace released her hand and reached to pour the tea. "I know a former courtesan who lived a difficult life. I helped her find a new identity. I wanted to help other courtesans escape sexual bondage, too. So I founded my school."

It was a simple tale. Laura suspected that there was much more to the story. "And the disguise?"

"I keep my two worlds separate. Very few trusted people know that I'm a duchess and a courtesan rescuer. It keeps gossips from digging into my privacy. That is why I ask for your discretion."

"Of course, Your Grace." This was a fascinating turn. Laura's respect for Miss Eva grew. She had everything a woman could ever want, yet she still made the trip to Cheapside nearly every day to help other, less fortunate women.

Her Grace smiled. "When I am at the school, I ask that you call me Miss Eva. Sophie knows the truth; the courtesans do not. The secret protects both them and me."

"Yes, Your Grace." It was almost impossible to reconcile Miss Eva as the duchess. Yet the warmth in Her Grace's eyes was the same as she saw in Miss Eva with her courtesans. Though she was often a tough taskmaster, she wanted only the best for her young ladies. And the young women adored their teacher.

The duchess looked at her husband over the rim of her cup. Laura glanced between them and saw the love in their eyes. Though she'd suspected that Miss Eva had a secret life, Laura never would have dreamed that the woman was the cherished wife of a duke.

How she envied them!

"I think we should get to the reason for your visit, Harrington," the duke said, breaking into her musings. "I believe you want to embroil my wife and myself in some scheme?"

"Perhaps you should hear my idea before you decide?" Simon offered. "You may not find it distasteful."

"So this doesn't involve the murder?" the duke pressed.

Laura wasn't sure if the duke was pleased or disappointed that the plan might not include a dangerous element. There was a wicked light in his eyes.

"I, too, would like to be privy to his plan," Laura said. "I am as curious as you are." The two men took a pair of chairs. The duke tapped his fingertips on the arms, showing his impatience. The three of them waited while the mantle clock ticked.

Finally Simon spoke. "I need for you to throw a party, a grand party here at Collingwood House."

Chapter Sixteen

H is Grace and Eva stared at him. Two pairs of eyes narrowed suspiciously. Simon waited for a protest, something, but they appeared content to wait for him to explain. Then they could refuse him outright.

Simon knew he was about to break Laura's confidence. He had no choice. In spite of his annoyance that she felt the need to warn him off for a second time, as if he were incapable of accepting her decision to remain chaste, he still felt extremely protective of her. Revealing her secret to Eva and Nicholas would further assure her safety. If anything happened to him, they would see her relocated away from London.

So he began, "As you know, Lord Westwick was murdered and his missing courtesan is suspected in the deed."

"This is the murder you mentioned in your note?" Eva asked. She shared a glance with her husband.

"The very one." Simon glanced at Laura. Her face had gone white. She'd shared her story with Eva, Noelle, and Sophie, but never mentioned Westwick by name. He plunged ahead, "Laura is the missing courtesan, Sabine."

"What?" His Grace sat upright in the chair. His sharp

eyes turned on Laura. "You brought a murderess to my home?"

Eva held up her hands. "Darling, calm down."

"I will not calm down." Outraged, the duke came to his feet. "You must leave at once."

Simon stepped between them, one hand up to block the duke from advancing toward Laura, and the other balled into a tight fist for her protection. "She isn't a killer."

"You are too close to this to see things rationally," the duke replied with a growl. "Your mind is clouded by lust."

Simon scowled. "My mind is clear. You know nothing about Laura. She is no murderess."

"Nicholas, please," the duchess begged.

The two men began arguing loudly. The duchess stood and pushed into the fray. Laura flinched at the melee, not sure how to calm the tension and worried that she was about to be thrown to the Bow Street Runners.

It took the duchess, small as she was, to settle the two men with a tone that was both firm and not much higher than a whisper. It was clearly meant to keep her husband and Simon from killing each other.

"Enough." With one hand on each chest, she gave a great shove, and they both stepped back. She glared at Simon but turned most of her anger on her husband. "Laura did not murder anyone. She does not have the darkness of a killer." She expelled a harsh breath. "Now if you both will sit down, we can calmly discuss the matter."

Laura watched the anger slowly fade in both men, from a flame to a slow simmer, as they moved to reclaim their chairs. As the men glared at each other, Miss Eva sent her an apologetic glance. Laura was certain then that as long as she had the duchess on her side, she might get through this troubling encounter unscathed.

Her Grace moved to pour the men each a large glass of some spirit, then took her seat. After a swallow or two, they appeared less inclined toward bloodshed.

Clearly satisfied, the duchess spoke to Laura. "I think both children have turned back into rational men. Now,

please tell us your story and how this ended with the death
of Lord Westwick and your complicity in the crime."

For the next hour, Laura told the duke and duchess
almost everything she'd told Simon, leaving out the more
shameful information about her captivity. By the finish of
her tale, the duke no longer seemed intent to have her
arrested and appeared somewhat sympathetic of her plight.
His relaxed posture confirmed her observation.

Still, this didn't mean he fully trusted her.

"That is quite a story," His Grace said thoughtfully.

The duchess nodded. "Many of my courtesans have
come from difficult situations and sometimes tell exaggerated tales to encourage sympathy from the other women."
She sighed. "I believe I can flush out lies when I hear them,
and I do not believe Laura is lying."

Though Laura still wasn't entirely convinced that His
Grace accepted that she hadn't killed Westwick, he appeared
ready to give her the benefit of his wife's wisdom.

"I will reserve judgment for now." He glowered at
Simon. "This may yet change. I expect that you will do
whatever is needed to keep my household free of turmoil."

Simon nodded. "I will do what I can, though I do need
your help. The case is stalled. I have come up with a way to
move it forward. But I need your agreement."

Her Grace faced Simon. "Does this have anything to do
with your request for a party?"

Simon sent Laura a reassuring glance. "Only Laura
knows the men who were at the town house the night of the
murder, and they have scattered like rats in daylight. Not
one has come forward as a witness to the events of that
evening. If we can get enough noblemen gathered in one
place, like here at Collingwood House, she should be able
to recognize one or two."

"That means we will have to invite a murderer into our
home," the duke said sharply. "I'll not put my wife in danger."

"Danger will not necessarily follow us here," Simon
countered. "The killer might be a merchant, a slaver, or a
ship captain. We know nothing of those men. And even

if he is someone we know, the bastard has already been moving in society without rousing suspicion." He scrubbed his hands over his head. "If we find Westwick's killer, Laura won't hang and the Ton will be a safer place for everyone."

The duke and duchess locked eyes. "We have to help," Her Grace pleaded. "Laura cannot come to harm. And if I am proven wrong about her, I will call for the Runners myself."

Laura saw the remaining tension leave His Grace. His wife had his complete trust.

"I will not do anything to cause danger to the duchess," Laura assured His Grace. "We will find a way to fulfill Simon's plan and be gone without anyone knowing I was here."

The duke stood and went to the fireplace, where Miss Eva joined him. Simon came to sit next to Laura as the duke and duchess talked quietly together.

"His Grace will help us. He may be settled in marriage and his ducal duties, but there was a time when he took a bullet for his wife. There is a man of adventure under those well-cut clothes. He'll help us for no other reason than to keep the killer, if he is indeed a nobleman, from living freely among us. He'll not want anyone he cares about put in danger."

Laura agreed. "His Grace is not weak willed." One glance was all she needed to discover that truth. He cut a powerful figure. "He really took a bullet for her?"

"He did."

She sighed. "What a romantic story. No wonder she loves him so much. He is her hero."

Laura's wistful sigh took Simon aback. In spite of the hardships she'd endured, she had a romantic heart.

He found that hard to believe. Her recent past had been anything but the stuff of sonnets. Yet she'd spent only about an hour with the duke and Eva, and was sighing wistfully, as if that one bullet were part of the greatest love story of the ages.

The beast, jealousy, rose inside him and pricked his emotions. Laura stared at the duke as if he'd flown down from the heavens on Pegasus to vanquish evil and save the world.

Simon pondered His Grace. He was handsome enough. Most women would think so. But it irked him that Laura's gaze had taken on a dreamy cast.

"The man is not a god," Simon snapped, far harsher than he'd intended. "He is just a man."

Laura turned away from the duke and duchess. She scanned his face for a long moment before a knowing smile spread across her face. "His Grace is very handsome. He saved Miss Eva's life. Why should I not admire him?"

"He is also arrogant and ill-tempered."

The patient smile remained. "Then the two of you are well suited to be friends."

Simon grumbled, "You have certainly changed from the woman I rescued from the footmen." He noticed he'd put an emphasis on "rescued." She seemed to forget that he was heroic, too. "I never suspected that beneath your reserve was a woman of such devilish humor."

"There are many things you do not know about me," Laura replied. "I used to smile quite easily. Now that the gray clouds have thinned and the sky has regained its blue in my eyes, I am rediscovering happiness." She gave him a curious look. "Perhaps you will grow to like the real Laura Prescott."

"And perhaps not." Simon crossed his arms.

"Come, Simon, it isn't as grave as all that," Laura said, her eyes dancing. "His Grace is handsome, but I find you more so. And you saved me from certain death. If anyone is heroic, it was you, charging out of the darkness to scoop me up onto your large gray destrier. I nearly swoon every time I think of that moment."

He said nothing. It still irked him that she'd cut him to the knees earlier, when the offer to find a room had been a half jest. Though he suspected her reasons had little to do with him and more to do with her desire to start a new uncomplicated life, her attention to the duke had not eased his injured ego. However, the last comment had certainly helped soothe his tweaked feathers.

Laura reached for his hand and continued softly, "It has been a long time since anyone cared about me as you do. You are my friend, my only real friend. I will always cherish you for your kindness. No man, not even a duke, will ever rise to your level in my eyes."

All the annoyance drained from him. He felt like an ass.

"I will forever be your friend," he said firmly and meant it. "I was born an arrogant bastard, confident in my charms. Of late, my inflated sense of importance has taken a battering." His mouth twitched. "First Lady Jeanette refused me and then you slobbered after the duke. I was certain I'd grown a horrid boil on the end of my nose."

Laura smiled. "No slobbering and no boils. Thank goodness. It's only that I have finally emerged from a dreadful situation and must plan my future with a clear mind. And you are very much a distraction. I hope you can understand?"

He did understand. It wouldn't keep him from lusting after her, but he did see her point. He had his own worries. Maybe keeping to friendship would help them both complete their goals.

"Then we shall put our focus on catching the killer," he agreed, trying not to notice her delightful scent. He suspected this self-imposed celibacy would be a difficult promise to keep. "Though if you become overwhelmed with desire for me, I'll not push you away."

Laughing lightly, Laura nodded. "I shall remember that should the occasion arise."

The duke and duchess returned and the conversation ended. Eva was obviously displeased. "We are not comfortable knowing that the two of you could be stepping into danger. However, we cannot in good conscience let a killer run about free. So on Friday next, we will throw a grand ball here at Collingwood House."

Laura looked at Simon. Apprehension marked her features. "I hope you understand how high the stakes are here. It would be easier for everyone if I simply left the country."

The idea of never seeing her again left him at odds. Having her out of his life would make his hunt for a perfect wife easier. She already spent too much time in his head. But was he ready to let her go?

"You escaped sometime during the murder," Simon countered. The killer may suspect that you fled because you witnessed something. If that is the case, he won't rest until he finds and silences you."

Chapter Seventeen

Laura shuddered. According to the *Times*, the killing had been gruesome. The thought of the murderer slicing her up like a Christmas goose stuck in her mind. She knew she'd never be safe until he was locked up in Newgate Gaol.

The arrival of the butler drew all eyes to the door. "Mister Crawford, Your Grace."

A tall and lanky man with a limp crossed the room on an uneven gate. He bowed to the duke, then turned to the duchess. Miss Eva's mouth twitched when he made a grand bow.

"I see you are doing well, Your Grace," he said and took her outstretched hand. "Marriage suits you."

Miss Eva smiled and her eyes took on an evil glint. "I am trapped in marriage to this arrogant man and it is all your doing. I should have you banned from the property."

He released her hand. "Alas, I have no regrets. Who'd have believed that my investigation of you would lead to such a happy union?" He glanced at His Grace. The duke was also smiling. "I suspect your husband would not have it otherwise."

Laura watched the curious exchange. This Mister Crawford did not look like a member of the gentry in his common clothing, yet he seemed very comfortable in the presence of the duke and duchess.

The duke smiled at his wife. "Indeed, I would not."

Mister Crawford cast a quick glance at Laura and Simon before turning back to the duke and lowering his voice. "I wish my call was under more pleasant circumstances, but I fear I have news of some concern. It is about the Earl of Westwick. May we speak privately?"

Laura's breath caught.

She darted a glance up at Simon. His face hardened as he stepped close and rested a hand on her shoulder. The action did not go unnoticed by Miss Eva. She sent Laura a reassuring smile.

"You may speak freely, Crawford," His Grace said evenly. "We were just discussing the matter ourselves."

This man, Crawford, shifted from foot to foot. He clearly preferred if Simon and Laura were not present. He lowered his voice again. "It involves a certain place of which the duchess is intimately connected."

"The courtesan school?" Simon interjected.

The stranger's eyes widened. Laura knew then that he was privy to the secret.

Miss Eva stepped forward. "Mister Harrington and Miss Prescott are aware of my school. If you have information that concerns my courtesans, please tell me now."

At her urging, Mister Crawford nodded. "I do not mean to upset you, Duchess, but this is a matter of great importance. A man came to me this morning, a servant by his clothing, and asked to hire my services to locate a missing courtesan. He believed she was involved in the murder of his master."

Laura froze. Her stomach pitched.

"What did you tell him?" His Grace asked tightly. He took his wife's hand and tucked it under his arm.

"As soon as he said 'missing courtesan,' I suspected the woman might have gone to you for shelter, so I put him off. I said I had too many cases to take on another."

"Did he give you her name or the name of the dead man?" Simon pressed.

Crawford shook his head. "He offered no further information, though I suspected he was speaking of Lord Westwick. His courtesan is a suspect who has gone missing, and I have heard of no other murdered men who fit that information."

Eva slumped onto the settee. "I trust your instincts. Thank you for your discretion."

The room fell silent for a moment. Then Simon asked, "How would a servant have the money to pay an investigator and why?"

"I was wondering the same thing," His Grace said. "If what I've heard about Westwick is true, the servants would be pleased to be rid of him."

Laura nodded absently. Westwick *was* a horrid master. He terrorized everyone in his employment just for the pleasure of doing so.

"It's true," Laura said, her voice thin. "They hated and feared him. If not for constant threats to hunt them down and have them whipped, or worse, they would have fled him in droves."

Crawford stared. Laura felt his keen eyes take her measure. After a long pause he spoke. "You are the missing courtesan?" He didn't wait for her answer. "I expected only an Amazon of a woman could take down Westwick. He was reputed to punish his courtesans with his fists."

Simon spoke up. "Do not let her size confuse you. Laura is a fighter." He briefly explained her history.

When Simon finished, Laura looked Crawford straight in the eyes. "I assure you that I did not kill Westwick. Unless wishing for his death is what killed him. When I escaped, he was still breathing."

"We believe the killer used her disappearance to cover his guilt and make her the main suspect," Simon added. "It was an unfortunate coincidence and may have saved her life."

The investigator crossed his arms. "Interesting. I thought

the servant's arrival was odd. Now I believe someone else put him up to the query, a man who wanted to distance himself from the crime."

"The murderer?" Miss Eva said.

"Possibly," Simon replied. "But other than the servants, and half of the fathers and brothers in London, why would anyone kill Westwick? He was just another spoiled lord who never had to account for his misdeeds. If every nobleman who fit that description were executed for those failings, half of the Ton would be dead."

"Yes," His Grace agreed. "*Why* Westwick?"

"That seems to be the question plaguing this situation," Simon replied. "I believe Laura is at the root of the crime." Crawford lifted a brow and Simon continued, "From what Laura told me about her time with Westwick, his evil deeds go back years. He'd collected enemies since boyhood, when he attacked his first housemaid. Surely there were many times since when someone wanted to kill him but hadn't the courage to murder a peer."

"It is the timing of the murder that I find suspect." His Grace briefly explained the auction. "The auction ended with the killing."

Crawford's eyes darkened with anger. He stared at Laura. "Lord Westwick received a just punishment. The killer should be knighted."

Heads nodded all around. Laura took comfort in the tide of sympathy from those gathered. If the Runners did find her, she'd have a small group of powerful voices speaking for her.

Simon stepped away to refresh his drink. "Though I have no proof, I think Laura became the object of a twisted desire. The man may have disposed of the earl to have her."

The investigator settled his attention on her. Laura tried not to fidget. The duke and duchess clearly respected Crawford. She somehow knew his opinion of her would solidify her innocence, or guilt, in the mind of the duke.

Finally, he nodded. "That is quite possible. Westwick was a man who did not discriminate with women. He

abused at will. He would find Laura's spirit challenging."
Crawford paused. "It isn't improbable that she could inspire
another man to feel the same passion. Throw shrews
together in the same bucket and eventually they'll canni-
balize each other."

"You know much about the man," Simon remarked and
his eyes narrowed. "How much?"

Looking at Simon, Crawford answered, "Years ago, I
worked a case for him. My only and last. I learned enough
about the earl during our brief association to keep clear of
him in the future."

Laura closed her eyes. Crawford did not look like the
sort of man to be intimidated by anyone. For him to consider Westwick dangerous confirmed that she was lucky
she wasn't dead.

"I would like to hire you to look into the murder." Simon
returned to his place beside Laura. "There were men at the
auction who travel in circles of which I am unfamiliar. If
you can find any information from that quarter, then we
can certainly cover more avenues. This could lead to a
rapid conclusion of this matter."

"Mister Crawford is a skilled investigator," Miss Eva
stated confidently. "He has helped on several cases of which
I am familiar."

Laura didn't like feeling more beholden to Simon than
she already was. And yet she hadn't the funds to hire Crawford herself. Although if he was as good as the duchess
claimed, he was well worth any cost.

"When I find a position, I will repay you for whatever
you spend," Laura said softly.

Simon shook his head. "I expect no repayment."

"I insist." She met his eyes. Her level stare showed she'd
accept no argument. "I will not allow it otherwise."

He frowned. "You are a stubborn woman."

She indicated her agreement with a wry smile. "I was
kept and imprisoned for over a year by a monster. I will not
accept charity from any man not my husband. We will
have an agreement, or I will not cooperate with this fool's

mission." She darted a glance at the other three people as they watched to see if Simon would agree. Miss Eva nodded her approval.

Finally, he tipped his head. "I agree."

Satisfied, she reached for her teacup. She glanced at the duke over the rim. She thought she detected a glimpse of admiration, but the moment was fleeting.

Though Miss Eva and Simon thought her innocent, neither truly knew her. They formed their opinion not on facts but emotion. The duke, however, had no connection to her and would look at her situation through facts alone. So far, he seemed to lean toward believing her. Hopefully, by the time the day ended, her innocence would be solidified in his mind.

The maid returned with a tray of mixed pastries. She fussed over Miss Eva before the duke dismissed her.

"Perhaps we should get to business." Crawford claimed a chair beside the fire. "There are still many paths to cover."

Simon would never take money from Laura, but knew she'd remain steadfastly stubborn if he refused. He also knew that unless she found employment, there was little chance she'd ever have funds for repayment.

The chances of her gaining a respectable position were minuscule. Who would hire such a beauty if the household was full of men? A wife or mother would see future trouble arising from her presence and chase Laura off.

He watched Crawford press Laura with clipped questions. The interrogation was meant to draw out facts. She held herself well, answering each with an emotionless tone.

"How many men were in attendance for the auction?"

"My guess is thirty. There may have been more," Laura answered, pressing her clasped fists to her mouth. "I was terrified by the tension in the house. Some of the men were frightening and I worried that I would be caught alone in a hallway or darkened corner and attacked. As for my escape, it was luck that left me unattended for those few minutes."

"You said the men were not all noblemen?"

She shook her head. "Some were dressed impeccably and others were a bit frayed. I wouldn't have known their occupations had I not eavesdropped on their conversations." She paused and scrunched up her face. "I remember there was an Italian merchant and at least two slavers from some faraway place. They were dressed in unusual clothing. I believe there was a French count and several merchants from America."

"And the rest?" Crawford pressed.

Laura rubbed her forehead. "I'm certain one of the men was a baron from somewhere south of London. A few others may have been noblemen, but I'm not positive. The rest were a mix of which I cannot claim knowledge."

Simon lifted a brow. "I am impressed. In spite of the trauma you faced, your memory is surprisingly clear."

Rubbing her arms, Laura said, "I had hoped to find an ally in the group. Unfortunately, I learned rather quickly that the men would not come to my aid. The earl had hand-picked them all for their discriminating tastes." Her mouth turned downward. "Once I was sold, I would never be seen again."

"Oh, dear," Eva said. Her face was pale.

"The bastard," the duke said.

Simon's jaw tightened. "I wonder how many other women have fallen prey to similar circumstances."

Crawford shook his head. "No telling. If the women are orphaned or without protection, they would be vulnerable."

"Thankfully, I am quite certain that I was the first." She worried her bottom lip. Then, "Westwick had a friend, a confidant with whom he plotted his evil deeds. They hoped the auction would be successful and, if so, would consider it the beginning of a new venture."

"Do you know this man's name?" Simon asked.

She shook her head. "Westwick called him Henry, but I suspect the name was false. The earl slipped once and called him Charles."

"Both are common names," Crawford said. "Can you describe him?"

"Medium height, trim, dark hair, cold eyes." She paused and picked through the bits of memories in her mind. "He spoke as if educated, though I believe he wasn't wealthy. His coat was worn and his boots scuffed. However, I would know him instantly if I saw him." She shuddered. "I spent many nights in his company. I think that had he the wealth to afford me, he would have outbid the others."

"Then we shall consider him a suspect," the duke said.

The room fell silent. The mantle clock ticked to fill the quiet.

"Wait." Laura's face brightened. "I don't know if this will help, but one of the merchants always wore a red waistcoat when he arrived during the week of parties. I thought it odd. Plain red, red and white stripes, some sort of pattern in red—he clearly preferred the color."

"How interesting," the duchess said. "It cannot be Byron Little. He prefers yellow."

Crawford smiled evilly. "I know the man of whom you speak. The man is a salvager and thief, though he calls himself a legitimate businessman. He sells stolen goods from cargo ships that have run aground. In fact, many believe he is a wrecker himself."

"Why hasn't he been arrested?" Laura asked.

"He gets away with it because the items have question-able ownership. Neither the local constables nor the Bow Street Runners have yet to catch him committing the crimes," Crawford explained. "He works out of a run-down warehouse in Whitechapel."

Simon stepped forward. "There is no time to waste. We can be in and out of Whitechapel before dark if we leave immediately."

His Grace agreed. "I shall call for a hackney. We will leave at once."

"Absolutely not!"

Chapter Eighteen

❧❦❧

Miss Eva came to her feet, a hand protectively over her abdomen. It was then that Laura realized the duchess was with child.

"I will not have my husband and cousin sneaking around Whitechapel chasing a murderer. It is too dangerous a place. You will be targets for thieves and cutthroats."

Both His Grace and Simon smiled patiently. Laura could tell by looking into the eyes of the men that they'd not be dissuaded by the protesting duchess. They were clearly looking forward to this adventure. Danger—or the duchess—be damned.

It was Simon who spoke up as he looked down at his expensive gray coat. "Eva's correct. We will be easy targets. We need to borrow some less costly clothes."

"We have some old servants' clothing that is destined for charity," the duke said. "There should be something that fits."

"That wasn't what I meant," the duchess snapped and was rewarded with a kiss on her brow from the duke.

"I shall return shortly, love."

Before she could launch a more zealous protest, the

three men hurried from the room. The duchess expelled an exasperated sound. She slowly turned and reclaimed her seat.

"Men. They are not happy unless they are plunged into danger," Laura said, agreeing with the put-out look on Miss Eva's face. "Thankfully, they are robust fellows. There are three of them and Mister Crawford looks like a man who has faced peril and survived. He will make certain that your husband comes back to you unscathed."

Worried herself, Laura put on a brave face and struggled not to pull her bottom lip between her teeth. She knew Simon enough to suspect that he could handle himself well in every situation. However, Whitechapel-bred men did not live by any set of rules. Until she saw his handsome face again, she'd worry.

"I know Mister Crawford," Miss Eva agreed. "He is a good investigator. Still, it displeases me to have His Grace running pell-mell around Whitechapel. The three of them could fall into all sorts of mischief."

Laura realized that the duchess wasn't worried about an attack on the duke, but that the men would seek out trouble purposefully. "Surely they will not seek a fight?"

The duchess gave her a sidelong glance.

This time it was Laura who sighed. "You're right, they would." She looked to the open door. From somewhere in the house, she could hear male laughter. She grimaced. "I am quickly discovering that men do not have the sense of a goat."

Miss Eva nodded. "True. Thankfully they have us to inject reason into their lives."

The two women shared a wry smile. "Will you stop His Grace from going?"

"As if he would listen to me." Her Grace slowly shook her head. "Let them have their fun. It will do them good to get their knuckles bruised. They will come back puffed up like peacocks and feeling like they can conquer anything."

Laura nodded. "I understand His Grace once took a bullet for you?" This was a story she was eager to hear.

Miss Eva was stoic for a moment before a grin widened over her beautiful face. Her eyes danced. "I must take Simon to task for spilling my secrets."

"I assure you, he said nothing until after I discovered who you were," Laura said, and turned back as the loud clomp of hurried footsteps came down the staircase.

Simon and His Grace paused only long enough to stop in the doorway and grin like naughty boys before they were off in a bustle of activity and humor-filled voices.

Simon and the duke were dressed in dusty trousers, stained white shirts, and a pair of similar scuffed brown coats that had likely spent time in the duke's stables. Wool caps, worn low, had completed the costumes. Laura hoped they would not be recognized as peers if they kept their heads down. And if they refrained from speaking to anyone in their lordly voices, the disguises might actually work.

"I suppose we are in for a long night," the duchess said glumly. "It would do me no harm to tell you the story of the night I rode off to rescue a kidnapped courtesan."

Whitechapel was a place for less fortunate souls— those who came from rural areas to London looking for work but couldn't afford the higher rents in the more prosperous sections of town. Some had fallen on difficult times for many reasons, and some were born into poverty. Whatever their stories, there was an overall feeling of sad desperation that cloaked the area.

Simon smelled the acrid mix of slaughterhouse and brewery as the hackney pulled to a stop before the address Crawford had given the driver. The three men alighted and requested the driver wait. It took the promise of a large fee to get the man to agree—that and a pistol he pulled out from beneath his seat to lay across his lap.

A few of the buildings clung to the façade of respectability, though Simon knew that after dark the façade would crumble as the dangerous element of Whitechapel came out to play.

"It appears as if Mister Smoot has let his property turn ramshackle," Simon remarked with a grimace. Soot already dusted his borrowed clothing. "I thought you said he was wealthy."

Crawford snorted. "Do not let the soot and disrepair fool you. In an area such as this, you don't show your wealth. You might end up with a crushed skull and empty pockets."

His Grace grunted his agreement. "Let us step lively, gents, before the ruffians sniff out the gold in my pockets."

They walked to the door and knocked. The next few minutes were spent arguing with the clerk in order to gain entrance to the building, It was coercion from Crawford, and the well-bred tones of the duke, that finally convinced the man that they weren't thieves and to let them inside.

"As I explained, Mister Smoot is not here," the clerk said smugly and swung out a hand to indicate no Smoot. "He, er, left the building, and I am unsure of his return."

Simon felt the clerk's deception. He clearly knew where Smoot was off to. Loyalty, or fear, kept him from speaking up.

Crawford didn't believe him either and peppered him with questions. The clerk answered with a whiny voice that grated on the ears. Simon took the opportunity to look around.

The room was a large warehouse, stacked from floor to roof with shelves holding goods from all areas of the world: carpets, bolts of cloth, tankards of ale, anything a lady or a gentleman in Mayfair or Berkeley Square could want. There was even a sarcophagus set out on thick stone slabs.

Unable to resist the pull of the ancient artifact, Simon walked over to examine the item closer.

He knew enough about Greek history to suppose that the figure carved on the lid was either a king or a god. He brushed his hand over the smooth stone and wished he'd paid more attention in school.

His Grace joined him. "It is a fascinating piece." The duke leaned to peer into the sightless eyes. "He should be returned to his homeland."

"The mummy has most likely already been ground up for some witch's tonic," Simon remarked. He hated the desecration of tombs for tonics and potions. It was a disgrace. "I understand some of the mummy potions are said to cure impotence."

"Anyone who believes that nonsense *should* suffer that malady." The duke straightened. "To drink the ashes of the dead as a cure for your ailments is foolish."

Simon nodded. He glanced at Crawford. "Has he been able to gain anything further from the clerk?"

"Only that Smoot has gone looking for a prostitute. He does so twice each day. Otherwise, he denies knowing what Smoot does outside of this business."

"Perhaps it is Smoot who makes his own potions," Simon jested wryly. "He sounds like a virile chap."

His Grace smirked. "That is something I'd rather not think about. It will give me night terrors."

The men walked back to Crawford and the clerk. The clerk had a stubborn set to his jaw. "You are welcome to search the alleys for a man with his pants around his ankles and a whore on her knees, worshipping his manly staff. Now if you gentlemen will excuse me, I have work that needs my attention."

Without another word, he spun and walked off toward the back of the warehouse.

Crawford expelled a breath. "I do hate the idea of wandering the seedier parts of this area, but I have a feeling that if we don't find Smoot before his clerk tells him of our visit, we may never find the man."

"If he believes we are secretly investigating his wrecking operation, he may flee," Simon concurred. "He has the means to hide out indefinitely."

His Grace nodded. "We still have some time until nightfall. We might as well get started."

They left the warehouse and the duke paid off the driver. There was no reason for him to wait. They weren't sure how long the search would take. It could be hours.

As he looked around the dismal area, Simon thought of

Laura. Her life could have ended in a place such as this, sold by Westwick as a prostitute to service any man with a coin in his pocket.

Rage burned hot in his belly. He hoped wherever Westwick was now, he was suffering for his crimes.

"You know Whitechapel, Crawford," he said gruffly. "You shall take the lead."

Simon desperately wanted to see the matter concluded. He hoped that Smoot would be a key to helping the case along. "Shall we begin behind the warehouse?" Crawford said. "If Smoot has gone off to find a woman, he shouldn't be far. If he is a frequent customer, the doxies will come to him."

"Lead on," the duke said.

Simon kept watch for footpads as they walked around the warehouse. The space between Smoot's warehouse and the one beside it was narrow. They stepped over a sprawled-out drunkard who was snoring loudly, the top half of his face covered by a worn cap. The smell coming from his filthy body and clothing made Simon's nose and eyes sting.

But the worst was yet to come.

"I smell blood," Crawford said as he stepped over a broken chair and cautiously peered around the corner of the building. He held out a hand to warn Simon and the duke to proceed with caution. "Keep alert, lads. I think a crime has been committed here."

The back of the warehouse was scattered with discarded crates and papers and anything that was of no use to Smoot. The rubble was riddled with rats that scampered out of sight.

Simon frowned. In this area, much of these discards would be of use to the poor. It was odd that the wood hadn't been touched. The question was answered when a chain rattled.

"Step back, Your Grace, Crawford." Both men took a few steps back, puzzled. Within seconds a pair of dogs, gray and brown and of undetermined ancestry, trotted out from behind the crates, heads low, bodies tense. They rumbled with low growls.

The first lunged at Crawford, only to be jerked upright by his chain. This sent the other into a barking frenzy. Soon both dogs were barking and growling. They carried on that way for several minutes before finally giving up their attempts to eat the men and settling back on their haunches to pant.

"This explains why the rubbish remains untouched. I suspect these beasts have eaten their share of crate thieves," Simon quipped. "Now we know the source of the blood scent. They have devoured Smoot."

"It is certainly possible," Crawford said. "Did you notice that the clerk didn't warn us of the dogs?"

Simon turned back to his companions and caught sight of a boot sticking out from behind a crate.

"Do not dismiss my observation quite yet, gentleman," Simon remarked as he walked slowly toward the boot. "I think I may have found the missing man."

The boot was still on a foot, which led to legs, as Simon stepped over a pile of junk and peered behind a broken crate. He found a man lying partially on his back, the upper half of his body, and head, slumped against the wall. His eyes were halfway open.

There was blood everywhere. "I don't think the villain in this case was dogs." Simon squinted. "There are no dog bites."

"His throat has been cut," Crawford said as he squatted down. A sudden choking inhalation brought Crawford stumbling to his feet. "He's alive."

Simon bent down. "Who did this to you, man?"

He received no answer. That one last desperate breath had been his last. Crawford squatted again and closed the dead man's eyelids.

"Is it Smoot?" the duke asked.

"In spite of the blood, I can see that his waistcoat is red. I am quite certain it is Smoot."

Gingerly, Crawford began to examine the body while His Grace went to alert the clerk to send for the Bow Street Runners. As a man attached to several crimes, Smoot's death would be of particular interest to the Runners.

Dropping down on his heels beside Crawford, Simon confirmed that the other injuries on his torso were not consistent with a dog attack. His open trousers and exposed cock left little doubt as to what he was doing when he was killed. "It appears all the wounds are from a knife."

Crawford nodded and eased Smoot's head to the side. There was a deep slash from one side of his neck to the other. "That explains the bloody spray," Crawford said. "His attacker used his blade well." He turned to Simon. "Smoot couldn't have lived long with that wound. I think we chased the killer off."

Simon rose. He began a search of the area. The killer had to be bloodied when he left Smoot. There was little doubt that the merchant had fought for his life. The cuts on his hands showed his attempts to save himself.

Unfortunately, except for several bloody footprints that ended at the street, there was no sign of the culprit.

He returned to Crawford. "The man got clean away. I did find smaller footprints, too. Whoever the woman was who was with Smoot, she either helped the killer or ran when he was attacked. She has also vanished."

The investigator nodded. The duke reappeared, dragging the protesting clerk by the coat. They stopped near the body. The clerk let out a whimper and stumbled backward.

"The whore killed him?" He wobbled. The duke jerked him upright.

"His killer wanted something from Smoot," His Grace said, holding the quivering man. "If he did not get the information he sought, he may come back for you. Tell us what you know and I will find you a safe place to hide."

The clerk began to blather as tears ran down his face. He answered their questions at a rapid clip. His information was thin. However, they did learn a few interesting bits about Smoot's last days.

By the time they'd wrung all the information they could from the clerk, he had nothing left and dropped to his knees.

The arrival of the Runners ended the interrogation.

Sometime later, Simon, His Grace, and Crawford were able to leave the Runners to their investigation. As they couldn't reveal the real reason for seeking out Smoot, they'd claimed to have been searching for a special gift for the duchess and had heard that the merchant dealt in all sorts of exotic items. It was by accident that they'd found the unfortunate Mister Smoot.

The explanation was accepted. The duke was a man of high standing. The Runners had no reason to question his account of their visit to Whitechapel.

It took an eternity to wave down a hackney and they climbed aboard for the ride back to Collingwood House.

"I need a drink." Simon leaned back on the squabs. The hackney headed back in the direction of Mayfair, but Simon shouted out the window for the driver to find them a tavern.

For several hours, Laura and Miss Eva shared stories of their childhoods, and laughed and groused over the troublesome nature of men. When the dinner hour arrived and still no sight of the trio, they ate and groused some more. The hour grew late before male voices, upraised in song, sounded from somewhere outside the front door. The two women rose and walked into the hallway as the butler swung the door wide.

It was almost impossible to distinguish the men as the same group who had left many hours previous. They were rumpled, bloodied, and scuffed. Yet they seemed to have managed to keep themselves somewhat hearty and hale, as they all walked in on their own volition—mostly.

"There is my darling wife," the duke said, his voice booming. "Lovely as ever. Isn't she lovely, Simon?"

Simon nodded. "She is indeed pleasing on the eyes," he agreed, but his attention was on Laura.

She frowned, her expression matching that of the duchess. Simon smelled as if he'd fallen into a barrel of ale.

Crawford gave the duchess a wink and withdrew from the house, clearly finding escape preferable to being party to any arguments that may ensue from bringing the duke home well into his cups.

"I see you found your mischief," Miss Eva said as her husband shuffled toward her, Simon on his tail. She gave him a brief examination and seemed satisfied the blood on his shirt was not his.

Laura's worry settled; she was pleased they'd not have to call for a surgeon. She frowned at Simon. "Thankfully, you are both unhurt. Whitechapel is a grim place."

He lifted a brow and peered at her through a swollen lid. "There are several sailors who are worse off than we."

The duchess clucked her tongue.

"Perhaps you should tell us about the merchant," Laura interjected before Miss Eva could reply. She tried, and failed, to keep eagerness from her voice. "Was he helpful? Did he have useful information?"

Simon's grin faded. "I'm sorry, Laura." Wobbling slightly, he took her hands. "We found the chap easily, though he was in no condition to offer any information. The bastard was quite dead from a knife wound to the throat."

The news was not what she'd hoped. She didn't attempt to hide her disappointment.

He continued on gingerly, "Let us just say that the man looked as though a moment of passion had been interrupted. His clothing was askew and a certain part of him lay flaccid against his thigh."

Laura's mouth gaped and Miss Eva scowled. At their expressions, Simon chuckled. "I apologize for my crudity, dear ladies. I seem to have lost my manners in a tavern near Whitechapel." He bowed slightly and swayed, just managing to keep on his feet. "We did speak to Smoot's clerk, who was surprised to discover that his employer was dead. Smoot often partook of the whores in that very spot behind his warehouse and always returned without a scratch."

"And you are sure this death was not connected to the earl's murder?" Laura asked sharply. She did not want to hear about a dead man's peccadilloes with whores in alleys.

"Crawford doesn't think so," His Grace replied. He was grinning at his wife. "Though he cannot know for certain. Simon and I share another opinion."

"We cannot come up with a reason why the killer would want to execute the merchant," Simon agreed. "True, the man is a thief and has enemies. As with Westwick, the timing of his death is suspicious. He was at the town house when Westwick was killed. Now he's dead, too. It can only lead to one conclusion. He must have seen something."

"I wholeheartedly agree," the duke said.

"And you discovered an agreement on this theory while partaking in"—Laura leaned forward and sniffed Simon—"ale at a tavern where the women wear cheap and offensive perfume."

Miss Eva leaned toward the duke. After a brief sniff, she settled back on her heels and crossed her arms. "I think you should explain, Husband."

His Grace's grin widened. "I shall fill you in on every minute of my evening, after you help me up that staircase to our room. I think I need to lie down."

There was no mistaking the seductive undertone in his words. Miss Eva harrumphed and turned her head to Laura. There was exasperation in her eyes. "I do apologize for their behavior. They are usually somewhat proper."

Laura twisted her lips and shook her head. "You have no reason to excuse them, Your Grace. They are certainly responsible for their own poor behavior."

With an audible sigh, Miss Eva slid under her husband's arm and began the tentative process of leading him to the staircase. The butler hurried over and took his other arm. In a matter of minutes, they managed to steer His Grace up to the second floor and out of sight.

"His Grace certainly tossed back large amounts of ale," Simon remarked. "I am surprised he has remained standing."

"You are only a bit less wobbly than he."

Simon snorted. "The man has been married for a year now. He deserved a night of drink and brawling. You know, he used to be a bit of a bastard before he fell in love with Eva. I have grown to like this less starchy duke."

Laura pointed a finger and scolded, "You two should be ashamed, frolicking about Whitechapel until almost eleven o'clock. The duchess was very worried. It is not healthy in her condition."

His brows went up. "So you know about the babe?"

"The babe is not my concern." She stepped close and turned him toward the light. "Obviously there was more than drinking tonight. Would you care to explain the blood, your swollen eye, and the condition of your knuckles?"

The silly grin deepened. "There were some sailors who were seeking an outlet for their repressed passions after months at sea. They were a bit rough with the tavern wenches, and we stepped in to help."

Laura rolled her eyes upward. She took Simon's elbow and eased him toward the door. "I want to know everything that happened, but first, I think I should get you home before you drop to the floor in a stupor. I'd hate to have to leave you as you lay."

Getting him to the waiting hackney was difficult, as he seemed more interesting in nuzzling her ear than walking. The driver patiently helped her get him inside the coach.

Once settled, she stared at him in the dim lamplight, not sure if she should scold him or leave him be. She fluffed her dress and smoothed it out, taking a moment to decide.

The driver called to the team and the conveyance rumbled to life. Soon Collingwood House was out of sight.

It was with the help of dim streetlamp light that she realized he was staring at her with one eye open and a smile tugging his lips. The warmth in his expression sent tingles dancing over her skin.

The battering hadn't detracted from his appeal in the least. If anything, it added to his rakish handsomeness. She wanted to crawl onto his lap and run her fingertips through his ruffled hair.

What was it about her and coaches? Why did she lose control whenever they were alone in one together?

In an effort to keep her hands to herself, she clasped them tightly together in her lap.

"What are you staring at?" she asked briskly. She shifted on the seat. His stare didn't waver.

"The duchess is not nearly as lovely as you."

It took her a moment to conclude that his words were no longer quite so slurred. She shot him a suspicious stare. "The duchess outshines me like the sun. Who knew there was such beauty under that dour disguise?"

The other eye popped open. "You underestimate yourself, Laura. Perhaps you should spend more time in front of a mirror. Then you will see what I see."

She ignored the compliment. "We have been in this coach for no more than two minutes and already you have become surprisingly sober. How did you manage that feat?"

He leaned back with a smug smile and stretched out his long legs. "We didn't imbibe in the ale nearly as much as we let on. The drunken duke and his raucous friends were an act to throw off anyone who might have followed us from Whitechapel."

Laura frowned. "Why would you be followed?"

The hesitation that followed pricked her ire. If he planned to lie to her, she'd not have it. "Tell me what happened or I shall find Mister Crawford and ask him myself."

Simon groaned and rubbed his face with his hands. "We tweaked the story so as not to upset Eva."

"Because of the baby?"

He nodded.

"Please continue," Laura said impatiently. She was not in the mood to discuss the duchess. "Finish with the story and leave nothing out."

There was a short pause, then, "The merchant, Smoot, was breathing his last when we found him. It looked as if our arrival had interrupted the murder and there was nothing we could do for him. As we said, the murder looked like a robbery that went awry. It was after we spoke to his assistant the second time that the man was more forthcoming. We realized then that there were darker matters at work."

His expression tightened her stomach. "Do not make me wait," she urged.

"Smoot had been complaining about being followed. He dealt in stolen merchandise, so at first it didn't concern him. But after several weeks, he began to see shadows where there were none. The clerk found it odd that Smoot would continue to meet with prostitutes behind the warehouse when he was jumping at every noise. Apparently his urges won over fear and good sense."

"He was worried for his life." Laura's hand shook as she plucked at her gown. "Do you truly think the killer targeted him and this wasn't just a simple robbery gone awry?"

"It's possible," Simon admitted. "The robbery was carefully orchestrated. Smoot's clothing was askew, his cock was displayed, and his pockets were turned out. We might have accepted the attack as it looked had we not spoken to the clerk. Suddenly the attack did not seem so random."

The coach stopped. According to Miss Eva, Simon's family lived only a short drive from Collingwood House. Laura glanced out the window. The house was largely dark but for the light of a few lamps.

Simon looked out the window. "My family is visiting a cousin for a few days. The house is empty. I want you to spend the night here."

Laura's neck prickled. "I thought we discussed this matter. I am not sharing your bed."

Simon leaned forward. "I am concerned with bringing danger to the courtesan school. I cannot be certain that any of us are safe now. If we were followed from the warehouse, we might be watched at this very moment."

Torn, a war waged in her mind. In the end, she chose to keep the school safe. "You must behave."

"I promise."

The way he looked at her left doubts. He wasn't as intoxicated as she'd initially believed, but he had still imbibed enough to leave him slightly soused. Many lines could be crossed when a man was in his cups.

"Do you want to hear the rest of the story?" Simon pressed. It was the last nudge she needed. Laura nodded and said, "I want a bedroom with a lockable door."

Simon grinned. "Yes, My Lady."

He helped her from the coach and paid the driver. Within a few minutes, they were safely settled in a sizable parlor, a sleepy maid pressed into service to bring tea and sandwiches.

When Laura protested and asked that the maid be allowed to find her bed, Simon waved off her concerns. "I am famished. It won't take Anna long to collect a tray. The cook always has food waiting for my late-night returns."

He was correct. The maid was back within minutes, then excused with profuse thanks. The young woman smiled brightly, clearly besotted with her employer, and left them alone.

"Do women always swoon at your feet?" Laura reached for a sandwich. The ham and cheese were slathered with some sort of herbed butter. The result was delicious.

"Not always." Simon quickly ate two wedges before continuing, "My reputation and family history cause many women to flee in my wake. The others are dragged off by protective mothers."

"But not Lady Jeanette?" It was an odd topic to be discussing with him in his family's empty home and at this late hour. She should be tucked in her bed at the courtesan school.

"Lady Jeanette's father likes to gamble. He keeps up appearances, but rumors are that he is deeply in debt. With creditors hounding his heels, even a reprobate like me is good enough for his dearest daughter."

"Hmm." Laura poured the tea. She tried to imagine Simon bouncing a baby on his knee, Lady Jeanette at his side, her pretty face smiling softly at the picture they made.

Her stomach tightened. Laura wondered if sometime in the future he'd ever think back fondly of her and their short adventure together. Or would she be swiftly forgotten once he took Lady Jeanette to his bed?

Jealousy prickled through her. She quickly tamped it down. "I think we should continue the story about Smoot. It's getting late and I grow weary."

Simon nodded. "Where was I? Oh, yes. We gleaned as much information as we could about Smoot. There were many people who despised the man, including his wife. Crawford will follow the information and see if there is any connection to Westwick's murder or if this was a random robbery."

"And the visit to the tavern?"

Simon cocked a brow. "After spending time with the murdered Smoot, I wanted to drink that sight from my mind. After we spoke to the clerk, we went to the tavern." He smirked and touched his swollen eye. "The fight was entirely unexpected."

"And clearly welcome." She leveled on him a shaming glare. "Why cannot men settle their differences with words?"

He shrugged and grinned. "Using our fists is much more rewarding."

Chapter Nineteen

Laura was seeing Simon in an entirely different light. He would never lift a hand to a woman, but he wasn't against fighting for sport. She wasn't entirely sure if she liked this newfound knowledge, but she was drawn to the hard edge it gave him. There was something raw and warrior-like about a man who would risk life and health in Whitechapel to find evidence to save her neck. She let out a small sigh. "I'll never again question whether you can defend me in any situation. Beneath the trappings of a nobleman lies the heart of a gentleman brawler."

He chuckled. "I do enjoy my position as your white knight."

A noise came from somewhere in the house. Likely the butler was waiting for them to retire before seeking his own bed.

She squelched a yawn. "If there is anything more you'd like to tell me about your grand adventure into Whitechapel, please do it quickly, for I am fading."

Simon shook his head. "There is nothing that cannot wait until morning." He rose and rounded the table to take her hand. Laura stood too hastily, not realizing that her

hem was under her heel. She wobbled. Simon chuckled and
settled her on her feet.

She looked into his eyes. He was standing dangerously
close to her. He smelled of ale and sweat and perfume. It
was an odd concoction that sent her senses reeling.

She swayed forward, her gaze locking on his damaged
mouth. Simon dipped his head and took her lips in a hungry
kiss.

A low moan broke from Laura as her hands rose to flat-
ten against his chest. The rough homespun of the borrowed
clothes added to the intensity of the moment. She kissed
him most willingly, her tongue intertwining with his, while
her body eagerly accepted his exploring caress.

The clock chimed midnight and Simon ended the kiss.
His eyes were passion dark, his face regretful. "If I do not
stop now, I'll carry you up to my room and make love to
you all night."

Laura made a noise that sounded agreeable to his sug-
gestion, but Simon shook his head. "I think you were right
when you said you should remain chaste. We both have
considerations that require clear thinking."

She hated that reason was taking over her desire. She
wanted to touch him intimately and be touched in return.
But she'd vowed to save herself for her husband, if one ever
came along, and save herself she would.

If only Simon weren't so desperately attractive. "Your
Lady Jeanette and my new life," she muttered acerbically.
She despised that her friendship proposal was now ruining
a perfectly wonderful kiss. "Yes, we must keep our focus
on the case and your hunt for an acceptable wife."

If the matter was settled, why then did she feel so out of
sorts? Perhaps it was her skin soaking up the heat from his
body as they stood close together. Perhaps it was the memory
of his mouth on her breasts, his lips tugging her hardened
nipples. Whatever was leaving her feeling terribly restless,
she had to extricate herself now or do something she'd regret.

Like fling her body against his chest and beg him to
make love to her, as he said, all night.

So she pushed away, shoving the chair backward with her shins, clutching the heavy table for support as she awkwardly stepped out of reach.

"I am dreadfully tired," she said, her voice thin. "Perhaps you should show me to my room."

Simon didn't move to take her arm. His gaze was thoughtful. It felt as if he were trying to read her thoughts. It would be a difficult task, as they were jumbled into a confusing tangle.

The walk to her room was very long. Simon would touch her back or shoulder as he guided her along, and she struggled to ignore the heat of his hand through her clothing.

By the time he stopped in front of her door, every inch of her was warmed and wanting him. She knew she should step inside the room and lock the door, but in a momentary lapse, she foolishly peered up into his eyes.

She wasn't certain if it was a squeak or a whimper that left her throat at the moment she launched herself against his chest, only that she forgot propriety and vows as she felt his arms close around her.

Somehow the door was kicked open and she was nudged backward across a candlelit room. The single candle flickered as her skirt caught the writing table and wobbled the candlestick. Simon managed to catch it before it toppled over and without breaking their kiss.

Laura smiled under his lips as he pushed her without preliminaries down on the bed and slid a hand up under her skirts. She felt a moment of reservation.

"Don't think," he said as his hands found her core. "I promised I will not take advantage. This is for you."

He played with her body, his expert fingers moving between her legs until she couldn't think. Somehow he loosened her bodice and kissed her breasts before tugging a nipple between his teeth.

Small sounds escaped her as she writhed like a wild thing in his arms. Her release came swiftly. She cried out, the sound muffled by his kiss.

As she smiled sleepily, he pulled down her skirts and

reached to caress his thumb across her jaw. "As promised, you are still untouched."

Laura narrowed her lids. "Not entirely."

He grinned. "I promised not to make love to you. Pleasuring you with my hand was never part of my promise."

"You are a cad," she said as he pulled her to her feet. "A handsome, arrogant, and seductive cad. I must learn the skill required to resist your seductions."

Simon led her to the door and placed a kiss on her forehead. "I hope you never do. Now lock the door and sleep well, sweetheart. We have much to do tomorrow."

Simon left Laura at the door, thankful to put some distance between them. He'd shoved his hands into his pockets during the walk upstairs to keep himself from reaching for her. Her seductive scent that had tickled his senses, the feel of her soft skin under his searching hands, and her big beautiful eyes, all together had left him undone.

And when she'd kissed him, it had taken every ounce of will inside him to leave her largely untouched.

He wanted her with a measure of insanity. Yet he knew that no matter how much they ached for each other, had he allowed himself to take her fully, she'd have regretted it in the morning. She was unsure of herself, her future, him. And he could promise her nothing. Even their friendship would end once he took a wife. Selfish desire would only be a temporary release. And he cared for her too much to press his intentions.

Damn chivalry.

He walked to his room on the far end of the hall. He shook off images of Laura undressing for bed and thought instead of the merchant. The horrific murder was the only thing that could distract him from his lustful thoughts.

The crime had been brutal. He envisioned the man lying among the rubbish, a death gurgle rattling in his slashed throat. As Crawford had bent over him, he'd tried to speak, but the words wouldn't form. He'd expired too quickly.

Had Smoot tried to name his killer?

If only their arrival had been better timed, they might have been able to save the man. But once the blade cut his neck, he was doomed.

Whoever killed the merchant had the strength no half-starved whore would possess. No, the killer was male; of that, Simon had no doubt.

He blew out the lamp, plunging the room into shadow, and walked to the window. He looked out into the darkened street. A light fog was settling over London, giving the city an eerie air. He had the sensation of being watched, though he couldn't see anyone lurking.

Dread filled him. Laura was in trouble. He'd thought her unease was simple worry that the Runners would find her. Now he wasn't certain she wasn't being watched.

She'd seen nothing the night of the murder. But did the killer think she had? Or was he merely obsessed with her, as Simon suspected?

A coach plodded past the house. Simon watched it vanish into the fog and let his mind turn to Westwick. He wasn't confident Westwick's story would fade away once the newspapers found another scandalous happening to intrigue readers.

Yes, the earl would eventually be forgotten as years passed and the courtesan-suspect would vanish into obscurity. However, the killer would always be a danger to Laura. She'd never feel entirely safe with him roaming free.

The door opened behind him. Dunston stepped into the room, his eyes squinting in the dim light. "Would you like me to help you undress, sir?"

"No, thank you. I am not ready for sleep." He turned back to the window. "Could you set a footman outside Miss Prescott's room? I have an uneasy feeling tonight. I'd rest better knowing she is guarded."

Simon caught Dunston's reflection in the glass and knew

the valet had questions. Though the servant had worked
for him for eight years and kept his secrets, he didn't feel
Laura's story was one to share. The valet would do as he
asked without question.

"Yes, sir." Dunston withdrew.

Alone again, Simon watched the street for what seemed
like hours before finally dropping, fully clothed, on the bed.
Sometime during the night, tired of staring at the ceiling,
he dozed. What followed was a nightmare of Laura, fleeing
a madman with a heavy blade.

Laura awakened to a sound from the street and startled
up on the bed. It took a second to realize where she was
and she slumped back on the pillow.

The Harrington town house. Simon was near. Still, as
she lay in the quiet, buried under soft sheets and a floral
coverlet, she found sleep elusive. Her mind was awhirl over
Simon's tale of the merchant's murder. She felt that he'd
kept something from her. Perhaps he didn't want to worry
her, as she was already unsettled. The fear of being watched
hadn't abated within the safety of this town house.

It was streaming moonlight that finally drew her from
the bed. A chill had come with the dying fire. She pulled a
blanket off a chair and wrapped it around herself as she
padded barefoot to the window. Pushing back the curtain,
she discovered a fog had taken over the night and blan-
keted the city.

She stared off across the empty garden and shivered.
Two murders followed her, mocking her, perhaps connected, perhaps not. Still, she couldn't shake the feeling
that danger was closing in on her.

Pressing her open palms against the cool glass, she
sought confirmation of her fears, her heart beating a little
faster. She saw nothing but fog and the dark shapes of trees
and shrubs. The creaks and groans of the old house added
to her uncertainty. Was she truly safe here?

Unable to summon up a desire to return to the bed, she let the curtain fall back into place and quickly crossed the room.

Peering into the hallway, she saw a young, strapping footman sitting outside the door. His head bobbed forward, then jerked back upright with a snore-snort. Laura smiled as she slipped out of the room and tiptoed down the hall.

It didn't take long to find Simon's room. The house was empty but for the servants, so she needn't worry about stumbling onto Simon's sister or parents. The last sputters of a dying lamp outside the door assured her that she was in the right place. She made very little sound as she slipped into the room and crossed to the bed.

He lay on his side on the coverlet. Quietly she slid in beside him, and snuggled close to his back. He rolled over and wrapped her in his arms.

"Couldn't sleep?" he asked.

She shook her head. "There are too many sounds in this house and the fog can hide many dangers. I feel eyes watching from the darkness."

Simon pressed his mouth to her forehead. "The doors and windows are locked. You are safe here." Suddenly, he frowned. "How did you get past Webster?"

Laura shrugged. "I learned to move stealthily about Westwick's bedroom. The longer he slept undisturbed, the less time I had to spend fending off his advances."

"You are quite a resourceful woman." There was admiration in his voice. She brushed her face against him.

His warmth comforted her. She rolled over and pressed back against his chest. He snuggled her close. "Would you mind if I slept with you tonight?"

She felt sure he smiled. "If you must, though there are only two hours until daylight."

"Then two hours it is." She rubbed her cheek against the coarse hairs on his forearm and closed her eyes. For the next few hours, she slept more peacefully than she had in weeks.

Chapter Twenty

꧁꧂

The sound of a crow squawking outside the window awakened Laura. She rolled over expecting to find Simon sleeping beside her. The bed was empty. There were female voices in the hallway that Laura assumed were the maids going about their duties. She stretched on the bed, wondering where Simon was and how she could explain her presence in his bed to the maids.

Luckily the women moved on and she hurried from beneath the warm covers. The floor was cool beneath her feet as she crossed to the door and eased it open. A peek outside confirmed that the hall was empty. She quickly hurried back to her room.

After washing up with tepid water from a pitcher and doing her best to detangle her hair with her fingertips, Laura pulled it back into a loose braid. With her toilet completed, she wriggled out of the borrowed nightdress and into her clothes. Slipping into her stockings and shoes, she made her way from the room.

At the top of the staircase, she stumbled upon a maid, who directed her to the breakfast room.

"Good morning," Laura said as she walked into the

pretty yellow room. The curtains were open and she could see that the fog was dissipating, with sunlight creeping through the remaining mist. The sun was welcome after several mornings of light rain.

Simon lifted his face from the newspaper and smiled. "Good morning." He met her eyes. "Did you sleep well?"

"Very well, thank you." She cast him a sidelong glance as she walked to the sideboard to examine the breakfast offerings. He was impeccably dressed, without even a hint of stubble to mar his perfect jaw. "And you?" She reached for a plate.

"Decently enough," he said from behind her as she loaded the plate with creamed eggs, bacon, and pastries. A maid poured her tea as she joined Simon at the table.

"Thank you." The maid nodded and left them.

Simon waited until they were alone before leaning forward on his elbows. "I had a bit of trouble sleeping with your backside pressed intimately against me."

Laura flushed and lifted her nose. "I was quite properly clothed and wrapped in a blanket." Her mouth twitched. "I do thank you for behaving. You were a perfect gentleman."

He snorted. "The bane of a proper upbringing, I assure you. I would have preferred we'd been naked and doing much more than sleeping."

She grinned. That he had behaved showed that he respected her and her wishes. Then she flushed, remembering his hand between her legs. Though he wasn't quite the pillar of propriety, at least he'd tried. "Unfortunately, I will never have the chance to thank your mother for raising such a gentleman."

Cocking a brow, he went back to his reading while Laura ate everything on her plate and returned to the buffet for another tart. She made no apologies for her hearty appetite. She was famished. When she'd finished, she cleared her throat.

Simon peered at her over the paper. "Yes?"

"I should get back to the school. Sophie will worry." She looked down at her dress. "And I would like to wash and change. I fear I am a bit rumpled."

Simon looked her over. "You look lovely."

"Next to you, I am a drab mouse." It was true. He wore a pair of cream breeches and a gray and cream striped waistcoat over a white shirt. His matching white cravat was perfectly tied and his cheeks freshly shaven. A charcoal gray coat hung casually over the chair behind him. "You must have dressed elsewhere. I didn't hear a sound."

"I didn't want to wake you. Your snores indicated your need for rest." His mouth twitched.

Her nose went up. "I do not snore." She knew he teased and found enjoyment in the easy banter on the pretty morning. After the strain of last evening, she needed a reprieve from the gloom of the case.

"I sent around a note to your Sophie, so all is well." He waved a hand at the footman lingering in the doorway and the man hurried over. "See that a bath is prepared for Miss Prescott and a clean gown found for her. My sister is about the same size."

"Yes, sir." The man walked away.

Laura opened her mouth. "I cannot stay here. It's unseemly. I am without a chaperone."

"There are plenty of servants to keep your reputation intact," he said, handily dismissing her concerns. He stood, rounded the table, and pulled out her chair.

"Servants are not the same as a chaperone and you well know it." She stood and faced him. "Your family will not be pleased when they hear gossip about the woman who stayed here when they were away. Who knows what they will think."

"I shall explain that I found you lost in the fog and came to your rescue," Simon teased.

"Not amusing." She crossed her arms. "I insist you return me to the school before my already tarnished reputation rusts completely through."

He frowned. The stubborn set of her jaw told him she was willing to fight over this. He sighed. "You may stay at the school for as long as you are safe. If I sense danger, you will move in here."

Her body relaxed. "I shall get my gloves."

"Not until we have found you a dress." At her puzzled look, he continued, "If we are to attend the ball at Colling-wood House, then you must be dressed properly."

Laura blanched. She'd forgotten the plan to look for auc-tion guests. Suddenly, the day dimmed. "I will not be a guest. Not even Miss Eva would risk her social standing for me."

"You needn't worry about Eva. And no, you will not be a guest." Simon led her from the room and up the stairs. "You will be in disguise. You'll not need to worry about discovery."

Laura's stomach soured. "It would be better if I watched the festivities from a landing above, or perhaps behind draperies. I cannot be seen; it is too high a risk."

Simon shook his head as he led her into his sister's room. A tub had been placed near the fireplace and a maid was laying out a towel on a chair. They stepped aside as the trio of footmen carried in buckets of steaming water and poured them out. Finished, they left again.

"It will be too difficult to spy when hiding behind drap-eries," Simon insisted. They watched as the footmen returned and finished filling the tub. "Trust me, you'll be perfectly safe." He nudged her toward the waiting maid. "I'll meet you downstairs in an hour."

Laura's scowl was her reply.

An hour and a half later, Laura came down the staircase, washed and fluffed and wearing a pale rose, slightly too long walking dress. Her hair was in a twist at her nape, and a small reticule dangled from her gloved wrist.

The frown changed to a grin. He knew she'd purpose-fully made him wait the extra half hour to irk him. But she looked so lovely that he couldn't hold on to his annoyance.

"I don't think Brenna has ever worn that dress quite so well," he remarked, admiring the fit. The bodice skimmed over her curves downward to where a matching rose ribbon circled her small waist.

"I really don't think taking me out is wise." She moved the reticule to her other wrist. "What if I am spotted by someone who knows me?"

Simon moved to take her hand. "The chance of recognition is small. Didn't you say that the earl never took you out in public? One ride through the city doesn't count. With the murder hanging over his little band of slavers and wretches, no one would dare come forward to admit knowing you, or become a suspect himself."

"Still, I am not comfortable with being seen publicly."

The anxiousness in her voice was clear. He looked around and found a solution. He walked over to a row of pegs by the door, removed the largest bonnet he could find from the row, and returned to place it on her head. "If you keep your head down, no one will suspect that you are the infamous Sabine, former courtesan and murderess."

Laura tipped her head back and met his eyes. "I do not find your humor amusing." She thinned her lips and adjusted the bonnet. "You'd better take care or you may be my next victim."

He chuckled and leaned down. The light scent of lavender swirled around her. "I will gladly fall at your hand, but only if you tie me up and torture me first."

With an exaggerated sigh, Laura shook her head. "You are horrible. I am a wanted murderess and still you cannot refrain from making light of the matter."

Reaching for her hand, he pressed a kiss on her gloved knuckles. "I jest to keep you from too much worry. I promise you, love, that we will find the real killer. Then you'll never again need to fret that your life, and neck, are in danger. You will be free to pursue whatever future suits you."

Her scowl faded. "Putting this matter behind me does sound wonderful. Still, we may never find the killer. He may hide away, never to kill again."

Though Simon suspected the killer was not finished, he wasn't about to admit his feelings. "Hopefully with your help we can find at least one member of the auction party. Smoot turned us to a new avenue of investigation. If he was the victim of Westwick's killer, there may be others who are in danger. Following a trail of bodies will eventually lead to the trail's end and the culprit."

Despite his assurance, she didn't appear willing to forgive him his jests. He sobered. "Darling Laura, I promise you that I take this situation very seriously."

Skepticism etched her features. "I would feel more secure if you explained the reason for this outing."

He took her arm and turned her toward the door. "All in good time, Laura; all in good time."

The dress shop was not crowded when Simon led her through the door. The scent of something exotic assailed her senses, as if the proprietress had sprinkled French perfume throughout the space. She nearly sneezed. "Someone should take away her perfume bottles."

"The widow Jensen likes to give the allusion of having been born on some exotic shore." He leaned in. "I have it on good authority that she was born to a merchant in Bath."

Laura looked around at the fashionable array of gowns displayed throughout the large room. "Then we shall allow her to continue her ruse. She is obviously a very talented seamstress."

"Indeed she is," Simon agreed. He glanced around the room. "I see a green silk that would look splendid on you."

She glanced up. "Should you desire to purchase it on my behalf, you will forget that notion. I cannot accept gifts from any man. Not even you."

He snorted. "I wouldn't dream of insulting your sense of propriety with gifts."

His tone convinced Laura that he had more than considered purchasing her a gown. Despite his words to the contrary, he'd likely been mentally counting the coins in his pocket.

Unwilling to argue, she let the matter drop.

It was early enough for the truly fashionable ladies to still be abed, so the shop was empty of customers. There was a flutter of activity from the back of the shop and a small woman burst from an open door. Clearly flustered, she mumbled something about not being able to find good assistants and hurried toward them.

At the sight of Simon, her eyes lit up. "Mister Harrington," she exclaimed and clapped her hands together. "It has been far too long since you've graced my humble establishment."

Simon gave her a knee-melting grin. "Sadly, Mrs. Jensen, other obligations have kept me from seeking out your talents."

The woman giggled girlishly. "You flatter me."

"I speak the truth," Simon countered. "You are the best seamstress in London. That is why we've come today."

Laura frowned as the woman finally jerked her eyes from Simon and turned to her. There was a flicker of jealousy in the pretty woman's face, which she quickly masked. "I see that situation has changed. She is lovely."

Immediately, Laura knew *exactly* what sort of services had previously brought Simon to the shop. The woman thought she was a mistress he needed fitted for a new wardrobe. There was a gleam in the proprietress's eyes in anticipation of a large sale.

A prickle moved from the back of Laura's neck and down her spine. She stiffened at the unintended insult.

As if reading Laura's thoughts, Simon quickly stepped between them. "I fear that you've mistaken the reason for our visit, Mrs. Jensen." The woman's face fell when he explained to her what he wanted. "We need a drab gown of an uninteresting color. Gray, brown, or tan would suit."

"Surely you would rather have something in blue?" the proprietress protested. "Or I have a delightful gown in yellow."

Simon shook his head. "Just the one I requested."

As she slunk off to find something befitting his request,

annoyance flooded through Laura. Her curiosity about the dress vanished under more pressing concerns.

"Do you often buy clothes for young women?" At his innocent expression, her annoyance notched up a peg or two. "This shop obviously caters to women. Unless you have a secret proclivity toward wearing garters under your breeches, then you have shopped here for someone other than yourself."

Simon smiled. "I may have passed through here a time or two. Mistresses do enjoy beautiful things."

She cocked her head. "How many mistresses have you had?"

His eyes filled with mischief. "Dozens."

Though she knew he was teasing her again, she didn't like the idea of his keeping multiple mistresses. Worse yet, that she'd been mistaken for one.

Until recently, she'd never given much thought to the institution of kept women. Men had always dallied with women outside of their marriages. However, after spending time at the school, her eyes had been opened wide. She felt sad for both the wives, for being tied to unfaithful scoundrels, and the mistresses, for having to sell themselves to survive.

Something in her face sobered him. He tipped up her chin. "There were only two, Laura." He released her. "Eventually, I will inherit the title and carry the responsibility for my entire family. I've felt the weight of it since Noelle's father died without sons and the line grew shorter. So if I ran a bit wild in my youth, I'll not apologize for those years."

Looking into his eyes, Laura understood his plight. She, too, had borne the burden of family while caring for her ailing father. His was just on a grander scale.

"Hmm. I've wondered about your protective nature. You see yourself as responsible for the welfare of everyone around you. You'll vanquish our enemies and keep us all safe."

"Brenna calls me overprotective."

"She is correct. Would you care to explain why?"

Simon took a moment before speaking. "When she was seven, Brenna nearly drowned in a pond. I should have been watching her. Instead, I was watching Miss Lizzy Mapplethorpe. I carry the guilt always."

This certainly explained much about him. "Is that when you donned your armor and started your knightly duties of saving damsels from dragons?"

He frowned. "No. It just made it worse."

Laura laughed lightly. "Then you were born to the sword. You, Mister Harrington, live in the wrong century." She imagined him on a great horse, dressed for war, wielding his weapons with skill and dexterity. A little shiver prickled through her as the image changed to his return to the castle to take his reward for keeping away invaders—tossing his lady over his shoulder and carrying her to his bed.

Curiously, the lady in the image resembled her.

"Perhaps," he said, interrupting her thoughts. "I have a feeling that you admire both my sword wielding and my persistence. If not for both, we would have never met."

Thinking about his steely sword quickened her pulse and sent parts of her twitching. Fortunately, *that* wasn't the sword he was speaking of.

"True. You did save me. My rescue had to appeal to your desire to protect. As for persistence, no matter how many times I tried to dissuade you from befriending me, you always returned. I cannot seem to rid myself of you."

Simon grinned. "You are not the least put off by my attentions. Perhaps at first. Not anymore."

After a pause, Laura shrugged. "You are pleasant to look at, if nothing else."

"When I pulled you onto my horse, I could not know what a tart-tongued termagant you would prove to be. It is trying to be your friend."

Her mouth gaped. "You—oh, you are impossible." Laughter bubbled up. "You are heads and tails more difficult than I."

"That cannot be true," he countered. "Women, by their nature, are the more difficult sex. They do not see things rationally as men do."

"Men, rational? You jest." She looked toward the back of the shop and lowered her voice. Mrs. Jensen was walking slowly toward them, an unhappy look on her face. Laura hurried on in a hushed whisper, "Men duel over the smallest perceived slight and rage over a difference of opinion. Men are not rational in the least."

She smiled brightly and turned to Mrs. Jensen.

"This was the best I could do," the woman said grimly. She held up a dress of dark brown wool. It was completely devoid of lace or ribbon, and unfinished, as the hem was full of pins. She spoke to Simon as she held the dress up to Laura to check the size. "Surely the young lady would prefer something in lilac satin?"

Laura stared at the drab gown. In spite of the lack of adornments, it was finer quality than the dresses she'd been borrowing from the school or, truthfully, her own. The question remained, what was Simon planning to do with her and that gown?

Simon waved off the woman's offer. "Just that dress. If you can quickly finish the hem, we will be off."

The woman held her tongue and walked off, muttering unhappily under her breath.

"She is terribly disappointed," Laura said, putting her hands on her hips. "Now will you finally tell me your intentions for me at the ball? I cannot attend the soirée dressed in that unpleasant creation."

Simon relented to her plea. "The ball, though last minute, will be attended by everyone. When a duke entertains, the masses flock. I tried to think of a way for you to attend without drawing attention. A maid will be limited to certain areas, and you possess too many curves to pass as a footman."

"I could still hide behind the drapes," she said dryly.

"That would make it impossible for you to move about and you'd risk detection. A lump in the line of drapes would certainly be noticed." He walked past her to the window and looked out to the street. "I think putting you in place as a companion is a perfect solution. You can attend the party and no one will give you a second glance."

Laura screwed up her face and joined him. "You cannot honestly think that will work. Even in a dress such as the brown wool, I will never be invisible."

Simon scanned her face. She did have a point. Hiding her beauty would be difficult. Even companions weren't entirely unnoticed.

"Eva can help with that." If anyone could find a way to make Laura plain, it was the spinster-duchess. "She has a way with disguises. Eva can turn you into a drab companion with little effort."

Laura didn't appear convinced. "So we have our disguise and I attend the party. And who am I supposed to be a companion for? I cannot be dragged around by you. I hardly think your society will accept that their scandalous Mister Harrington needs a companion—a chaperone perhaps, but not a female companion. They will think you are bedding me."

"I *have* bedded you," he offered.

She shot him an exasperated glare.

"I know a woman who needs your help," he said, quickly turning the topic back to the ball. "She is desperately in need of watching. It is only a matter of getting her to agree, and I have the perfect temptation to wave in front of her."

Suspicion welled in Laura's eyes. "Who is she?"

"I have an aunt who is, shall we say, an interesting character. She tends to tipple the sherry a bit too much. If anyone needs a chaperone-companion, it is she."

Laura's face twisted into a grimace. "Perfect. Not only will I be putting myself in peril, but I shall spend the evening keeping your drunken aunt from knocking over the vases."

Simon chuckled. "The image of you diving after falling vases does amuse. It sounds like excellent fun, doesn't it?"

Her eyes narrowed dangerously. "I am so pleased that you are enjoying yourself at my expense."

A long-suffering sigh followed. He reached out a hand to her when the door opened and two women walked into the shop. Simon saw the hawked beak of the older woman and dread gripped him. He pressed forward, the motion of his body pushing Laura behind a table stacked high with bolts of cloth.

"What are you doing?" she said, lifting her hands to push him back. He caught her wrists.

"It is Mrs. Howard," he whispered harshly. "She is a notorious gossip. Worse, she never gets a single fact correct when spreading her news. If she sees us together, it will be unpleasant for us both."

His body blocked Laura from view as the women passed deeper into the shop. It also put him in direct contact with Laura's pleasing curves.

His body twitched. His hardening extremities reminded him of her against a stormy background, sans clothing, gasping beneath him. His eyes warmed as his hands slid to her waist, forgetting Mrs. Howard entirely.

"If you kiss me, I'll be forced to slap you," Laura hissed. "It will not be pleasant for either of us."

Surprised she'd read his thoughts, his eyes widened. "I wasn't going to kiss you."

A low grumble passed her perfect lips. She met his gaze. "Your eyes gave your thoughts away, though I think your imagination went well beyond kisses."

A kiss *wasn't* what he was after, but he had been staring at her mouth like a man starved. Their one night together had done nothing to assuage his lust. If anything, it made things worse.

"My thoughts are my own, my dear Laura," he said drolly. "If I wish to imagine you in my bed, there is nothing you can do about the matter."

Feminine voices caused Laura to take another step backward. She pulled Simon along with her. The stack of bolts provided an ideal barrier if one didn't look too closely.

"I am *very* happy I cannot read your thoughts," she offered with a pained expression. "For I'm certain I would not be pleased with what I learned."

Her expression was serious, but her fingers were playing with his coat. He'd believed that her mind and body often warred when it came to him. The frequent stolen kisses in coaches confirmed his belief.

He leaned forward and her hand went flat on his stomach.

"I think we both know that I cannot keep from desiring you. I am a man and you are very beautiful. Seductive thoughts are always present when I'm with you." He shrugged and lowered his voice further. "Truthfully, you need not be in eyesight for those thoughts to emerge and my body to arouse. You, love, are never far from my heated imaginings."

Her eyes warming, she flexed her fingers, and her mouth quirked. "Can you not behave?"

"It is proving more difficult with each passing hour."

Her mouth opened and her breath fluttered. "For me also," she whispered. Her other hand joined the first. Her heat burned through his waistcoat and shirt to mark his skin.

"I must kiss you," he said tightly.

Warmth welled in her eyes. Finally, she nodded. "One kiss."

He glanced around quickly to see if their privacy was assured, then pulled her into his arms. As he closed his mouth over hers, she let out a breathless sigh of welcome.

The touch of her lips lit a spark in him, and he eased her one final step backward until her back pressed against the wall.

The voices of Mrs. Howard and her companion faded away. Laura moaned lightly as she rose up on her tiptoes and wrapped her arms around his neck.

He kissed her deeply and desperately, knowing the shop was not the best place to steal a kiss. But it had been so long since their last one that he wasn't about to quibble.

Approaching footsteps broke them apart.

* * *

Simon released her and put an arm's length between them.

Laura patted her hair and pretended to examine a bolt of yellow cloth as Mrs. Jensen assured the other women that she would return shortly and returned to Laura and Simon with the dress.

A flush stained Laura's cheeks. Again, she'd jumped willingly into his arms, a bad habit she'd thought she could overcome. Clearly, not even the possibility of getting caught by a notorious gossip could force her to behave.

"Here is the dress," Mrs. Jensen said and passed the package into his hands. Her lips were pressed into a disapproving line. "If you ever desire to purchase something for the lady that will bring you to your knees, come back. I have a red French silk that would be stunning on her."

Simon grinned and Mrs. Jensen's starchiness slowly melted. He lifted her hand to his lips. "I shall remember your kind offer if there is ever a need."

Laura was convinced that the pretty widow was smoldering. If not for Laura's presence, the shopkeeper might have convinced Simon to go into the back room to discuss something other than fabrics.

Annoyance burned as Simon released Mrs. Jensen's hand. They concluded their business and Simon led Laura from the shop.

"You *would* look splendid in red."

A noncommittal grunt was all she could manage. Then, "Have you ever shared a bed with her? She looks as if she'd like to cover you in clotted cream and eat you."

She hated her tone. It was puzzling, even to her. She had no claims on him. Yet she sounded like a jealous wife.

"Mrs. Jensen is nothing more than someone whose shop I have visited." He steered her toward the coach. "Though I do find the pink flush of jealousy on your cheeks quite charming."

A denial sprang to her lips. She held it down. At the

moment, she was muddled with a mix of emotions. His scent was present on her clothing. His taste still lingered on her mouth. In the heat of midday, a light sheen of perspiration covered her skin. She was heated and achy and frustrated.

There would never be innocent public touches between them. She'd never laugh into his eyes as he spun her around a ballroom. She'd never openly share his bed—all the things that Mrs. Jensen or Lady Jeanette could do quite freely. She would always be relegated to the secret part of his life, always a mistress, never his wife.

Yet she hungered for him. His body called to her and hers responded. Even now, she struggled to resist the pull, the fight stealing her energy.

Laura said nothing as he led her to the coach and helped her inside. Even then, as the coach jolted into motion, she remained silent. Still, she saw his eyes on her in the dim light and could not read his face. But there was something in his eyes. . . . Before she knew what was happening, she was on his lap, again, and kissing him with all the passion she'd felt since the night of their lovemaking. He only had a moment to clasp her against him when she deepened the kiss and was lost.

Chapter Twenty-One

※

Laura knew she was making a mistake by kissing Simon—a grave mistake. Still, she couldn't stop herself. The warmth of his arms, the strength in his body, the way he tasted, kissed; it was what she suspected flying felt like.

The scent of sandalwood and spice teased her mind while his warmth teased her body. He drugged her and tormented her, and all she could do was kiss him breathless.

His hand clasped her neck and she clutched his shoulders. Even with his arms around her, she couldn't get close enough. There were far too many layers of clothing between them.

After a moment, she broke the kiss. "I should move back to my seat," she groaned and dropped her head back.

Simon nuzzled her neck. "You should. Or you can continue to kiss me until we reach our destination."

She smiled and ran her hand through his soft hair. He lifted his head and their gazes locked. "That is the first of your recent ideas that pleases me most."

His mouth came down to claim hers again and her lids closed. They kissed as if these were their last moments on earth. They made free use of their hands, with touches both innocent and not so innocent. Panting breaths mingled.

Simon slid his hand up her leg and tugged at her garter. "You drive me mad," he said as she nipped his jaw.

"I feel the same." She kissed him again.

The horse plodded onward, finding the courtesan school all too soon. The coach lurched to a stop.

It was Simon who noticed they'd stopped first. He ended the kiss and looked into her eyes. "Sadly, we have arrived."

Laura frowned and smoothed out his coat at the shoulders, where she'd crumpled it with her hands.

"You should have asked the driver to take the longest route." She adjusted his cravat where it had gone askew. "I don't want this to end."

Simon touched her mouth with his thumb. "If I'd have known what was awaiting me on the ride back, I would have." She made a regretful sound and rubbed her cheek on his palm. "Why do I feel this way? You torment me like no other. I cannot think when you touch me, Simon."

He grinned and tugged a curl. "And you are a beautiful witch who has wriggled into my mind and taken control of my body. This game we play has no satisfactory conclusion."

"I know." She nodded. "I have no expectations."

"Were we a smithy and milkmaid . . ." He left the rest unsaid. "Come, I must return the coach before my friend requires it."

The borrowed conveyance was chosen not for comfort but because it had no markings to lead back to his family. With Laura in danger, they had to keep vigilant, especially in public. Hackneys and hired coaches helped to keep from drawing attention to his family and the school.

Sadly, Primm was waiting in the open door. There would be no more kisses. She collected the package. Simon opened the door and climbed down, turning to assist her.

He took her hand. "I will ask Noelle to help you ready yourself for the party. The rest of the details will be mine to prepare."

Laura watched him lift her hand to his mouth and press a kiss on her gloved knuckles. She ached to kiss him again. Unfortunately, the street was not the place to steal kisses.

"Until the party then," Laura said. She stepped back.

"Until then." Simon tipped his hat, returned to the coach, and climbed inside. As the coach rumbled away, she hugged the package tightly to her chest and sighed long and deep.

If she didn't gain control of her actions, she'd soon find herself in love with the man.

And that would be entirely unacceptable.

The day of the party had arrived as any other day, with daylight seeping into her window and a bird or two peeping outside the pane. Laura assumed there was a nest hidden somewhere in the tree and smiled while thinking about downy baby birds.

It was many hours later when Miss Noelle arrived to help her dress that Laura wished she could climb out that very same window, make the great leap to the tree, and disappear into the garden.

At present, her stomach flip-flopped beneath the brown dress and threatened to sour her midday meal. This added to the tremors in her hands and wobbling knees.

"Thank you for your assistance, Miss Noelle," Laura said, placing a hand over her abdomen. The gesture did nothing to settle her worries. "I cannot help thinking this ball is a mistake. I know nothing about being a companion. My ineptitude will certainly give me away."

The two women locked eyes in the mirror. "I'm not happy you're being put into this situation," Miss Noelle said glumly. "Unfortunately, Simon believes this will help your case."

Laura twisted her fingers together. "I'm not so certain I shouldn't flee from London and take my chances in hiding. I understand America has vast wildernesses and mountains that climb up to the clouds. There are many places there for one woman to hide."

Miss Noelle took her elbows. "You must decide this for yourself. If hiding is your choice, I'll see that you are sent to someplace far from here. If you choose to stay and attend the party, you will be well guarded in Collingwood House. Eva will make sure of it." She leaned back and scanned Laura from head to toes. "There, finished."

With those parting words, Miss Noelle left her.

Laura slumped on the bed. Having had everything dictated to her by the earl, her decision making was out of practice. Before that, her father had been her guide. Now that she had some control, this possibly life-altering decision left her baffled.

She could easily choose coddled eggs over poached or tea with or without sugar, but deciding whether to endanger her life for the chance at complete freedom went beyond such simple choices.

Stay or flee? Simon would be arriving shortly and she wanted to be confident in her decision.

If she fled, her life would never be completely hers. There would always be moments when she'd jump at every sound, peer behind every door, and look under every bed. This unknown stranger would be no better than Westwick. His control would be complete.

However, if she did stay, she could be killed. That was the part she couldn't settle in her mind.

Laura sat for a quarter hour struggling to find a solution when Westwick's face welled in her mind. A chill rippled through her and, with it, memories.

With her defiance came beatings. And there were moments when she couldn't fight him and had curled up like a wounded kitten, braced for more abuse. But through all of that, she'd not succumbed to his will. Not completely. No matter what he demanded of her, deep inside, she'd known she'd someday be free. That distant light had kept her alive when her sanity was threatened.

Never again would she be that kitten. No matter what troubles arose from the murder investigation, and beyond, she'd face them with an unbroken spirit.

As she straightened slowly upright, Laura knew what she had to do. She would fight. She'd fight her fear, she'd fight her weaknesses, and she'd fight the killer. She deserved nothing less than a life without darkness.

B y the time Simon arrived, Laura was ready for battle. He stared at her as Sophie found an old blue cloak and settled it around her shoulders. In addition to the severe dress, Sophie had secured her hair in a tight knot at the base of her neck and Noelle had settled on her a pair of spectacles. They'd powdered over the few freckles on her nose and deemed her disguise complete.

"Keep her safe," Sophie warned and left them.

Simon continued to stare.

"Is there something the matter?" she asked. She patted her hair. Everything seemed in place.

"There is something different about you." Simon looked puzzled. "And it has nothing to do with the dress."

She pushed the spectacles in place. "You wanted drab and you have drab. Unless you wish to put a sack over my head, there is little else we can do."

He shook his head. "The disguise is not it. You have changed somehow since I saw you last. I cannot put my finger on what it is exactly."

Laura shrugged. "I have done nothing but reclaim my spine. This killer will not frighten me anymore. It is time I stop jumping at shadows and floor squeaks. And if the murderer has his way and I am killed, at least I will have put up a strong fight."

While Laura watched, a slow smile drifted over his face. Dressed largely in black, he was immeasurably handsome. Her fingers twitched to touch him.

"Bravo, love. Though I intend for you to survive this ordeal intact, I welcome knowing that you will not fall to the floor in a frightened puddle in the face of danger. The lamb has claws."

This time Laura smiled. She reached down to bunch up

her hem, exposing her garter and a small pearl-handled knife strapped to her thigh. "Claws . . . and this. I am not entering the fray tonight without protection."

His bark of laughter caused her to giggle. "You continue to shock and surprise me," he said. "I know of no woman who goes to a ball with a knife. I fear for the safety of our killer."

Laura's eyes took on an evil glint. "I worry less about him and more about the rest of the guests. I have heard that members of the Ton can be a brutal lot. Even a simple companion can fall prey to jabs and barbs from abusive tongues."

Simon shrugged. "The gossips *can* cut to the quick. But they will hardly notice a companion." He led her outside to the waiting hackney. "Truthfully, you will be so busy looking for familiar faces, and making sure that Aunt Bernie doesn't trip and fall flat, that you'll not have to worry about catty women and their bitter gossip."

"Aunt Bernie?" She climbed into the coach and settled on the seat. "Is she the aunt you mentioned before? The one who enjoys too much sherry?"

Simon waited for the coach to start before answering. "She is the one, my maiden aunt. I assured her that the only way she would be allowed to go to the party is with a chaperone. She gets into mischief, and my female relatives have refused to escort her out anymore."

"Excellent," Laura grumbled. "This explains why you have held back more dismal details of the plan until I was trapped in this coach. She is not eager to play your game."

"To be fair, I did mention her tippling at the dress shop." He leaned forward to pat her hand. "You need not worry, love. Aunt Bernie is an amiable sort and quite entertaining. If you steer her clear of the port, she should do quite well."

Laura desperately wanted to tell him what she thought about his idea. Instead, she said nothing as they rolled toward Berkeley Square.

She'd accepted that she'd spend the evening looking for auction guests. As a drab companion, there was little chance that anyone would recognize her as Sabine. And if she was exposed, the presence of Simon and the duke and duchess would minimize the danger.

The chances of drawing attention to herself would rise if his aunt misbehaved. That was what most concerned her.

In spite of his assurances, she was quite certain the woman wouldn't be pleased to have Laura foisted upon her. It appeared as if she was already resentful over her with-drawal from society.

"Don't look so grim, sweet." Simon remarked. "Aunt Bernie does not have fangs. She is looking forward to the party after months of exile in Kent."

Minutes later, Laura's mood lightened considerably when she met the tippling Aunt Bernie.

The woman was somewhere near sixty, clearly favored the color yellow, and had gray and brown hair that defied any attempts by her maid to sweep it back into some sem-blance of order. Several strands danced in tight coils around her head, where yellow feathers had been tucked into the curly mass.

It looked as if she'd been caught in a tussle with the wind, and the wind had won.

Laura pressed her fist to her lips as the woman flounced down the staircase on the arm of a footman. Simon had mentioned his aunt's lengthy exile. By the look on her face, the woman was clearly impatient to be freed of her opulent cage.

"It is about time you returned, young man," she snapped. "I have been waiting for several hours."

Simon snorted. "I was gone and back in no more than an hour. It probably took that long for the maid to put those feathers in your hair."

Aunt Bernie lifted her nose and glared. "It takes longer for a woman of my advanced age to look presentable. The feathers are meant to distract from my wrinkles."

Laura bit her lip to keep from laughing. The grousing woman was delightful. The evening ahead looked brighter.

He walked to his aunt and pressed a kiss on her cheek.

"You look lovely. All the other matrons will envy your plumage." He took her hand to lead her to Laura. "Aunt Bernie, I'd like you to meet Miss Prescott."

Aunt Bernie looked Laura over quite thoroughly. "So you are my guard for the evening? I have been told by my nephew that I am not allowed out without a chaperone." She sniffed. "Tripping Lady Marbry was an unfortunate accident. No harm done."

"No harm?" Simon sighed. "She sprained her wrist as she toppled over her new Chippendale chair. That is why you were sent off to Kent. We clearly cannot leave you unattended."

"I sent Lady Marbry flowers," the aunt said with another sniff. She plucked at the lace on one wrist. "She sent around a note that I've been forgiven."

Laura felt badly for her. Obviously the woman wasn't mean-spirited. She'd made mistakes.

Stepping around Simon, Laura presented herself to Aunt Bernie. "I am so pleased to meet you, My Lady," she said. "I think tonight we will have a grand adventure together."

Aunt Bernie's eyes widened as an invisible cloud of rose-scented perfume whirled around her. "Oh. It has been months since I've had any adventure, grand or otherwise. I have been collecting dust in the country."

Laura nodded. "Then we shall dust you off. According to Simon, this will be the event of the season. There will be no sitting in the corner. We shall laugh and be gay. And by the time the clock strikes three, there will be no adventures left to experience."

Aunt Bernie's face slowly melted into a smile. With an up-tipped nose, she turned her back to Simon and slipped her arm through Laura's. "I like you. My nephew is far too stuffy. He wouldn't know fun if it nipped him on the bottom."

Laughing, Laura watched Simon scowl at his aunt.

The two women proceeded out of the town house, Aunt Bernie condemning Simon, and all the Harringtons for that matter, for their lack of understanding of her condition. Her stiff hands and sore feet required an occasional nip from the bottle.

"Have you ever sat through a musicale where the family daughter had the voice of a strangled cat?" Aunt Bernie said as Simon helped her into the Harrington coach. "If there was ever the need for the sherry, a musicale is the perfect time."

Laura laughed and wondered if she should check the aunt's reticule for bottles.

By the time they'd made the short ride to Collingwood House, the two women were fast friends. Simon's mouth twitched as he watched them. Laura sent him a secretive smile as his aunt chattered on and Simon grinned his approval.

The foyer of the mansion was already filled to the seams when the trio entered with the flow of guests. The duke and duchess had only a moment to greet Simon and Bernie as the crush pressed in behind them. They gave no notice of Laura, per her lowly position. However, as they moved on, Miss Eva did indicate her approval of the disguise with an almost imperceptible nod and Laura knew she'd passed inspection.

Collingwood House was as she remembered, yet different, too. There were flowers on nearly every surface, and guests filled every nook and corner.

"It is overwhelming," Laura said, her heart beating hard in her chest. "I shall look for drapes behind which to hide."

"Calm yourself," Simon said over his shoulder as he escorted his aunt toward the ballroom. "I shall settle you in a corner until you can get accustomed to the crush."

Music played and people mingled while Laura kept her eyes mostly down at her feet. Aunt Bernie spent the first hour greeting acquaintances and friends and learning the latest gossip. She lamented her months of isolation on the thousand-acre estate to anyone who would listen.

The crush of people who wanted to speak to Aunt Bernie kept Laura from enjoying her company. Time proceeded slowly.

Laura struggled not to tap her foot beneath her gown or show too much interest in the passing guests. The spectacles hid her eyes enough for covert glances at men, but she saw no one she recognized. Whether it was good or bad remained to be seen.

"I would love some punch."

Laura turned her head. "Pardon?"

Aunt Bernie patted her hand. "I am parched. It is hot in here." She waved to a woman in an ostrich plum hat. "Perhaps you could get us punch and ask the duchess to open a few more windows. There are never enough open windows."

Laura was pleased for a reprieve from boredom, and yet concerned about wandering alone amid the room full of potential murderers. She walked with a stilted gait in the general direction of the dining room, keeping vigilant for knife-wielding party guests. She got about halfway through the packed space when Simon appeared at her elbow.

"See anyone familiar?" he asked casually, making certain not to appear too interested in her.

"Sadly, no. The one man I recognized is a member of Parliament. I knew this only because of the disparaging cartoons of him depicted in the *Times*." She shrugged at his curious look. "The artist portrays him quite accurately."

Simon peered out over the crowd. He was several inches taller than most men. It gave him an advantage that she lacked. She fought to keep her hands demurely clasped together. "I expected Aunt Bernie to keep you locked to her side. She does like an audience."

Laura's snort was most unladylike. "Thankfully, she has sent me for punch. I thought it a perfect opportunity to walk around the room and see what I can discover."

He frowned. "I would walk with you but it would draw attention. If a Harrington man spends too much time attending to a woman, it sets tongues wagging. If the woman is my aunt's companion, the gossips will be speculating on how quickly I will ruin you."

Laura bit back a cynical smile. "I am already ruined. You are too late to accomplish my deflowering."

Eyes dancing, Simon coughed behind his hand. "You have a wicked sense of humor and are far more entertaining than the women of this company." He reached for a glass of port off the tray of a passing footman. "Unfortunately, I must go before I draw notice to you."

He turned and slipped into the crowd. Laura pressed onward until she found the punch and claimed two glasses for herself and Aunt Bernie. She walked gingerly past a group of women in brightly colored gowns, feeling like a sparrow among peacocks.

She gave them a cursory glance and realized one of the women in deep blue was the duchess. They locked eyes for an instant as Laura passed by.

Though she felt the familiar tug of unease she'd been experiencing since her escape from Westwick, as always there was nothing noticeable to give her pause.

The dancing was fully under way when Laura returned to the ballroom. Eager to make the evening successful in her hunt for clues, she took the long way around the room to get back to Simon's aunt. She covertly peered at every male guest, hoping to find someone she recognized. The quicker she sent Simon on the trail of another suspect, the sooner the investigation could turn away from her.

Alas, her efforts gained her nothing.

She spent another two hours suppressing yawns, and envy, between brief and amusing comments made by her companion. She desperately wished she could join the guests on the dance floor. Occasionally, Simon would whirl past, a woman in his arms, and jealousy would burn in her breast.

She wondered if one of them was Lady Jeanette. No chit of marriageable age would ever miss an event of this size.

Although Laura grew up in a small village, she knew that mamas with eligible daughters would have to be felled by the plague before they'd pass up this opportunity to prance their little darlings in front of dozens of eligible men.

Simon could be engaged before night's end.

Even with Laura at the party, he'd not pass on the chance for an engagement should the opportunity arise. Lady Jeanette was too grand a prize for him to lose because of his fondness for an impoverished former courtesan.

Her eyes burned and she blinked away tears.

It was then that Laura realized she had fallen headlong in love with Simon. With this newfound information came a bitterness that soured her stomach. She'd gone and done exactly what she'd feared she'd do: become emotionally attached to him, the one man she could never have.

"Are you feeling well, Miss Prescott?" Aunt Bernie asked. "You look pale." She pushed a drooping feather out of one eye.

Laura blinked. "I think I need some air."

Aunt Bernie pressed her fan into Laura's hand. "Take this."

Her hand closed around the item. "Thank you, but I fear I need to step outside." She stumbled to her feet and walked briskly across the room toward the patio doors. As she got close to freedom, she bumped into a woman in lavender who stepped into her path. "Excuse me."

The woman turned and Laura gaped. "Miss Noelle?"

As quickly as the words were out, Miss Noelle's arm hooked around hers. She was ushered out the door, across the terrace, and into another door, which turned out to be a library.

Shock at finding Miss Noelle at the duchess's ball kept her from speaking. Miss Noelle had transformed from a woman who helped school courtesans to a peacock in silk and jewels.

Laura knew Simon and Miss Noelle were cousins. She just assumed Miss Noelle was an impoverished member of the family. She certainly dressed the part at the school.

"Come, sit." Miss Noelle pressed her into a chair. "Would you like a brandy? I know the duke keeps some somewhere."

Laura shook her head and sat the fan on the table. "Who *are* you?" she whispered.

A smile flashed. "Lady Noelle Seymour, but more recently, Mrs. Gavin Blackwell. I do play my part of the helpful widow quite well, don't you think? The courtesans accept me as such without question."

Before Laura could ask the myriad of questions bouncing about in her head, the terrace door flung open, startling both women.

Chapter Twenty-Two

Simon stepped quickly into the room and clicked the door closed behind him. He crossed the room with brisk steps.

"What is happening?" he asked, his face concerned. He quickly looked Laura over. "I saw Noelle pull you out of the ballroom. Are you ill?"

Laura shook her head. "It was nothing. Well, unless you consider my shock at finding out that Miss Noelle is a Lady." She scowled. "I am beginning to realize that there is a vast array of secrets hiding in the courtesan school and in your family. Is there anything else I should know?"

Simon looked at Miss Noelle. "You know Noelle is my cousin. We haven't hidden that information."

"I do," Laura replied. She pressed a gloved hand to her forehead. "Is Sophie your sister? Is Thomas your long-suffering bastard brother?"

He chuckled. "Sophie is not my sister. She is no relation at all. And I am positive Thomas is not the product of my father stepping out on Mother. She'd kill him."

"Perfect." She glanced at Miss Noelle. "How closely are you related to the duchess? You have the same color eyes."

The two cousins briefly stared at each other, as if trying to decide what information to share. Finally, Miss Noelle spoke. "The duchess is my half sister. We just met about a year ago. We've kept it secret for now."

If loving Simon had been an impossible dream before this moment, it was as far out of reach as the stars now.

Though she'd known he was to be an earl someday, as the cousin of a duchess and Lady Noelle, he'd need someone like Lady Jeanette at his side. He might care for Laura, but ultimately, he would do his duty to his family.

Her shoulders slumped. Why couldn't she have been rescued by a footman or a farmer? Why did it have to be Simon?

"Will you leave us?" Simon asked and Noelle slipped quietly out onto the terrace. He crouched down onto his heels and closed a hand over hers. "Will you tell me why you look as though your best friend has just died?"

"My only friend *has* just died." She sighed deeply. "You cannot be my friend. Not really. It's a game we've played these last few weeks. Don't you see that, Simon? It doesn't matter how deeply I care for you, or that you are still only third in line to become an earl, you and I will never be able to socialize publicly without drawing scandal."

"We've know this from the first. It hasn't stopped us from caring for each other. Why is this coming up now, tonight, when we have suspects to uncover?"

She closed her fists. "Because I've come to the horrible realization that I'm falling in love with you. Every time you danced with a young woman tonight, I wanted to pull her hair out. Every time I overheard Lady Jeanette's name, I wanted to push her in front of a coach." She stood and rubbed her eyes beneath the spectacles and said angrily, "Don't you see, I knew better. I knew that our time together was a mistake. You are too charming and handsome to resist. How could I not love you?"

Simon chuckled softly. "Is loving me as terrible as all that?" He pulled her into his arms. "It isn't as if the condition is fatal."

"It is when one day soon, you and I will part forever and my heart will shatter into bits," she grumbled and met his eyes. "I truly expect nothing from you, Simon. My feelings are mine alone." She plucked at his coat. "I understand the way of this world and will go away quietly when we are done. I only wish that I had protected my heart a little better."

Simon lifted her chin. The surprise of her stunning confession had taken him aback. It shouldn't have. Laura always spoke openly about her feelings. At least she'd never held back when scolding him for his forward behavior.

Still, he never expected her to love him.

"I cannot marry you." He looked softly into her beautiful gray eyes. Even the drab disguise couldn't hide away her loveliness. He'd been watching her all evening, barely able to tear his gaze away, wishing it were she dancing in his arms.

"I know." She smiled wistfully. "I wouldn't marry you if I could. I need a life free of gossip and social stigma. If my time with Westwick was ever to become news, I would be ostracized by everyone you know."

Sadly, she was correct. And in spite of his fondness for her, they both had to be practical. Though her situation hadn't been her fault, she'd always carry the title of courtesan, if only in her mind.

"Then we shall continue forward with our investigation and speak of this no more." Simon leaned forward and impulsively pressed a light kiss on her lips. "Come, let us return to the ballroom before Aunt Bernie notices you are missing."

The hallway was quiet when they emerged from the library. Laura excused herself to go to the retiring room, wanting a few minutes to settle her emotions before returning to the ball.

There were several women already there but they barely gave her a glance. Laura walked over to a mirror and adjusted her spectacles. For the first time, she'd confessed to loving a man and nothing had changed because of it. The sun hadn't broken through the clouds to cast them in shimmery light, and birds hadn't chirped a happy song to celebrate her love.

No, life would go on as it always did.

She exited the room and realized she'd left the fan in the library. Retracing her footsteps, she found the fan where she'd put it down. She hooked it over her wrist and turned toward the door.

A flutter of curtains caught her attention.

Miss Noelle had left the terrace doors open. She walked across the room and reached for the handles. She had only a moment to realize that she wasn't alone when a pair of hands caught her arms from behind and jerked her back against a hard chest. She let out a surprised squeak.

"Say nothing," a voice commanded. His breath smelled strongly of ale. His plain brown coat gave no clue as to his identity as she tried to look over her shoulder at his face.

Yet there was something familiar about the voice. Though she couldn't immediately place it, a cold trill of alarm went down her body.

The man released one arm for an instant. She hadn't time to begin to struggle, or to reach for the knife in her garter, when a blade was pressed against her throat. She went still.

"Imagine my surprise to find the beautiful Laura attending the duke's ball in the accompaniment of Lady Bernice Harrington. You have obviously taken up a new profession," he hissed into her ear. "Isn't playing Harrington's whore enough to keep you occupied? Now you are a lady's companion to his aunt?" He snickered. "You are a woman of many talents."

"Please, what do you want?" Laura asked. Her mind reached out, trying to put a name or face to the voice. It was just out of grasp. But she knew him. Somehow. And he knew her.

With the knife pressed to her flesh, it was difficult to think of anything but saving herself.

A low chuckle filled her ear as he pressed his mouth to her lobe. She shuddered. "What do I want? I want you, Laura. From our first meeting, you have haunted me, a vision in a simple cream dress. I can still see the sadness and acceptance in your eyes as you went stoically to your fate."

"I don't know you," she pressed. "You have mistaken me for another." The churn of panic kept her frozen. One slip of the blade and she'd be dead. "Please release me."

He nipped her ear. She winced.

"There are too many guests for us to get reacquainted properly." The knife trailed from her neck to her shoulder blade. She clutched her throat with her free hand.

"We will talk again," he said. "Soon."

Spinning her around, he shoved her into the room and escaped out the terrace doors.

Laura didn't wait for him to change his mind and return. She ran across the room and into the hallway. A couple stepped back in surprise as she raced passed them. She had to get to Simon before the stranger escaped.

Never had a hallway seemed so long as she hurried away from the library. She just made it to within a few footsteps to safety when a faded image slipped to the fore and his words became clear. She'd married in a simple cream dress. Only a few people knew that information and two of them were dead.

A face rushed into her head and with it a name.

Henry.

Bile burned in her throat.

It took Laura forever to find Simon. He was in an alcove talking with a pair of gentlemen when he caught her eye. Fear must have been evident on her face, for he quickly excused himself and walked toward her.

"I—" She struggled for words and touched her neck. "I was accosted in the library."

That was all it took for Simon's face to tighten. "Come with me." He turned and led Laura from the room.

For the third time, she found herself in the library. Her eyes darted to the open doors, half expecting to find Henry hiding, ready to attack her again.

There was nothing to indicate his presence. Clearly he'd had the sense to flee after accosting her.

Simon locked the door behind them. "Tell me everything."

Laura rubbed her arms. "I returned for the fan and a man snuck up behind me with a knife. He must have been lurking outside and crept in here after we left. It was unfortunate that I left Aunt Bernie's fan behind."

Simon's jaw pulsed. "Did he hurt you?"

She shook her head. "He pressed the blade to my neck. He said he desired me from our first meeting and mentioned a dress I used to wear. At first, I didn't know what that meant. And he called me Laura, not Sabine."

"Did you know him?"

"It wasn't until after he fled that it came to me." She looked up, her fear rising. "It was Henry."

"Henry?" Simon scowled as he walked over to pour her a glass of wine and handed it to her.

She drank to clear her dry throat. Then, "Westwick's friend. I spoke of him before. He witnessed our marriage and was often a guest at the town house. I never considered that he could be the killer. The way he'd held the blade . . . I'm certain he could use it with deadly accuracy."

Simon clenched his fists. "You are lucky to be unhurt. I never should have left you alone."

"You could not know I'd be accosted here. There are hundreds of possible witnesses." She drained the glass. Her hands shook. "Though he attacked me, I believe it wasn't his intention to harm me." She set down the glass. "He wants me; he is playing with me. He will do me no harm while his desire is unsatisfied."

Laura felt Simon's rage, saw it in his eyes.

"The bastard." Simon walked to the sideboard and poured a drink. "Does this Henry have a full name?"

She stared at his back, tense and stiff. She tried once more to remember what she could about Henry and recalled very few details. Yet she knew his face well. She'd seen it many times. Otherwise, she had little information that would help Simon find him.

"I do not know it." A helpless feeling followed. "He is somewhere his early twenties and has dark hair. I don't think he is a noble as his clothing is modest, though well cut, and he doesn't have the air of a man born to privilege."

Simon turned around. "Does he have any scars or oddities that would make him noticeable?"

"Not that I can remember. He was ordinary. Well, as ordinary as one can be with a streak of evil in his heart. He often brought women to the town house and abused them. It was as if he were the other half of Westwick. In fact, they somewhat resembled each other in coloring."

"Is it possible that they are related?" Simon walked over to claim a chair. Only the light from a pair of sconces kept the room from darkness.

"It's possible." Laura stood near the cold fireplace. "I'd never considered it." She ran a fingertip along the mantle. "They were as unalike as they were alike. Westwick was clearly the leader and Henry was the one led along. Even so, he had an arrogance about him that led me to believe he wasn't entirely happy to be the follower."

Simon fell silent. After a moment, he said, "If he is a guest here, he should be easy to find."

"I wish I knew more," Laura said. "I was struggling to survive during those months in captivity. I paid very little attention to anything beyond my own suffering. Henry was merely another background player. Had I known that Westwick would be murdered, I would have paid closer attention to the man he called a friend."

Fortunately, the rest of the evening went without incident. Against Simon's wishes, she'd stayed at the party. She knew Henry; he did not. Unfortunately, her continued presence led them no closer to finding the mysterious Henry. If he was a guest, he'd left after confronting Laura.

Simon spoke to both the duke and Eva, but they were as puzzled as he was. The duke vowed to call for Crawford in the morning and give him the new information.

It was nearing two o'clock when Simon escorted the women back to the Harrington town house. He thought it best if Laura spent the night there, and Laura agreed. As a companion, she was found a room on the upper floor and the maid was instructed to find a nightdress for her to use.

Aunt Bernie bade them good night.

"If my sleeping away from the school continues, I shall have to start carrying a valise with a change of clothing," Laura remarked as Simon led her upstairs. She yawned.

"I think you should move in here."

"What?" Her exhaustion faded.

Simon stopped outside the bedroom door. "I no longer think you'll be safe at the school. I believe it will be best if you are here, where I can keep watch over you."

Laura bristled. "I can watch over myself."

He grinned. "I know you can. However, I find the appearance of this Henry at the ball more than a coincidence. If he is not a member of society, then he was not an invited guest. He attacked you in the library. That leads me to believe he was watching you through the windows this evening. He saw you leave the fan and expected you to return for it. He lay in wait."

"Then he knew I'd be at the ball," Laura said. "He watched me all night, waiting for his opportunity to confront me."

"Tonight, and likely every day over the last few weeks. If so, he knows about the school, whom you talk to, everything about your life."

The idea of her presence at the school endangering the women outraged her. "I knew someone was watching me. I felt him. But I never saw anything suspicious." She pressed her fist to her mouth. "I rarely leave the school. Is it possible that he followed us the night of my escape?"

"I don't believe so. I was careful."

A terrifying thought came to mind. "Oh, dear. He was in the coach." Her eyes widened. The crushing truth became clear and she paced. "He must have seen me escape the town house. He was there when the footmen tried to reclaim me and saw me ride off with you." She rubbed her hands together. She was very sure that she was right. "It wouldn't be difficult to discover the owner of Horse. He is a distinctive animal."

"Then he not only has been watching you, but he found you by following me to the school," Simon ground out. "Had I left you alone, he'd still be futilely searching for you."

Laura shook her head. "You couldn't know."

"I *should have* known," he countered. "You warned me of the danger you faced that first night. I didn't take enough precautions to keep you safe."

She felt his anger and knew it was directed inwardly. "We can do nothing about that now. And we do not know for certain how he found me. It will be a time waste to speculate. We need to figure out what brought him out of hiding tonight."

He expelled his held breath. "I'm more curious to know why he let you go and what he intends to do next."

A memory tugged. "I thought I saw something at the manor the night we spent together. I made myself believe that it was you standing beneath a tree outside the attic window. It wasn't, was it?"

He shook his head. "I tended the horses, nothing more. If he was there, and has been stalking you, then there is little about either of us that he doesn't know."

"This could put you in danger, too. It would certainly give him reason to come out of the shadows," Laura said. Her heart twisted. "If he sees you as my lover and an obstacle in his way, he may kill you to have me."

Simon cupped her face. "Do not fret about me, love. We Harringtons are a hearty lot. I do not plan to die with a knife buried in my back."

Laura placed her hands over his. The puzzle grew more confusing with each new piece. "He would have had many opportunities to kidnap me. Tonight was part of some vile game."

Simon nodded. "Passion, greed, desperation are all possibilities. We shall return to Collingwood House when His Grace meets with Crawford. Perhaps between the four of us, we can get our answers."

Chapter Twenty-Three

✦

"Henry is a common name," His Grace said after the foursome gathered a day later in the library at Collingwood House. "I suspect I know eight or more in my circle. And there are certainly several with dark hair. It isn't much to work with."

Laura had spent the better part of the morning trying to remember everything she could about the mysterious man. She'd spent hours in his company but paid him little mind. Her thoughts during those days were mostly on working through opportunities to escape.

"He had an ordinary face." She glanced at Mister Crawford. The investigator and His Grace had gone over the guest list and found nothing unusual. Before the duchess left for the school, she went through the guest list, too, and tried to remember the names of the guests of her guests. There were very few she didn't know and certainly no one who fit the description of Henry and his clothing.

Neither the duke nor the duchess remembered more than a few faces they didn't recognize. And no one stood out as particularly interesting, and certainly not threatening.

It solidified their belief that Henry had been following Laura.

"I think it is time I visit Westwick's town house," Crawford said. "Though the house has been abandoned by most of the staff, I believe there are a few servants still in residence."

"Hasn't someone stepped forward to claim the estate?" Simon asked. "Usually a death has family members salivating over the prospect of adding to their coffers."

Crawford shook his head. "The inheritance has yet to be distributed. The court wants to see the matter of the murder settled before they render a ruling."

"Do they suspect a family member in the murder?" Simon asked. "That would be an interesting twist."

"That is unlikely. According to records, most of his family is either dead or old," Crawford said. "There is a distant cousin who would be pleased to inherit the title, but there may be very little fortune to be gained. Westwick burned through his inheritance at a staggering pace. The barristers are still untangling his muddled financial records."

"I would not be surprised to know Westwick was teetering on financial ruin," Laura said. "There wasn't anything, no matter how costly, that he wouldn't purchase if he desired it enough." She screwed up her face. Her stomach soured. "Perhaps he hoped to stave off creditors by selling me."

With her emotions no longer raw, she could coldly talk about Westwick as if she were discussing a stranger. Her scars were still fading and she hoped one day not to see them every time she stood naked before a mirror.

"It's possible," Simon agreed. He looked softly at Laura. "You were his most valuable possession. It would have taken desperation to force him to part with you."

A shimmer went through her as their gazes held. There were moments when his eyes fell on her that felt almost like a caress.

She tore her gaze away. "I did not feel valued." Her hand came up to the hidden scar on her collarbone. Simon had kissed the spot with such tenderness. "Though he did consider me his possession."

A flash of emptiness filled her eyes and was gone just as quickly. Though Simon knew Laura's pain was fading, it would take time for her to completely recover.

The fire in his chest burned. For the thousandth time, he wished the earl were alive to take his punishment.

Crawford's voice brought him back to the present.

"I know the address of the town house," Crawford was telling His Grace. "I'll go there now and see what I can find out from the servants."

"I'll go, too," Simon added. He wanted to be directly involved in the investigation. Truthfully, he wanted to be the one who found this Henry. That way he could be on hand to wring his scrawny neck for what he'd done to Laura.

"I have an appointment, so I'll leave you two to the matter." His Grace glanced at Laura. "You are welcome to remain here until they return."

Laura nodded pensively, her eyes brooding. Then she shook her head vigorously to clear it and stood. "You will take me, too."

The three men stared before a heated debate began about whether she'd be at risk. Simon was adamant that she stay at Collingwood House. Laura was adamant she wouldn't. Crawford stood back for a moment before joining the argument.

"Her personal knowledge about the house and staff could benefit us if we search the house," Crawford said. "If Westwick had secrets, Miss Laura would be better able to flush them out. She will notice if anything is amiss."

His Grace broke in, "Her face is well known by the servants. They could alert the Bow Street Runners."

In the end, Laura won. "I promise to wear a bonnet, keep my face covered, and refrain from speaking. As Crawford said, I have knowledge of the household. I can help."

Simon grumbled under his breath during the hackney

ride to Cheapside, up the walkway, and to the door of West-wick's town house. "If even one servant recognizes you, the Runners will be on your trail before the coach is half-way back to Eva's mansion."

"Have faith, Simon," Laura urged. "We will conquer both the house and my demons and survive brilliantly."

"You are taking a serious risk," Simon whispered to her as Crawford clacked the knocker.

Laura peered out from under the bonnet brim. "I know. You have said so at least two dozen times."

True, and it clearly didn't matter. She was determined to return to the place of her confinement to look for clues and vanquish ghosts. Proving her innocence was more impor-tant than the unpleasant memories the house would bring.

"You can still wait in the coach," he said.

"I think you should not worry so much or you will sour your stomach," Laura remarked tartly. "I will be careful to avert my face. But you cannot expect me to hide away when my future and life may depend on what we find out today."

Simon pondered her words and couldn't fault her argu-ment. If it was he who was in trouble, he'd feel the same.

"Remember, not only might the servants alert the Run-ners, but Crawford and I could face arrest for helping you if you make a misstep."

Laura nodded. "I will be the perfect woman of mystery. Not one servant will know me. I promise."

In spite of her declaration, his chest tightened when a grizzled old butler answered the door.

"Yes?"

Crawford introduced himself and explained the reason for his visit. He kept silent on the identities of Simon and Laura.

"This should not take long if you cooperate," the inves-tigator said firmly. "Round up the servants and I will con-duct interviews."

The butler drew to full height. He still couldn't look Crawford in the eyes. "There are only four of us and we know nothing about the murder. We have no master at the moment and I cannot let you wander about the house. We are in mourning."

Laura peeked at Hamm and bit back a smirk. She recognized the waistcoat the man was wearing. It formerly belonged to Westwick. The servants likely waited only long enough for the body to be removed before stealing what possessions they could take without rousing suspicion.

There was no mourning here.

"I did not ask for your permission, my good man," Crawford said. "You either let us in or we will find a Bow Street Runner and let you explain how a man of your income can afford such a fine pocket watch."

Hamm paled and his hand fell involuntarily to the watch hanging on the bob just inside his coat. His jaw worked beneath mottled skin.

Slowly, the fight left him. He said nothing as he stepped back and swung the door wide. "Excellent choice, my good man," Crawford said. "And I never saw the watch."

Crawford, Simon, and Laura trailed inside. She faltered as the familiar aroma of Westwick's favorite candle scent took her aback. The candles had been imported from the Orient, and she hated the musky smell.

Simon touched her arm and barked at Hamm, "Leave us."

The command sent the butler skittering off in the direction of the kitchen. Crawford followed.

"It is not too late to wait in the coach," Simon said, placing a hand on Laura's shoulder. "Crawford and I can do this without you."

For a moment she hesitated. It would be simple to accept the offer. Instead, she steeled her spine and patted his hand. "I need to face my fears. It is time to flay Westwick from my mind. There is no better place to do so than the scene of my captivity."

Simon smiled. "You have great strength, My Lady."

"I would hold your opinion until we have finished here," she said, looking up the staircase. "I may yet run screaming from this house."

He chuckled. "As long as you do so without alerting the staff to your identity, screaming is acceptable."

Laura expelled a hard breath, looked at him askance, and straightened her shoulders. "I'm ready."

The house was as she remembered it—masculine décor, dark, somewhat brooding. The wallpaper was still worn and the drapes frayed. She knew Westwick had kept the town house as a place to play his vile games out of sight of society. She assumed he had a respectable residence elsewhere, though he never spoke of it to her.

She heard raised voices coming from the kitchen as Crawford questioned the servants.

His threat had hit its mark. Likely all the servants had stolen from their dead master and wouldn't want a close inspection of their possessions. They'd tell him what they knew, if only to be rid of him.

"A silver picture frame is missing," she said as they passed a gilt side table. "It held a painting of his mother."

When she arrived at the library, Laura hesitated on the threshold and touched the scar on her shoulder.

"I find it fitting that he died here," she said, her voice barely above a whisper. "This was the room he considered his sanctuary and where he plotted most of his evil deeds."

She stepped over the threshold. Crawford joined them.

Without Westwick to infuse evil into the room, it was almost like any other library. Dusty books lined the shelves, a large desk sat in one corner, and a rug lay before the fireplace. She jerked her eyes away from the rug, tamping down unpleasant memories.

"Laura?" Simon stepped close.

"I'm fine," she assured him. "Where was he killed?"

Crawford walked to the desk. "Here." He waited for Laura and Simon to walk over and pointed behind the desk. "The Runners report indicated that a footman found him stabbed to death behind the desk. Rumors have been buzzing about whether the servants sent for the Runners immediately, or waited an hour or two to make sure he was good and dead."

Her mouth twitched. "I would have waited."

She knew saying such a thing was cold and scandalous. However, she also knew the two men understood her bitterness. Though she'd kept most of the tales of suffering from Simon, and had never spoken frankly to Crawford about her past, they both knew of her abuse and wouldn't judge her for speaking frankly.

"There are bloody patches on the rug." Crawford stepped around the desk. Simon followed. "His last moments were gruesome."

Laura left them to examine the spot, for in spite of her relief that Westwick would no longer haunt her, she didn't want to see the blood. She wandered around the room, looking for anything out of place.

"You don't really think the killer left clues to his identity here, do you?" she asked. She touched the books, knowing the earl never read. The books were more to give the impression of a learned man than to actually teach him anything useful.

"Probably not," Simon answered. "Whatever clues were present were carted off by the Runners."

Crawford agreed, "We will probably find nothing. However, I'd like to get a greater understanding of the man."

"Knowing he was evil isn't enough?" Laura quipped dryly.

The investigator smiled. "Not if we are to add to our suspect list." He claimed a pen and parchment from the desk and opened the inkwell. "According to the butler, Hamm, Westwick had shady business dealings that angered investors. Several had come here to confront the earl. We will also add abused former lovers. Perhaps even one of the maids got tired of his tyranny and killed him. We cannot discover the truth without first looking in all the corners of his wicked life."

The pen scratched across the page as Crawford made notes.

Laura touched a book and nodded. "There will not be enough hours in your day to investigate all the people he wronged. Westwick was a vile man. The list must be endless."

"Hamm should be willing to help me trim the list."

After a thorough examination of the books, Laura wandered into the hallway, leaving the men to their investigation of the contents of the desk. A maid poked her head out of the parlor, saw Laura, and skittered back inside. Laura kept her head down as she walked up the stairs and trudged toward Westwick's room. Once outside, she took a few deep breaths before pushing the door open.

The first thing she noticed was that the sheets and coverlet were askew. The second was that her stomach rolled as she stared at the large bed. She closed her eyes and leaned against the door frame, willing herself to be strong. She'd once suffered his attentions in that bed with stoic silence and passionless dread. Not once, in all the time she'd spent in this room, had she felt anything other than revulsion in his arms.

Thankfully, that was over. This was just a room like any other master's chamber, large and ornately decorated.

Striding purposefully inside, she began a search of the room. She peered in every drawer, inside the wardrobe, beneath the mattress, looking for anything that might lead to the reason behind the killing.

There was very little to find: clothing, boots, and a few drawings of naked women hidden in a rosewood work box. She ran her hands beneath the mattress, discovering a pair of loaded pistols. She smiled wickedly. If only she'd known of their presence sooner, it would have saved her much aggravation.

"There you are." Simon arrived as she laid the pistols on the bed. "I was concerned that you had gotten into trouble."

"Nothing so dire, I assure you. I've been facing my fears,

and winning." She cast one last glance around the room. "Regretfully, I have also found no clues."

Simon moved to the bed and lifted the pistols. He examined them. "These are fine, indeed. You should take them."

Laura frowned. "What will I do with them?"

He handed them to her. "Sell them, keep them, use them to deter Henry from threatening you; you decide. The earl owes you more than he can ever repay. And since the servants have likely stolen all of the household monies, you should take these. They have some value."

She considered his argument, then slipped them into her pockets. The pair bumped against her legs. She scrunched up her face, her eyes dancing. Without another word, she walked to the fireplace, where a statue of an elephant sat— an ugly and distorted artist's rendering of a magnificent creature.

"I've always hated this thing." She held it up. It was small but weighty. "Westwick boasted that it was made of pure gold. It should go far to finance my new life." Her mouth twitched. "Suddenly, I find it a beautiful piece."

Simon chuckled as she clutched it to her breast.

"Take whatever you like," he said. "Burn down the house. Westwick is gone. Who will care?"

Laura's heart lightened. "I think the elephant will suit me well enough. It can help me pay Crawford's fee." She shot him a knowing look. He grinned. "Thank you for making yourself an accomplice to my thievery."

"What else would I be?" He was rewarded with a grin. "If you'd like, we can stuff the coach full of stolen goods. The servants are already fearful of arrest. They will not protest."

She shook her head, amused. "I think I shall settle for the pistols and elephant."

Leading him into the hallway, she headed for the staircase. "I have had enough of this house to last my lifetime. I would like to leave now."

Simon went to fetch Crawford. The investigator had learned nothing about Westwick to whittle the list down to a firm suspect. As they walked to the coach, Crawford explained that the volume of men and women who hated the earl was endless.

Drawing from his strength, she kept her eyes on Simon as they pulled away. She clutched the elephant as she closed the final door on that part of her life.

"Now to find Henry and confront him," she said when the town house was well behind them. "There is no proof that he is a killer. He might, in fact, be innocent. But he is as close to a serious suspect as we have presently."

Simon stretched his legs. His reached out his hand. She twined their fingers together.

"If he isn't the killer, then I'm not a Harrington." He peered at Crawford. "If Henry was as close to Westwick as Laura believes, and has not called for the Runners to arrest her, then he has much to hide."

"I agree." Crawford dug into his coat and withdrew a folded note. He opened it and held it up. "I found this in the desk. It is a deed to a property in Suffolk. What is odd is that it was affixed to the underside of a drawer. I think I shall travel there tomorrow to see what I can find."

Laura took the deed. She scanned the page. "I've never heard of this place. Westwick didn't mention it to me."

"It may be nothing," Simon cautioned. "Westwick comes from an old family. They must have properties scattered throughout England. However, it is curious to hide the deed, unless there's a reason he didn't want it discovered."

Dread fell over Laura. "Westwick carefully kept his darker proclivities hidden from society, so I suspect the property must have a disreputable history. I believe that as we delve into the cracks and crevasses of Westwick's life, more evil deeds will come to light."

The coach stopped at Collingwood House, and Crawford stepped down. "I shall advise His Grace of our findings and prepare to leave for Suffolk. I don't expect to be gone for more than a few days." He looked at Laura. "Keep yourself safe."

"I will."

Crawford closed the door and the coach rolled off. Laura leaned back on the squabs and met Simon's eyes. "I wonder if we were followed today."

Simon squeezed her hand. "I assume so, though I saw no one. There is no reason to hide our activities if Henry has been watching you. He already knows everything about you."

Her stomach knotted. "Do you think he really does know about the courtesan school?"

Simon paused before answering. "Yes."

"Then we must alert Miss Eva and Miss Sophie immediately. They must be on guard in case he attempts to confront me there."

"Already done." He met her worried eyes. "Guards will be watching the school and Thomas will be ever vigilant. But I have reason to believe he'll not go there. You will be staying with me at our town house through the conclusion of this case."

Laura's eyes widened. "I cannot. I thought I was to stay only for a few days. This matter could last weeks, months even."

"Aunt Bernie likes you and you've already been established as her companion. As such, I can keep watch over you while we continue our hunt for an auction guest, or until we unmask your mysterious Henry."

He did have a point. Still, "My presence at the town house will bring danger to both you and your aunt." She worried her bottom lip. "I should take shelter at an inn until this investigation has been concluded."

Smiling, Simon leaned forward. "It would be difficult to guard you in such a public place. People arrive and depart at all hours. Henry could sneak in without notice." He drew her hand to his mouth. "I promise to keep both you and my aunt safe."

The confidence in his voice eased a few of her concerns. Staying in his family's town house would certainly be safer than the school or an inn. "I hate the thought of anyone endangered because of me."

"Eva has already arranged for some clothing and necessities for your stay and has advised Sophie of your change in residence. All you need to do is agree."

She watched him draw a finger down her arm and claim her hand. She shivered. "I'm not certain that living under your roof is an ideal solution. It will give you many chances to misbehave."

"I promise to be a pillar of propriety."

The words fell flat when he turned her palm up and found a bit of exposed skin just above her glove. He nibbled the place.

Laura's knees wobbled. "I can see how much your promise is worth," she scolded lightly and her mouth parted slightly. "You cannot even behave for a few minutes in a hired hackney."

With his mouth still on her skin, he looked into her eyes.

"You cannot fault me for a nip here or a kiss there. I am male after all."

She grinned. "You are shameless."

"Unapologetically so," he agreed and glanced out the window. "I think we have less than a minute before we reach the town house. If you'd like to be kissed, you need to lean in quickly before our moment is lost."

Laura was still smiling as he pulled her into his arms.

Chapter Twenty-Four

꧁꧂

T he house is lovely, my dear," Aunt Bernie said happily
as she greeted Mrs. Peet, her old friend. The strains of
music swirled from somewhere in the house as guests filed
into the manor. "I do love the new paper. Is it silk?"

Laura stood a few feet away as the two women discussed wall coverings and other things. Simon lingered
politely beside his aunt but sent a covert glance at Laura,
his amusement evident. After kissing her for that full minute in the coach, he'd dropped her at the town house and
left without explanation.

She scowled at him from behind the spectacles. She suspected he'd known exactly how she'd spend her day and
wanted no part in the arduous hours ahead.

She'd suffered the entire afternoon in the garden with
Aunt Bernie, discussing plants and birds until her head
ached. Afterward, she only had time for a quick toilet
before a maid came to dress her in a new gown of uninteresting gray and they were off to a musicale at the home of
Mister and Mrs. Peet.

As she listened to the musical warbling of the oldest
Peet daughter, Laura understood why Aunt Bernie imbibed

in sherry to soothe her frayed nerves before these performances.

And as the days followed slowly after the Peet rout, Laura learned that once released from her opulent prison in Kent, Aunt Bernie could not turn down an invitation. From the Peets, they went to the Baneses the following night, then to Lord and Lady Malbury's the evening after, and on and on it went for the rest of the week.

By Saturday, she was exhausted.

"I cannot sit through another social function," Laura grumbled over breakfast with Simon. "Another week of this and I shall drop dead."

"You are bearing up well, sweet." He chuckled.

She grumbled some more under her breath and arched her back. "At least you get to dance. Do you have any idea of how uncomfortable it is to sit for endless hours in too-small chairs? It is torture." She rubbed her neck. "This would be worth the discomfort if I'd managed to flush out at least one auction guest. Not one all week! I'm beginning to think they all live outside London."

He nodded, his eyes sympathetic. "I suspect the murder has sent those men fleeing from town; otherwise, you would have recognized one before now. They must want to put as much distance between themselves and the crime."

Her frustration welled. "This charade has been futile."

"It is disappointing."

Laura was saved from replying by the arrival of a footman with a note. Simon opened the missive and read it. She stabbed at a sausage as her spine ached beneath her corset.

"It appears Crawford has returned from Suffolk." He folded the note and laid it on the table. "Our presence is requested at Collingwood House posthaste."

Simon stood silently as Crawford arrived. The man looked as if he'd ridden all day. He was rumpled and dusty, his face grim.

"Would you care for a brandy?" His Grace asked and

pressed a glass into Crawford's hand without waiting for an answer.

"Thank you." Crawford drank down half, sighed, and looked at Miss Eva. "I apologize for my appearance, Your Grace. I knew you wouldn't want to wait for my report."

The duchess waved her hand. "My sensibilities have not been offended. Please do tell us what you've found."

Leaning against the mantle with his arms tightly crossed, Simon braced himself for bad news.

"It wasn't difficult to find the house. The small local populous called the place haunted," Crawford began. "It was a run-down manor set far off the road, with a small tumbledown stable behind it. I went in through a broken door and discovered it had been years since anyone had called it home."

"No one lived there?" Laura's shoulders drooped.

"No one," Crawford said. "I searched for an hour or so and discovered nothing that gave any indication why its ownership should be kept secret."

"That is regretful," Simon remarked. He'd hoped to discover something that would help Laura. The case was a series of clues that went nowhere. "The trip was fruitless."

"Not exactly." Crawford looked from Simon to Laura to Eva and the duke. "There was a farm some distance up the road. It was there that I learned the truth about the house."

Simon saw how eagerly Laura clung to Crawford's words. He wanted to hurry the investigator along for her sake, but clearly the man enjoyed building anticipation.

"Oh, do go on," Eva snapped. She wasn't as patient as he.

Crawford nodded sheepishly. "Yes, Your Grace. The farmer had lived there all his life and he was quite old. As such, he wasn't reluctant to discuss the elder or current earl with me. He knew both father and son. His own son worked in the earl's stable and was privy to bits of gossip."

He sipped his brandy. "Though his tale was long, and his memory spotty, the basic story was that Westwick's father had bought the place many years ago. He housed a young woman there who was very beautiful. Mary. She was his lover and, according to the farmer, a reluctant lover. She was no more than fifteen and innocent."

This time, Eva did not urge Crawford on. They all took a moment to ponder this. After refreshing his drink, the investigator continued, "Mary was a frail creature, shut up in the house with only the servants and occasional visits from the elder earl to keep her company. She eventually bore him a son, just days before the old earl died."

Laura's stomach pitched. Her heart ached for the young woman not old enough to leave the schoolroom and forced to bear the old man a bastard child.

"How horrible," she said. She felt Simon move up behind her. He placed a hand on her shoulder.

"The farmer said the child was sickly but survived the birth. He was about three months old when the younger Westwick came. He'd discovered the deed and hoped to find a property of some value. Instead he found *her*." He paused. "Without the old earl to pay the bills, the household was slowly decaying and food was becoming scarce. Most of the servants had left, leaving only a few to care for mother and child."

Laura saw Crawford's inward struggle. Some topics were not fit for polite company. Laura braced herself for what was to come.

"Westwick took Mary into his bed. Her already frail mind and body broke. The next morning, she was found in a pond behind the manor. There was some speculation that she hadn't killed herself but was murdered. Regretfully, there was no proof and the last of the servants ran off right after the body was found. The farmer's son took the baby to a foundling hospital and that was the last he was seen."

"Do you think Henry is that boy?" Miss Eva asked.

"Perhaps. Henry would be around the right age. The farmer thought the lad would be about twenty-three or so.

He wasn't certain, as his memories were a bit muddled," Crawford said. "I tried to find the foundling hospital, but the place burned to the ground ten years ago. If there was any information about the child, it was destroyed in the fire."

"Poor child," Laura said. Simon's hand tightened on her shoulder. "Westwick has damaged so many lives. If Henry is his brother, it would explain the darkness in him. The entire family breeds wickedness."

"This would certainly explain why he's focused on Westwick and why Henry had a reason to kill him," Simon added. "If the farmer's tale is correct, then Westwick was only twenty or so himself and already ruining lives. Even if he had no direct hand in killing Mary, he certainly drove her to her death."

The room fell silent. It was a dismal tale with many twists. Laura wished both Westwick and his father were alive to pay for their crimes against Mary. Even if the girl had gone to the elder earl as part of an arrangement, she was far too young to have successfully protested the matter. And Westwick? He would have seen her vulnerability and taken advantage, taking her to his bed as his right.

"We are left with finding Henry." Simon walked to the sideboard and refreshed his glass. "If he is the brother, he might hope to inherit from the estate."

Laura shook her head. "If Westwick didn't care enough for the boy to raise him, and left him to an uncertain fate, he would not be kind enough to leave him a portion in his will."

"I agree," Simon added. "Still, Henry purposefully hunted down Westwick. He might have hoped to gain something from his death. We already think Laura was part of his plan. Perhaps jewelry or property was the financial motivation? There are ways to forge documents."

Laura tucked a stray curl behind her ear. "I wonder if Westwick ever knew the truth about Henry. He never said anything to me and never would have looked into the background of his new friend. As long as Henry showed himself a loyal supporter of depravity and abuse, he'd be welcomed."

"It's also possible the man came to him under false pretenses," Simon added.

"True," His Grace added. "Unless Henry chooses to share his tale, we may never know the true reason he aligned himself with Westwick."

The maid came in with a tray of cakes. She laid them out and withdrew.

Crawford reached for one and took a bite. "We are basing this speculation on Henry being the lost brother. He might be just a man who has an unsavory obsession with Laura."

"And who displayed his poor taste in choosing Westwick for a friend," Miss Eva said.

After a few more minutes of speculation, the party disbursed. Simon and Laura took the duke's coach to the Harrington town house. There was no need to travel in hired hackneys when Henry was well aware of Laura's every movement.

Aunt Bernie was napping when they arrived. The housekeeper explained to Simon that Laura's possessions had been delivered, sparse as they were, and had been put in her room.

Laura looked down at her drab dress, one of many she'd been wearing since she was a girl. Children teetering on the edge of poverty did not wear gowns trimmed in silk ribbon or fine lace. "Once I am no longer a suspect and my life is my own, I will never again wear anything but red satin and silk."

Simon smiled. "You would look lovely in red. Though I suspect you would also look stunning in blue."

She scrunched her face. "Anything but gray, brown, or white." Even when Westwick brought her clothes, they were often well-mended castoffs. He paid out very little money for her upkeep. He'd vowed that would have changed had she been more "agreeable." Not even silk would have made her *that* agreeable. "I want color, lots of deep rich color."

Reaching up, she smoothed his lapel. She enjoyed the feel of him under her hands. What would it be like to love him openly, to be free to choose him as her husband, and to share his bed without censure?

"What do we do now, Simon?" She reluctantly drew her hand back. "All of our clues come to nothing."

Simon cupped a hand on her neck. He toyed with her earlobe. "Crawford will keep looking for Mary's missing son and for new clues. However, I fear we may have to wait for Henry to show himself again. He continues to be our only suspect."

Simon wanted to erase the defeat from her eyes. There had to be a way to lift her spirits. An idea took root.

"Go change into a habit. We are going riding."

Laura paused too long. He spun her around and nudged her toward the stairs. "You have fifteen minutes. Hurry."

He sent a passing maid after her and called for horses. He had just enough time to change himself, with the help of a rushed Dunston, when he met Laura at the top of the stairs.

"Where are we heading?" she asked.

"We have spent too many days thinking about murder and lost souls. We need to spend the rest of our afternoon finding fun." He escorted her down the stairs and out the door. "Now ask no more questions. Just enjoy the lovely day."

Dressed in a blue habit that belonged to Brenna, Laura looked lovely. A matching hat sat atop her upswept hair. She'd been correct. She needed color in her wardrobe.

As he followed her out of the town house, he couldn't help noticing a place at the back of her neck perfect for nibbling.

Perhaps he'd find a private moment today and steal a taste.

A pair of horses stood at the ready with the groom

as they exited the town house. Simon helped her mount a chestnut gelding, then swung himself onto Horse. "Off we go."

The streets were crowded with coaches and carriages, as many residents of the city had the same desire to take advantage of the sunshine. Simon took the fastest route out of town and soon they were free of the bustle.

"Will you tell me our destination?" Laura patted the horse and looked at him askance. Her pretty eyes had brightened considerably already. Being on the back of the fine gelding seemed to put her at ease.

"Patience," he scolded lightly. "You will see soon enough."

They'd ridden for almost an hour when Simon turned Horse and led them through a massive stone gate. Beyond was an estate of a magnitude Laura had never seen. She gaped openly at the stone castle, turrets and all, that sat perched atop a rise.

"What is this place?"

Simon chuckled. "It is the home of the Marquess St. John. One of his ancestors saved the life of a king and was rewarded handsomely for his service."

"Quite handsomely," she repeated in awe. The drive was made of stone, wide enough for two coaches to pass comfortably. They passed by gardens breathtakingly beautiful and well tended as Simon led the horses to a trail that circled right of the castle. "Will the marquess mind us trespassing on his property?"

Simon winked. "He is a close friend of my father."

Laura settled back to enjoy the day. They tied up the horses for a brief sojourn from riding to play in the castle's maze. Laura got terribly lost and Simon rescued her with laughter, kisses, and a nuzzle of that perfect spot on her neck.

"Kisses are always required when a damsel is rescued

from a maze," he said when they finally found their way out. He lowered his head and Laura eagerly kissed him back.

They reclaimed the horses and raced through the endless ribbons of interconnecting trails that covered what must have been hundreds of acres of open land and forests.

Laura's carefree laughter filled the quiet forest as they frightened a quail and startled a pair of deer.

When the horses were lathered and in need of rest, they slowed to a sedate pace and turned back toward the road.

"I don't know when I've last enjoyed myself this much," she said, smiling at her handsome companion. "Truthfully, I have never had this much fun."

Beneath his hat, Simon's eyes were full of mischief. Her heart swelled as they approached the gate. She did love him so!

Simon stopped Horse and locked on to her eyes. "I never tire of hearing your full and unguarded laughter. Today, you have succeeded my expectations splendidly."

Flushed under his attention, she realized he was right. She'd laughed more today than she had in years. He was fully responsible for this happiness. "I've grown weary of frowning. I know that we have much to do before I am completely free, but from this day forward, I promise to laugh at all your jests and smile politely even when I do not find you amusing."

Simon looked put out. "I am always amusing."

Laura made a face. "Only you find yourself so."

He struggled to remain serious, then grinned. "The only person required to amuse me is me. As long as I amuse myself, nothing else should matter."

"Truer words have never been uttered."

He leaned to brace his hand on her knee. "I think you should give me one last kiss before we return to town."

There, beneath a brick and steel arch, Laura pushed herself up from the saddle and met him halfway with a most loving kiss.

* * *

Simon hated to return to the town house. The afternoon was more than he'd imagined. Hearing her laughter and seeing the open happiness in her eyes had pleased him immensely.

It was sometime during those hours that he realized he cared for her as more than a casual friend. Was it love? He wasn't entirely convinced it was. But his affection for her was deepening. Suddenly, he no longer wanted to marry for position. He wanted Laura in whatever form that would take.

He'd skip past Lady Jeanette and get Chester under heel without sacrificing himself. There had to be a way to drag the man before a parson. It was the matter of discovering the man's weakness. Hopefully, by the time his uncle's title came to Simon, Brenna would be married off and no longer his worry.

Mother never liked the idea of him marrying Lady Jeanette. Both his parents wanted their children happy. And Laura wasn't a courtesan, not really, and she loved him. If he did marry her someday, it wouldn't be the worst of the Harrington misdeeds. There was no certainty that her history would ever get out. Besides, the Harrington family could survive another scandal.

Years from now, when he was earl, they'd be long past whispered speculation about how their relationship had come to be.

Looking over at Laura, he felt something that he hadn't felt in a long time. Hope for his future.

First, he needed her free of the murder. He'd not start their life together on a bleak note.

"You've become quiet," she said, drawing her horse to a stop before the stable behind the town house. "Should I worry?"

The groom and a stable boy rushed over to take the reins. Simon dismounted and walked over to swing her down. She brushed against him and he felt her warmth. He wanted to steal a kiss but lack of privacy prevented it. So he took her hand and walked her out of the mews and into the town house garden.

"I've been thinking about you."

She looked at him askance. "Now I am worried," she teased.

Simon narrowed his eyes. "I suspect that no matter how old you become, you'll always be a troublesome wench."

Her eyes flashed. "That is my intention."

Chuckling, he led her around the house. "I have come to a decision. It involves my future." ·

"Oh?"

He nodded. "I have decided not to marry Lady Jeanette." He stopped on the path. Shadows from the town house blocked the late afternoon sun and hid them from view of the windows.

Laura stared at him, clearly puzzled. "When exactly did you make this decision? I thought you were firmly settled on the girl."

He thought of all the reasons why he should keep quiet, marry Jeanette, and forget Laura. And not one of them made sense. "I cannot marry her when I care for someone else."

Her face clouded. "Simon, no." She pulled her hand free and walked over to a nearby bench. She sat. "You have to marry her, or someone like her; if not for your sister, then for yourself. You need a woman of impeccable breeding to bear your children and host your parties and run your massive manor home. You cannot allow your feelings of responsibility for me to distract you from what's important. You will be an earl someday. You need a proper countess."

Simon sat beside her. "You think my feelings for you are due to some misguided sense of responsibility?"

She said nothing.

Exasperation welled. "Isn't it possible that my affection for you has grown not because I saved your life but because I find you fascinating and intelligent and beautiful?"

He watched her stiffen and press a hand to her forehead.

"This cannot be happening." She stood, removed her hat, and looked into his eyes. "My presence has upended your careful plans. Please tell me you haven't considered marrying me." He paused long enough to give her answer. "I will not do it."

She turned and lifted her hem. Simon caught her before she could take a step. He spun her around and pulled her into his arms. He didn't care if the entire household was watching. He kissed her. Hard.

Laura struggled against him for a moment, then went slack. She opened her mouth to deepen the kiss. Simon splayed his hand on her lower back and pulled her closer.

She fit perfectly in his arms. No other woman would ever take her place. Laura was his destiny.

Slowly, he lifted his head. Her eyes were warm as they met his. "I won't marry you, Simon," she whispered.

"Have I asked?" he countered.

Slowly, she lost some starch. "Then we are in agreement. We will speak no more about the matter."

She pulled away and continued down the path and around the house, Simon on her heels.

"I have not agreed to anything," he said. "I will take all the time needed to convince you that a future together is a possibility." He followed her up the steps and moved around her to block the door. "And when I have convinced you that you will make an excellent countess, then I will ask."

Sighing, she shook her head. "You are a stubborn man."

"And yet you love me."

Laura frowned. "It is my deepest regret."

He laughed as he opened the door and they stepped inside the foyer. The once quiet house had been taken over by a bustle of activity. Chaos had erupted during the few hours they were away. Maids rushed about, and from somewhere in the house, he heard weeping. His father stepped out of the parlor and spotted Simon. He walked to him, his face bleak.

Father glanced briefly at Laura and dismissed her. Whatever had sent the house into upheaval was more important than any curiosity Father might have about Laura.

"You've returned early," Simon observed.. His stomach twisted. Something was terribly wrong. This kind of upset could not come from his parents' discovery of a stranger, Laura, living under their roof. There had to be more. "What has happened? Is it Mother? Brenna?"

Father shook his head. "We have received terrible news. Your Uncle Arthur is dead."

Chapter Twenty-Five

❧❧❧

"We aren't sure exactly what happened," Simon's mother, Kathleen, said and dabbed her eyes with a handkerchief as the family gathered in the library. "All we know is that he was attacked by a local man he'd hired as a guide. Apparently there was some dispute over his fee. Arthur was pushed into a river and drowned."

"Uncle Arthur was killed over money?" Simon couldn't believe this was happening. "Arthur was known for being tightfisted. But to be killed over such a thing is a tragedy. . . ." He let his voice trail off. How do you put into words the absurdity of the situation without sounding callous?

"If it is any comfort, the perpetrator was hanged by the British Army," Father said. "They don't take kindly to the death of a peer."

Simon leaned his head back against the chair. The implications of all this were unbelievable. His father was now Lord Seymour. Mother was a countess. Simon was now a titled viscount. Brenna was Lady Brenna. The wealth, the properties, everything held by Arthur was now Father's.

He looked over at his sister. Her red eyes stared back

at him. They'd lost an uncle they never really knew, and their world had changed drastically because of one senseless act.

"Has anyone informed Noelle?" Brenna asked.

"She and her mother have been notified," Father said and walked to the window. Of everyone in the room, he seemed the most disheartened by the news. He'd lost his only remaining brother—first Noelle's father and now Arthur.

"Perhaps you should give us a moment," Mother whispered to her children. Her beautiful face was filled with sadness as she walked to her husband. She slipped her hand into his and leaned against his shoulder.

Simon and Brenna left them. Once in the hallway, they faced each other. "I can't believe Uncle Arthur is dead," Brenna said softly. "He was always the missing earl. I was an infant when he left. Now he is gone forever."

"I should do something for Father." Simon rubbed his jaw. The shock of the news still lingered. "I'll contact Gabriel. He should be with us."

"Do you know where our brother is currently?" Brenna asked.

"The last I heard, Spain." Time was long past for their wayward brother to return. It had been four years since he left to find adventure.

The weight of Simon's new responsibility was staggering. He wasn't certain of his new position, nor could he fathom what all this would mean, for himself or Laura. Becoming a viscount had always been a distant consideration. In a matter of minutes, his life had changed. "Has anyone made arrangements to get Arthur home?"

"The army has taken care of it." Brenna pressed her clasped hands to her mouth. "We will be notified when he arrives in London." Weeping sounded from above. "I should go to Bernie. She has lost her brother."

Brenna went upstairs. Simon felt adrift. He looked up to the second floor and knew he should see to Laura. During the melee, she'd slipped away.

Somehow, he couldn't bring himself to seek her out.

There were preparations to be made and he needed to make certain his father's other sister, Aunt Clara, had been notified of the death. Arthur was her brother, too. His family needed him now, more than Laura did.

With shoulders slumped, he headed toward the library. He really needed a drink.

Laura packed her things and left the house with her valise clutched tightly against her chest. She hailed a hackney at the end of the street and gave him directions to the school.

She pressed her face into her hands. Her heart ached for Simon's family. They'd suffered a great loss. Aunt Bernie was devastated. Laura had sat with her until Simon's sister arrived, then removed herself to pack. She had no place in the household. Not really. It was best she return to the school and leave the Harringtons to grieve privately.

Miss Eva was sipping tea when she arrived. The few remaining courtesans were absent. The house was quiet.

"Simon has sent you back?" Eva asked. She slid her skirts aside so Laura could join her on the settee.

Laura shook her head. "I thought it best if I left. The household is in turmoil. His family is in mourning. He doesn't need questions about me to add to his troubles." Eva poured her tea. She accepted the cup and added some sugar. "I wish I could help him."

Miss Eva nodded. "It is an unusual situation. Arthur has been away so long, he was almost a phantom to his family. Now he's gone. There are some big changes coming."

"There are," Laura agreed sadly.

The duchess glanced sidelong at her. "This changes things for you, too." She refreshed her tea. "I know Simon cares for you, but he is a viscount now. With what little I know about Simon, I suspect he is already feeling torn between the title—and you. Has he made you any promises?"

"No." Laura swallowed deeply. She wondered how much

she should share with Miss Eva. The burden proved too heavy and she explained their earlier conversation. "He left open the possibility of marriage, yet I knew it would never come to fruition. He spoke out of desire, not practicality. We are too far apart in circumstance—now more so than ever. Once he has a chance to see things clearly, he will see that I am right. We are not meant to be together."

The duchess sent her a knowing stare. "I would not be so sure about his intentions. Yes, he is currently in turmoil. However, the Harrington family is not like other members of the Ton. If he wants you, he will have you, in spite of his new title."

Laura frowned. "With time, he'll see reason."

Miss Eva smiled. "Have you ever known a reasonable man when he thinks he is in love?"

"Simon doesn't love me," Laura protested.

"Give him time. He will."

This conversation wasn't as comforting as she'd hoped. She'd thought perhaps the duchess would impart some wisdom about how to discourage Simon. Instead, she seemed to encourage the relationship.

"You don't understand," Laura said firmly. "He is a viscount now. He needs his Lady Jeanette."

"And a duke needed a wife with a perfect pedigree," Miss Eva said lightly. "Sometimes life doesn't work out as planned."

An hour later, Laura went to her room, somewhat comforted by Miss Eva's story of how a courtesan's daughter found love with her duke. Yet Laura was still locked in the muddle that was her life.

She grew weary of uncertainty. She was being stalked by a man who could be a killer. She was living in a courtesan school. She had very little money, two pistols, and an ugly elephant statue. And she was in love with a man who clearly had a knight-in-armor affection for his rescued damsel.

All she could hope for now was that the death of his uncle would make him see her, and his own world, more clearly.

*   *   *

Simon paced. The town house had become a prison. Har-ringtons were arriving daily from far afield and the staff was harried. While trying to ease the burden borne by his parents, the servants relied heavily on his guidance, and the pressure to prove his worth was intense. He bore the weight of his inadequacies with rising frustration. "Three days since Arthur's death and I'm already feeling chains hanging around my neck."

Brenna sat in a chair, watching him. "Father has asked nothing of you. He knows you need time to adjust to your new role as earl-in-waiting."

The censure in her voice brought him upright. He turned to see her scowling at him. He replayed the last few days and realized she was right. Father had taken the full respon-sibility of everything on his own shoulders. Aside from send-ing out a missive to the last known address for Gabriel and directing the staff, he'd done very little.

"This is a shock for all of us and I'm only thinking about myself," he grumbled unhappily. "I thought I had years before I became next in line. We all hoped that Arthur would return to reclaim his position and live a long life."

"Think of how Father feels," Brenna said tightly. "He has lost his two brothers. He never suspected he'd ever lose them both." She tapped her fingers on the chair arms. "Truthfully, I believe you are more worried about losing your mysterious woman than becoming viscount."

After a brief pause, she continued, "I do find her disap-pearance odd. She should be eager to lift herself from com-panion to viscountess."

Simon stopped pacing. He glared. "You know nothing of Laura. She asks nothing of me."

Brenna stood. "I know you placed her as Aunt Bernie's companion and attended several parties with her in tow. You think we didn't hear the rumors? Then we return home and she vanishes. If you expect us to understand what's happening, you could explain yourself."

He raked his hands through his hair. "It is not the time or place for this. There may never be the right time."

Their last moments together played in his mind. Laura assured him marrying Lady Jeanette was his future. He'd refused to consider the notion. Sadly, with his uncle's death, Laura may have been right. Choosing a viscountess was a task not to be entered into lightly.

Without waiting for Brenna to press him further, he walked out of the library.

Laura was gone, his aunt couldn't stop crying, and his father had disappeared into his study with Noelle's mother, estate managers, secretaries, and whoever else might help figure out the jumble of disorganization that was Uncle Arthur's life. Brenna had been wandering London, likely in search of a pirate to father her child, and Mother felt responsible for them all.

The only thing he did know was that Laura was safe for the moment. The school was well guarded. Still, he worried. The only way he'd be confident she was fully protected was if she was with him. Hell, as distracted as he was, not even that was certain. She was best left to the paid guards. For now.

He'd suffered through three days of a headache. Noelle's mother was a harridan who'd somehow taken control over parts of Arthur's life. The rest had fallen to bankers and stewards and Father. Unfortunately, Father hadn't paid the attention he should have to the estate after their oldest brother, Noelle and Eva's father, had died. Arthur had inherited, and as the youngest son, Walter was left to make his own fortune from an inheritance and prudent investments.

Now the whole estate was in disarray, and it would take months to pull it into some semblance of order.

Since the moment they'd received the grim news, the household had been overwhelmed. Simon was overwhelmed. He needed a moment to breathe. He called for Horse and turned him toward the courtesan school.

Neither Sophie nor Eva protested his arrival, as the former led him through the house to the garden. Laura sat in a chair beneath a tree, a book open in her lap, looking devastatingly beautiful in the mottled sunshine.

His heart skipped. Lud, how he'd missed her!

With his attention drawn to her, he barely noted the guard loitering by the back gate as Laura looked up from her reading.

"I had to come," he said awkwardly. She placed the book on the table and rose. Without a word, she slipped into his arms and laid her head on his chest. He lowered his face to her hair and inhaled her sweet scent.

"How is your family?" she asked softly.

"We have fared better." He kissed her head. The headache that had plagued him faded. "I wish you hadn't left."

"I had to." She lifted her face. "Your parents didn't need a stranger in their home while they were dealing with their grief. And how would you have explained me?"

He smiled grimly. "Your leaving didn't silence the questions. They know you were Aunt Bernie's companion, but nothing more. But you're correct. Mother and Father will wait to press the issue of you until after the chaos has settled."

The wind fluttered through the garden, and birds chattered overhead. After days of sober silence and tears, the small space was a welcome respite.

"Is Aunt Bernie well?" Laura eased from his arms and reclaimed her seat. Simon joined her in an open chair.

"As well as she can be. She was closest to Arthur. I believe she hoped one day he'd surprise her and come home. Now she will never see him again."

Laura's eyes clouded. "I am sorry for her loss."

"I will tell her." Aunt Bernie had asked after her. Simon told his aunt that Laura was called away on a family matter.

During the short time they'd been together, Bernie had developed a fondness for Laura, even insisting she call her "Aunt Bernie" as the family did. And his aunt had not once indulged in sherry while under Laura's care. That was an added benefit of placing Laura as her companion.

"His Grace spoke to Crawford last evening. The investigator met with a former footman who knew where Henry was staying before the murder. Crawford went to the inn and missed him by a day. He has vanished again. Fortunately, Crawford has new information as to where Henry might be hiding."

"Surely we can worry about this later," Laura said and took his hand. He rubbed her soft skin with his thumb.

"I need to keep my mind occupied. My father currently refuses my assistance and my mother is caring for relatives who are arriving from all corners of England." He grimaced. "I cannot go back."

Laura sympathized. "I've never had more than my parents. I can only imagine how overwhelming so many family members in one town house can be." In spite of his grumbling about his large family, she envied him. She'd longed for siblings while growing up—sisters to share confidences, brothers to frighten off unsuitable suitors, and cousins to come and fill their small house on holidays.

A pang of longing tugged at her heart.

"Hmm." Simon watched a bird land on a rosebush. "It's odd how life can change in an instant."

"I know that well," she agreed. She wanted to kiss away his hurts, ease his mind, speak wise words to make his situation easier. However, it wasn't her place. Now that he'd taken one step closer to the title, any future for them was impossible. "What will you do now?"

"I will hide here with you for a few hours. Then, I will plunge back into the fray. Hopefully in a few days, when Arthur has been interred in the family crypt, all will settle again."

Laura raked her gaze over him. Her heart squeezed painfully. She hated throwing another topic into the conversation while he was already troubled, but there was no better time. She had to know his thoughts about her.

"No, I meant what will you do now that you are a viscount? You cannot push aside the fact that you are directly in line to inherit. You must plan for your future."

Simon stared thoughtfully at her for a moment. "You are wondering what I intend to do with you?"

If only there were another option. "You cannot hide from your responsibility. Eventually, you will have to say good-bye."

Sadly, he did not deny it. There were too many obstacles to overcome: her past, her poverty, his title, his family, society.

"Must we speak of this now?" he said. "I have many things to worry about in the next few days. My uncle's funeral and catching a killer are only two. Once both have been settled, the picture will be clearer. Until then, I intend to enjoy your company."

Simon left two hours later. Laura was no closer to accepting his loss. She was deeply in love with her viscount. That would never change. However, she had to be practical. The end was bearing down on them. A broken heart was in her future.

Thankfully, he did not love her. One of them had kept a sensible head, and it wasn't she.

"Laura?"

Jane walked toward her, her timing impeccable. Laura wondered if the three remaining courtesans had been watching her and Simon from the window. They were concerned for her.

The courtesans were told only that Laura was in danger through her former patron. This was to explain the guards and to keep them vigilant. Laura hated to put them in this situation.

"Miss Noelle is taking Mariette, Polly, and me shopping. We were wondering if you wanted to join us." Jane glanced at the guard at the gate. "Miss Noelle has arranged for Thomas and a second guard to go with us. You will be perfectly safe."

Her first thought was to refuse. Her second was that she could use a distraction. The tension in the household was nerve fraying for everyone.

Besides, how could she win over her fear while hiding away at the school? "I would like that very much." She reclaimed her book and followed Jane into the house.

Laura didn't know Polly well. The blue-eyed blonde was almost as shy as Jane. With everything happening in her own life, Laura hadn't taken the time to get to know the young woman as perhaps she should have. Now it was too late.

Bess and two other former courtesans had already married and were gone. Polly was matched and marrying tomorrow, and Mariette and Jane were in final arrangements to do the same, sometime that week or next. Soon the house would be empty but for Sophie and the small staff. Laura knew she'd miss them all very much.

The positive of their leaving was getting them out of harm's way. The negative was losing their companionship.

"I thought the ladies would enjoy an outing," Miss Noelle said as she pulled on her gloves. "It will be their last as unmarried women."

Laura's eyes met hers. Tension had etched lines around Miss Noelle's eyes. Laura realized the frivolous shopping day was as much for the courtesan rescuer as for the courtesans.

"I cannot believe I will be a wife soon," Jane said. Her excitement lifted spirits all around.

Laura smiled, relieved for the lightened mood. "Mister Adams is an ideal match for you, Jane. He is clearly smitten."

Jane flushed. "I am as well." The sweet-natured courtesan would make Mister Adams a wonderful wife.

"My Mister Albert has readied his home in Bath for my arrival," Polly said with ill-concealed excitement of her own. "He assures me that his children are eager to meet me. Since his wife died, the poor little dears have been left in the care of a nurse. I cannot wait to be their mother."

This was the first time Laura had heard of this. She

knew Polly's Mister Albert had two very young children. She didn't know that Polly looked forward to motherhood with such enthusiasm. Her respect grew.

"You will make them an excellent mother," Mariette said. "And they will adore you."

Polly smiled shyly as Miss Noelle shooed them out the door and into the coach. "I do love children."

Bond Street was relatively quiet when the five women arrived a short time later. For the next several hours, they went from shop to shop with no destination in mind. They looked at gowns, hats, and gloves. Small purchases were made. Even Laura managed to find a pair of lace gloves for herself.

"I had reservations about inviting you today," Miss Noelle said to Laura during a private moment. "However, you appeared so forlorn these last few days. I worried that you might slip into melancholia without a distraction."

Laura toyed with the fine white gloves. "You need not fear for my sanity. I am quite hale." She paused and sighed. "I do fret about how my situation will affect the school, Simon, everyone. I could not have imagined how the repercussions of my escape would negatively affect the people I'd meet henceforth."

"Posh." Miss Noelle lifted a scarf to the light. "None of this is your doing. Now, let us think of something else. Oh, look at that yellow fabric. . . ."

Smiling, Laura followed her across the store and temporarily forgot her troubles.

Thomas kept watch and carried the packages to the coach. The other man lingered, out of sight, on the ready to protect Laura should the need arise. Nearing the close of their shopping day, they went into a milliner's shop after Miss Noelle spotted a hat adorned with ostrich feathers in the window.

The last one to enter the shop, Laura paused to look up the street for Thomas. He was taking a long time to reappear.

Disquiet settled over her. With a killer still free, she'd

taken comfort in the presence of the servant. It was late afternoon and people were now filling the street. She hoped he hadn't gotten turned about somehow and lost them.

She let the door close and stepped back onto the walk. She'd wait for him outside in case her hunch was correct.

Minutes ticked by. No Thomas. Worried, she decided to walk back to the coach. With the street full of shoppers, she didn't fear for her safety. And she knew the guard was nearby.

The unadorned coach wasn't hard to find in a row of fancy equipages. Miss Eva didn't like to draw attention to her ladies. Laura waited for a moment for the street to clear before readying herself to dash across.

A sound brought her upright. She turned to see a young girl of no more than eight or nine, standing near an alley at the side of the milliner's shop. Her tiny face was clearly distressed. By her clothing, Laura suspected she was poor and was probably begging for coins.

Laura had heard that some parents beat their children when they didn't earn their keep. If giving a few coins to the child would keep her from harm, Laura would be happy to oblige.

She reached into her reticule and walked toward the girl. As she approached, her heart tugged at the sight of dirt-smudged cheeks and a frayed coat.

"All is well, dearest." She held out a coin. It was then that Laura noticed there was blood on her coat, near the child's wrist. "You've hurt yourself."

She cleared the last few steps when the girl spun and darted down the alley. Surprised, Laura stood rooted to the spot. She looked around for Thomas with a tug of apprehension. He was nowhere in sight.

The girl needed tending. A killer was lurking. A war raged in her mind. The child won over her fear.

Cautiously, she walked forward. The alley wasn't deep and there was no hint of danger. She saw the girl slumped against a wall with her injured wrist cupped in her other hand.

The child stared helplessly up at Laura.

"How did you get such a cut?" she asked gently. The girl flinched against the wall as Laura approached. "Let me have a look and perhaps I can make it feel better."

Truthfully, she had no idea what she would do with the child. She had very little experience with children. Still, she had to do something to aid her.

The girl clutched the injured arm tightly against her body. She opened her mouth to speak, and when she did, the words were not words at all but gibberish. Laura realized immediately that the girl was mute.

Sympathy and pity welled. She forgot everything else but seeing to the child as she knelt in front of her. "Everything will be fine. Now let me see your hand." The girl shook her head. Laura smiled. "Please?"

With some hesitation, the child finally held out her hand. Thankfully the cut wasn't deep. But Laura was shocked to discover that it was straight edged, as if made by a sharp tool.

"Did someone do this to you, dearest?" It horrified Laura to think that anyone could intentionally hurt the little one.

The girl met her eyes and nodded slowly. Outrage welled in Laura. She needed to get the child out of the filthy alley and find some help. Miss Noelle would know what to do.

A sound grabbed her attention. The girl pointed behind Laura and rolled into a tight ball.

"I knew you couldn't resist her."

Chapter Twenty-Six

※

Laura's stomach lurched. She knew the voice. Henry. She'd allowed herself to be led into a trap.

He was the one who'd hurt the girl. Somehow he'd known about the shopping outing and had lain in wait for a chance to get her alone. Leading her into the alley had been well planned.

"How did you know how to find me? Who is the girl? Why would you hurt an innocent?" she asked, the questions tumbling from her. She did not turn to him but stayed crouched in front of the girl to shield her from further harm.

Laura looked around for a weapon in the filth. There was very little to use for protection.

The closest thing to a weapon was a shard of glass just out of reach. It wasn't large, but if she could get to it, the sharp points just might persuade him to back away.

"If I told you my secrets, then you would take the measures needed to protect yourself." There was a sneer in his voice. "It is great fun to know that I can take you whenever I wish."

Sickening dread washed through Laura. She looked

down at the girl and then at the glass. "Please do not hurt us." She hoped the weakness she portrayed in her voice would be enough to make him believe that she would not fight him.

He chuckled. "Oh, my dear Laura. You have no idea what I plan for you—"

Any further verbal torment was cut off as Laura lunged forward on her knees and closed her gloved hand over the shard. Without pause, she spun around, gained her feet, and swung the piece out like a saber.

Partially masked, Henry's eyes widened in surprise.

"I fear you will have to change your plans," she sneered. "I have no intention of playing your game."

An ugly leer split his face as his eyes casually dropped to her breasts. Her flesh recoiled, but she didn't waver.

In his hand was a knife. If he lunged for her, she wasn't certain she could escape unharmed. The shard would provide very little protection from the knife and his greater strength.

"We are at a stalemate," he said, snorting. "Bravo. You have won a point. But I intend to win the match."

"Then you will be sadly disappointed, for I intend to see you hang."

His confidence briefly faltered. He quickly recovered.

"*Tsk-tsk*. And I thought we were friends. It saddens me to know that you do not share my affection." He skimmed his gaze over her face. "If you put down the shard, we can speak calmly about my expectations for you."

She tightened her grip. She felt the sharp edges through her glove. "Or perhaps *you* should give yourself over to the authorities. I think the Bow Street Runners would be pleased with your confession. Unfortunately, they have focused too long on the wrong suspect."

They stood facing each other, each armed and unwilling to stand down. Laura sensed his arrogance and knew that if she showed fear, he would win.

"Come to me, lamb," he said to the child. He cocked his finger. The girl whimpered.

"Stay put," Laura commanded. She clutched the glass. It shook slightly in her hand. "Touch her again and I will carve you up like a goose."

His eyes darkened. He took a step forward, just out of reach, yet close enough for Laura to see the sweat dotting his lip. Perhaps he was not as confident as he portrayed.

He bit out through clenched teeth, "I will enjoy torturing the defiance out of you."

"You will never get the chance."

It was the intervention of a stranger that ruined Henry's plans. "What is happening here?"

The voice drifted from the street and Henry jumped. The girl skittered out from behind Laura and ran down and out of the alley.

Laura's relief to see the child safely away diverted her attention from Henry for only a blink, but it was enough for him to take advantage. She felt pressure on her arm and swung her attention back. Henry fled like a startled hare seconds after she felt her arm sting. She looked down to see that in that instant of distraction, he'd cut her.

The pain quickly followed, though it wasn't great. The cut was no more than a scratch.

Dropping the shard, she hurried from the alley. The stranger who'd spoken was elderly, but he held his cane with a young man's grip. Clearly he'd planned to help her if Henry hadn't run off.

"He has hurt you." The stranger took her hand and looked at the wound. "You must get that cleaned and bandaged."

"I will." She clutched her arm and met his eyes. "Thank you for your assistance, sir."

"Laura?" She looked past the stranger to see Simon bearing down on them. He glanced from her to the stranger and back. "I spotted the coach and found Thomas inside with a lump on his head. I worried for your safety."

"Is Thomas badly hurt?" she asked.

"Thankfully, no. He was rousing when I found him." His gaze dropped downward. "Lud. What happened to your arm?"

She shook her head. "In a moment." She turned to the stranger, only to discover he'd gone. Disappointed, she sighed. "Please take me to the coach and I will explain."

In a matter of minutes, Simon sent an angry Thomas off to find Miss Noelle and the courtesans, and Laura was settled on the coach seat. The women arrived in a flurry of concerned chatter.

"Where is the guard?" Miss Noelle said angrily as she climbed into the coach.

"There is no sign of him," Thomas explained. He helped the courtesans inside. "He seems to have vanished."

There was no time for further explanation or speculation as the coach, Thomas at the reins, was off to Cheapside.

Once Laura, Simon, and Miss Noelle were settled into the parlor, with Sophie getting bandaging and salve, Laura told the full story. When she'd finished, Simon was fit to murder and Miss Noelle was livid.

"The bastard hurt a child and used her to spring a trap." Simon's check pulsed. "I will wring his scrawny neck."

He tore open Laura's sleeve to expose the cut as Sophie returned with the items. All four looked at the wound. As Laura suspected, it was a scratch.

"He could have done much worse," Laura said.

Sophie scowled. "He's marked you. Every time you look at the wound, you will think of him. It is his way of possessing you."

Three pairs of eyes stared. Sophie shrugged. "I once knew a woman whose lover bit her. He told her that his marks were a way to warn off anyone who'd seek her bed. They were proof that she belonged to him."

"Animals are marked in a way to prove ownership," Simon added. He clenched his fists. "I'll kill him."

Miss Noelle placed Laura's arm on her lap and began to dress the wound. "You will have to line up behind me. No one hurts one of my young ladies. I will hang him myself."

Laura smiled at the fierce protectiveness in her face. "You will both have to wait for your revenge. I'm first to extract my own chunk of flesh." She winced slightly as the salve stung. Miss Noelle wrapped the strips of cloth around her arm and tucked the ends under.

"It should heal nicely. In a week or so, it should fade away." She squeezed Laura's hand. "It was a terrible idea to take you out. This would not have happened had I been sensible."

Laura covered her hand with hers and shook her head. "This wasn't your fault. It was daylight on a well-traveled street. I was only a few steps outside when I spotted the girl. The alley wasn't deep and I saw no threat. He must have been hiding in a doorway." She stood and walked to the window.

"He has had several chances to kidnap or kill me, yet he only threatens," Laura said. "I do not understand his hesitation to finish this. By waiting, he risks much." Henry was taking dangerous chances with his life. Had Simon or Thomas found them together, instead of the elderly gentleman, they likely would have killed him.

Simon nodded. "I think your terror drives him. He darts in and out, leaving you fearful of what he may do next. He'll not hurt you until he is ready to finish the game."

"This man is far more devious than we suspected," Laura said. "I wish I knew what was driving him to such desperation." She spun to face the trio. "It isn't just a great desire for me. I saw no hint of lust in his eyes."

"Did he say anything helpful?" Simon asked.

"No. But bedding me is not his greatest goal." Laura paced. She struggled to put together what he said during their two encounters and find some link, a hint to solve the riddle. There was nothing. "Whatever his intentions are, he's keeping them secret."

Simon walked to her. "There was a reason I came to Bond Street seeking you out. After an exhaustive search of inns, and your sketch in hand, Crawford has discovered where he thinks Henry is staying. He, His Grace, and I have decided to go there tonight. We hope to finally catch Henry."

The previous day, Laura had met with the artist who did the sketches for Miss Eva's Husbands Book. She did her best to explain Henry's face and was satisfied with the drawing. After the artist left, Simon had sent off the sketch to Crawford.

"Crawford saw him there?" Miss Noelle interjected.

"Unfortunately, no. He was likely out putting together this attack on Laura." Simon's voice trailed off. "How did he know where you would be today? In order to use the girl, he had to be forewarned of your intentions. He couldn't get the information from peering into windows."

Miss Noelle's eyes widened. "No one outside of this household knew of our plans. The idea for an outing came to me after breakfast, and I didn't confirm the plan until about an hour before we left."

"Then you have a spy under this roof," he said.

The household was soon awhirl. Simon had sent for His Grace and Miss Eva, and the two men interrogated everyone until the courtesans and the maid were in tears and even the normally unflappable cook was frazzled. Thomas had fully recovered—headache aside—from the surprise attack and took the questions stoically. Primm answered with affronted dignity.

"I cannot believe that a monster has breached the serenity of this household," Noelle said. "Could the spy be the guard? He is still missing."

"It is possible," Simon answered. "Until we find him, everyone must be considered a suspect."

When the interviews were over, Laura, Simon, and the duke and duchess were convinced that the home was secure. If anyone had given information to Henry, it hadn't been a member of the household staff.

"I didn't feel deceit from anyone." Simon raked his hands through his hair. "Yet we are certain that someone from here has spoken to Henry. There is no other explanation."

Miss Eva walked over to close the parlor doors. "My staff

has worked for me for years, save Sophie and Thomas, and I trust him with our lives."

"I understand Sophie's loyalty. Why Thomas?" Simon asked. "How did he come to be employed here?"

She sat on the settee beside Laura. "He came from a desperately poor family. At fifteen, he became a soldier to earn income for his family. Sadly, it wasn't enough. While he was in the peninsula, his older sister sold herself to a wealthy merchant. Thomas was devastated."

Laura understood poverty. "How sad."

Miss Eva nodded. "Though she'd chosen her path, she couldn't live with what she'd done. After their parents died, she ran away from her lover and came here. I matched her. She now lives just outside London with her husband. According to Thomas, she is content."

The duke turned to Simon. "Thomas is fiercely loyal to my wife. He would never cause her, or the courtesans, any harm."

It wasn't difficult to see why Miss Eva earned such devotion, Laura thought. She took women out of difficult situations and gave them new lives.

Soon, Laura would ask for assistance finding employment. Taking a position would both offer independence and free Simon from his vow to protect her. He could wed Lady Jeanette without worry.

The duchess knew many people throughout London and beyond. If there was a position open where she could use her household skills to support herself, Her Grace would be able to find it for her.

Laura glanced at Simon. Until then, she would consider every moment with him a gift.

"I am satisfied that we have disrupted this household for naught," Miss Eva said, coming to her feet. "I am off to soothe ruffled feathers. If you will excuse me."

Once the duchess had retreated, the topic turned to Crawford and his discovery. Miss Noelle listened with alarm growing on her face. She turned to Laura. "I didn't realize the full gravity of this situation. You must watch yourself."

"I will. My mistake today will not be repeated." She still worried about the child. Perhaps she could ask Crawford to see what he could find out about her. A mute child would be noticed. It shouldn't be difficult to uncover her identity.

"The innkeeper has looked at the sketch and assured Crawford that it is the same man who took a room three days ago," Simon interjected. "If we are to catch him, this will be our best opportunity."

"Then we will ready ourselves," the duke replied. "I will hire a hackney and pick you up at your town house at ten. It should be dark enough then to spy without alerting our prey."

Simon nodded. "With luck, we will turn him over to the Runners by morning."

Chapter Twenty-Seven

❧❧❧

Simon sent a footman to make a sweep around the Harrington town house for spies as he collected his hat. Though he was certain that Henry was watching Laura, and they'd taken added steps to secure the school, he had to be cautious. They couldn't take a chance that Henry was watching him, too, and would discover they were on his trail by following Simon and His Grace to the inn.

Surprise had to be their advantage if they were to catch him.

"Are you certain the school is now secure?" His Grace said. "The guards hired previously proved to be woefully inadequate. Henry still managed to get to Laura."

"That is why they were let go. The new guards are retired soldiers and trained fighters. Henry will not dare approach the school," Simon said. "I think we are ready for every event."

"Why were they not hired first?"

"I just learned of their existence through a friend," Simon replied. "I am confident there will be no further trouble at the school. I only wish I could convince Laura to stay here, with me."

A few minutes later the footman returned to report that nothing suspicious was found around the town house.

"Then we are off," the duke said and led the way.

The night was dark and quiet, with only an occasional coach clomping down the street to break the silence. There was a ball at Havenwood House, and most of the neighborhood citizenry were in attendance.

His Grace paused for one last look around as Simon climbed inside the hackney. It took a second for his eyes to adjust to the darkness. When they did, he startled. Seated farthest from the door, pressed against the wall as if doing so would hide her from sight, was a slight figure in a homespun coat and breeches.

He knew her instantly. "Laura."

Dropping into the seat opposite her, he waited for His Grace to join them. A pair of dark brows went up as the duke took note of their uninvited guest.

"I see we have a visitor," the duke muttered and called for the driver to stay put. He settled back and crossed his arms. "Shall I toss her out, or will you?"

Simon scowled. "Please allow me. I know the perfect bush to assure her a prickly landing."

Her eyes narrowed. "If either of you places so much as a finger on me, I shall scream so loudly that your ears will suffer for a week."

The two men glanced at each other and back at her.

"Why are you here, Laura? Haven't you had enough danger for one day?" Simon's scowl deepened. "How did you get past the guards at the school? Does Eva know of this little adventure?"

"Miss Eva knows nothing and I left a note for Sophie before I escaped out so she won't worry. The new guards were more challenging." She smiled, her eyes alight with mischief. "After spending weeks in that garden, I knew which bushes could provide effective cover in the darkness. Then I had to wait for one of them to look away long enough to sneak out the garden gate and into the mews."

"You are lucky Henry wasn't waiting for you," Simon growled. "He could have taken you with no one the wiser."

The smile faded. "I am not silly-minded enough to chance my life," she snapped. "I had a hackney waiting at the end of the street. And before I took a single step away from the garden gate, I made certain no one was watching. Besides, Henry would have to be a fool to lurk anywhere near the school. You must have hired a full dozen men to watch over us."

"Clearly a dozen was not enough," Simon grumbled. "And you still haven't explained why you're here."

Laura glanced from Simon to His Grace and back. Simon knew the answer but wanted to hear it from her. Then he could refuse and toss her into the aforementioned bush.

There was no hesitation. "Why, I'm coming with you, of course."

He knew his fearless Laura well enough to know that she had made up her mind. She'd also need to convince the duke to take her side in the matter. Once she had His Grace convinced to allow her to tag along, she'd have a two versus one advantage.

"It's too dangerous," His Grace said.

"I agree," Simon insisted. "I shall hire a coach to return you to the school."

Pointedly ignoring him, Laura leveled her pleading gaze on the duke. "Surely you can understand my need to correct the wrong that has been perpetrated upon me, Your Grace. If Miss Eva had been mistakenly accused of murder, wouldn't she do anything to clear her good name?"

"His Grace would never allow his wife to put herself in danger," Simon interjected.

Laura frowned. "What would he do? Keep her caged?"

They glared at each other. Her gaze didn't waver. Her spine was made of steel bars.

A grin broke from His Grace. "The point is taken, and she does know Henry better than anyone."

The duke was turning in her favor. Simon would get no more help there.

"I spent over a year cowering, wondering which blow might prove fatal. I'll not cower again." Laura drew in a deep breath. "Henry is the devil, hurting women and children for his game. I do not fear him anymore."

The urge to shake her warred with his desire to kiss her pretty mouth. She knew the danger of her situation, yet she wanted to play a part in Henry's capture.

Admiration welled. Yet as strong as she was, he still worried. He couldn't bear it if she came to harm.

She kept her eyes locked on Simon and expelled an exasperated breath. "I am either going with you," she stated, "or following behind. Watching over me will be easier if I ride with you. Not that I need watching. But if it makes you feel better to think of yourself as my protector, who am I to argue?"

Laugher sputtered out of His Grace. "Do let her come, Harrington. She will add a measure of liveliness to our little trio."

Simon's glare deepened. "I shall remind you of those words the next time Eva runs off to rescue one of her courtesans. Then we shall see if you don't drag out that cage."

The duke grinned. "If I have learned anything about women in the time I've spent with my headstrong wife, it is that she seldom heeds my counsel when dealing with her courtesans. Though I have extracted the promise that if there is ever a need for another rescue, I would like to learn of it before she trots off on Muffin."

Laura smiled at the image. "Then you can understand why I want to go with you tonight. I know Henry and am angry enough to clock him with a candlestick." She pushed back Primm's cap, which she'd used to cover her hair. It was too big and wanted to slide down over her eyes. "But I promise to behave."

Skepticism and frustration etched lines around Simon's mouth. "When have you ever behaved?"

Her smile turned saucy. "You'll just have to trust me."

* * *

The inn was raucous, filled with sailors, merchants, and travelers from all over the world. It was far enough from the wharf to keep from bearing the brunt of the bitter winds that would come with winter, but close enough to draw in the oddly mixed crowd for ale and trouble.

Laura resisted the urge to lean into Simon as a sailor stumbled toward the door, nearly knocking her over.

The man had a prostitute tucked tightly under his arm. The woman gaped at Simon and the duke, taking their measure in spite of their worn clothes. For a moment it looked as if she would send her companion away for a better class of client, then thought better of it when both men scowled. She and her sailor vanished into the night.

Simon stepped farther inside, with Laura following closely behind. A fascinating new world was displayed before her.

Laura's face flushed at the sight of scantily clad women speaking to the men with language that would make the bishop blush. Yet her heart filled with excitement at this risky adventure.

Keeping her cap low and her hair secured inside it, she hoped the borrowed clothing would make her appear like a cabin or stable boy. From beneath the brim, she immediately scanned the crowd for Henry.

It was a difficult task made worse when a pair of large breasts stepped into her line of vision to block her view.

She slowly lifted her eyes up to see a painted visage on the tallest woman she'd ever seen. The woman was nearly the same height as Simon and His Grace but had curves that went on forever.

Laura gulped as the woman reached out a hand and ran a long fingernail down her cheek. She smelled of ale and sex. "Ye are a young one," she said saucily as she raked her eyes up and down Laura. "By yer blush, I think ye are yet untried. I'll give ye a free ride if ye'll let me be yer first."

Beneath the cap, Laura's face burned.

"Be off, woman," Simon barked and stepped between them. "There are other men here to pester."

The prostitute shrugged and flounced away.

"I shouldn't have brought you here," Simon growled. "This is no place for a lady."

"I brought myself, remember?" she said, stunned by the encounter. "I have never been propositioned by a woman, and never by an Amazon certainly." Laura's mouth twitched. "I will remember this night always."

He shook his head. "You are an odd chit. Most young women of good breeding would be horrified by all of this, but not you. You see this as an adventure."

"Oh, I am horrified, shocked, and terrified that at any moment, Henry will appear brandishing his blade and murder me where I stand. Until then, I intend to make memories and live my life as if every moment is my last."

For a pause, he looked into her eyes. Then, "If there wasn't a chance that I'd be arrested for crimes against morality with my stable boy, I'd kiss you now."

Their eyes locked and she winked. "And I'd let you."

Everything outside of the two of them faded into a whirl of color. It took a drunkard with his voice spewing out a very loud and slurred ditty to remind Laura where they were.

"Later," she promised.

Sobering, Simon stepped back. "We should take our post."

He led the way to a corner near the staircase and called for ale. When the tavern wench ambled away, he leaned down to be heard above the din.

"Are you certain Henry will come?" Laura asked. "Surely he will not stay in one place long."

"Crawford confirmed with the innkeeper that Henry is staying here and paid up for tonight. There is no reason to believe he will not return."

They stared out into the room. The crowd was a seedy mix. It was a perfect hiding place.

"His Grace should have found Crawford by now and let

him know we're in place," Simon added. "They'll watch for Henry at the front and back entrances. If you see anyone you think is the bastard, point him out, even if you are not immediately certain. He could be disguised."

"I will." Laura began to scan the room. The large space was filled with faces, none of them Henry's, but she refused to lose hope. It was still early and people were arriving steadily. Simon sipped his ale as she casually leaned against the wall and kept her head down. "What happens if we catch him?"

"Crawford will question him for a confession, then turn him over to the Runners." A woman sauntered past, her eyes raking over Simon. He ignored the blatant invitation.

"And what if we're wrong and he isn't the killer after all?" Laura's stomach soured. "If Henry is nothing more than a man obsessed with me, then our investigation of him will be in vain."

Simon looked down at her. "It's possible, though unlikely. We have seen nothing to indicate another man was involved. All clues point directly to him."

Laura nibbled a thumbnail. A man walked in and her breath caught. When he turned his face toward the light, she slumped back. It wasn't Henry.

The night continued on in much the same manner for an hour, then two. Laura pointed out men that could be Henry, and Simon would head off for a closer look. When midnight approached and still no sign of him, Laura started to twitch. Her legs were weary from standing and her patience grew thin. The room was hot and the stench of questionable hygiene overwhelmed her.

She tried to catch Simon's eye across the room, hoping they could finish up and return home. She was ready to admit defeat.

He was closing in on her latest suspect, but she knew it unlikely that the man was him. The coloring was the same, but his carriage wasn't. Henry had a long-boned walk that this man didn't have.

Several men pushed in through the open door and Laura

settled strained eyes on them one by one as they headed off in different directions. It was the fourth man who stepped over the threshold who brought her upright, her senses alert.

Henry. Though he was unshaven, she knew him instantly. She'd not forgotten his face.

Trying to keep watch over him and searching desperately for Simon in the crush, her eyes darted back and forth. Henry crossed the room, elbowing aside a prostitute who had the misfortune of approaching, and headed for the staircase.

Laura turned her face toward the wall as he passed. He took the stairs up and disappeared.

Following his trail, she paused on the first step and turned to find Simon.

He was heading in her direction, the advance slowed by a group of men shouting at one another. The argument built in intensity as the shouts dissolved into shoving.

Clearly impatient to return to Laura, Simon stepped sideways to avoid a stumbling figure and hurried toward her. She tipped her head, indicating her intention, and hurried up the stairs.

Earlier, the innkeeper had given Crawford the room information and he'd passed it on to Simon. Laura quietly walked the dim and narrow corridor, stepping gingerly to avoid tripping over an uneven floorboard.

Careful not to arouse suspicion, Laura leaned an ear against the door as Simon came up behind her.

"It's him," she whispered.

A door farther down squeaked open, and a man and woman stumbled into the hallway. They moved off toward the staircase and vanished from sight.

"Are you certain?" Simon whispered. He leaned to listen at the door. There were sounds of movement inside.

"Completely."

Without another word or any indication of his plans, Simon pulled her away from the door, stepped back, and kicked the panel open with a crash.

Henry cried out as Simon and Laura spilled into the room. However, his stunned surprise lasted only for a moment. He lurched into motion and dove for the open window.

Simon was fast, but Henry had fear driving him onward. Simon caught his boot as he scrambled over the sash. Laura rushed over and clawed at Henry's trouser leg for a handhold. Unfortunately, his flailing and falling body jerked the leg free. There was a cry as Henry hit the ground below.

His Grace appeared in the doorway as Simon went out the window behind him, feet first. "It's Henry," Laura cried.

"I saw him enter the inn." His Grace bolted for the window and leaned out. "He was moving too fast for me to catch up with him."

Laura wasted no time dawdling. She spun and ran out the door, along the corridor, and down the stairs. His Grace brushed past her on the landing, shoving bodies out of his way and moving Laura forward in his wake.

The cool night air hit her face when they pushed out the doors and into the street. They paused long enough to see a pair of men running in the distance, with a third not far behind. The uneven gait was Crawford's.

His Grace bolted after them, Laura at his heels.

Night encompassed them away from the lit inn, and yet they didn't slow. There were shouts ahead and Laura recognized Simon's voice. They rounded a warehouse and Laura smelled the brackish Thames on the breeze. Henry was heading for the wharf.

"Stand back," Henry cried out. The pair made a last turn and discovered that the chase had ended. Laura and His Grace lurched to a halt behind Crawford.

Henry stood on the pier, a gun in his hand, pointed at Simon. Simon had his hands out, palms up.

"You have nowhere to go, Henry." Simon's voice was surprisingly calm. "If you shoot me, you will hang."

Henry's face contorted with pain. Laura realized he'd hurt himself when he'd hit the ground. How much, she couldn't tell, but he was rubbing one thigh with his free hand.

"To hang me, you have to catch me." He fired, turned, and jumped into the Thames.

Laura cried out and ran to Simon. He caught her against him. "I am unhurt, love. The shot went wide."

Unwilling to take his word, she pulled back and quickly assessed him from head to toe. Then she stepped back into his embrace. He pressed his lips to her temple.

"You gave me a fright," she scolded. "He could have shot you at any time during the chase." They turned to see Crawford and His Grace searching the darkened water for Henry.

"I gave you a fright? I thought you were going out the window with Henry. You had quite a grip on his leg." He lifted her face. "You are positively fearless." He kissed her soundly.

"I did not need my knife," she said, easing back. "Everything happened so quickly."

"He *is* a slippery fellow," Simon agreed and kissed her again. She clutched his coat, her strength slowly fading.

"There is no sign of him," Crawford said as he and the duke returned. "If he didn't drown, then he's made his escape."

Chapter Twenty-Eight

❧

The night brought dreams of Henry, choked in seaweed, reaching up for Laura from the depths of the Thames. She woke up at two in the morning, drenched in a chill sweat, her body shaking.

The dream had felt real, down to his cold dead hand locked on to her wrist.

Worried that he'd survived the river and had come back for her, she rushed to the window and scanned the garden. Seeing nothing to cause alarm, she ran barefoot down the stairs to peer out every window of every unoccupied room of the school.

"Nothing," she whispered. She proceeded to backtrack, checking the locks. The school was secure, with guards watching the perimeter, just out of sight.

Feeling foolish, she returned to her room for a few more hours of restless sleep.

You have a visitor, Laura," Sophie said later that afternoon in the garden. "It is Lady Seymour."

Laura frowned. "Lady Seymour?" According to Simon,

there were Harringtons all over England. But how many Harrington women would know about the school and travel to Cheapside to see her? One by her calculation. Her heart dipped. "It cannot be Simon's mother."

"She didn't say," Sophie replied. "I'm not privy to any further information."

Laura stood and walked up the garden path to the back door. As she passed through the kitchen and into the hallway, she stopped briefly to check herself in a mirror over a hall table. Outside of sleep-rimmed red eyes, she looked reasonably presentable—if she were entertaining a flower vender or a shopkeeper.

If the guest was indeed the countess, Laura was badly in need of the attentions of an experienced maid.

Sadly, she lacked both a ladies maid and a fancy dress to change into. And decent breeding left her knowing it was rude to dash off and hide. She'd have to face the countess with pride and courage.

With a sigh, she stopped outside the parlor, smoothed her dress, and stepped into the open doorway.

Lady Seymour was not a matronly mother, nor was she a pinch-faced noblewoman in a too-tight corset. The woman was lovely in a simple blue day dress. As she sipped her tea and chatted with Miss Eva, her smiles were warm and genuine.

Remembering the story Simon told her about how his parents met, Laura could easily see why Simon's father had been so enamored of Kathleen that he'd married her the day they met.

It was the countess who first spotted Laura in the doorway. Her smile faded to open curiosity as she seemed to take Laura's measure.

Any discomfort Laura felt notched up with each ticktock of the clock. Miss Eva sat quietly, watching them both, with a half smile on her face.

"Please come and join us, Miss Prescott," Lady Seymour said finally. She slid over on the settee.

"Yes, My Lady." She squelched a resigned sigh.

Laura braced herself and took a seat beside Simon's mother. She clasped her hands primly in her lap and waited.

"You are not at all what I expected," the countess admitted. "I'd heard that there was a woman in Simon's life and thought he'd finally chosen a wife. It came as a surprise to discover she was the same woman who was Aunt Bernie's new companion." Lady Harrington paused. "It was through gathering bits of information from my aunt and the staff and then pressing my son for details that I discovered you were not my future daughter but a mysterious woman my son helped flee a difficult situation."

"I am anything but mysterious, My Lady," Laura countered gently. "I am just a poor squire's daughter who became the victim of an unfortunate situation."

"So I understand." Lady Seymour set down her teacup. "My son has an attachment to you."

"He has placed himself in the position of my champion. Nothing more," Laura assured her. She was certain any feelings Simon had for her would fade once the case was finished. "Since my rescue, he has decided that he is the one person who can disentangle me from this unacceptable situation."

"Hmm." Lady Seymour glanced at Miss Eva. "Would you excuse us for a moment?"

Miss Eva smiled and stood. "Of course."

When they were alone, the countess turned in the seat to face Laura fully. "I think you underestimate my son. There is something about you that has pricked his interest as no other woman has."

"You must know that I expect nothing from him."

Lady Seymour nodded. She held Laura's gaze. After a moment she said, "Will you tell me your story?"

Laura wanted to refuse. It was kindness in the woman's eyes that finally led her to agree. Her history had been told many times of late. What would one more time matter?

"It is an unhappy tale. Not the sort of story one usually shares over tea."

"Please," Lady Seymour urged.

For the next half hour, Laura told Simon's mother about her life. There was little she left out, including the murder. When she was finished, she slumped back in the settee, completely depleted of emotion.

"As you can see, I am nearly penniless and am certainly homeless. I am living off the kindness of Miss Eva. No matter how many loaves of bread I bake or dresses I wash, I will never be able to repay her for all she's done for me."

"I don't believe Miss Eva expects repayment."

"No, she does not," Laura agreed. "As for your son, I care very much for him. However, he is not in my plans for my future. Our lives are too divergent."

"You are a sensible young woman." The countess pulled on her gloves and stood. "Perhaps you should wait until after the case has been resolved before you firm up any plans. You cannot know what the future holds." She smiled. "It was a pleasure to meet you, Miss Prescott."

Laura watched her walk from the room.

She waited until the door closed behind Simon's mother before she dumped several lumps of sugar into her tea with shaking hands, swallowed down the sweet concoction to calm herself, and puzzled over the exchange.

Lady Seymour left her with as many questions as answers. Why had she come and what did she expect from the meeting? Was she hoping to assure herself that Simon's plans to marry Lady Jeanette would not be thwarted by a courtesan?

If that was the case, the countess had no worries.

Simon arrived shortly after his mother left. He found Laura in the parlor. She was staring off at a painting of a landscape and didn't immediately notice his arrival.

"Laura? Is something the matter?"

She frowned and turned her head. "I'm not sure." He moved to sit beside her. "Your mother came for a visit. It was very strange. She asked me about myself and then left."

His mother was here? "How did she know where to find you?"

"I have no idea. She told me nothing." Laura rubbed her arms. "She may have gone off to summon the Bow Street Runners. Who would want their son mixed up with a murderess?"

"She would not do that," Simon assured her, though he wasn't at all certain what his mother had planned. Her visit was as much a surprise to him as to Laura. "She knows you are innocent. I explained it well."

"I wouldn't be so convinced of that. She has only your word that I'm not a killer. Mothers will go to great lengths to protect their children."

He stretched out his legs. "Whatever her reason, I'll find out soon enough. Mother does nothing without a purpose behind her actions."

A commotion sounded from outside—a shout and then a second. Simon jumped to his feet and hurried to the window. He watched two guards race past the house toward the garden.

"Something has happened." With Laura following, he ran to the kitchen and outside. A guard was on the ground and several other guards circled him. Simon brushed them aside and bent to the fallen man. He had a gash on his shoulder.

"What happened?" Simon asked.

"I heard the gate open and went to investigate. I was attacked from behind by a man with a knife." He winced. "We fought briefly and I chased him off." He gave a brief description of his attacker.

"Henry, the bastard," Simon growled. He pulled a handkerchief from his pocket and pressed it against the wound as Laura knelt beside him. Concern and fear were etched in her features.

"Only a coward doesn't face his foe," Laura said. "He is getting brazen and desperate. There are guards everywhere."

"Desperation notches up the danger," Simon agreed.

"Whatever is driving this risk taking will explode eventually and everyone around him will suffer."

Sophie arrived, pushing through the men. She quickly assessed the guard's injury. "Bring him into the house. I will tend him."

With Sophie leading the way, Simon and another guard half carried the injured man into the town house, while the rest of the men took up watch outside.

Once the man was settled in the parlor, Simon pulled Laura aside. "Gather your things. I'm taking you to my town house."

Laura nodded. "I cannot stay here. It risks Sophie and the ladies." She hurried away.

Within a few minutes, Simon shuffled Laura off into a hackney, making a grand production of doing so, hoping that if Henry was still lurking, he'd follow her away from the school.

Once settled, Laura pressed her fingertips to her temples. "Henry has proven he will do anything to get to me. Neither guards nor witnesses will stop him now."

"We cut him off from what few possessions he had when we chased him from the inn. Unless he has help, he is without funds and a place to hide." Simon took a breath. "Crawford has set the Runners on his tail, claiming that he received information about a new suspect in the murder. Though skeptical, they have confiscated Henry's things from the inn and are following this new information."

"So we wait?"

Simon shook his head. "He is running headlong towards something and you are the key. It won't be long until he makes a mistake and is caught."

"Then I will sit like bait in the Harrington town house and wait for the rat to come out to play."

When they arrived at the town house, Simon left her in the foyer and went to seek out his parents. Laura fidgeted, staring at the walls, the ceiling, and the paintings, trying to calm her nerves. She sniffed a vase of flowers and fidgeted some more. She passed her valise from hand to hand before finally setting it on the floor.

After what seemed like an eternity, Simon reappeared. "My parents would like to see you."

Laura's stomach dropped. She picked up her valise. "Wouldn't it be quicker to just have me ejected out of the house from here?"

Simon shook his head. "You are not to be ejected. My father wants to see if Mother was correct about your character."

"Excellent."

He took her arm and escorted her to the library. The warmth of the familiar room didn't clear the chill from her limbs as she faced the new earl.

The man was tall and handsome. The paternal connection between father and son was clear on their faces. They resembled each other remarkably. She curtsied. "My Lord. My Lady."

"Miss Prescott." Lord Seymour stood and rounded his desk. He looked at her over a pair of reading glasses. "I understand that you have gotten my son into all sorts of mischief these last few weeks, including a race about the wharf last evening on the tail of a possible murderer."

With knees shaking, she managed to meet his eyes. "In all fairness, My Lord, Simon got himself into mischief when he rode in to rescue me from Westwick's footmen. Had he dropped me off at the school and never returned, he would not have risked his neck by jumping out that window last night."

Lord Seymour nodded, amusement in his eyes. "My son is impulsive. And I can see why he is fascinated with you. You are very unlike that simpering Lady Jeanette."

"Father," Simon warned. "We did not come here to discuss Lady Jeanette. We came to seek shelter for Laura."

The countess stepped forward. "Of course Laura will stay here. It will give the two of us time to get better acquainted."

Never had Laura heard a more ominous comment. Though Lady Seymour appeared kind, she was a mother first. If she saw any indication that her son was falling in love with a courtesan, she'd have Laura kidnapped and dropped off somewhere in the wilds of Northumberland.

"It will be my pleasure to get better acquainted with you, Lady Seymour," she managed through a tight throat. The countess's smile was a touch mischievous, as if she saw Laura's discomfort and enjoyed it immensely.

"Excellent." The countess crossed the room and passed Laura. "Come, I shall see you settled."

Laura shot Simon a pleading look. He shrugged. The silent plead turned into a frown. He'd dropped her into a lion cage without a weapon to fend off the sharp-toothed felines.

"I have just the room for you." The countess led the way up the stairs to a tastefully decorated rose and white room. The color was subtle and warm and overlooked the street. Laura placed her valise on the bed for the maid, who quickly unpacked her meager possessions.

Shamed for the countess to see her poverty displayed in the old clothing, Laura spent a minute putting her parents' miniatures in just the right place on the writing desk. When she finally turned back to the countess, the maid was gone and Lady Seymour was wearing a curious expression.

"You should never be ashamed of where you come from, Miss Prescott." She settled on the bed and patted the coverlet. "Please join me."

Apprehensive, Laura took a seat beside her.

"Let me tell you a story," the countess began. "My family was large and as poor as church mice, though some would say the mice had better lodgings. I worked as a milkmaid and housemaid since I was eleven to help support my family. We all worked very hard to keep food in our stomachs."

Laura pondered the information and waited for her to continue.

"Oddly, in spite of the harsh conditions, my family was

happy." She smiled. "One afternoon I was walking back from Henley Hall when a man rode past on a large bay horse. I thought nothing of it until he turned the animal around and rode back to me." Her eyes took on a faraway cast. "Though he was very, very handsome, I had been chased by some of the finest bucks in Ireland. I wasn't about to be seduced and left with child by this arrogant Englishman with a charming smile."

"The earl sounds very much like his son," Laura said.

"He was, is. But he had other plans for me. He climbed down from that horse and for the next two hours told me about his life, his family, and his plans to marry me. By the time he returned me to my father, I was smitten. We wed a few hours later."

"What a romantic story." Laura sighed.

The countess nodded. "I took a leap of faith that day. I only knew that when I looked into his eyes, I would always be loved and cared for."

Tears prickled behind Laura's lashes.

"The point I am making with my long-winded tale is that I went from a tiny house my father had built to an estate in Kent. When I met my husband, I was barefoot and wearing a dress Lady Henley's daughter had outgrown and gifted me." She took a deep breath. "I will judge you for your character, not whether you have a large dowry or are weighted in jewels."

Laura sat a little straighter on the bed. She smiled wryly. "I'm pleased, for I have nothing other than my character *to* judge."

Lady Seymour stood. She peered askance at Laura through narrowed lids. "We shall see."

Caught up in the whirlwind that was Lady Kathleen, Laura spent the next two days in her company and in that of her daughter, Brenna. They shopped, went to a museum, and even called on Mrs. Fairchild, who had recently lost her elderly pooch.

Simon, His Lordship, or the guards were always present and wary. Though the outings were meant to bait Henry, Lady Seymour struggled to treat each as if nothing dark was lingering just out of sight. In public, she appeared more interested in learning about Laura than worrying that a killer might be stalking them. In the privacy of the town house, Lady Seymour fretted about Laura's safety.

The family wanted to keep her sheltered. It was Laura who insisted they continue life as if nothing were amiss. After a long and somewhat heated argument, they reluctantly agreed.

"Is your mother always so enthusiastic?" Laura had asked Brenna after the visit to the museum when the two younger women slumped, exhausted, in the carriage.

"Always," Brenna replied as her mother was helped inside. "Mother has the energy of six women."

The countess righted her hat. "It keeps me young, dearest."

Laura eventually discovered Simon's plan to marry off Brenna to one Chester Abbot and, by his sister's description of the man, stood firmly with Brenna against the notion.

"How can you consider him a husband for your sister?" Laura confronted Simon later that evening. She made a face. "He sounds positively dull."

Simon scowled. "It is as I feared. You have come under the negative influence of my mother and sister. Soon you will be taking me to task for my choice of coat or how to better use my spoon. Perhaps I *should* consider moving you elsewhere until Henry has been captured."

"You wouldn't dare." She glanced at the open door of the sitting room and stepped close. She took his hands. "I feel safe here. If I promise not to speak a word about your spoon or coat, will you let me stay?"

Laura knew he'd not remove her from the town house and the threat was only jest. But it gave her an excuse to lean in, feel his warmth, and enjoy the touch of their hands together. In such a busy household, and with the lack of privacy, their contact had been minimal.

He let his gaze roam over her face. "An inn would be

more private. I cannot get close to you without tripping over Mother or Brenna."

She warmed. It was comforting to know his ardor for her hadn't waned. She intended to steal many more kisses.

"They want to assure themselves that you will not take advantage of my good nature." She walked backward, drawing Simon behind the open door. She pulled her hands free and placed her palms on his muscled chest. "Or perhaps they hope to keep me from taking advantage of you."

Simon growled low and dipped his head for a kiss. She moved against him and slid her arms around his waist.

The kiss deepened quickly, infusing her with tingles. Then just as quickly, it was over.

Laura didn't try to hide her disappointment. "I've missed you terribly. Making lively conversation over meals or speaking politely about the weather is not enough."

Her Grace's voice drifted in from the hallway.

Cupping her face, he pressed a last hard kiss on her mouth and drew her back into the room. "I have employed an estate manager for my manor and the hiring of a staff has begun. I also have two pieces of news. Uncle Arthur has been returned to London and will be buried tomorrow."

"That is good news. Your family has him home." Laura sat in a chair. "And the second piece of news?"

"Crawford has discovered that Henry's real name is Charles Henry Innes. He has passed the information to the Runners."

"The name certainly fits with what I know. Westwick did slip once and call him Charles. But why the ruse?"

"We suspect Westwick and Henry of nefarious deeds beyond their desire to kidnap and sell young women for profit. There are rumors about cheating at cards and selling shares in worthless shipping investments, to name two. Charles may have used 'Henry' to keep his true identity secret. Both names are as common as tea is in England."

"And yet Westwick had no such qualms about revealing his own identity," she interjected. "He must have thought his title would keep him safe if he was caught committing crimes."

Simon snorted. "He got away with so many misdeeds in his life. Why would he not think he was safe from prosecution?"

Laura nodded. "And yet he wasn't safe from an assassin's knife."

Chapter Twenty-Nine

❧

"Aunt Bernie still has a touch of a fever and is sleeping," the countess said. Clad in black, she pulled on her gloves. Her face was grim. "I have promised to take her to pay her respects to Arthur once she is feeling better."

Laura nodded. Aunt Bernie was beside herself when she realized she'd have to miss the funeral. Unfortunately, she could barely rise from her bed to take care of her most basic needs. She'd never be able to sit or stand several hours upright.

"I will check on her frequently," she promised.

Lady Kathleen patted her arm. "You are a dear."

Simon stepped forward and took Laura's hands. "I don't like leaving you alone in this house. Henry could be anywhere."

The family was gathered in the foyer, a sea of black. Miss Eva and the duke and Miss Noelle and Mister Blackwell had all come to travel together with Simon's family to the funeral. The rest of the extended family had already gone off to the church.

"I am well guarded," Laura said. She squeezed his hands. "I promise to stay inside and keep vigilant."

"I'd rather you came with me," he said softly.

"The funeral is for family and friends. Besides, I can comfort Aunt Bernie should she awaken," she said. "The house is full of servants, and guards are posted outside. I am better watched than the king."

Laura worked to present a confident tone. Henry was a man capable of any misdeed. If he wanted to find a way into this house, he would. She could only hope that the sheer volume of the staff, having been alerted to watch for anything suspicious, would ensure her safety.

"I will be back as quickly as I can." Simon pressed her hand to his mouth as the family filed out the door. He glanced at Hardy. "Bolt the door behind us."

"Yes, sir." The butler did as he was told.

Her first order was to check on Aunt Bernie. She went upstairs.

The lady was sleeping, her cheeks flushed and streaked with tears. Laura placed a hand on her forehead. The fever seemed to be abating from a high the previous day. It was a happy sign of recovery. Laura tucked a blanket around her and left her to sleep.

Laura walked to her room and collected the volume of poems she'd finished last evening. She went downstairs to the kitchen and the cook made her a snack of scones with jam, left over from breakfast.

"These are the most delicious scones I have ever tasted," she said and the cook smiled. "Perhaps you should take the rest away, lest I have to let my dress out."

Satiated, she walked to the library to return the book and select another. After a thorough search, she chose a book that chronicled the history of pirates and walked to the parlor.

A footman stood at the end of the hall, clearly alert for trouble. Another was posted at the top of the staircase. Laura appreciated Simon's thoroughness.

She wandered into the yellow parlor, took a seat on the settee, and was soon immersed in the fascinating tale of the life of Edward Teach.

An hour passed and then two as she delved in the stories of Calico Jack Rackham and Anne Bonny. She was half-way through the history of Captain Kidd when her unsettled nights caught up to her. Her head bobbed and the book hit the floor with a clunk.

The sound startled her awake.

Rubbing an eye, she bent to retrieve the volume and heard a noise from the open doorway connecting the parlor with the library next door.

Curious, she rose and walked toward the doorway.

She was nearing the opening when a shabby figure stepped into the room. Alarmed, she opened her mouth to cry out when the man lifted his arm and aimed a pistol at her face.

Chapter Thirty

"Henry." Laura's heart raced.

Nodding, he lowered the weapon and stared into her eyes, his face tight. "Your lover is determined to protect you. It is lucky that I spent my youth as a housebreaker. There is not a wall I cannot climb or a window or door I cannot unlock."

"How did you avoid the guards?" Laura took a step backward. Fear burned in her stomach.

"Save for one visit to the courtesan school, I've been hiding in the attic since I dragged myself out of the Thames. I figured the last place anyone would look for me was in this house. And I was correct. No one thought to look up there when they made a sweep of the house and grounds." He shrugged and indicated his dusty clothing. "I've slept in worse places."

She shuddered at the idea of him hiding in the upper floor for the last few days, with her and the Harrington family living below.

Clearly she'd underestimated him. They all had. A life of criminal pursuits had honed his ability to get in and out of every situation.

"Why did you wait to confront me until now?"

"There were far too many people about," he admitted. "A few minutes ago, I noticed the house had suddenly gotten very quiet. I decided to find out why, so I snuck down the servants' stairs and crept through the kitchen. Getting to you was simple with all these connecting rooms. No one thought to post a guard in an empty parlor or library."

The man was brilliant. Insanely brilliant.

"I see I have finally done something you admire."

"What do you want?" Laura snapped. She hated the quiver in her voice. She would beat him at his game. She had to win for the sake of them all.

"I have come for my due," he said, moving across the room. "I watched Westwick put his hands on you, kiss you, and carry you to his bed. It's my turn."

Laura braced herself as he neared. The stench of stale sweat and dirty clothing permeated him. He was scuffed and water stained. "You will never have me," she vowed.

He smirked. "And what will you do about it, Lady Laura? Fight me? I am both stronger than you and armed." He lifted the pistol. "You will either come willingly or I will tie and carry you from the house. Either way, we will be well away from here before your lover returns."

"You may be able to slip into the house alone unnoticed, but you will never get away while carrying me. You will be seen."

The smirk turned evil. "The guards will not interfere when I'm holding a pistol to your head."

Worry kept her from calling out. She knew the footmen would come to her aid. But who would die before he was subdued? Could she risk a life to save herself?

For now, she had to rely on her wits.

Moving closer, he came within reach, yet still far enough back to keep her from lunging for the weapon.

She met his eyes. "How did you become so evil? I know you killed Westwick. We found the maid who saw the murder," she lied. "She has made a statement to the Runners. You will be caught and hanged."

Smugness flashed to rage on his face. "Westwick was my brother. He murdered my mother as if he'd held her under that water himself." He rubbed the pistol against his temple. Madness welled in his eyes. "I was orphaned and still he left me to rot, forgotten, in that foundling hospital."

In spite of his evil, Laura felt for the baby he once was. Growing up orphaned had twisted his mind.

"How did you find out about Westwick?" Leaving the town house with Henry would mean certain death. If she could keep him distracted, she might find a way to escape.

Henry grinned. "The home kept records, such as they were. When I was fifteen, I discovered that I'd been left there by a farmer from Suffolk. I'd thought I was his unwanted son. Imagine my surprise when the truth came out."

"How much do you know about your history?"

"Everything." He drew the pistol down the side of his face as he stared down at her breasts. "I learned that I come from a long line of lechers." Before Laura could see his intention, he stepped forward and tore her delicate bodice open.

She cried out. The swell of her breasts above her corset was exposed. She reached out to claw him, but he stepped back just as quickly as he'd advanced. She clutched the torn fabric together.

"Bastard."

He leered. "You have beautiful breasts, Lady Laura. Later we shall remove your gown so I may worship your perfection."

"You will have to kill me before you take your pleasure," she ground out. "I'll never come willingly to your bed."

One lid narrowed. "Still a fighter? And I'd thought Westwick had beaten it out of you."

Deep inside her, hatred flamed. "Westwick was weak. He had to use his fists to get me to comply. A real man does not need to use brutal tactics to win a woman."

If the insult hit home, he didn't show it. Her breasts held his attention. Her flesh crawled.

"Westwick was a spoiled fool." He lowered the pistol to his side. "I knew what he had planned for you. He would allow the highest bidder some time with you before stealing you back. He thought you'd finally break and be pliable to his demands. But I had my own plans. I couldn't allow Westwick to take that chance. The purchaser might have killed you. I needed you alive. So I killed Westwick."

To hear the murder confirmed by his words came as some relief. Once he was arrested, her nightmare would end. She'd be free of Westwick and his evil brother forever.

"You killed him to have me?" She snorted. She had to remain calm. Any sign of fear and he'd be on her like a mad dog. "Surely there are other women in London who would make you a more willing companion."

For a moment, he stared. "Do you think I killed Westwick just to use your body?" He let out a bark of harsh laughter. "I did not go through the trouble to find and befriend my unsuspecting brother just to steal his courtesan, though bedding you will be an added treat. No, this plan was hatched long before he met you."

Laura had suspected he was mad. This confirmed it. If he'd planned to kill Westwick before she'd met him, how then did she become tangled in this plot? She pressed on for answers. "I do not understand."

Smiling, he shook his head and clucked his tongue. "I wanted to take away everything he had—his wealth, his property, and you. You are the key to my revenge, to it all, Lady Laura."

"This makes no sense. I was his courtesan and will get nothing upon his death. I cannot help you steal his wealth."

His smile changed to a smirk. "My dear Lady Laura, you were much more than his lover. You were his wife."

❦

Chapter Thirty-One

Y ou should be locked in Bedlam," she said softly. There was an unsettling glint in his eyes. "As you well know, the wedding was a farce. You helped him fool both my father and me. The parson was an actor hired to play the part."

Henry lifted a finger. "That is where you're wrong, Lady Laura. The parson *was* a drunken sot. That part of the tale is true. But he was, in fact, a parson. Your wedding was legally binding. You are indeed Lady Westwick."

Her body trembled and she dropped into the nearest chair. All the months of thinking she was only Westwick's whore were false. Was she his wife all along?

"How can that be?" she whispered.

"The plan was simple," he began. "Westwick would never have legally married you. If he ever married, it would be to a woman of his class. But he had to have you. From first sight, he was a man obsessed. Though he could have taken you once your father died, he liked his games. So I suggested he marry and bed you. We planned the farce wedding for his amusement. He took satisfaction knowing he'd take your innocence and make you his whore while you suspected nothing."

"Why?" Her head began to throb. "What did it matter to you whether or not I was his legal wife?"

He shook his head. "My dear Laura, in order to access his fortune, I needed for Westwick to beget an heir. Then, as his grieving brother, once thought dead, I would step forward and petition for guardianship after Westwick's and the mother's sad and untimely deaths. A babe would not fight me when I emptied its coffers."

Laura couldn't speak. Stunned, her throat closed up.

"The day you met him, you all but fell into his lap, a perfect victim—poor, innocent, about to be orphaned. Though he'd spread his seed throughout the land, only a few very distant cousins have any legal connection to his fortune. I realized that you could pull the threads of my plot together. And though you failed to bear his fruit, you are entitled to whatever is left of his wealth."

The words rolled around in her mind and brushed aside concerns for her safety, the pistol, everything outside of the news she'd received. She was Westwick's heir?

"How could Westwick fall for such a hoax?"

"I paid the parson well to pretend he was an actor. It was brilliant. Westwick thought he'd gained a courtesan, and I had the wife I needed to steal his fortune. All I had to do was wait for the right moment to end him. After you ran away, I killed him and left the ear bob next to his body. You became the suspect and I was free to continue making plans for us."

Even as she'd protested, she knew Westwick hadn't known the truth of the wedding. Much of his torture came from reminding her that he owned her body without the legality of marriage.

"Why would you want to frame me for the murder?" she continued. "Wouldn't my hanging ruin your plans?"

"No one except me knows you as Sabine," he said. "I could use the ear bob evidence to force you to do my bidding."

Laura's mind spun. "I cannot be Lady Westwick. I cannot." Saying the title made her ill. She'd rather be a courtesan than Westwick's widow.

Reaching into his coat, he pulled out a rolled parchment paper. He tossed it to her. "This is a page torn from the church ledger that you and Westwick signed. If you look at the parson's signature, you'll see his name. I assure you the man was qualified to wed you. He lives about half a day's ride from your old home."

The paper lay at her feet but she didn't reach for it. If he'd gone to such measures to fool Westwick, she knew that his information was accurate. She'd have laughed over Westwick's comeuppance if not for the gravity of the current situation.

"Westwick didn't live to learn of the betrayal," she said. She wondered what he would have done had he known. Would he have killed Henry? Her? "How stupid had he been to trust you? Couldn't he see the evil in you, or had he been too blinded by his own wickedness to recognize it in others?"

"Opium was wasting his brain. I suspect he would have died from it eventually. I did not like waiting."

The weight of this was monumental. She'd gone from a courtesan to a Lady, and Westwick's estate was hers. Her life was no longer a shameful secret. The nights spent in Westwick's bed were sanctioned by God.

There was nothing to stop Simon from wedding her if he desired. Though her blood wasn't old and blue, she was a titled lady nonetheless. No one would question their marriage.

And she probably wouldn't live long enough to tell him the truth unless she could extricate herself from this danger.

Laura lifted her eyes. Defiance boiled in her blood. "You think I will simply hand over his estate to you."

"I am not that dense," he said simply. "I will have to wed you first."

Wed, bed, and murder. She had little doubt as to what her fate would be. He did not love her. Why then would he keep her alive?

"If I thought you would not kill me, I'd give you everything. Alas, I think the only reason I am alive now is because you need me. No one will hand his estate to you without my continued good health."

A slow demonic expression crossed his face. "I will gain the estate with or without you. I have my parson ready to wed me to a prostitute if you fail to follow my instructions. She looks much like you. I'll not be questioned when I present her to the bankers as the widowed Lady Westwick. With your father dead, there is no one left alive to challenge her identity."

"You bastard."

"*Tsk. Tsk.* Is that language proper for a Lady?"

Laura wanted to scream out in frustration. She was trapped in the Harrington parlor with a madman.

Someone had to come along soon. A footman, a maid, a guard. She'd have to delay him for as long as possible.

"Is she the woman you used when you killed Smoot?" His grin faltered. "We know that he was engaged in a carnal act with a prostitute when he was murdered."

"She has been very helpful," Henry admitted. "Perhaps you've heard her name spoken by the courtesan Mariette. Josie is her sister and the whore-mother of the ignorant mute girl. I paid Josie well to glean information from Mariette about the courtesan school. They speak daily over the back garden fence. I suppose you don't know that?"

This explained how Henry knew of the shopping trip.

"Mariette betrayed Miss Eva?" Laura asked.

"Not knowingly. Josie is a clever girl. I will reward her loyalty by making her my wife."

As if he'd let Laura or Josie live once he had what he wanted. He'd silence all witnesses.

"I'll not help you." She glanced at the pistol. "You'll kill me either way. I'd rather it was here than to suffer your abuse before my death."

He scowled. "Now I understand why Westwick wanted to sell you. You are a difficult woman."

This time it was Laura who smiled. "Westwick would have been better served to have found a more pliable victim."

She could see his frustration and sensed his impatience

rising. He'd mistakenly expected her to submit to his will without question. Fool.

"You will come with me," he said tightly.

"I will not." For all his evil and bluster, he was nothing more than a petulant, murderous child. She expected him to stomp his feet at her refusal. "You'd better decide my fate, and quickly. The family will be home soon."

Without another word, he aimed and fired.

Chapter Thirty-Two

❧

Laura screamed as the bullet ripped through the chair near her head. She dove off the surface and spun to her feet. Her heart squeezed painfully as her eyes met his.

"To show you how serious I am, Milady."

A footman appeared in the doorway. Henry threw the empty gun aside and pulled a knife from beneath his coat. He pointed it toward Laura. "I'll kill her."

The footman stepped back and retreated. Henry rushed over and locked the door.

Deep gasps did little to fill her lungs. She knew he was capable of murder and would harm anyone foolish enough to try and stop him.

"If you kill me, Simon will kill you." Her heart squeezed. She loved Simon with everything in her. It terrified her to know that she might never again see his beloved face.

"He'll not live long enough to kill me."

Laura flinched. "You are a coward. You'll not face him as a man. You'll wait until he's alone and shoot him in the back."

His face turned red. "I grow weary of your insults. Come with me or die. Your choice."

Desperate, she said in a rush, "All your plotting will

now come to naught. The footman has seen you. Witnesses will gather as we leave the house. You have lost. Flee now or be hanged."

His face burned red. He knew he was trapped. "You bitch. You ruined everything."

He lifted the knife as a rustle sounded in the open doorway to the library. Both of them spun around. Expecting a footman with the guards, Laura's eyes widened in terror as she recognized the sweet face.

"I heard a pistol shot." Aunt Bernie stood steps away, wearing a dressing gown and robe, hands on her hips, glaring at Henry through red eyes. "Who are you?"

Without thinking, Laura launched herself at his back. "Run!" she screamed as he pitched forward, taking her down with him. He grunted and hit the floor. The knife flew from his hand and clattered away.

"Run!" she shouted again. Aunt Bernie vanished.

Laura had no time to waste. He rolled over, throwing her off, and lunged for her leg as she scrambled free. She turned onto her back and kicked him in the jaw. His head snapped back. But he wasn't finished with her. With an outraged growl, he launched himself on her, oblivious of her pummeling fists.

With a free hand, he backhanded her across the face. She cried out and brought her knee up between his legs.

He arched back and clutched his damaged cock. But her reprieve was short lived. Spitting in rage, he dove for her neck, wrapping his hands around her throat.

"I'll kill you." He squeezed. Laura clawed his hands. She fought for her life as her throat narrowed, cutting off her breath. The room dimmed. She was dying.

From a far-off place she thought she caught a glimpse of Simon's face. She felt Henry's weight lift from her. Rolling to her side, she coughed and clutched her throat.

It took several deep, welcoming breaths to clear her mind and observe what was happening around her. She pushed to her knees, realizing that Simon wasn't a vision and was locked in battle with her attacker.

The fight was violent and brutal. The men were well matched in their determination to kill the other. Laura suspected that Henry had learned to fight while in the foundling hospital and on the brutal London streets.

She darted a glance around and spotted Aunt Bernie in the doorway, clutching a cooking pot as upraised voices sounded in the hallway. Laura raced across the room and grabbed the handled pot. "Get help!"

Laura spun and ran toward the men. Simon had the advantage, but only for a moment as he backed Henry against the wall and gave him two quick jabs to the stomach. But Henry leveraged his body and pushed Simon off. Laura took the opportunity and raised the pot. She hit him with a glancing blow to the shoulder.

He grunted and turned on her with a fist to the jaw. Laura jerked back and heard Simon's outraged bellow.

Simon watched Laura strike the edge of a chair and crumple. He had no time to tend her. He lunged forward and knocked Henry sideways. They landed hard.

All he could see was the bastard's face as he hit him in the nose, the jaw, anywhere he could find a target. The man was a street fighter and tougher than he'd anticipated. But Simon had two women to protect and wouldn't falter.

However, Henry wasn't finished. He managed to get Simon off balance and pushed him away. They rolled to their feet as shouts filled the house.

Fists upraised, they faced each other.

"I'll take pleasure in killing you," Simon growled.

Spitting out blood, Henry smirked. "You will not kill me unarmed. You noblemen have too much honor. It will be me who takes pleasure showing your beautiful lover every depraved way there is to please a man."

Simon grinned evilly. "Give me your best, you bastard, for you'll never live to take her."

Henry grinned through bloody teeth and reached to lift his pant leg. He jerked a thin blade from his stocking. He bent for an attack but never got the chance to take a step. The bark of a pistol echoed through the room. His eyes widened and he pitched forward on his face.

Simon looked down at the man, then back up. Behind the dead man, smoking pistol clutched in her two hands, stood Laura, her angry eyes flashing. "I'm weary of men controlling my life. It was time I take charge of myself." She dropped the spent pistol. Taking a shaky step forward, she wobbled toward Simon. He stepped over the body and caught her in his arms.

"Is he dead?" she asked, her words muffled by his chest.

Simon looked down. The large bloody hole in the bastard's back confirmed what he suspected. "He's dead."

Laura sighed and held tight. "I could not let him murder anyone today."

Relieved and pleased she was largely unharmed, he leaned back and stared into her face. "I take insult. I had no plans to let him kill me."

She pressed her hands to his chest. "Oh, I am well aware that you would have won the fight. My concern was that you'd bleed to death after. Your face is quite damaged."

Reaching up, he found his lip split and his nose bleeding. Wiping the blood off on his cravat, he knew that neither was potentially fatal. He looked in her eyes and realized she was teasing him.

"So you came to my rescue," he said and wrapped his hands around her waist. He glimpsed the library doorway filling with guards and footmen. They all stood frozen, staring at Henry's prone form.

"I had to. And no, I was not rescuing you. The fight had to end before Aunt Bernie returned with another pot and endangered herself. I saved *her* life."

Chuckling, Simon led her away from the body, through the library, and into the hallway. The crowed parted.

"I never thought of my aunt as a fighter." He escorted Laura to the drawing room and pulled her inside. Closing the door, he eased her back against the panel. "You, on the other hand, I would want guarding my back in a fight. You are well trained in the use of both pot and pistol."

"I had to live." Laura pulled him close. "I have a title and estate to collect."

Simon's brow when up. "What is this?"

"Kiss me first and I'll tell you my news." She rose onto her tiptoes as he willingly complied.

It was a little more than an hour later when the rest of the Harringtons arrived home. They were stunned to find Bow Street Runners in their parlor, questioning their son, Laura, and the servants.

Crawford quickly explained the matter to the family. Simon had sent for him first, before the Runners, knowing he could help sort out and explain the situation. Everything.

Kathleen went first to her son and then to Laura. Lady Seymour took her into her arms. "Thank goodness Simon returned home early. He couldn't settle his fear that you were in trouble." She pulled back and darted a glance to the covered body. "Though it looks like you had the situation well in hand."

Laura peered at Simon. He was telling the Runners the entire story. For Laura to be truly free, Sabine had to be cleared of the crime and buried in the past. The two Runners didn't seem willing to end Laura's rule as their suspect, but with the evidence turning toward the dead man as the murderer, and the viscount vouching for her character, they were willing to listen.

"I'd hoped to end the case with an arrest. Unfortunately, it wasn't to be," Laura said as the countess released her and took her hands. "Thankfully, your husband keeps a loaded pair of pistols behind a set of books by Huntley. I'd found them just yesterday morning."

The countess lifted a brow.

Laura smiled and pulled a second pistol from her pocket. She placed it on a table. "They are lovely pieces, and quite accurate. My father would be proud to know I remembered his training and managed to vanquish Henry before he could harm others."

Kathleen nodded. "My husband does like his weaponry. Thankfully, you managed to get to them in time."

The women shared a smile before returning their attention to the activity around them. A pair of footmen gathered up the body after rolling it up in the expensive, and bloodstained, Oriental rug on which it lay.

"We shall look through this new evidence and make a determination of guilt." The shorter of the two Runners sent Laura a warning frown. "Stay in London until this matter is concluded." They followed the body out.

Once the household was left to the family once again, they all gathered in the library.

"Will someone please tell us everything that happened here?" Miss Eva said. She and the duke had arrived late. "We return from the funeral to a household in upheaval and a dead man in the parlor."

"Laura shot the man," Simon informed them.

His Grace settled his wife in a chair. "I assume he was our missing murderer?"

All eyes turned to Laura. She sat on a settee, her hand in Simon's. "Yes, he was Westwick's killer and boastfully admitted such. Henry came to kidnap and wed me, hoping to steal Westwick's fortune."

"How odd," Brenna said.

"At first I thought he was mad," Laura said. "Now it appears my marriage to Westwick was official after all. The false ceremony had been part of an elaborate ruse." She quickly explained everything Henry had told her.

"Then you are Lady Westwick?" Brenna asked and darted a glance between Laura and Simon. A small smile tugged her mouth. "You never were a courtesan. Imagine the implications of that news?"

Laura didn't take offense. "It's true, though it changes nothing about my life with Westwick. He was still a vile man."

"True, but now Simon can wed you," Brenna pressed. There was a wicked glint in her eyes.

Simon leaned forward to scowl at his sister. "What

Laura and I do is none of your concern. And it does not change my wish to see you marry Chester Abbot. He will open many doors for our family."

Brenna's mouth turned downward. She glared at her brother. "Then I am off to the docks. I understand that an entire fleet of pirates has just landed on these shores. Surely one of them has the virility to get me with child."

"Brenna!" the countess gasped. She stood as her daughter strode from the room, and frowned at her son. "Did you have to get her riled? The last time you fought about this, it took me two days to convince her not to row a boat out into the channel in search of a Jolly Roger. Pirates indeed."

She walked quickly after Brenna while the duke, the earl, and Simon all chuckled in her wake.

Laura frowned. "You are horrible, Simon." She indicated Miss Eva. "You have a duke and duchess to polish up the family reputation. You do not need Chester Abbot. Certainly you can allow Brenna to choose a man for love."

He grinned. "Perhaps. I'll give it some consideration."

The conversation turned back to Laura, with the men commenting on her skill with pistols and the women just happy that Laura and Aunt Bernie were safe.

Finally, the duchess turned to her husband. "I am very tired. I think it is time to return home."

Walter rose and helped Miss Eva to her feet. The duke walked to her and took her arm. He led his wife away.

"I think I shall post a footman outside Brenna's door," Walter said. "That girl is far too headstrong for my comfort."

"You might also set a guard in the bushes below her window," Laura offered lightly. "I do not know her well, but she is most determined to thwart a marriage with Lord Abbot. She may use the window to make her escape."

The earl nodded, his eyes filled with humor. "Too true. That girl is the reason my hair is sporting gray."

The family dispersed, leaving Simon and Laura alone. He stood, pulled her up from her seat beside him, and then eased her down into his lap.

"Simon, this is entirely inappropriate. Someone could return and catch us." She pushed against his shoulder. It was no use. He already had his hands locked tightly around her. She stopped struggling. "You are impossible."

"Taking into consideration my promise to keep my hands to myself, I will forgo seduction and be the first man to steal a kiss from the new Lady Westwick."

Laura's lids narrowed. "I will allow one kiss. However, if you call me Lady Westwick again, I shall rearrange your nose."

"Such a violent nature you have." He nuzzled her neck. "Now that we are free of the shadow of Westwick and his evil brother, I intend to marry and compromise you for the rest of your life."

Marry her? Laura's stomach flipped. She put her hand between them as he leaned in for the kiss. "Oh, Simon. You are only proposing because I am no longer a courtesan."

His eyes darkened. "Is that what you think?" He slid her off his lap and stood. "You think my feelings for you have changed because you're titled?"

Laura didn't know what to believe. He'd mentioned a future together, but she'd assumed as lovers. Any thoughts of marriage had been just that, fanciful thoughts. Now he was proposing marriage on the same day they'd finally rid her of the terror of arrest?

The proposal was ill-timed and suspicious.

She crossed her arms. "Your entire focus since I've known you has been to marry well. You've never spoken seriously of marriage to me until now. Suddenly, my position has altered and you cannot wait to wed me. What am I to think?"

With angry strides, he walked several steps away. She saw his anger in his posture, felt it in his carriage.

When he finally turned back to her, there was resignation in his face. "I've been falling in love with you since the morning after I left you at the courtesan school. You were standing at the window with such sadness in your eyes that it tugged at my heart. I felt drawn to you as I'd never been drawn to any woman. I couldn't stay away." He reached into his pocket and pulled out a small box. Leaning, he placed it on the sofa table. "I never saw you as a courtesan, a whore. You have always been so much more to me."

As Laura sat, stunned, he left the room.

Slowly, she reached for the box and opened the lid. The ring was magnificent, a ruby surrounded by diamonds in an intricate gold setting. Tears came and, with them, shame. How could she have doubted his feelings? How could she have questioned his desire to wed her? Everything he'd done since the night of the rescue had been for her. Everything. And he'd never asked for anything in return.

"Simon," she exclaimed as she slid the ring onto her finger, jumped to her feet, and ran from the room.

She darted through the house, drawing the curious stares of the servants. She was halfway up the staircase when Dunston called up to her from below.

"My lord has gone to the mews," he said and stepped back as she took the steps down and brushed past him.

"Thank you, Dunston," she called out as she rushed to the door, jerked it open, and hurried out of the house.

Thankfully, Simon was still waiting for Horse to be saddled when she stumbled into the stable. She stopped, catching her breath, relieved she'd not have to chase him all the way to Surrey to have her say.

"Simon." She slowly approached him. He stood with his arms crossed, leaning against a stall, his annoyance palpable.

The groom must have sensed the tension. He left them.

"I'm so sorry," she began, a hand on her chest. "I've spoken without thinking and made you angry." She clasped her hands behind her back to hide the ring. "Not once since you rescued me had I considered that you'd ever truly want to marry me. And when you blurted it out, I was stunned. If you would like to ask me again, I promise I will give the matter careful consideration."

Simon snorted. "Why would I marry you now?"

Laura looked at him sidelong. "Because you love me?"

His eyes flicked upward and he sighed. "There are several women out this season who would make me an excellent wife—all sweet natured, lovely, and ready to bear my children. I would never suffer a moment's aggravation with one of them at my side."

"Yes, those are excellent points." Laura walked over to him and reached a tentative hand out to his chest. "Still, what about passion and fire and love? Are those not important, too?" She slid her palm down to his waistband. "I do love you madly, Simon Harrington. I want to be your wife."

A low grunt rumbled in his throat. "I should have left you to the footmen that night in the rain."

She smiled. He was bending. "You'd not change a moment of adventure with me."

His hands moved up to span her waist. He drew her nearer. "No, I would not. You've stolen my heart. I love you."

With that, he dipped his head and kissed her. Laura melted against him with a whisper of a moan. "And I love you."

The kiss lasted only long enough for Horse to get restless and nudge Simon. They broke apart with a laugh as the beast nudged him again. "No you don't, you jackanape. You hurt me once. I'll not have a repeat of your bad behavior."

Simon shifted them out of reach and snuggled her close. "We need to get the ring. I want everyone to see proof of my devotion."

She lifted her hand and wriggled her fingers. The ruby sparkled in the dim light. "I'd hoped you'd still want to marry me, because I'm never taking it off."

The engagement was met with tempered happiness. Of course, the family was thrilled. However, until the investigation was officially closed, the threat of Laura's possible arrest cast a lingering pall over everyone, mixing with the sadness over losing Uncle Arthur.

It was the pleasure Aunt Bernie showed to Simon and Laura upon hearing the news that ultimately eased their minds. The loss of her brother was not diminished, but she knew life continued forward, and she was eager to see Simon and Laura happy.

Laura was relaxing in a small sitting room at the back of the town house when Simon found her a week after their engagement. She was curled up in a chair overlooking the garden, a book in her hand.

"There you are." He walked to her and kissed her head. "I was told I might find you here."

She smiled and smoothed out her deep blue dress, one of several new and colorful gowns gifted to her by Simon. She'd first felt out of place with the other women all adorned in black, but the countess insisted she not let their mourning shadow her wedding day. She was entitled to be happy.

Laura reluctantly agreed, though wore only the darker-colored gowns out of respect.

"Your mother and Aunt Bernie are twittering over wedding plans, and I found that I needed a reprieve. Though your family is wonderful, you were right. It takes time to get used to the bustle of your household."

Simon pulled up a chair beside her. "As soon as the wedding is over, we will use the house in Surrey as our primary residence. It will be more peaceful there."

"I am not complaining," Laura rushed on, her eyes troubled. "I adore your family."

"I know you do," he said to ease her mind. "Still, we must get you used to them slowly. Until we are wed, you may yet flee in terror."

Laura smiled and set the book aside. She scanned his face. "You did not come to speak about the many colorful Harringtons. What did you find out from the bankers and solicitors?"

Simon rubbed the side of his neck. "That they are a humorless lot."

"Simon," Laura said with thinly veiled impatience. "You know that wasn't what I was asking. Will you leave me in suspense forever?"

He grinned. "I fear I have both good and bad news. First, you have been recognized as Lady Westwick, legal heir to the late Lord Westwick. The parson was found and the page from the registry confirmed to be official."

"That gives me some comfort," she admitted. "As comforted as I can be while knowing that for over a year, I was tormented by thinking I was a courtesan."

It was impossible for Simon to believe any man would not treasure her as a gift. As he looked into her sweet, upturned face, his heart tugged. He would cherish her always.

"You not only won, sweet, but exacted your revenge." He hadn't been allowed to beat Westwick for his mistreatment of Laura but savored a small measure of revenge anyway. "The squire's daughter became a countess. Westwick would be livid to know that you now carry his name."

"There is some satisfaction in knowing Westwick is likely haunting his town house, rattling chains and raging over this turn of events," she admitted.

They shared a smile. Then Laura pressed, "Please continue."

Simon quickly obliged. "The second piece of news is that Crawford found Josie. She admitted that she'd led Smoot behind the warehouse, but denied knowing Henry planned to kill him. As Henry's puppet, she is unlikely to face much imprisonment over the matter, and Mariette is keeping her daughter, Marie, until the case is resolved."

This was grand news. Knowing little Marie was safe and well was worth everything she'd been through. "If there is anything we can do for them—"

"Eva has assured me that Mariette's husband will care for them both. Eva has also offered to help Josie find a more suitable situation for her and the child once her troubles have been settled."

Laura sighed. "Your cousin is an angel."

Simon screwed up his face. "After what she put me through with you these last weeks, I would not call her angelic."

She knew he deeply admired his cousin and any barbs

they leveled at each other were all in fun. He'd grown fond of the prickly duchess over the weeks Laura had been in her care. "For Eva's help and protection, I will always be grateful."

Laura realized everything that happened to her from first meeting Westwick, to her escape and the murder, had led her here. Fate had certainly pushed her down a rutted path to happiness.

The wind fluttered the curtain as Laura stared at the muted sunshine streaming through the window and finally placed the last of the pieces of the mystery together in her mind.

"Though I am relieved to have been cleared of the murder and legitimized as a wife, I will forever hate the name Westwick. We must wed quickly so I can shed it. I want to be Lady Seymour instead."

"All in good time, love. First, we must present you to society at tonight's party. Please do not scowl," he urged. "With the family in mourning, there will only be one hundred of our closest friends and family, so you will not feel overwhelmed."

One hundred? She pinched the bridge of her nose. "Do not remind me. I have had knots in my stomach since your mother announced I'd be presented at a soiree at Collingwood House. Thankfully, I know how to laugh prettily and discuss the weather; otherwise, I'd be racing for the Scottish border."

Simon cocked a brow. "You are a remarkable woman. Everyone will see that. And I will not leave your side all night." He paused. "Now do you want to hear the bad news?"

"Yes, please."

"The missing guard was found dead in an alley just down from the dress shop. He'd been covered by some refuse. We suspect he was somehow lured there by Henry and killed."

"How dreadful," Laura said sadly. "He died protecting me."

Simon squeezed her shoulder. "And you gave him justice."

Silence fell over them. Henry had hurt so many in his brief life. Both he and Westwick would not be missed. Finally, she lifted her head. "There is more news?"

"Unfortunately, Westwick was financially incompetent. He was a man who fell into bad investments," Simon paused. "There is little left in his coffers."

"This was not unexpected." Still, it irked to think of the misfortune that might have been avoided had this news been known to Henry. "After all Henry went through to steal the Westwick fortune, there was nothing to steal." Her fists balled. "I spent over a year under Westwick's heavy hand, followed by weeks of watching behind me while the killer haunted me. Then I killed the man in the Harrington parlor and it was all for a grand estate that wasn't."

"Do not look so grim, love," Simon urged. "There are three properties Westwick owned: the one in Suffolk, which is dilapidated; one in Kent, which is fairly profitable; and the town house. You will certainly share a portion of those with whatever Westwick cousin inherits the title."

Laura sat for a moment in contemplation. "Whatever I inherit will be sold immediately. I want to be free of anything Westwick touched." She unfolded from the chair and settled in Simon's lap on the settee. "I never want to think of him again."

She pressed a kiss on his cheek. "I have another reason for wanting to marry quickly. We have not made love since the night of the storm. I am eager to share your bed."

Simon ran a hand down her side, taking a moment to cup her breast. "As am I. However, I will not touch you again until you are my wife."

"You are a noble man, Simon Harrington."

With a last caress, he removed his hand. "There are times when I wish I wasn't." He kissed her soundly, then eased her off his lap. "We must ready ourselves for the party. Eva will be put out if we are late."

The sounds of music drifted up the stairs as Laura paused on the landing, smoothing the bodice of her gown before settling her gloved hand over her fluttering stomach. This was her entrance into society, and she was certain she wasn't ready.

"You look lovely, my dear," Kathleen said, placing a hand on the small of Laura's back. "My son will not be able to take his eyes from you."

The words were meant to encourage her, yet she felt no comfort. "I told Simon that when I was finally free of poverty, and Westwick, I'd never again be drab." She looked down at Mrs. Jensen's bright scarlet French satin creation, bedecked in tasteful ribbons and bows. "Now I think I should change into something more demure. It will be easier to pass the evening unnoticed."

"Nonsense." Kathleen stepped in front of her. The countess was wearing mourning black. "You will soon be Simon's wife and my daughter. Hold your head high. If you want to wear red every day for the rest of your life, I will see to it that every bolt of red cloth from here to China is at your disposal."

Laura blinked to keep back tears. "Thank you." She hugged Kathleen tightly, then stood straight and confident. With the Harrington family's support, she could face any challenge. "I think we should hurry. Your son is waiting."

The look in Simon's eyes as she walked down the staircase was the final encouragement she needed. Her breath caught at the heat in his eyes. She barely noticed Kathleen leaving them as she ran an appreciative gaze over him. He was dressed in a black coat and trousers, a gray and white waistcoat, and a white shirt and cravat. He was most handsome.

"You are beautiful." He took her gloved hand and pressed it to his mouth. A twitter went up among the guests who loitered in the foyer. Clearly she'd caused a stir.

"It is you who are beautiful, my love," she replied and smiled when he made a face. "I shall have to keep you locked at my side all evening lest another woman try to steal you away."

"They can try all they wish, but my heart is taken." He reluctantly released her hand. "Come, we are late. There is a matter that needs immediate attention."

Curious, Laura took his arm and allowed him to escort her to the ballroom. The guests parted and Simon grinned as he handed her off to his father without explanation, then promptly vanished into the crowd.

Thoroughly befuddled as the earl led her forward, she was halfway through the room before she realized what was happening when Brenna stepped into her path with a bouquet of white roses.

"She is not quite ready, Father." She handed Laura the roses as the countess's lady's maid placed a veil over her upswept hair. In seconds, she was transformed into a bride. "Now, she is ready."

Brenna smiled and stepped back. The earl led Laura forward. Her steps faltered.

"Steady, Laura," the earl whispered. "There will be no fainting at your wedding."

Stunned, Laura found the duchess and Lady Noelle in the crowd. They smiled happily, as if they'd had a direct hand in the surprise. Kathleen dabbed her eyes and Aunt Bernie sniffed loudly as Walter handed Laura back to Simon at the end of the room. Flowers covered a makeshift altar.

"When did you plan this?" she whispered.

"I've had the special license since the day I purchased the ring. After you expressed your eagerness to bed me this afternoon, I knew I could wait no longer."

"Simon, shush." Laura's face burned as she looked over at the man she assumed was a priest or parson. The man winked and she wanted to cover her face with her hands. Instead she glared at Simon. "You are terrible."

"Yes, but will you marry me now? The guests are waiting."

She indicated the dress with her hand. "This dress is inappropriate wedding attire. I should be wearing something sedate. White, blue . . . brown."

"Then you will start a new fashion—red wedding gowns." He took her hands and pressed his mouth on her knuckles. "Marry me, Laura, here and now."

With a backward glance at the gathered company, she nodded and whispered, "Yes."

L ater, during a quiet moment in their bed, Laura, sprawled on his bare chest, settled her head on her crossed hands and looked into his blue eyes. Her body was sated and her heart full. Never had she felt such wondrous joy and contentment.

He'd kissed her and loved her with all the tenderness reserved for a cherished new wife. He'd whispered things that made her blush, did things to her that she didn't know a man could do to a woman, and taught her how to pleasure him, too.

She loved him so.

"What are you thinking, Wife?" He slid his hands over her rump and up her back to weave his fingers in her tangled hair.

"I was thinking of how you managed such an elaborate surprise without me suspecting anything. Even your mother gave no indication that she was hiding a secret."

Simon grinned. "There was very little to do to carry it off. The party was in place and I didn't think you'd miss not marrying in a church. My biggest challenge was finding a parson willing to perform a last-minute ceremony. Once I told him that you were with child, he was all too happy to oblige."

An outraged sound escaped Laura and she pushed herself up to face him. He winced when she dug her elbows into his ribs. "You did not tell him such a thing."

"I did. He raced to Collingwood House." He winced when she playfully socked him in the shoulder.

"I cannot believe I married you," she said with mocking-serious outrage. "You are horrible. By morning, half of society will be atwitter about how you had to rush the marriage before the baby arrived."

Simon chuckled. "It *will* be scandalous. Thankfully, we Harringtons do enjoy a good scandal."

Laughing, Laura scrambled up to straddle his hips. She felt his cock stir against her. She smiled wickedly and leaned to kiss his chest. "I thought you wanted to positively alter the family reputation? You cannot do so if you continue with your scandalous behavior."

"True. Thankfully, I've changed my mind." He shifted her to press his hardening erection against her core. "It is much more exciting to embrace scandal than to be dull."

Laura laughed, remembering their long-ago conversation on the day of her adventure into the country with Muffin. "'Tis true. I despise dull." She covered his chest with kisses. "What about the baby? Everyone will be disappointed when the little mite doesn't make an appearance next spring."

He pondered her comment for a moment. "I was thinking the very same thing. We should start making a new little Harrington immediately."

Laura gasped with shocked laughter as he rolled her onto her back and pressed her down on the bed.

Read on for a special preview of
the next School for Brides romance

A Convenient Bride

Coming January 2013 from Berkley Sensation!

The first thing Lady Brenna Harrington noticed was the pistol. The second was the unusual shade of blue eyes of the man holding the pistol. The third was the way those eyes bore into her with such an intensity that her heart beat at a rapid clip.

Then, without warning, the highwayman cursed, lowered the pistol, and slammed the coach door shut without demanding either bauble or coin.

It took a few deep breaths for her heart to stop pounding in her ears and to recover her senses.

"That was odd," she said, screwing up her face. "I may not know all the particulars of coach robberies, but I am certain highwaymen always steal valuables."

Her new maid, Tippy, let out a whimper of relief.

Brenna had the opposite reaction. "What sort of thief steals nothing?" As puzzled as she was, it was her next thought that forced her out of her seat with a burning sense of urgency. The solution to her woes had appeared in front of her, complete with a pair of bright blue eyes, and she was not about to let him get away.

He would make a perfect substitute suitor! If she pretended to be smitten with an unsuitable stranger, he'd provide the distraction needed to put off Father until she could find a way out of a marriage to the dreadful Chester Abbot.

If she could get the highwayman bathed, buy him some decent clothing, and teach him a few phrases of proper English, she might be able to successfully fool Father into believing she was deeply infatuated with a handsome stranger.

Father would be outraged, believing the man was a rogue, out for her fortune, and would be fit to kill. Who knew better how to keep his neck safe from an irate father than a highwayman?

Taking a deep breath, she carefully pushed the door open and peeked out. The thief was urging the coachman to continue their journey with clipped words and a wave.

The coachman, Fletcher, an elderly man who'd served the family for as long as she could remember, was obviously in the throes of his first robbery, too. He sat frozen, with his hands still uplifted over his head, in spite of the highwayman's insistence that all was well.

Her mouth twitched at the corners. Lud, the fact that he'd not shot Fletcher made him perfect. A killer of coachmen just would not do.

She gathered her skirt in one fist and clutched the doorframe with the other.

Taking advantage of her coachman's temporary paralysis, she made a hasty climb from the coach in a flurry of gray muslin and white petticoats. Mud squished beneath her boots from an earlier rain, but she ignored the possible ruination of the fine leather and focused instead on the back of the retreating thief.

"Pardon me. Sir?" Soiling her hem in her haste, she rushed over to him as he collected his waiting horse. She kept her eyes averted from the pistol in his waistband, so as not to lose her courage, and boldly faced him, close enough to touch his dusty coat. "Sir, if I could have a moment."

The highwayman paused and scowled down at her. He was tall, not overly so, and unshaven, with several days of beard growth marking his hard jaw. His clothes were those of a laboring man, though cleaner than most. He smelled better than a groom or farmer, too, like strong soap, leather, and rain.

Most important, though, was his clear lack of wealth: worn gloves, scuffed boots, not a bit of lace on his cuffs. He was likely without the means to give up his life of thievery, even though he didn't steal her jewels. That information worked well in her favor.

"Please, I must speak to you privately." Emboldened by desperation, she pressed ahead. "I'd like to propose a financially beneficial arrangement between us that will thicken your purse and keep my life from ruin."

His icy glare set her back on her heels. Why did he not seem intrigued with the offer?

He was an odd fellow. Perhaps he was new to thievery and inexperienced? She needed to do something to pique his interest.

Brenna tucked the stray hairs on either side of her face behind her ears so that the diamond earbobs were clearly visible for his inspection. The pair, and her pearl necklace, were worth a tidy sum; certainly enough to intrigue a thief.

She braced herself and waited for him to pluck the necklace from her neck.

He ignored the expensive items and held his angry expression.

"Young lady, return to your coach." He claimed the loose reins and walked around the horse. Brenna stepped back as he passed her. Her baubles were as uninteresting to him as stones on the muddy road.

"Wait, I beg of you," she continued, ducking under the horse's neck. "I am in a dire situation and am desperate for help. My father and brother intend to marry me off to a man I find unfavorable. I cannot be his wife."

His expression didn't improve. "Perhaps your father and brother know what's best for you." He removed his gloves and jerked the stirrup into place. "Women often let emotion muddle their judgment."

Brenna grabbed the bridle and ignored the insulting comment. She wasn't about to chase this thief off by arguing with him.

Without the highwayman, she'd need weeks, maybe months, to find another disreputable character that wouldn't be intimidated by her father's title. By then, she could be Lord Chester's new marchioness.

"Release my horse," he demanded. She shook her head.

"Not until you listen to my proposal." She tightened her grip on the bay gelding. Even if he shot her, it would be preferable to wedding Chester Abbot.

His exasperated sigh must have carried all the way to London. He briefly closed his eyes—she hoped for patience and not because he was about to shoot her—and crossed his arms across his chest.

"State your business," he said gruffly. "I do not have time to waste while you whine about the unfairness of your life. If you need a sympathetic ear, look elsewhere."

Brenna's back stiffened. If she had any other choice, she'd tell this arrogant clod where to take his boorish manners and be done with him. But desperation held her tongue.

She pulled in a deep breath, knowing that what she did in these next few moments could either save or ruin her.

"As I previously explained, my family intends for me to marry this man, a dolt of high standing. He is dull and weak and about as exciting as the mud currently wetting my feet. I would rather throw myself under the hooves of your horse than to suffer that fate."

His jaw clenched. "What has this to do with me?"

Clearly his controlled temper was faltering. She rushed on, "The wedding cannot happen. I need you to compromise me."

The stranger twitched and his brows shot up.

Brenna's heart raced at the shocked surprise in his eyes. Finally, she had his full attention. She prayed she'd not just made a grave mistake.

"Have you lost your senses, young lady?" He shook his head slowly and stared as if she'd sprouted horns. "You think that my tossing up your skirts and violating you on this sodden ground will be a superior choice over wedding the man your family has chosen? Are you mad?"

The words and the way he looked at her left her feeling foolish and a bit childish. Still, Brenna held fast. Simon was already making overtures to Abbot. This man *was* her only option. It mattered not what he thought of her, only that he'd help her.

She fingered her expensive necklace. "You will not actually take my innocence," she clarified, her body recoiling at the thought of him touching her intimately. "You need only misbehave just enough to convince my father and brother that you are a cad, a bounder, out to ruin me. While they are focused on trying to rid me of you, I will be free to choose my own husband."

JENNIFER ASHLEY

The Madness of Lord Ian Mackenzie

*Most women heeded the warnings.
One woman was tempted by them . . .*

It was whispered all through London Society that Ian Mackenzie was mad, that he'd spent his youth in an asylum, and that he was not to be trusted—especially with a lady. For the reputation of any woman caught in his presence was instantly ruined.

Yet Beth found herself inexorably drawn to the Scottish lord, whose hint of a brogue wrapped around her like silk and whose touch could draw her into a world of ecstasy. Despite his decadence and his intimidating intelligence, she could see that he needed help. Her help. Because suddenly the only thing that made sense to her was . . .

The Madness of Lord Ian Mackenzie

From *New York Times* bestselling author
of *Sinful in Satin*

MADELINE HUNTER

Dangerous in Diamonds

Outrageously wealthy, the Duke of Castleford has little incentive to curb his profligate ways—gaming and whoring with equal abandon and enjoying his hedonistic lifestyle to the fullest. When a behest adds a small property to his vast holdings, one that houses a modest flower business known as The Rarest Blooms, Castleford sees little to interest him . . . until he lays eyes on its owner. Daphne Joyes is coolly mysterious, exquisitely beautiful, and utterly scathing toward a man of Castleford's stamp—in short, an object worthy of his most calculated seduction.

Daphne has no reason to entertain Castleford's outrageous advances, and every reason to keep him as far away as possible from her eclectic household. Not only has she been sheltering young ladies who have been victims of misfortune, but she has her own closely guarded secrets. Then Daphne makes a discovery that changes everything. She and Castleford have one thing in common: a profound hatred for the Duke of Becksbridge, who just happens to be Castleford's relative.

Never before were two people less likely to form an alliance—or to fall in love . . .

penguin.com

LOVE

ROMANCE
NOVELS?

For news on all your favorite romance authors,
sneak peeks into the newest releases, book
giveaways, and much more—

"Like" Love Always on Facebook!

f LoveAlwaysBooks

Enter the rich world of historical romance with Berkley Books . . .

Madeline Hunter

Jennifer Ashley

Joanna Bourne

Lynn Kurland

Jodi Thomas

Anne Gracie

Love is timeless.

berkleyjoveauthors.com